D0951710

Also by
EMILY MARCH

The Christmas Wishing Tree

EMILY MARCH

St. Martin's Paperbacks

THE CHRISTMAS WISHING TREE

Copyright © 2018 by Geralyn Dawson Williams.

All rights reserved.

For information address St. Martin's Press, 175 Fifth Avenue, New York, NY 10010.

ISBN: 978-1-250-13172-0

Our books may be purchased in bulk for promotional, educational, or business use. Please contact your local bookseller or the Macmillan Corporate and Premium Sales Department at 1-800-221-7945, ext. 5442, or by e-mail at MacmillanSpecialMarkets@macmillan.com.

Printed in the United States of America

St. Martin's Paperbacks edition / October 2018

St. Martin's Paperbacks are published by St. Martin's Press, 175 Fifth Avenue, New York, NY 10010.

10 9 8 7 6 5 4 3 2 1

For Blake and JD.

*May your Christmas wishes
always come true.*

Part One

Chapter One

Christmas carols played softly in the background. The scent of spiced cider perfumed the air. Shoppers munched happily on gingerbread cookies and perused the bookshelves for that perfect gift.

Dr. Jenna Stockton imagined ripping the halo off the angel's head and choking her with it. Instead, she reached deep within herself for patience and managed to find a smile for the costumed character behind the bookstore counter. "If I could speak with your manager, please?"

"She's awfully busy."

Jenna thought of the ridiculous length of her own to-do list as she fought to keep her smile from turning into a sneer. "Yes, well, it's that time of year, isn't it? Your manager?"

The little angel gave a haughty sniff, and then said, "If you'll step out of line, please?"

Without missing a beat, the angel turned a bright smile toward the woman waiting behind Jenna. "I'm *so* sorry for this unfortunate delay, ma'am. I'll be as quick as I possibly can."

Jenna didn't snarl like a rabid dog. She didn't. She smiled at the woman behind her in line. Sweetly. Without canines.

The woman and the four people behind her each gave Jenna an annoyed glower. She gave them all a smile too, then reached for the nearest book, which she pretended to read until the clerk returned, accompanied by a fiftysomething woman dressed like an elf. The angel gestured toward Jenna and said, "This is the one, Ms. Thomas."

The elf spoke in a harried tone. "May I help you?"

"I hope so." *Especially considering that I went out of my way to support a local business rather than ordering online.* Jenna set down the paperback. "I placed a special order two weeks ago and someone from this store called me last week to tell me it was in. However, your . . . angel . . . can't find it in your computer system, so she insists I'm mistaken."

"Do you have your receipt?"

"Not with me, no."

"Well, if you'll come back—"

"I don't have time to come back. I ordered the books for an event that begins"—Jenna checked her watch—"in forty-five minutes. I'd like you to check your stock room. My name is Jenna Stockton."

"Ms. Stockton, I can't—"

"I ordered thirty copies of *New Adventures in the Christmas Angel Waiting Room.*"

"Oh." The manager pursed her lips. "Oh. I recall that order."

"Good."

Then the manager winced. *Uh-oh. Maybe not so good.* Jenna drew a deep, calming breath, then asked, "If you will get it for me, please?"

"Oh dear."

Jenna closed her eyes.

"I'm afraid we had some internal miscommunication. We sold out of our stock of that particular title and an employee unfortunately failed to notice the hold notice on your order. She put them on the shelf."

"How many are left?"

"It's a popular title," the manager hedged.

Jenna leaned forward. "The books are for pediatric cancer patients at Children's Hospital. The Christmas party is at four o'clock."

"Oh dear," the manager repeated. "Four o'clock you say?"

Jenna nodded curtly.

"I'll call our distributor. If you can stop back by—"

"You'll need to deliver them directly to the hospital. To the attention of Dr. Jenna Stockton." She removed a card from her purse and handed it to the manager. "Here's the address. Take them to the information desk in the lobby. I'll tell the volunteers working there to expect them."

"But we don't have a delivery—"

Jenna folded her arms and gave the manager her best take-no-prisoners look.

"I'll do my best to have them there by four, Dr. Stockton. I apologize for the inconvenience. Now, is there anything else I can help you with? I saw you looking at the new Liza Holcomb thriller." She picked up the book and handed it to Jenna. "It's a fabulous book. Scariest stalker story I've read in years."

Jenna quickly returned the book to the display table. *A stalker story?* That was all she needed. "No, thank you. All I need today is what I ordered. Thank you for the help. You have my phone number. I trust if there is any further problem, you will give me an immediate call?"

"Yes. Of course."

"Perfect. Merry Christmas, Ms. Thomas."

"Merry Christmas to you too, Dr. Stockton." The manager gave her a bright smile that didn't quite hide the worry in her eyes.

Jenna headed for the door, glancing over her shoulder before pushing it open. The elf was on the phone, the angel had been replaced at the register by a reindeer, and Frosty the Snowman was on hands and knees beside the urn of mulled cider wiping up a spill. She sighed. Angels with attitude aside, she liked this little store. She really hoped they didn't let her and the children down.

Outside, the jangle from the Salvation Army bell ringer mingled with the shrieks and laughter of children embroiled in a snowball fight in the park across the street. Jenna tugged leather gloves from her coat pocket and pulled them on as she walked to the street corner and waited for the light to change. Her gaze drifted back to the snowball warriors. It did her heart good to see healthy, happy children playing, especially after a morning like this one.

When the walk signal flashed on, she crossed the street and cut through the park headed for her car, which she'd left in a lot a block away. Her thoughts returned to her to-do list. She could save a few minutes if she bought cookies at the grocery store instead of making the extra stop at the bakery before picking up Reilly from daycare. But she'd promised Reilly a gingerbread man from—

Whack.

Something cold and wet stung her cheek. *What in the world?* Reflexively, Jenna lifted her hand to her face and the remnants of . . . a snowball. She'd been hit with a snowball. Had the battlefield moved without her noticing and she'd been struck by an errant shot? Or had the attack been deliberate? If that was the case, one of these heathens was about to get a piece of her mind.

But when she turned to identify the culprit seconds after the snowball landed, her gaze skidded over a group of youngsters to an adult standing nearby. The pockets of a black wool coat concealed the man's hands. A black knit cap pulled low on his brow and the matching scarf looped around his face shielded everything but his eyes.

Eyes that watched her.

A shiver of fear skidded down Jenna's spine. She whirled around and picked up her pace. By the time she reached her car, she was all but running. She thumbed the key fob and unlocked the door as she approached, then locked it again the moment she was inside. She sat behind the steering wheel breathing hard, her heart pounding. Her gaze locked on the path through the park.

Nobody had followed her. Chased her. She'd let her imagination run wild.

"You didn't imagine the face full of snow," she muttered.

She should call the cops. File a report.

Sure. Be one of "those people." Tie up a law enforcement officer's time over a child's prank. Because surely, that's all it had been. One of those kids probably threw the snowball, and the guy dressed in black probably saw it as it flew by. He'd watched her to see if she'd pitch a fit about it.

She slipped her key into the ignition, started the car, and did her best to dismiss the incident. Forty minutes later—after stops at the dry cleaners, grocery, bakery, and party store—she made it back to the office in time for her one-thirty appointment with five minutes to spare. If she'd checked her rearview mirror more often than usual and paid close attention to those around her as she completed her errands, well, she was simply being responsible.

Whenever she had a few free minutes during the rest of the afternoon, her thoughts drifted back to the troubling events of recent months. The harassment had begun in October, although for the first few weeks, she hadn't recognized the threat. Everyone got hang-up calls. She explained away the texts as wrong numbers. But once on-line orders she hadn't placed began showing up on her doorstep, she realized she had a problem.

She'd thought she'd been a victim of identity theft. She'd spent an entire weekend canceling cards and changing accounts. Then last week when a particularly difficult case kept her at the hospital until early morning hours, she came out to the physician's section of the parking garage and found the air had been released from each of her tires.

Random vandalism, the police said. Teenage pranks. Jenna wasn't so certain, but she didn't know who would be doing this to her or why.

As she exited Exam Room 4, her receptionist met her with the news that her three o'clock was a no-show, which meant she was done for the day. Jenna tucked away her dark worries and turned her thoughts to the light and bright. Now she'd have time to pick up Reilly from school rather than have his after-school caregiver drop him off at the hospital.

Luck was with her for a change because a parking place became available just as she pulled up. As she got out of her car, a bell rang, and the door to the kindergarten class-room opened. Reilly was the third youngster out.

"Mom!" exclaimed her six-year-old son. "You're here! It's time for the Christmas party, isn't it? Is it time for the party? Is Santa going to be there? I have my list all ready."

"Hello, little man. Yes, it's time for the Christmas party and yes, Santa has promised to make an appearance."

"I'm *so* excited!"

"Me too, Reilly. Me too."

She'd been trying to make the Santa visit happen for two weeks now. Because kids grew up so fast these days, she knew that this might be the last year that Reilly believed in Santa Claus. Jenna had wanted to make it a special event for them both.

For the initial effort, she had planned an all-day Saturday holiday adventure beginning with breakfast at a pancake house, followed by shopping for gifts for Reilly's friends, then a matinee performance of *Rudolph* at the children's theater, and culminating with a visit to Santa's Wonderland and a conversation with the big man himself. They'd had a great time eating and shopping and watching the play, but as they left the theater, her pager had gone off. She'd tried again the following Saturday with a different itinerary, but with similar Santa results. She and Reilly both were counting on "The third time is the charm" axiom working today.

Arriving at the hospital, she took advantage of valet parking due to the amount of party supplies she had to tote inside. She loaded up a collapsible wheeled cart with gifts and decorations and bakery boxes, then Reilly helped her tug it inside, where she approached the information desk with trepidation. "I'm Dr. Stockton. Do I have a package waiting, I hope?"

"Books," the volunteer said. "Yes, they're here."

Yes!

She reached beneath the counter then pulled out a box. Jenna spied twice as many gift-wrapped items as she'd expected. The folded note taped to the front of the box read, "*Your complete order is enclosed. In addition, please accept these thirty copies of the first book in the Christmas Angel Waiting Room series as a gift to the children from the staff here at Hawthorne Books.*"

"Well, isn't that nice?" Jenna murmured.

"Isn't *what* nice, Mom?"

"The Christmas spirit."

He nodded in all seriousness. "I love the Christmas spirit. I wish it could last all year long."

"You and me both, little man. You and me both."

The Christmas party that followed was a bittersweet

success. Local and a few national celebrities showed up to shower attention and gifts and good cheer on the patients of Children's Hospital and their families. It was always nice to see the smiles, but invariably, tears were shed too. The what-ifs and if-onlys were unavoidable. Hospital events always caused Jenna to hug Reilly a little tighter and spend a little more time on her nightly prayers.

The books Jenna gifted were well received by parents and patients alike. Reilly finally had his visit with Santa, and Jenna shed a tear or two of her own while she snapped photos of the moment with her phone.

In the car ride on their way home, Reilly bubbled about the party—the food, the games, the gifts. "There were a lot of dads there," he observed. "Did you see, Mom? There were a whole bunch of dads."

"Yes." Then, in an effort to alter the direction of the conversation, she said, "I was surprised to see how many football players attended. How many autographs did you get?"

"I don't know," Reilly answered with a shrug before proving that he was not to be distracted. "I thought Dr. David would be there. Why didn't Dr. David come?"

Oh, Reilly. Dr. David Henderson was Reilly's pediatrician, a widowed father whom she'd dated briefly last summer. "I told you he moved back to Minnesota to be closer to Bella and Jessie's grandparents. Dr. Larimer is your new doctor."

Reilly gave a long sigh. "I pretended I forgot. I thought he would make a really good daddy for us, Mom."

"Oh, Reilly."

"We really do need a daddy."

"Reilly," Jenna said, warning in her tone. "Please. It's been a long day. Let's not get started on that subject again."

"But, Mommy . . ."

She silenced him with a stern glance. Her son could be

a terrier when he got an idea in his head, and lately, every time she turned around, he'd been yipping and yapping about needing a daddy.

How about I just order one online? Everything else was showing up at the house. She'd certainly have more use for a daddy for Reilly than a yodeling pickle electronic noise-maker.

She switched on the radio, which was tuned to the Christmas music station. Listening to Alvin and the Chipmunks hope that Christmas wouldn't be late wasn't much better than the yodeling pickle. However, the music did manage to distract Reilly, who sang along the rest of the way home, so she wasn't about to complain.

Her son helped her unload the car, and then he dashed about the house turning on the lights of all of their Christmas decorations while Jenna sorted through the mail. One envelope in particular caught her notice. Whitewater Adventure Rafting on the Snake River? Her stomach took a sick little flip.

Dread filled her as she stared down at the envelope addressed to JENNA M. STOCKTON, MD.

This was coincidence, surely. Just bad timing of an advertisement that probably went to everyone in her zip code.

She slid the letter opener blade beneath the envelope flap and removed the folded paper.

A reservation for one. Paid in full. January 23rd at 10:00 a.m.

She dropped the paper as if it were on fire. Her hands trembled. Her heart pounded.

Her always-adventuring parents had drowned in a whitewater rafting accident seven years earlier . . . on January 23.

"Mom, can we read a story?"

Jenna saw her son standing in the doorway with his stuffed Rudolph beneath his arm. His request was a life preserver tossed to a drowning person. "Absolutely. I have a new book for us."

Because she wasn't on call tonight and she had no patients she suspected of being in imminent need of her services, she poured herself a glass of wine, traded her shoes for slippers, and settled into the overstuffed easy chair in the family room with the copy of *The New Adventures in the Christmas Angel Waiting Room* that she'd reserved for her own family. "In my lap, little man."

He bounded over to her, his face alight with joy.

Story time was special for them both. She'd finished the first book and allowed herself to be talked into reading a second and a third. They were negotiating a fourth when she answered the doorbell to a pizza delivery she had not ordered.

By nine thirty, her doorbell had chimed eleven more times with deliveries of eleven more cheese and mushroom pizzas. Jenna was allergic to mushrooms.

At nine forty-five she called the police.

Chapter Two

ETERNITY SPRINGS, COLORADO

Devin Murphy dreamt about home, about the warmth of the sun on his shoulders and the taste of salt in the air as he sailed his boat on a sapphire Coral Sea. A handful of puffy white clouds dotted a true-blue Australian sky. The breeze was stiff, a steady fifteen knots, as he turned into it. He was on a busman's holiday, free of tourists to guide in a dive of the Great Barrier Reef or fishermen on the hunt for something huge, but he wasn't alone.

In Devin's dream, a woman waited for him in his bed. She lay naked and needy and just beyond his sight, but he knew she was there. Knew she waited for him. A redhead, which was unusual because he'd never dated a redhead. Her scent drifted through his senses like a song. Exotic, like the beaches of Tahiti, and as sweet as a mango fresh off the tree. He wanted to lick that sweetness off her lips, to— *whoomp!*

Something heavy pounced on his back. "Wake up, Dev! It's Christmas Eve!"

The dream evaporated, Devin dragged his head off his pillow and aimed a hairy eyeball at his five-year-old brother. His voice gruff with sleep, he said, "Get off me and out of my room or die."

"You can't kill me on Christmas Eve. You can't kill me

ever. Mom would be mad. She told me to come wake you up. You promised to do a favor for Celeste today and Mom said daylight is wasting."

"Go. Now." He dropped his head back onto his pillow. "Or I'll slit your gullet from stem to stern and feed your entrails to the sharks."

"Oooh. I'm scared." Michael Cameron Murphy grabbed the ends of the pillow, yanked it free, then hit his big brother with it once before giggling his way out of the room.

Devin grinned. One of his favorite parts of the visits to see his family in Eternity Springs was horsing around with Michael. Devin had little use for kids as a rule. He certainly didn't want any of his own, but this kid hero-worshipped him. It was good for a man's ego. He figured that being a big brother must be sort of like being a granddad. Play with the curtain-climbers when you want, then give 'em back to Mom and Dad.

Though he probably shouldn't mention that theory to his parents, Cam and Sarah Murphy.

With a groan, he tossed back the comforter and shivered in the morning cold as he climbed from his toasty warm bed. Downstairs, his mother bustled around the kitchen and his father was locked in his study wrapping gifts. Devin ate a quick breakfast of oatmeal, kissed his mom on the cheek, twisted his brother's ear, then bundled up and headed over to Angel's Rest Healing Center and Spa to do a favor for a friend.

It was a picture-perfect December day—windless, with temperatures in the twenties and a blue sky dotted with puffy white clouds. At the resort's main building, Cavanaugh House, Devin hoisted a long, skinny box over one shoulder and carried it out onto the porch. There he paused a moment to appreciate the beauty of the winter scene. "It's like living in a Christmas card," he murmured.

Three inches of new snow had fallen overnight, frosting rooftops and tree limbs and shrubbery and giving Angel's Rest and Eternity Springs beyond the perfect Victorian snow-village look. This was a whole different world from Christmas where he'd come of age. Cairns, Australia, was hot and rainy as a rule on the twenty-fourth of December. So too was Bella Vita, the island in the Caribbean where he'd lived for the past few years.

Devin climbed down the porch steps and made his way to the stone walk that led toward Angel Creek. Groundskeepers had been through here already this morning and the pathway was clear and lined with candy canes tied with sparkling gold bows. Angel's Rest's owner, Celeste Blessing, did like to get her sparkle on, didn't she?

And yet, candy canes—even ones with sparkling gold bows—invariably made him think of his dad. How many times had he seen Cam Murphy at the wheel of the *Bliss,* his face into the wind and the hooked end of a candy cane hanging from his mouth? More times than Devin could count. Originally, his dad had used peppermint sticks to help him give up cigars, but one habit had replaced the other. Now, Devin kept a supply of canes on his own boat, *The Office,* in honor of Cam.

Or at least, he had kept them there until Danielle, the vicious Category 4 bitch, had sent *The Office* along with the *Lark* and the *Sunny Luck,* Devin's other two fishing boats, to the bottom of the harbor on Bella Vita Isle.

Devin looked out over the sea of white covering the grounds of Angel's Rest and imagined an ocean of blue with a rainbow of colors below. The Coral Sea and the Great Barrier Reef. He yearned for them. The Caribbean was a beautiful place and he'd been happy living there, just like he'd been happy living in Eternity Springs for a stretch of time prior to that. But Australia was home, the place where he'd been born and raised and never thought he'd leave—until the day an American tourist and her daughter booked a tour on his dad's boat and turned his world upside down.

At the sound of jingling bells, Devin twisted his head to see Celeste headed his way dressed in a fluffy gold jacket with matching boots and a knit hat with a rolled brim worn with a cocky tilt over her silver-gray hair. Gold bells trimmed the scarf draped around her neck. He grinned. People liked to say that she was Eternity Springs' very own angel.

He wouldn't argue the fact. Without Celeste, Cam and Sarah might have never found their way back to each other, and he wouldn't have the family he treasured, or this Victorian Christmas village complete with a white Christmas. And candy canes. And angel cookies. *And our very own angel.*

Devin truly did love Eternity Springs at the holidays. He would be happy to come back for Christmas at least every other year. And that's what he planned to tell his mother when he broke her heart after Christmas and finally confessed his intention to move back to Cairns.

"I brought box cutters," Celeste said as she approached.

"Thanks." He carried the box across the footbridge, and then set it onto the ground atop a large, flat, snow-dusted rock. He took the tool from Celeste and moments later removed sections of aluminum tubing along with a half-dozen smaller unlabeled boxes. Inside those he found strings of twinkle lights, LED lights, battery packs, rolled vinyl, glitter tape, and zip ties. He didn't have a clue where to start. "What exactly is this supposed to be, Celeste?"

"I don't really know." She clapped her hands, her blue eyes sparkling with delight. "It's a gift from one of my repeat guests. Isn't this a wonderful surprise?"

"It's something." He hunkered down and sifted through the contents, looking for a set of instructions. Just as he spied a folded piece of paper tucked inside the roll of vinyl, his cell phone rang. He fished it from his pocket and checked the screen. His mother. He thumbed the green button and lifted the phone to his ear. "Hey, Mom."

"Devin, are you still at Angel's Rest?"

"Yes." He shook the paper open, revealing a child's drawing done in colored pencils instead of the instructions he was hoping for.

"Good. I called Celeste, but she isn't answering her phone. Will you track her down for me? I'm about to leave Fresh with these cookies, but I neglected to ask her if she wants the extra pinwheels I baked this morning too."

Fresh was the bakery his mother owned and operated, and her mention of his favorite cookies was enough to distract him from his search for the package instructions. "Um . . . Mom . . . you do remember that your strawberry pinwheels are my favorite, right?"

"Oh really?" Sarah observed in a dry tone. "I'm sure I didn't notice that you've plowed through more than a dozen since you came home the day before yesterday. Don't worry. I restocked our pinwheel tin."

"I love you, Mom. And Celeste is here with me. I'm helping her with a new decoration for the Angel Creek footbridge. How about I just hand her the phone?"

The older woman glanced up from the pile of supplies she'd sorted into a semblance of order and took the phone from him. "Yes? Hello, Sarah. Merry Christmas!"

Devin paid scant attention to the phone conversation as he turned his attention to assembling Celeste's newest holiday decoration using the drawing for guidance. It was to be a lighted, decorated arch placed on the town side of the bridge. The rolled vinyl was a welcome sign. He decided that Celeste should do the official unfurling, so he went to work piecing together the poles.

Celeste's conversation with Sarah proved to be more

involved than answering a simple pinwheel-cookie question. Devin had the arch's aluminum framework completely assembled when he realized that Celeste was standing at the center of the footbridge, leaning over and peering down into the frozen stream as she talked to his mother.

Unease snaked through Devin at the sight. He felt the urge to call out and tell her to be careful, but he stilled his tongue. Celeste wasn't Michael's age. She was an adult.

Tuning into the conversation, he heard her say, "Yes, I know. It's been a while, but I do remember. Hot flashes are simply not any fun."

Quickly, Devin tuned right out again. TMI. He focused his attention on the box, and that was why less than a minute later he didn't see what happened. He only heard it.

The bump. The screech. The crack and the splash. Devin glanced up in horror to see that Celeste Blessing had fallen facedown into the icy water of Angel Creek.

"Celeste?" Devin tossed aside the Christmas decoration and scrambled to the bank and down its icy slope. His heart raced. His mouth had gone dry. A fall of ten feet onto a rocky creek bed could be disastrous for anyone of any age. For an older woman like Celeste . . . *Please, God* . . . three feet of water wasn't much to break a fall.

She moved. Devin exhaled in relief.

"Talk to me, Celeste," he demanded as he stepped into the creek, his boots breaking through honeycombs of ice into the freezing water. She rose up onto all fours. *Okay, good. That's good.* "Celeste? You okay? Where are you hurt?"

"I'm all right," she replied in a voice that was reassuringly firm. "I'm not hurt. But . . . ooh . . . this water is cold."

"Careful . . ." Devin took quick, but cautious, steps on slick stones through the icy water toward the woman who was trying to find her feet. "Hold what you have, Celeste. Let me help you up. We don't want you falling again."

"True. I've given my poor guardian angel enough of a workout as it is." Celeste gave Devin a shaky smile as he reached her side and steadied her as she climbed to her feet. "Thank you, Devin. I don't know what happened. I'm not ordinarily so uncoordinated."

"We're lucky you didn't break something." *Like your neck.* "What matters now is getting you to dry land without taking any more spills. I think the going might be just a little easier if you head upstream just a tad. I'll let you find your footing and you can use me for balance. Okay?"

"Yes. Thank you, dear. I just—oh—look."

Devin was prepared for Celeste to lose her balance again. He didn't anticipate that she'd halt mid-step, bend over, and scoop something out of Angel Creek. His phone, he realized. He'd forgotten she'd been talking to his mother on his cell phone when she took her dive.

Handing it to him, she said, "I spotted it because your phone case is so cute and colorful."

Devin's Scooby-Doo phone case had been a birthday gift from Michael. Watching the classic on the Cartoon Network together was a favorite brother-bonding activity. Too bad the case wasn't waterproof. "I'm glad you rescued it, but please, Celeste. Let's get out of this creek while we can still feel our feet. Watch your step, now."

He firmed his hold on her elbow. It took another couple of minutes and a pair of precarious slips, but Devin finally managed to lead Celeste to dry land. She was visibly shivering as he tugged her up the slick, sloping bank of the creek, and the wail of an approaching siren was a most welcome sound. "Either someone saw you take a tumble or Mom called in the cavalry."

"Oh dear. That wasn't necessary, but Sarah wouldn't

have known that, would she? I do have such wonderful friends."

"It won't hurt to let the doctor look you over."

"I suppose you're right."

The ambulance pulled to a stop and two EMTs exited the vehicle. Celeste waved at them and called, "All is well. Merry Christmas!"

The medical personnel's expressions relaxed at Celeste's greeting. Devin called, "She fell from the bridge into the creek. She needs to get warm and dry, and to see the doctor."

As one EMT opened the back of the ambulance, the other approached saying, "Miss Celeste, are we glad to see you up and walking. Sarah's phone call gave us all a fright."

The second EMT approached, carrying a silver emergency blanket, which she wrapped around Celeste. "Let's get you into the ambulance."

"Devin, you need to get out of those wet things too," Celeste observed. To the EMTs, she added, "He should ride along and we can drop him by his parents' house on our way to the clinic."

As the two shared a look meant to obviously frame a protest, Devin jumped in. "No, Celeste. You go on. Mom or Dad is sure to be right behind the ambulance. In fact"— Devin gestured toward the pickup that had just made the turn from Fifth Street onto Cottonwood—"here comes Dad's truck."

"Excellent." Celeste gave a satisfied nod. "In that case, I'll toddle along to the clinic. I am terribly cold."

She was halfway to the ambulance when she turned and said, "One thing, dear. About your phone . . . I'm aware of a method . . . it's possible I can save it and return it to working condition, if you'll allow me the opportunity to try?"

Probably the old rice-in-a-bag trick, Devin thought. He

didn't have a lot of hope for its success, but then, she *was* Celeste Blessing. "Sure." He crossed the distance between them, handed her the phone, and bent down to kiss her cheek. "Thanks, Celeste. But I don't want you to worry about it. Take care of yourself first."

"I will."

The EMTs helped her into the ambulance as Cam Murphy braked to a stop behind it. He jumped out of his truck's cab, and just before the ambulance door closed, he heard Celeste call out, "Merry Christmas, Cam."

After waving at Celeste, Devin's dad gave him a quick once-over. "Don't *you* look like a drowned wallaby. What happened here? Your mother is scared to death."

Devin gave his father a quick summary of events, and then repeated the story to his worried mother upon reaching home. He took a long, hot shower, then dressed and went downstairs to find a bowl of hot tomato soup and a grilled cheese sandwich waiting. Comfort food. "You are the best, Mom."

Sarah smiled. "You're today's hero. Thank God you were there to help. That's as frightened as I've been in a while. Celeste had mentioned that she was standing on the bridge, and we were talking about tonight's open house. She said something about seeing a reflection in the water, and the next thing I know, she yelps and the phone goes dead."

"We're lucky the phone is the only thing that died," Cam observed as he entered the kitchen carrying gift tags and in search of a pen. "May it rest in peace. Though I'm compelled to wonder how the young women of the world will survive the loss."

"Very funny, Dad."

"You'd better go buy another phone before the stores all close for Christmas," Michael said as he intently watched his father write a name on a tag.

Devin's lips twisted. This was Eternity Springs. The stores all closed for Christmas yesterday.

"It might be nice for Devin to have a break from tending to his harem," Sarah observed.

"What's a harem?" Michael asked.

"Not a topic for Christmas Eve," Devin declared before smoothly changing the subject. "So, have you had an update on Celeste? Everything check out okay?"

"Yes, she's on her way back to Angel's Rest with dry clothes and a clean bill of health. She told me she's ready to dive back into party preparations."

"As long as that's the only diving she does," Cam said. "What do we put on the tags for the senior center angel tree gifts?"

Sarah responded. "Put 'To a woman' or 'To a man' and add 'from the Murphys.'"

"Got it."

Displaying wisdom beyond his age, Michael observed, "It would ruin Eternity Springs' Christmas if Miss Celeste got hurt."

The adults nodded their agreement, and then Devin asked his mother what was on the agenda for the afternoon. Sarah summarized the day's itinerary—a happy blend of traditional activities and new events that reflected the changes to their growing family.

Cam spoke to Devin. "I need to deliver our senior center gifts. Want me to drop you by Angel's Rest on my way so you can retrieve your truck?

"Thanks. While I'm there, I might as well finish setting up that decoration Celeste had me working on when she took her tumble. Shouldn't take more than a few minutes."

"Celeste will appreciate that," Sarah said. "You know how she is about her holiday trimmings."

"She's the decoratingest person I've ever known," Cam observed.

Devin finished his soup and sandwich, then borrowed dry outerwear from his dad and hitched a ride back to Angel's Rest. He finished assembling and installing the welcome arch, tested the lighting, and shook his head in amusement at the twinkling, flying angels. "The decoratingest person," he repeated to himself. His father had that right.

With the task finished, Devin gathered up the trash. He had just tossed the cardboard box into the bed of his truck when he heard Celeste call his name. He turned to see her rushing toward him. He started forward, praying he'd intercept her before she slipped and fell and, to quote Michael, "ruined Eternity Springs' Christmas." Devin yelled, "Slow down, Celeste!"

"It's Christmas Eve! There's no time for slow."

Devin swept her with a studious gaze. "You're feeling well?"

"Fit as a cherub's fiddle. I saw the welcome sign. Thank you so much, Devin. You truly are my hero today."

"Glad I could help."

"I have a little something for you."

When she reached into her pocket, Devin took a step back. "I don't need—"

"Yes, you do need this." She handed him a prepaid phone. "I keep a few of these for emergencies. I'm afraid it doesn't have text messaging or the Internet, but it will keep you connected until we know whether my efforts with your phone will prove successful."

Devin grinned down at the gift. "A burner phone? You keep burner phones around the house?"

"I always try to be prepared."

"Celeste, you are amazing." As he tucked the phone into his pocket, she gave him a smile so brilliant and bright that it warmed him from the inside out.

"I've a special Christmas message for you this year." She

took his hands, her blue eyes gleaming with a mesmerizing intensity that had Devin holding his breath as she said, "Christmas is a promise. Christmas is a gift. Don't be a prisoner of the past. If at first you don't succeed, don't be afraid to make another run at the dream. Open your eyes and heart and imaginings to the possibilities that await. You must believe. Wishes can and do come true. And when the Christmas bells ring, Devin Murphy, don't you fail to answer."

He responded the only way he knew how. "Yes, ma'am."

Later that afternoon as he searched through his mother's craft room for the tape he needed to finish his gift wrapping and "Carol of the Bells" began to chime from his pocket, he recalled her words.

Part of him didn't want to answer. He'd been around Eternity Springs and Celeste Blessing long enough to know that when she started talking weird, weird things tended to happen.

He touched the green button to connect the call and brought the phone to his ear. "Hello?"

A small voice asked, "Is this Santa Claus?"

Devin's gaze locked on a roll of wrapping paper—red with white Santa silhouettes. *Okay, genius, how do you handle this?*

He cleared his throat. "Who is asking?"

"I'm Reilly from Nashville. Remember? I gave you my Christmas list at the hospital last week. At the party for sick kids?"

A party for sick kids. Devin sat down abruptly. "Hello, Reilly from Nashville."

"So you remember me?"

"Santa has a great memory."

"Okay. Good. I'm sorry if that sounded mean. I didn't mean to be mean. I'm scared to be calling you."

"No need to be scared, buddy. Talk to me like I'm a normal dude."

"Okay. Sure. I can do that."

Devin waited, but Reilly didn't appear to be in much of a hurry to continue. After a pause of more than half a minute, Devin prodded. "I expect you had a reason for calling Santa Claus?"

The boy spoke on a heavy sigh. "I do. We were supposed to go to see *Charlie Brown's Christmas* at the hotel and throw snowballs and ride the slide. We had tickets and everything. But Mom got called to work—she *always* gets called to work—and we're not going to have time. So that's why I thought maybe . . . well, I wanted to ask you . . . is it too late to add to my list, Santa?"

Well, crap. "It *is* Christmas Eve."

"I know. It's too late, isn't it?"

The boy sounded so dejected that Devin found himself wanting to fix the problem. He gave the lazy Susan on his mother's craft table a spin as he formulated his response. "It's complicated, what with the sleigh already loaded and everything. Let me ask you a few questions, and I'll see what I can do. First, how did you get this phone number?"

"An angel gave it to me."

Devin stopped the lazy Susan mid-spin. *Why does this not surprise me?*

"Not a real angel," Reilly clarified. "There's this store at the mall where little kids can buy presents, and the lady who wrapped the perfume I picked out for my mom was dressed like an angel. She's the one who told me your phone number is North-Pole-One."

An angel. *Christmas is a promise. Christmas is a gift. . . . Open your eyes and heart and imaginings to the possibilities.*

Except this angel worked at a store in Nashville. Devin wondered if Celeste had a sister. Or maybe a cousin. She *was* from the South, wasn't she? "Are you calling from your own phone, Reilly?"

"No. I don't have my own phone. Mom won't let me have one until I'm at least eight, and that's two whole years away. This is Mom's phone. She lets me play games on it when I'm waiting for her at work."

Okay, that was good. That meant Devin had the mother's phone number. He could call her later and let her know about this conversation. "All righty, then. Now, back to your Christmas list. I need you to understand that I can't make any promises. My sleigh is all loaded up and most of my elves have already clocked out and are taking off for vacation."

"It's not really a list, Santa. It's a wish."

"I think fairy godmothers are the ones in charge of wishes."

"Not Christmas wishes. This is a Christmas wish."

A Christmas wish, huh? For a kid who visited Santa at a hospital party for sick kids. *Murphy, you are so in over your head.* Devin cleared his throat, closed his eyes, and braced himself. "So, Reilly. What is your Christmas wish?"

"A daddy. I want a daddy of my own."

Devin let out a long breath. While he searched for the right words to respond, the boy continued. "If Mom and I had a daddy, everything would be so much better. She wouldn't have to work so much, and I wouldn't have to stay with Mrs. White so often."

"Mrs. White?"

"My sitter. And if I had a dad, he'd throw a football with me and take me fishing and we could go on vacation and camp in the national parks. And when we had tickets to the ice show and Mom got called in to work, my dad could take me."

"Have you talked to your mother about this wish of yours?"

Glumly, the boy replied, "Yes. She told me that daddies don't grow on trees—not even Christmas trees."

Smart mom.

"So what do you think, Santa? Can you make my Christmas wish come true?"

Noise outside in the backyard caught Devin's attention, and he glanced out the window to see his little brother chucking snowballs and taunts at their dad. *Reilly from Nashville doesn't have a Cam Murphy in his life.*

But he did have ties to a hospital.

Devin rubbed the back of his neck. "Well, I'll tell you what. This is a tough one. Even if this wasn't Christmas Eve and my sleigh was already packed up, I couldn't very well wrap up a dad and leave him beneath your Christmas tree, could I?"

"I guess not. Unless you put him in one of those big bags like bicycles come in."

"He couldn't breathe if I did that," Devin pointed out. "By the way, never put a bag over your head, buddy. That's dangerous."

"Yessir."

"Now back to this wish. Someone reminded me today that Christmas is a gift. It's a promise. There's the answer to your Christmas wish question right there."

"I don't understand."

"You gotta believe in the promise, Reilly. You gotta hold onto your hope, even when what you wished for isn't under your tree on December twenty-fifth. Because Christmas isn't just a day. It's not just a season. It's the love that's in your heart."

Following a moment of silence, Reilly said, "I still don't understand."

Devin closed his eyes. *That's because I'm not making sense. I've been hanging with Celeste way too much.* "It's a good wish. You hold onto it. Keep wishing it. Believe it will come true."

"And then it *will* come true?" Reilly asked, his question full of hope.

"You believed enough to call Santa on Christmas Eve. What do you think?"

"I think I'm gonna believe!"

"There you go. And now, I have an elf giving me the stink eye. It's time for Rudolph and his pals to do their thing. Goodbye, Reilly from Nashville. Merry Christmas!"

"Merry Christmas, Santa Claus."

Devin disconnected the call and let out a low, slow whistle of relief as out on the back lawn, his little brother gave a delightfully terrified squeal. Devin glanced out to see that Cam had the boy in an armlock and was washing his face with snow.

In that moment, Devin remembered Celeste's advice. *Don't be a prisoner of the past. If at first you don't succeed, don't be afraid to make another run at the dream. Open your eyes and heart and imaginings to the possibilities that await. You must believe. Wishes can and do come true.*

"It's a nice idea, Celeste," he murmured. But like the saying went, *If wishes were horses beggars would ride.* And little boys wouldn't be going to hospital Christmas parties.

And somewhere in another part of the world, another little boy built sandcastles on a beach with his daddy. The daddy who wasn't Devin after all.

Chapter Three

"One more," Jenna murmured as she measured the box against the roll of wrapping paper to gauge where to make the cut. Every year when she found herself wrapping packages on Christmas Eve, she promised herself that next year she'd do better. Of course, the Christmas Eve wrapping problem wouldn't be so bad if she'd do something about her Christmas Eve buying problem.

It was a bad habit. Invariably as the final hours ticked by toward Christmas, no matter how many packages sat beneath their tree, panic kicked in. Jenna worried she hadn't bought enough or purchased the right thing. Guilt had gotten the better of her again this year because she'd had to drag Reilly to the clinic when she got called in to cover for another doctor. On the way home, she'd stopped by the bookstore and covertly purchased three more books.

"It's always okay to buy books," she justified as she skimmed the scissors along the paper with precision. That's what her mom had always said, anyway. At the thought, a wave of grief rolled through her. She missed her parents every day of her life, but holidays always sharpened the sense of loss. The ugly gift in last week's mail had made the pain unusually acute. If Mom were here today, she would tell Jenna not to fret over her last-minute purchases, but she'd also add, "Next time, get them gift wrapped."

Jenna was tying a bow of green yarn around a wrapped book when she heard the muffled ringtone of a cell phone coming from her handbag. She shot a worried look toward it. This couldn't be good. Who would be calling her at four o'clock on Christmas Eve? Only a handful of people had this number, and they'd all be busy with family this afternoon. A call on that phone at a time like this might well mean somebody she cared about was ill or hurt.

She dug her phone out of her bag and checked the number. She didn't recognize it. She didn't recognize the area code.

Her stomach did a sick flip.

She'd changed her phone number after the harassment started in the fall. This number was unlisted. Anyone who had this number knew to phone her work line in an emergency. If the caller was a friend with a problem, her pager would go off any second now. Her friends all knew what to say to have the answering service put their call through.

This caller wasn't a friend.

Maybe it was simply a wrong number. It could be that simple. Everything didn't have to be part of the prankster's assault on her.

Whoever the jerk was, surely he had better things to do on Christmas Eve than to prank call her. "Even sociopaths have families," she muttered before tossing the phone back into her bag. She wasn't going to answer it. She had presents to put beneath the tree and a six-year-old boy to get to the children's service at church.

She didn't hear the phone ring a second time ten minutes later because she was on her hands and knees looking beneath Reilly's bed for a missing shoe. The next time it rang, Jenna had it silenced for the church service, and since she neglected to switch it back, she didn't hear the fourth or fifth calls either.

It wasn't until the evening of Christmas Day that she pulled her phone out of her purse and checked the display. Five missed calls from that same number. She froze as tension washed through her.

In the den, Reilly cheered and called excitedly, "I did it, Mom! I put the train track together all by myself. It works!"

"Awesome. I'll be right there, Reilly."

Jenna tossed the phone back into her purse. She wasn't going to let these phone calls bother her. She and Reilly had enjoyed a perfectly lovely holiday, and she wasn't going to spoil the mood by fretting over something that was probably nothing more than a wrong number, somebody wanting to wish Merry Christmas to someone he or she obviously seldom called. Since she'd never set up voice mail for her new number, he wouldn't know he had the number wrong. If the phone calls continued into next week, well, she could worry about it then.

She went into the den and played trains with her son.

The following day, she never heard her phone ring. With Reilly out of school, Jenna had cleared as much of her work schedule as possible. She stayed so busy with her son that she forgot all about the unsettling calls—until a friend phoned three days after Christmas and she took a good look at her call history.

In the days following Christmas, it turned out that Reilly from Nashville had a lot to say to Santa. Devin didn't quite know what to do about it.

He'd tried to get hold of the boy's mother on Christmas Eve to tell her about the dad request, but she never answered the phone. Once Christmas was over, Devin figured his responsibility to inform her of Reilly's call was over too.

But then the day after Christmas when Devin was up at the Rocking L summer camp helping his brother-in-law repair damage done to one of the cabins by some mischievous raccoons, the boy called again. "Hi, Santa. This is Reilly from Nashville. Thank you for all the nice presents. I really love everything, especially the book about Yellowstone National Park. That was a really great surprise. I want to go there some day. I want to visit all the national parks. There are fifty-nine of them. Did you know that?"

"I did not know that," Devin replied. He propped a hip on a sawhorse and set his hammer down.

"You should read the book you gave me. I learned it there. Did you have a good Christmas, Santa?"

"I had an excellent Christmas."

"That's good. I'll bet you were tired. Were you tired?"

"I *was* tired."

"Because you went all over the world delivering presents. You have to go to lots and lots of places. What's your favorite place in the world to visit? Is it Orlando? Because of the Magic Kingdom?"

"No." Devin's lips twisted. Personally, he wasn't a fan of theme parks. Give him real parks anytime. "My favorite place to visit is a little town in Colorado called Eternity Springs. For me, it's the most magical place in the world."

"Because it has magicians and wizards and superheroes?"

Devin thought of Celeste and he grinned. "Not exactly. Eternity Springs has family magic. People who come to Eternity Springs think it's very special."

As the conversation continued, Devin tried to subtly pump Reilly for information in an attempt to ascertain the state of the boy's health. *Was* he a cancer patient? And if so, how sick was he? Devin desperately wanted to know.

But nothing Reilly said answered the question, and when he mentioned his mother, Devin cut to the chase. "That reminds me. I'd like to speak with your mother. Would you put her on the phone, please?"

Following a moment's silence, Reilly said, "You're not going to tell her I've been bad, are you?"

"No, that's not why I want to talk to her." Devin waited a beat and asked, "Have you been bad, Reilly?"

This time the silence lasted longer. Finally, the boy said, "No, I haven't been bad. But Santa, she can't come to the phone. She's talking on her work phone so she can't talk to you. She's supposed to not be working this week because I'm out of school, but that never works out. She works all the time. That's why I need a dad. I gotta go now, Santa. And don't worry, I'm still believing! Bye!"

The call disconnected. Devin stood staring at his phone when Chase Timberlake walked into the cabin toting a two-by-four. He gave Devin a quick once-over, then asked, "Something wrong?"

"No. Not really." Devin considered explaining the call, but before he decided what to say, his phone rang again. The call was from his own number. "Hello?"

"Good news, Devin," Celeste Blessing said. "I fixed your phone."

"Wow. I'm impressed. You have a magic touch, Celeste."

"Like I said, I had a little trick. The bad news is that it's ringing off the wall. You're missing a lot of calls."

Devin realized he didn't really mind. It had been nice not to be tethered to his screen these past few days, though it might have given his social life a hit or two. Wonder if his New Year's Eve date with the ski instructor at Wolf Creek was still on?

He shrugged, not really caring one way or the other. *Message there, much?* "That's okay. They've waited this long, they can wait a little longer. I'm up at the Rocking L helping Chase with a project. I'll pick my phone up on my way home."

"That sounds great. I'll leave it at the front desk." With amusement in her voice, she added, "On silent."

As he drove to Angel's Rest later that afternoon, Devin considered the problem of the burner phone. He couldn't very well return it to Celeste. What if Reilly called again? He couldn't have Santa going MIA. But neither could this Santa Claus hotline go on forever. Well, unless the boy was sick. He'd talk to him every single day if that was the case and talking to Santa helped him.

He really needed to get in touch with the little guy's mom. When he parked his truck, he dialed Reilly's number hoping his mother would pick up. After twelve unanswered rings, he gave up. Maybe tonight he'd get on the Internet and see what sort of luck he'd have tracking her down. If worst came to worst, he'd ask Daniel Garrett to help him. The former police detective could probably track her down in minutes.

Celeste did indeed have his phone working like new, and he spent the rest of the evening returning calls and soothing ruffled feathers. The New Year's Eve date was off but he didn't mind. Ringing in the New Year with family and friends at Murphy's Pub had more appeal than hitting the slopes, so to speak.

The following morning he tried Reilly's number again before meeting his sister and brother-in-law for a couple hours of cross-country skiing. Again, nobody answered. That afternoon, he offered to do errands for his mom. He had just tossed a twenty-pound sack of dog food into his basket at the Trading Post grocery store when the burner phone rang. "Hello, Reilly."

"How did you know it was me? Magic?"

Or caller ID. "Something like that. Why are you calling today, buddy?"

"I wanted to tell you about a show. It's on TV and you need to watch it, Santa. I watched it last night even though it was after my bedtime because Stephanie lets me stay up later than Mrs. White."

"Who is Stephanie?"

"The Stephanie who lives next door. She stays with me sometimes when Mom has to go to work. She's in high school and she talks on the phone to her boyfriend a lot. My mom had to go to work again last night even though she wasn't supposed to. Anyway, the show is so cool. It's all about Yellowstone. Did you know that underneath Yellowstone is a volcano? You probably know that because you gave me the book, but Mom just reads me one chapter a night so we haven't gotten to that part yet. So I learned it from the show. It's on the National Geographic Channel. You should watch it, Santa."

They talked about volcanoes while Devin finished grocery shopping and checked out. When he loaded his Jeep, the conversation moved to camping. He'd just pulled to a stop in his parents' driveway when the topic of Reilly's new bike came up.

"Mom is going to take me and my friend Dustin to the church parking lot so we can ride our bikes where it's safe. I'm almost ready to take off the training wheels, Santa."

"That's great."

"And after we ride bikes, Mom is going to make us chocolate chip cookies!"

"She is?" Devin seized the moment. "You know, my elves have a secret ingredient that makes chocolate chip cookies taste magical. Would you like your mom to add it to her cookies?"

"That'd be great, Santa!"

"Okay. Put her on the phone, and I'll tell her what the ingredient is."

On the other end of the line, Reilly went silent. After a long pause, he said, "If I do that, she'll make me stop calling you."

"Your mom doesn't know about these calls?"

"No."

Devin grimaced. He'd been afraid of that. "That's not good, buddy. You can't hide things from your mom."

"I know." Reilly's voice held a world of misery. "Because of the bad guy."

Devin's brow furrowed. Had he heard wrong? "Did you say 'bad guy'?"

The boy's voice went small. "I'm not supposed to know, but I do. She got a whole new phone because of him. He's playing mean jokes that scare her, but the policemen can't find him. They don't know who he is."

With that, Devin knew that the phone calls to Santa had to change. "Reilly, I like talking to you, but we can't—"

"I gotta go, Santa. It's time to ride my bike. Goodbye! I'm still believing!"

Devin stared down at the phone. Crap. What the hell had he gotten mixed up in? He didn't regret playing Santa for Reilly and he didn't want to spoil the boy's fantasy, but this had taken a strange turn. It couldn't continue.

A bad man who played mean jokes?

Devin needed to get ahold of Reilly's mother. She wouldn't answer his calls, but maybe she'd respond to a text. He considered the problem as he unloaded the groceries. What to say without writing a novel? 'Lady, your kid is in trouble. Call me.' He didn't want to scare her, but if that's what it took. . . . Devin placed the last grocery sack on the kitchen counter and said, "Mom, if you don't need me for anything else, I think I'll walk over to the store. Dad said he has a new line of fishing tackle he wants me to check out."

"I'm done with you, thanks," Sarah replied. "Remind Cam that there's a high school basketball game this afternoon. He's promised to take Michael."

"Will do."

The scent of wood smoke drifted on the air along with the sound of laughter from children taking advantage of the sunny afternoon to play touch football in Davenport Park. As Devin walked up Spruce Street, he found himself wondering what the weather was like in Nashville. Probably pretty good since Reilly said he was going bike riding.

Reilly. This whole situation plagued Devin. As much as he hated the idea of letting the boy down, he really couldn't answer Reilly's calls again until he'd talked to the boy's mother. With that decision made and a short, but hopefully compelling, text message composed, he reached into his jacket for his phone. When he pulled out the burner phone instead, he hit redial one more time. He almost dropped the phone when on the second ring a female voice demanded, "Who is this!"

Devin opened his mouth to give his name, but the woman didn't give him a chance to speak. "Who are you? Why are you doing these things? What have I ever done to you? I swear, if I find out you're a pervert who's been preying on my child in any way, I will hunt you down and carve you up like a coroner."

"Whoa," Devin muttered.

"I don't know what your motive is, mister, but when you decided to drag my son into this twisted little game of yours you went too far."

"Hold on, lady," Devin fired back. He crossed the street and aimed for the relative privacy of a park bench, temper revealing his Aussie roots as he continued, "If you'll quit your whinging for just one minute I'll tell you what you need to know."

"Quit my what?"

"Whinging! Bitching. For a woman who can't take time to be a proper mother to her kid, you sure are quick to throw around accusations."

The woman on the other end of the call gasped in outrage.

Devin was full of outrage himself. "I assume you're Reilly's mother. Well, if you will hold your tongue for one bloody minute, I will tell you about my motive. Your boy called me. On Christmas Eve. He believed he was phoning Santa Claus and he had something he wanted to add to his Christmas list."

"And you talked to him?"

"It was Christmas Eve! He told me he's six! I wasn't going to ruin his Christmas by telling him he had the wrong number. So yes, I played along and I let him think I was Santa. And the minute we were done, I did what any responsible person would do. I tried to call you! Only you were too busy flossing your teeth to answer the damn phone!"

"Excuse me?"

"Yeah, well, I've been doing that for days and now I'm done with excuses. Why don't you answer your phone, lady? Do you know how lonely your little boy is? Care to guess what his Christmas wish was? A daddy. The boy wished for a dad."

The sudden silence on the other end of the line indicated that Devin might have gotten through to her. He was tempted to keep talking, to roll out some of the truths he'd been chewing on for days, but he forced himself to wait for her response.

Finally, she cleared her throat. "Mr., um . . ."

After her threats, Devin wasn't all that anxious to give her his name. "Why don't we stick to Claus?"

When she spoke again, her voice was tight. "It appears I am missing some important information. I would very much appreciate it if you would explain from the beginning."

"I'll be happy to do so." If his voice had a note of moral superiority to it, well, she had it coming.

Devin started with the Christmas Eve phone call and detailed the conversation as best as he could remember. Reilly's mother let out a little groan of misery when he repeated Reilly's daddy wish. She murmured a pained moan when Devin brought up the boy's complaints about her work hours. He told her that he'd asked Reilly to put her on the phone. "He wouldn't do it. He said you'd make him stop calling me."

"Well, of course I'd make him stop calling," she fired back. "This is just unacceptable. Sneaking my phone out of my purse, calling strangers, and lying about it—I can't believe he'd do this."

"Well, technically, I'm not a stranger. I'm Santa. And you are . . . ?"

"What?"

"Your name. Reilly only calls you Mom. I imagine I could track you down, but I haven't gone snooping. I'd like to know your name."

There was a long pause. "I don't know what to do about this. You could be the guy."

"The one who the police can't find?"

She gasped. "It *is* you. Who are you? Why are you doing this to us? How did you get this number?"

Devin's eyes rounded upon hearing the fear in her voice. "Whoa. Hold on. Wait a minute. I don't know what game you're talking about. All I've done is answer the phone when your kid calls and try to get hold of you to tell you about it. I'm not the bad guy here. Reilly told me some lady dressed like an angel in a department store gave him this number. It's North-Pole-One."

"How do you know about the pranks?"

"I don't. Not really." He told her about Reilly's mention of the bad man. "That's when I knew I had to keep trying until I connected with you. I don't know what sort of trouble you are in, but I'm invested in Reilly at this point. I don't want to rip the Santa rug out from under him. However, I need some guidance. I need information. First of all"—Devin closed his eyes, braced himself—"is he sick?"

"Six. He's six years old."

"That's not . . . I said 'sick.' Is he sick? He told me he saw Santa at a hospital party for sick kids."

"Oh." Reilly's Mom sighed heavily into the phone. "No. No. He's fine. I'm a . . . volunteer."

"Thank God." Devin's breath fogged on the winter air as he lifted his face to the sky and blew a heavy sigh of relief. "I'm so glad to hear that."

For a long moment, neither of them spoke. Motion in the fir tree above him caught Devin's notice and he watched a pair of squirrels scamper from limb to limb. In a quiet voice, Reilly's mother said, "Your number really is North-Pole-One, isn't it?"

"I wasn't lying."

"Do you get a lot of these types of calls?"

"Actually, Reilly is the only one. It's a new number for me."

"Ah. I see. Me too. A new number, I mean. I had to change mine. I'm being harassed, and it started with phone calls. That's why I didn't answer on Christmas Eve. I didn't recognize the number. And a couple of weeks ago someone sent more than a dozen pizzas to our house."

"Oh. I see." Devin did see. *Asshat.*

"The police call it doxxing. It was a new word for me—the modern word for pranks—and I don't think this guy is necessarily dangerous, but his pranks could be. He slashed my tires and that has a sinister feel."

"That's more than harassment. That's criminal behavior."

"And in the midst of all this I'm standing here talking on the phone to a total stranger."

"I repeat. I'm not a stranger. I'm Santa."

"Well, Santa," she said with a laugh that had a hint of despair in it. "What am I going to do about this hotline of yours?"

"We need a game plan. I'm happy to keep talking to the little guy, but I'm afraid we have a bit of a ticking clock to deal with. I'm scheduled to leave the country next week. I won't be able to talk to him after New Year's Day."

"Oh. Well . . . I need to put a little thought into this. And . . . oh dear . . . Reilly just fell and skinned his knee. Can I call you back later? After Reilly goes to bed?"

Devin had plans to watch tonight's college football bowl game with some friends from high school. He wasn't really interested in the matchup. "Sure."

"It'll probably be around nine. We're central time. Goodbye." Before the call disconnected, he heard her say, "Oh, honey."

Oh, honey. She'd sounded just like Mom when Michael hurt himself. Lots of love in those two words.

A mother's love. He closed his eyes as an old pain wrenched his heart.

Breast cancer had taken his biological mother when he wasn't much older than Michael. If not for Cam Murphy . . .

Then Devin gave his head a shake, drummed his fingers against the park bench, and brought his thoughts back to the phone call. This situation had taken an unexpected turn. The tire-slasher thing worried him. He'd have to quiz her about it when she called tonight. Sounds like Reilly's Mom wasn't the neglectful mother after all, but a woman with a lot on her plate.

He hoped she actually called. He liked the sound of her voice.

Bet she's a redhead.

Chapter Four

"Hey, Santa."

"Good afternoon, Reilly, my man."

"Guess what? I told Mom about calling you, and she wasn't too mad. I'm only in a little trouble."

"That's good."

"You were right. I needed to believe. So guess what we're going to do tomorrow? We are going to a big cave! It's huge and we get to go inside it. It's a national park like Yellowstone only there's no volcanoes. It's called Mammoth Cave National Park. Did you know that there used to be big elephants called mammoths, but they all died? I don't know if they lived in the cave or not. Mom says we'll learn about it on our tour."

"You'll enjoy that."

"Hi, Santa."

"How's my spelunker?"

"I know what that is! I learned it today at Mammoth Cave National Park. It's the funniest word."

"So tell me all about your visit."

"You're not too busy? It will take me a long time."

"I'm not too busy for you, little man. So tell me, why is it called Mammoth Cave National Park?"

* * *

"Hi, Santa. Guess what? I told my mom what you said about the Great Barrier Reef, and we went to the bookstore today and got two books about it!"

"You're going to love those books."

"And you know what else? I'm going to have a big brother! Not a real big brother who you have to share a bedroom with like my friend Jason. This big brother will take me places and do guy things."

"Guy things are the best."

"I don't think having a big brother will be as good as having a dad, though. I'm still going to keep wishing for that. I told Mom."

"You keep talking to your mom, Reilly. You have a really great mom and it's important that she knows what you're thinking."

"I will. I wish I could keep talking to you too, though. I hate that we only have one more call. Mom says it's not a real vacation if you have to take your phone with you. But Santa, I'm worried about something. What will you do if you have a 'mergency and you can't call nine-one-one?"

"Oh, you don't need to worry about that, Reilly. My elves take excellent care of me."

"Like my mom does me."

"Like your mom does you."

"I'll talk to you tomorrow, Santa. Happy New Year."

"Happy New Year, Reilly from Nashville."

At twenty minutes after eight on New Year's Eve, Jenna finished reading a chapter about Big Bend National Park and kissed Reilly good night. When she checked on him fifteen minutes later, he was sound asleep. She went downstairs, brushed her hair, and rummaged through her makeup drawer for her lipstick.

"You're an idiot," she murmured at her reflection in the

mirror. This wasn't a FaceTime call. He couldn't see her. She could call him with her hair in a rat's nest and with mascara running down her face and spinach stuck between her teeth and he wouldn't know. Nevertheless, she reapplied her lipstick before walking into her kitchen and pouring herself a glass of wine. At quarter to nine, she dialed North-Pole-One for the fourth time.

He answered on the second ring and she could hear the grin in his voice when he said, "Happy New Year, Reilly's Mom."

"Happy New Year, Santa."

By an unspoken agreement, they'd never breeched the anonymity of their contact by exchanging names. When Jenna phoned him that first night, she'd been filled with suspicion and skepticism as he repeated his explanation of events. Her focus had been on Reilly and his safety, and she'd shared nothing about herself.

In the end, she'd believed "Santa's" story. They'd developed and agreed upon a strategy for going forward. Only after they'd ended the call had she realized that he had never shared his real identity. During the subsequent calls, she'd learned that he was visiting family in the Colorado Rockies for the holidays, that he was single and in his late twenties, and that he loved *Star Trek* and *Lord of the Rings* and *Game of Thrones*. He'd never shared his name, where he made his home, or what he did for a living.

He did have the most delicious accent, and she'd spent a ridiculous amount of time analyzing it, finally setting on a Hugh Jackman Aussie sprinkled with an occasional Bob Marley Caribbean flare. If he occupied a lot of real estate in her imagination at the moment, well, that was understandable, wasn't it? He was a mystery who, unlike the doxxer, wasn't threatening or frightening. He'd inserted a little sparkle into her holidays, and she'd decided to enjoy the experience.

"So what are you and the little caveman doing tonight?" he asked.

"We have an exciting night planned. Reilly is already asleep. I'm going to binge watch *The Carol Burnett Show* and maybe splurge and have two glasses of wine."

"You wild woman, you."

"Carol makes me laugh. I've decided I don't have enough laughter in my life, and that's something I'm going to work on during the coming year."

"So that's your New Year's resolution? To laugh more?"

"I don't do resolutions, but lately, I have been taking stock. This doxxing business has me rethinking a lot of things."

"Did you call that private investigator?"

"Not yet." Jenna propped her legs on an ottoman and stretched them toward the fire. "Santa" had a detective friend who'd recommended someone based in Nashville whom she could enlist for help in tracking down the jerk. "I thought I'd wait until next week. Things have been quiet this week. I think this guy must have taken the holidays off. Honestly, I needed the break from worrying about all that, but I will make the call early next week."

"Promise."

"I promise."

She decided to change the subject. "So, how about you? What is Santa Claus doing on New Year's Eve?"

"My night is a little more exciting, but not much. I'm meeting my sister and brother-in-law at a local pub. I'm told the proprietor is breaking out a new microbrew in honor of the holiday."

"That sounds lovely," Jenna said, her tone wistful. "Are you close to your sister?"

"Lori and I are friends, which based on our beginnings says a lot. We fought like angry cassowaries when we first met. We were teenagers."

"Cassowaries? What's that?"

"Huge bird. Think ostrich, only bigger. They have razor claws and spikes on their wings. Nasty fighters when provoked."

"Tell me about your sister. I take it yours is a blended family?"

"Not in the traditional sense. Both my sister and brother are my parents' biological children. My dad adopted me after I was orphaned as a tyke. Mom officially adopted me after she and Dad married, but I was all but grown by then. Lori and I had some serious sibling rivalry to work through before we became friends."

"It's no wonder you and Reilly hit it off. You have a lot in common."

"He has an evil sister?"

Jenna laughed. "No. It's just the two of us. I adopted him after his mother died."

Following a moment of silence, he spoke in a quiet but warm tone. "Tell me about it."

Unexpectedly, tears sprang to Jenna's eyes. "His mom was a troubled young woman. Too young. A runaway. I met her through some volunteer work I did. She was . . . lost."

Jenna's throat closed up. She rarely spoke of Marsha Rocheleau. The events that brought Reilly into her life still left her emotions raw.

"And Reilly's father?"

"He was the reason she was a runaway." Jenna sighed heavily. "It's an ugly story, but the bottom line is Reilly's mother gave him to me, the monster who fathered him signed away his parental rights, and I'm blessed to be Reilly's mom."

"Sounds like he's a pretty lucky little boy too."

"That's my goal. I want Reilly to grow up believing he's the luckiest boy in the world. I may not pull it off, but I'm going to try."

"It's a worthy goal. So, let me ask you a question. Hold on a minute, if you don't mind."

Jenna heard what sounded like footsteps on a staircase. Next she heard a door open and a screen door creak. They both banged shut.

"Whoa, it's cold outside tonight, but I needed to move. So, back to my question. Say you hit a home run in the parenting department. Reilly grows up happy and healthy, and he has a great life. That security you've given him has made him strong and independent. He decides to move half a world away, so your visits will be cut in half at best. You'll probably be crushed, won't you?"

"Probably, yes."

"How do you deal with it? What could Reilly do to make it easier for you?"

Jenna's heart did a little dip. "This trip you're going on tomorrow. It's more than a vacation, isn't it? You're moving."

"Yeah. I'm going home."

"To Australia?" she guessed.

"How did you know? I'm told my accent has softened a lot and most people peg me as Irish."

"Your vocabulary is a hint, but mainly it's the way you shared the Great Barrier Reef with Reilly. It's obvious you've spent a considerable amount of time there."

"Ah. Yes, I have. I grew up diving the reef." He told her about his role in his father's tour boat business. "We came to the States when I was sixteen. I loved the mountains, but I missed the sea. The Caribbean was my compromise. It's a long flight, but it's manageable for visits with the family. Then Danielle blew into my life changed everything."

Frowning, Jenna put the clues together. "The hurricane."

"Sank my boats. Damaged my home. It's the second storm in three years. I'm done with it. I'm not rebuilding in the Caribbean again. I'm going home, and it's going to break my mother's heart, make my brother and sister cry, and give my dad a tick. Any suggestions on how to soften the blow?"

Jenna sipped her wine, and then gave him her best advice. "Be honest with them, but let them be honest with you in return. Acknowledge and respect their emotions."

"In other words, be a man and stand there and take it."

"Maybe bring some cotton to protect your eardrums."

He sighed. "Too bad I'm not really Santa. I could live where I want, then hop onto my sleigh and have Rudolph and friends zoom me to Eternity Springs for dinner once a week."

"Eternity Springs? You mentioned that to Reilly. That's your little mountain town?"

"Yes. It's pretty much in the middle of nowhere, home to less than two thousand people—and that's after a growth spurt the past few years. It's a beautiful place and I do love to visit. Eternity Springs is a safe harbor, but I need a rolling deck beneath my feet."

Jenna rose and walked to the bedroom that served as Reilly's playroom, where the lighted globe she'd given him for his birthday last spring sat on top of a bookshelf. She sent it spinning with her index finger, watching the blue oceans and colorful continents roll by. She stopped it on Australia.

"Something tells me your parents won't be as surprised as you fear."

He sighed again, then said, "You know what? That's a worry for tomorrow. It occurs to me that I've neglected my Santa Claus duty this evening. Want to hear what Reilly and I discussed this afternoon?"

"Of course."

"Well, he's planning a birthday present campaign."

"What?" Jenna sent the globe spinning once more.

"He's hardly played with all of his Christmas presents yet. And his birthday isn't until March."

"Apparently he's going to need every minute to convince you to approve his request."

Jenna couldn't imagine what . . . oh. Of course. "That boy," she groaned. "Let me guess. He wants a puppy."

"Got it in one."

"We can't have a dog. Never mind that he's too young to be responsible for a dog or that my plate is already overflowing as it is. His babysitter doesn't like dogs, so that's the end of the argument right there."

"He thinks he can change Mrs. White's mind. He's *believing*."

Jenna closed her eyes and groaned again. "I swear, I've heard that word more since Christmas than in the entire previous year. Thanks, Santa."

He chuckled. "You're welcome."

She hesitated a moment, then added, "Actually, I do want to tell you again how much I appreciate all that you've done for my son in the past week. I don't know that you understand what an impact you've had on our lives."

"I'm glad I could help, but as far as I'm concerned, it's been a two-way street. Who knew I had so much to learn about caves?" As Jenna laughed softly, he added, "This has been the best holiday I've had in years. I'm going to miss talking to Reilly and to you too, Reilly's Mom."

She traced the outline of Australia with her finger. "You still want him to call you tomorrow at noon?"

"I do. He's going to love my special goodbye message."

"Just promise me you won't make him any promises that include a dog."

"Santa's honor. I . . . oh, wow. I just saw a shooting star."

"I'm jealous. I've never seen a shooting star. Eternity Springs sounds like a really cool place."

"Cold. Bitter cold this time of year, but the homes are warm and welcoming, as are the people who live here."

Jenna's eyes filled with tears. "That sounds so lovely. If it were my home, I doubt I'd ever leave. Well, speaking of leaving, I'd better let you go so that you get some of that microbrew before it's all gone. One last time . . . thank you for your kindness to my son. May you have fair winds and following seas in this New Year, Santa. Goodbye."

"Good—wait. One more thing. Can I ask you a personal question?"

My name. He's finally going to ask my name. Should I tell him? "Okay."

"What color is your hair?"

"My hair!" Surprised, she blurted out. "Auburn. I'm a redhead."

"I knew it," he replied, satisfaction in his tone. "Goodbye, Reilly's Mom. I wish you and your boy nothing but peace, joy, and happiness in the New Year. And, no pizza."

The line disconnected.

Jenna sent the globe spinning once again, the writing on its surface blurred by both motion and the tears flooding her eyes. It was ridiculous, really, for her heart to tug with such loss. She'd spoken to the man four whole times!

But he'd been kind. He'd been funny and entertaining and . . . that accent. He'd been a fantasy. An escape.

After the past four months, she'd needed an escape.

And Reilly . . . he'd been so sweet to Reilly.

Jenna gave the globe one final spin, and then retraced her steps to the family room. She topped off her glass of wine, searched through her DVD collection for Carol Burnett, and then settled in to work on that New Year's non-resolution of hers.

She was laughing at Tim Conway playing a dentist when Reilly came downstairs. "Mom?"

"Reilly, what are you doing out of bed?"

"I'm hungry. Can I have a banana?"

Bananas were the boy's favorite middle-of-the-night snack. "Sure, buddy. Help yourself."

"Thanks, Mom."

She heard his Thomas the Train slippers scuff against the kitchen floor and the fruit bowl slide across the granite counter top. A moment later, he spoke with a mouth full of fruit. "Mom, can I watch TV with you?"

She opened her mouth to repeat her ordinary "No," but reconsidered. It *was* a holiday, after all, and not too long until the ball dropped in Times Square. Except, she hadn't watched it in years. Was the broadcast family friendly? Guess he could watch Carol Burnett with her. She could pay attention to the clock and switch it over a few minutes before eleven their time.

"Yes, you can. This one time since it's a holiday. C'mere, little man."

He was halfway across the room when the noise began. Loud hammering. Alarmed, Jenna set down her wine and started to rise.

The next few seconds were a firestorm of fear and confusion. *Bang. Wham.* Light flashes. Sound booms. For a moment, Jenna was stunned into inaction.

Men shouted, "We're in, we're in. Clear!"

Reilly screamed, "Mommy!"

Men with guns poured into the room and ran right over Reilly. Jenna lunged for her son.

"Halt! Halt! On the ground! On the ground! Now!"

A little boy's scream of pain reverberated across the air and terror gripped Jenna.

"Now! On the ground! Show your hands!"

"Get the boy. Get the boy."

"Mom-my!" Reilly wailed. "Mommy! Mommy! Mommy!"

"Reilly!"

Footsteps thundered down the hall, up the stairs. Sirens approached. Jenna's heart pounded.

"Separate your feet. Hands on your back."

"Clear! Clear!"

"Reilly!" *Oh God, oh God, oh God.*

"Be quiet. Don't move."

"Don't shoot! Please, don't shoot. My son . . ."

Whop, whop, whop, whop. Bwee bip bip bwee!

"Who else is here?"

A knee pressed at her back. Her arms jerked. Cold metal slid against her wrists. Handcuffs snapped.

"Got one in custody. Who else is here?"

Jenna trembled, her teeth clattered. Fear was a copper taste in her mouth. "No one. No one. It's just me. Me and my son." *Oh God.* "Reilly. Where's my boy?"

"Any weapons in here?"

"No."

"What's your name, lady?"

"Jenna." Her heart pounded. "Jenna Stockton. Doctor Jenna Stockton."

"We're clear upstairs."

"Clear downstairs."

Faintly, she heard Reilly crying and his panicked voice call, "Mommy! Mommy! Mommy!"

Rage welled up inside Jenna. Reilly! She wanted to yell and scream and pull a Wonder Woman and burst out of the handcuffs. Common sense made her remain still and silent until the activity around her calmed down.

The crystal ball had long since dropped in Times Square before the situation was finally sorted out. The 911 operator had received a call from a child who claimed his mother had just shot and killed his father and sister. He said she was searching the house for him and he was hiding.

"It's called swatting, Dr. Stockton," the team leader explained once all had been sorted out. "Prank calls on steroids. That said, it is seldom done as a random act like the prank calls I used to make when I was in elementary school. 'Hey, lady, is your refrigerator running? Better go catch it.' These calls take a level of sophistication in that often, the callers know how to shield the origin of the call. Bottom line is someone has something against you."

No, Jenna told herself as she thought about the SWAT team leader's comment while she waited in the emergency room for her son's broken arm to be set. The fact that someone had something against her was not the bottom line.

Reilly was.

The scum-sucking rat bastard had gone too far this time. Police had pointed guns at Reilly. Six-year-old Reilly. They'd pointed guns at him and knocked him over and broken his arm.

Six years old and he'd had eight police officers pointing a gun at him because he was near the front door. Six years old and frightened so badly that he wet himself when the stun grenade went off and he thought he was being kidnapped.

Six years old and trampled and broken and carried screaming away from her.

He clung to her like a toddler on their way home. *This could scar him for life*.

The crazy excuse for a human who had targeted her for some unknown reason had gone too far tonight.

Reilly had been traumatized. Reilly could have *died*.

That was the bottom line.

So Jenna intended to make sure something like what happened tonight would never, ever happen again.

Devin hadn't been this nervous since his first skydiving jump, but all in all, telling his parents about his move had gone about as well as could be expected. His mother had teared up, but she never allowed the tears to fall. His sister had bubbled and smoked like a volcano threatening to blow, but his brother-in-law managed to calm her down. His dad hadn't been surprised, which had surprised Devin.

Michael . . . ah, hell . . . Michael had broken his heart.

Michael cried every time Devin left following a visit. He cried every time the family came to visit Devin. The little boy's tears always broke Devin's heart, so this wasn't really anything knew. Michael was too young to understand how much farther Cairns was from Bella Vitae Isle, but he was bright enough to realize that the reactions of his family meant he wasn't going to like it.

Michael's tears stabbed Devin's heart like nothing else.

So after the morning family meeting and with three hours remaining before he needed to leave for the airport, Devin took his brother sledding. They had a great time, and as a result, Devin failed to watch the time closely.

At the end of one particularly laughter-filled run, he glanced at his watch. Eleven minutes past eleven? *Oh, crap.* Had he missed hearing Reilly's call? That would be so uncool for this, their final exchange.

Devin fished in his pocket for the burner phone and checked the display. No, no calls yet, thank goodness. "Hey, squirt," he called to his brother. "It's time for a hot chocolate break."

"Hurrah!" Hot chocolate was one of Michael's favorite things.

Their mother had packed a thermos of hot chocolate, plastic cups, marshmallows, and Devin's favorite brand of trail mix. They sat on a picnic bench out of the wind and dug in. Michael chattered away about his scheduled return to preschool at Gingerbread House the following day and the gifts that his friends had received for Christmas. Devin was happy that sledding had managed to distract the boy from his sadness. Oh, he'd blubber up again when Devin left, but at that point, Devin wouldn't be around to watch.

Devin checked the burner phone once again. Eleven twenty-seven. Scowling, he double-checked the reception. Four bars . . . plenty of connectivity. The ringer was on. No missed calls.

Maybe he'd misunderstood. Maybe Reilly's Mom had meant noon Mountain Time.

That had to be it. He should have listened closer. That's what he got for spending his time fantasizing instead of paying attention. "You about finished with your snack, squirt? We have time for one more run."

"I think two more, Dev."

"All right. Two more fast ones. No dillydallying at the top." In the end, they had time for three more runs.

Noon Mountain Time came and went without a phone call. Devin told himself to be patient while he showered, dressed, and finished packing. He kept the burner phone close during lunch, but saying goodbye to his family distracted him for a time after that.

"Sure you don't want me to drive you to the airport?" Cam asked as Devin tossed his duffle into the backseat of his Jeep. His blurry-eyed mother and whimpering little brother watched from the front window.

"I have to return the rental car, Dad."

"Mom and I can do it. It'll give us an excuse to drive to Gunnison for Mexican food."

"Thanks for the offer, but you know Michael would want to tag along. I don't know that I have the energy for another round of goodbyes."

"You're right. Well . . . you be careful, son. We'll see you in June." Cam extended his hand for a handshake, then wrapped his arms around his son in a hard hug. "Fair winds and following seas."

"Thanks, Dad," Devin managed without choking up. Barely.

Fair winds and following seas. It was Cam's traditional farewell. But as Devin took the highway north out of Eternity Springs, his thoughts returned to the other person who recently had offered him the sailor's wish. Why hadn't they phoned?

On another day, he'd have already placed a call to Reilly, but Devin had put a lot of thought into this final contact between them. It was well choreographed to ensure that Reilly's Santa calls ended on the right note. Devin didn't want to screw that up. So he waited. And fretted, especially during that forty-five minute stretch of road with no cell connection.

But when he emerged into civilization once again, his phone showed no missed calls, no voice mails. No nothing. He drummed his fingers against the steering wheel. "What the hell, Reilly's Mom?"

At the airport, he kept the phone in his jacket pocket when he turned in his rental car. He held it in his hand as he checked his luggage and stood in the security line. At the restaurant near his gate, he set the phone on the bar as he ordered and drank a beer. Time ticked by.

Ten minutes before he was due to board, he threw in the towel and hit redial. It rang twice, but when the call connected, the voice on the other end wasn't Reilly or his mother. The canned recording said, "The number you have reached is no longer in service."

He called again, this time dialing the number himself. Same result. Next he called the phone company, fought his way through to a human being, and checked for a service outage. *Nada.*

They made the boarding announcement for his flight as he waited in line to inquire about a flight to Nashville. He dialed her number again. "The number you have reached is no longer in service."

Dammit. Temper churned inside him. Why? If she didn't want Reilly to talk to him again, the least she could have done was call him and explain!

But that didn't make sense. Reilly knew his number. Reilly could call him from any phone. Why would she disconnect—

The stalker. *Oh holy hell.*

"Final call for flight three forty-seven to LAX."

Devin stared at his boarding pass and rubbed the back of his neck. What the heck did he think he could do? He didn't know her name. He didn't know what she did for a living beyond work long hours. He'd talked to her four times. Spoken with Reilly only a few times more than that. It was nonsense to think she needed his help.

"Sir?" The gate attendant gave him a chiding look. "Your boarding pass?"

"Yeah. Okay." Devin handed the slip of paper to the attendant. He didn't need to decide this very moment. He had a layover in LA.

He made his way onto the plane and took his seat. He was feeling around for the seat belt when the burner phone rang. He didn't recognize the number, but he didn't hesitate to answer. "Hello?"

Reilly's Mom's voice sounded rushed and harried as she said, "You've been kind. It seemed only right to let you know. Reilly won't be calling today. His arm was broken and he's . . . sedated. So, goodbye. Good luck in Australia. Thanks for the fantasy, Santa."

The connection went dead.

Chapter Five

ONE YEAR LATER

At the summit of Sinner's Prayer Pass, Jenna pulled into the observation point parking lot and said, "I need a little break before I tackle the descent. Let's get out and explore a few minutes, shall we?"

"Okay." Reilly unbuckled his seat belt and scrambled out of the truck. Immediately, he bent and scooped up a handful of snow, made a snowball, and threw it at the nearest target—the wood sign declaring the pass's elevation.

"Get your gloves if you're going to play in the snow."

"Mo-om," the boy protested.

She lowered her sunglasses and gave him a warning stare. He returned to the pickup and dug around for his gloves as Jenna walked to the edge of the scenic overlook. The town lay nestled at the center of the narrow valley, snuggled up against a meandering creek that flowed into a frozen lake to the south. She counted four main avenues and a dozen or so cross streets. Garlands of greenery bedecked with twinkling white lights and big red bows stretched across the intersections. Instead of one central business district, commercial structures appeared to be interspersed with residences. All over town, wood smoke rose from redbrick chimneys.

From this vantage point Eternity Springs appeared to

be the quaint Christmas village in a department store display window. The only thing missing was the train.

Reilly threw a snowball over the guardrail and stood beside her to watch it fall into nothingness. After it disappeared, he stared down at the little town. "Is that it? The place where we're spending Christmas?"

"Yes, it is. Eternity Springs." Jenna waited, holding her breath for his reaction.

He had none. Jenna's sigh fogged in the cold mountain air. She had high hopes that this Christmastime visit to Colorado would revive her son's excitement over the holiday. It was just wrong for a seven-year-old boy to be so ambivalent about the holiday season.

Not that she blamed him. Even she had trouble disassociating the trappings of Christmas with assault rifles and masculine shouts. It had been a bitch of a year.

After the New Year's Eve SWAT raid, she'd transferred to a new OB/GYN group in Memphis and hired a private nanny for Reilly and a private investigator to find the jerk who was terrorizing them. But after identifying three likely suspects—all men with professional ties to Jenna—the PI had cleared them each of any wrongdoing.

For seven months, they'd led a peaceful life. Reilly's arm healed, and he stopped waking from nightmares in the middle of the night. Jenna settled into the new practice and found a new church for her little family to attend. Then in July, she received shipments from a fruit-of-the-month club, a jelly-of-the-month club, a razor club, a coffee club, a salsa club, and a jerky club—none of which she requested. In August, she began receiving text notifications from social media accounts she'd never created. She reengaged the private investigator, but when eighteen pizzas arrived at their front door on September the third and Reilly's nightmares resumed, she packed up their belongings and moved to Tallahassee.

While waiting for her Florida license to be processed, she worked screening phone calls for a physician practicing concierge medicine. In October, she and Reilly had accepted an invitation to attend a Florida State football game with the divorced CPA who lived in the apartment next door. They'd had a fabulous time and that date led to numerous others. Jenna had grown fond of Joel Mercer, especially because Reilly had thrived under the man's attention. After she'd cooked Thanksgiving dinner for the three of them, he'd invited Jenna and Reilly to join him and his children on a Disney cruise over Christmas.

Then last week, Joel had rescinded the invitation after his children pitched a fit about sharing the cruise with their dad's girlfriend and her son. Reilly had been crushed. Jenna was steamed. Boy, had she misjudged Joel's character. When had—

Reilly tugged on her sleeve. "Mom, look! Is that a bear?"

Alarmed, Jenna whirled around. "Where!"

"Nowhere. Scared you!" Reilly giggled, his eyes sparkling with happiness she hadn't seen in days.

"Reilly James Stockton!" she scolded, her hands on her hips, her expression schooled into a fake scowl. His laughter was music to her soul. "You shouldn't scare your poor mother like that."

"You shouldn't have been fooled. Bears are hibernating now. It would be very unusual for us to see one. Didn't you pay attention to what the park ranger told us yesterday?"

"Obviously, I didn't pay close enough attention."

This morning they'd visited the Great Sand Dunes National Park and Reilly had peppered the ranger with questions. His enthusiasm had reassured Jenna that the decision to come to Colorado for Christmas had been a good one. After the Joel disappointment, she'd wanted to do something totally different from Disney. She'd considered taking Reilly to New York City, but decided the crowds wouldn't suit. They lived near the beach, so that wasn't a solution.

Then she'd recalled the praise Reilly's Santa had given his parents' mountain hometown. She'd recalled the wonder and yearning in her son's voice when he told her about Santa's favorite place to deliver toys. *Santa's favorite place is Eternity Springs, Colorado, Mom. Because it's magical. It has family magic.*

Since Jenna's little family could use some magic, she'd picked up the phone and booked a Christmas trip to a place called Angel's Rest Healing Center and Spa. *So, here we are, Eternity Springs. I hope you're ready to do your thing.*

"It's starting to snow, Mom. Isn't it cool?"

"Frigid." For the next few minutes she watched her boy catch big fat snowflakes on his tongue, and hope filled her heart. Maybe this would be a good Christmas, after all.

"Better load up now, Riley. We're running out of daylight. Plus, we need to get down off this mountain pass before it starts snowing any harder."

Half an hour later, they were introduced to Celeste Blessing, the Angel's Rest innkeeper. She wore her gray hair in a stylish bob. Gold filigree angel wings dangled from her ears and friendliness sparkled in her light blue eyes. Jenna liked her immediately.

"We had a last-minute cancellation so we've upgraded you to our best two-bedroom cottage at the same charge as your regular room. It has plenty of space for a lovely, large Christmas tree. I hope that's all right with you?"

"That's fabulous. Thank you."

Celeste chattered on about holiday events in Eternity Springs as she ferried Jenna and Reilly and their luggage in a golf cart to a cottage sporting a plaque beside the door that read BLITZEN.

"We absolutely love Christmas here at Angel's Rest,"

Celeste explained as she led them into the cottage. "All our cottages get a special holiday name. I trust you'll be comfortable here. Don't hesitate to ask for anything you need."

Jenna looked around and her spirits took flight. She saw a fireplace with a mantle built for stockings, a spot in front of a picture window made for a tree, a bar separating the kitchen from the living area that cried out for a plate of cookies and a glass of milk for Santa.

"This is fabulous. Just fabulous."

Celeste reached into the pocket of her gold ski jacket and removed a Christmas-green ticket. "As part of your rental, you are allowed to harvest one Christmas tree from the Angel's Rest property. If you wish to take advantage of this offer, you need to make an appointment with our Christmas tree elf. I'm sure he'll have time to take you tomorrow. Just pick up the house phone and dial X-M-A-S."

Jenna glanced at her son. He'd gone quiet in the face of all the Christmas talk, shoved his hands into his pants pockets, and started scuffing his boots against the cabin's wooden floor. *We'll get through this, buddy. I'm going to make this such a good holiday that you'll forget all about last year.* "I love that idea. We'll do that."

"Let me recommend our local Christmas shop, Forever Christmas, for trimmings. You'll find a tub with tree-trimming basics in the downstairs closet, but I'm sure you'll want to buy a few things to make the tree your own. At Forever Christmas you'll find everything you need to trim the tree and deck the Blitzen halls—lights, garland, ribbons and bows, ornaments, and of course, the Twelve Dogs of Christmas. Mention you're guests at Angel's Rest and receive a ten percent discount."

"Dogs?" Reilly repeated.

"Yes. Forever Christmas has an entire room dedicated to dogs. It's called the Dog Haus. If you like dogs, you need to pay it a visit, and be sure to check out the special collection of ornaments that features the dogs of Eternity Springs. They can be purchased individually or as a set."

"I love dogs," Reilly said.

Celeste gave him a warm, gentle smile. "You're going to love Eternity Springs, Reilly. I can just tell." Glancing up at Jenna, she added, "It's where broken hearts come to heal."

The statement resonated through Jenna's mind as Celeste finished the tour of the cottage and departed. It stayed with her as she fixed supper, negotiated a bedtime with Reilly, then built a fire in the fireplace and read aloud two chapters of *Harry Potter* before overseeing bath time and tucking the boy into bed.

She checked on him twenty minutes later and found him still rosy cheeked from his hot bath and sleeping peacefully.

Peacefully. *Where broken hearts come to heal.*

Jenna went to bed with a smile on her face.

The following morning, she and Reilly had breakfast in the dining room at Angel's Rest and registered for a slot to choose and cut their own Christmas tree. They arrived at Forever Christmas shortly after it opened for the day. In short order, *finally*, Reilly got his Christmas on.

It was the Dog Haus that did it. Everywhere you looked, you found something related in some way to dogs. Gifts for pets, apparel for dog moms and dads. Ugly-Christmas-sweater dog costumes and chew toys and bubbling dog-bone tree lights and ornaments celebrating dozens of different breeds. Reilly was in heaven, and it quickly became apparent they'd have a dog-themed Christmas tree.

Reilly had been lobbying for a dog almost since he learned to talk, but a pet was one too many responsibilities for single mother Jenna. So far, she'd managed to withstand his numerous requests. But now as she watched him load up his shopping basket with dog-themed trimmings, she wondered if the time had come to relent. Maybe a puppy from Santa was just the medicine her son needed to bring joy back to the holiday.

"Isn't that little dachshund ornament cute?" asked the woman behind the checkout counter. She'd introduced herself as Claire Lancaster, the store's owner. "It's one of my daughter's favorites. She loves her some wiener dogs. One of our local residents owns a dachshund whose hind end is paralyzed and the dog gets around in a wheelchair. She's the sweetest little thing. Her name is Penny."

"What happened to her?"

"I believe the story is that she jumped down off some lawn furniture and landed wrong. Broke her back."

"That's sad."

"Yes, but it honestly doesn't appear to bother her. She's a happy dog."

"Do you have an ornament that has a wheelchair?" Reilly asked.

"Not this year. I'm having one made for next year, though." To Jenna, she said, "If you'd like to join my mailing list, you'll be notified when they become available."

As a rule, Jenna didn't join mailing lists, but she couldn't resist Reilly's reawakened enthusiasm for Christmas. This was the most animated he'd been about the holiday since his last phone conversation with Santa. "Yes, I'll sign up."

While Jenna recorded an email address in a notebook Claire kept beside her register, Reilly said, "We're going to cut down our own Christmas tree this afternoon."

"You'll enjoy that. Do you have one of the national park permits?"

"I honestly don't know," Jenna answered. "It's something arranged through the place where we're staying."

"You must be at Angel's Rest."

"Yes." Jenna snapped her fingers. "The innkeeper told me to mention that."

"You get a ten percent discount," Claire said with a cheery smile. "The forest where you'll choose your tree is acreage that Celeste recently purchased from a rancher that expands the Angel's Rest resort. You are going to love your trip into the forest. It's a gorgeous section of land and you have perfect weather for it. Sunshine and crisp, but not bitter, temperatures. Two inches of new snow to make everything pretty. My friend Cam Murphy handles the tour for Celeste. He takes you in a horse-drawn sleigh and it's a beautiful ride."

"That sounds great. Don't you think so, Reilly?"

"I guess," he said with a shrug, but Jenna didn't miss the note of interest in his eyes.

On the way out of Forever Christmas, Jenna noted that Reilly slowed as they passed a Santa-themed room. When he stopped and stared, she held her breath. Was he about to make a breakthrough?

He had not asked to visit Santa this year. He had never mentioned last year's Santa calls. He certainly had never mentioned the final phone call that never happened because the Nashville SWAT team had burst through their front door, screaming and sweeping the house at gunpoint. The break in her son's arm had healed just fine, but mentally, he still had a ways to go. He'd gone from being fearless and friendly before the SWAT team raid to fearful, suspicious, and shy—especially around men. It had taken him weeks to warm up to Joel—and then that had turned out to be another kick in the teeth.

Jenna wanted her son to find the right balance between caring and carelessness. She wanted him to find his sense of security. She wanted him to rediscover the innocence and magic of being a child. She prayed these ten days in Eternity Springs would help in that regard. If they could just have a normal Christmas, it would do Reilly a world of good.

To that end, she walked past him into the Santa room. She picked up a red and green plate with the words COOKIES FOR SANTA written at its center. "I think we need this. Don't you?"

He stood there for a long moment before he shrugged. "You haven't made cookies in a long time. I bet Santa likes chocolate chip cookies."

"I'll bet you're right. Let's do it!" Jenna carried the plate back to the register and paid for it.

She exited Forever Christmas with a spring in her step and hope in her heart.

"We sure wish you were coming home for Christmas, son," Cam Murphy said, watching Devin's image on the computer. Devin had called to pick his father's brain about a recurring engine problem he'd been having on the *Out-n-Back*, and the two had talked shop for almost half an hour before the conversation turned to more personal matters.

"I know. I'll miss you guys." Because Devin had taken time away from work to come home for Brick Callahan's wedding in October, returning two months later simply wasn't doable. "If our foolish friends ever wise up and stop getting married, maybe we can stick to that visit schedule we planned when I decided to move home."

"Foolish friend, my ass. Brick Callahan is so happily married, his smile can power a generator."

"Hey. I smile plenty myself and I don't have a ball and chain to haul around."

Cam shook his head. Devin was the very definition of a rolling stone who never hid his lack of interest in marriage. Cam figured he'd really enjoy it the day his boy met his match. *Hard heads fall harder.*

"You're still planning to come over at Easter, aren't you?" Devin asked.

"We are," Cam said. "I'd like to make a trip before then, but with your brother in kindergarten now that puts a hitch in our git-along. He'd never forgive us if we went to Australia without him."

Devin laughed. "When Mikey's not happy, nobody's happy."

"Tell me about it," Cam said. "He and your mother are locked in a battle royal right now."

"Oh yeah? Over what?"

"Cell phones. He thinks he needs one. Sarah isn't having any of that."

"I should hope not. The kid lives in Eternity Springs. If he needs to get hold of you or Mom all he has to do is raise his voice."

"Well, he's not getting what he wants, though he's made the end-around play and asked Santa to bring him one."

Devin burst out laughing. "Why does this not surprise me?"

"Well, I'm afraid the surprise is going to be on him. Santa might bring him a cell phone, but it won't be a smart phone. No camera. Mrs. Claus is adamant about that."

"Good for her. By the way, this reminds me. Remember that phone I gave you when I was back in the States for Brick's wedding?"

"Celeste's burner phone. Yeah."

"Don't forget to turn it on."

"I already have." Cam had been touched by the story Devin told him about playing along with a little boy's Christmas Eve wrong number. "I charged it up and turned it on four days ago. Not a peep so far."

"I don't expect it to ring," Devin said. "The mom knows I moved, so I imagine she'll have run interference. But, just in case . . ."

"I'll take care of it."

"Thanks, Dad."

They spoke a few more minutes, and then Sarah entered the room and shouldered Cam out of the way. Mother and son were still talking ten minutes later when Cam went upstairs to change his boots prior to departing for Angel's Rest and his two o'clock tree-cutting trip. Sitting in the easy chair in front of the bedroom suite's fireplace, he bent over to tie his laces. Michael burst into the room and made a running leap onto the bed. "Hey, Daddy. You going somewhere?"

"I have an appointment at Angel's Rest."

"Can I go?"

"Nope."

"Aw, Daddy." Michael went up on his knees. "Please? I'm so bored."

"Then go do your homework."

"I don't have homework. We're on Christmas break. Let me go with you, Dad."

"Nope. This is work."

The boy bounced on the mattress.

"You'd better hope your mom doesn't catch you jumping on the bed. She'll tan your hide."

"She's downstairs talking to Devin. Dad, after you finish your work, will you take me to Forever Christmas?"

Cam sensed a trap, but dang it, he couldn't see what it was. "Why?"

"It's the Saturday before Christmas."

"Yep. What does that have to do with anything?"

"Ms. Claire is going to have gingerbread cookies and hot apple cider, and Santa is going to be there!"

Bingo.

"You've already visited Santa."

"Yes, but I need to tell him something else."

"Nope, doesn't work that way. You get one shot at Santa, boyo."

"But—"

"Zip it. Tell you what. I'm taking a lady and her son to cut their Christmas tree. I think the boy is around your age. If you promise to behave and do exactly what I tell you to do when I tell you to do it, I'll bring you along."

Michael's eyes lit up. "I'll behave! I promise."

"If you don't, I'll ask Mom to make liver and onions for supper."

"Ick. I'll be good, Daddy."

"Go get your gear on and meet me downstairs." The boy was off the bed like a rocket and almost ran down his mother, who had come to stand in the master bedroom doorway. Cam looked at Sarah and let out a weary sigh. "I'm too old to be raising a little kid."

"That sentiment is going on seven years too late."

"Just think. We still have the teen years to go through. Devin almost did me in and I swear, for boys who aren't blood related, those two couldn't be more alike."

"Well, if Michael grows up and moves to Australia, I'll be the one who goes Down Under."

"Excuse me?"

"You'll be burying me in a shallow grave. I won't survive losing another son to Oz." She gazed at Cam with watery violet eyes. "I miss Devin so much!"

Cam opened his arms and Sarah walked into his embrace. His wife undid him. Devin had been a seventeen-year-old with an extra load of teenage baggage when he came into Sarah's life. Sarah couldn't love him any more if she'd given birth to him herself.

Cam hugged her tight, then put his fingers beneath her chin and tilted her head up to meet his gaze. "No shallow grave for you, my love. I'll dig you one nice and deep."

"You're so good to me, Cam Murphy."

"Aren't I though?"

She snorted, and he playfully slapped her butt. "Actually, something tells me if we manage to survive Michael's teenage years, we'll be ready for our heavenly reward."

"Teens? I might not survive grade school."

"Like I said at the beginning of this conversation, I'm too old to be raising kids."

"It's the school holidays that make it so hard. The 'I'm bored' complaint is getting old. Seriously, I don't know what I'm going to do with him next summer."

"That's easy." Cam shot her a wicked grin. "We ship him off to Devin."

Sarah laughed. "Mr. No-Kids-for-Me? It would serve him right. I don't know why he's so adamant about not having children, anyway. He's great with Michael."

"I don't know why you're worrying about that. Boy needs a wife first and from what I can tell, he likes having a harem too much to settle down."

"Men." Sarah said it like a curse.

"Hey, don't paint me with that brush. I married my high school sweetheart."

"Eventually."

"Hey, better late than never. Am I right?" He swooped down and captured her mouth in a lusty kiss.

From downstairs came the sound of their son's impatient voice. "Daddy, let's go!"

Cam met Sarah's gaze. "Military school is always an option."

He headed downstairs and was in the truck watching Michael buckle his seat belt when a rap sounded on the driver's side window. He glanced up to see Sarah holding the Santa phone. Cam winced. That's the second time he'd forgotten Devin's phone.

"What's that, Daddy? Is that a phone? You already have a phone. Why do you have two phones? I don't have any, and I need one!"

Cam gave his son a sidelong look. "It's the Santa hotline. I'm bringing it along in case you don't behave and I need to report."

Michael's eyes went round. He zipped his lips. Cam whistled "Santa Claus Is Coming to Town" all the way to Angel's Rest.

"Here it comes," Reilly called down from the cottage's loft bedroom. "I see the sleigh, Mom."

"Well, come on downstairs and get your hat and gloves."

"I'm gonna go pee first!"

"Good idea." Jenna took one last sip of hot tea, then decided to follow her son's example and made a quick trip to the downstairs restroom.

She was kneeling to help Reilly zip his coat when a rap sounded on their door. "Come in!" Reilly called loudly before Jenna could manage a word.

The door opened, and Celeste Blessing was there carrying two ceramic mugs sporting the Angel's Rest logo. "Merry Christmas!"

"Merry Christmas, Celeste," Jenna said.

"Are you ready to go?"

"We are."

"I hope you don't mind if I tag along with you. I have an errand to do in that part of the forest, and as much as I enjoy taking a snowmobile out for a spin, nothing beats a horse-drawn sleigh."

"We're happy to have you join us."

"Wonderful." Celeste smiled down at Reilly. "I'm thinking I might harvest one more tree for the main house if we find the perfect specimen. There's a spot on the second-floor landing that cries out for a tree. Reilly, do you like marshmallows in your hot chocolate?"

"Yes, ma'am."

"Good. I had a feeling you might. I put a couple extra in yours."

Outside, Celeste introduced them to their driver, a handsome man with friendly, forest green eyes, and his young son Michael, who pinned a blue-eyed gaze on Reilly. "There's a Reilly in my school. She's a girl."

"Don't be rude, Mike," his father said. "Don't forget I have the phone."

The boy appeared honestly insulted. "What's rude about that? She *is* a girl!"

Jenna quickly changed the subject by asking, "How old are you, Michael?"

"I'm almost seven."

"I'm almost eight," Reilly informed them in a superior tone.

"Scoreboard," Cam said to his son.

Michael shrugged that off. He turned back to Reilly. "Do you have a cell phone?"

"No. My mom won't let me have one."

"Me either!"

With that, the boys bonded.

The sleigh was something right out of a Dickens novel, red with gold accents, seating for nine plus the driver, runners that curved on the front end, and jingling bells on the harnesses of the two sorrel horses hitched to it.

Reilly accepted Cam's invitation to sit up front with him and his son. Celeste topped off everyone's hot chocolate from a thermos, then Cam took up the reins and, to the jingle of bells, the sleigh glided smoothly across the snow.

Celeste pointed out valley landmarks as they crossed the main area of the resort. When they entered the forest and the winding trail began a gradual climb in elevation, she fell silent. Even the chattering boys spoke more softly. Snow frosted the branches of evergreens and

sunshine dappled the ground. The fragrance of fir . . . of
Christmas . . . drifted on the air. Jenna sipped her hot
chocolate and enjoyed the peace of the snow-dusted afternoon.

"It's beautiful here," she murmured.

Celeste beamed at her. "We call it a little piece of heaven
in the Colorado Rockies."

"I can see why. In some ways this forest reminds me of
a cathedral."

"That's a keen observation, Jenna. Many people find
that communing with nature enables them to tap into spir-
ituality. I like to say that while God is everywhere, in
some places He's a little more obvious."

Just then the sleigh rounded a bend to reveal a scene
right out of a postcard. Majestic snowcapped mountains
stood against a brilliant blue sky. Jenna was suddenly so
glad they weren't on a Disney cruise. "It's breathtaking."

Gently, Cam pulled up on the reins, slowing the horses.
He gestured to the left. "Look, boys. Through the trees,
just beyond that big boulder. See him?"

"Him?" Instinctively, Reilly went stiff.

Michael asked, "See who, Dad . . . oh. I see." He tugged
the sleeve of Reilly's jacket. "Look, Reilly."

Jenna saw the animal at the same time Reilly did. The
boy sat forward on his seat. "Wow. Is that a reindeer?"

"He's an elk," Cam answered. "Majestic, isn't he?"

"Those are really big antlers."

"They're called a rack," Michael informed Reilly. "My
brother Devin says guys really like big racks."

Jenna made a strangled noise in her throat. Michael
continued, "I've seen lots of elk and deer and mountain
goats. Once I saw a bear. I was spending the night with
Mr. and Mrs. Callahan at Stardance Ranch and one of the
campers didn't put the lid on the trash can the right way
and the bear got into it. He was licking a can of barbecue

beans. He almost got his nose stuck in it. Have you ever seen a bear?"

"No. I'd really like to see one."

"I want to see a shark. One time, my brother caught a great white shark. He lives in Australia."

Jenna pulled her attention away from the elk and focused on the boy. "Australia? That's a long way from Eternity Springs."

Michael nodded. "I know. It makes me sad that he wants to live there. It's so far away that I don't ever get to see him. And you know what? It's summer there now! On Christmas, he's going to church on a beach and he'll wear flip-flops."

"Wow." Reilly's brow furrowed in thought. "I don't know if I'd like that. Seems like Christmas should have snow."

As Cam gave the reins a slap, the horses moved and the sleigh slid forward. Jenna watched the passing scenery, though her thoughts were turned inward. Could the world be that small? What were the chances that two men with younger brothers from Eternity Springs lived in Australia?

Slim, she imagined. Very, very slim.

She gave Cam Murphy a studied look. So, he was Reilly's Santa Claus's father. Michael was his brother.

Reilly's Santa Claus's name was Devin Murphy.

Celeste leaned toward her saying, "The Murphys are close. This will be the first Christmas holiday that Devin isn't spending with his parents and siblings. They're planning a nice long visit to Australia in late June, but that seems a lifetime away to Michael."

"Holidays make the absence of family members all the more acute," Jenna said, her thoughts drifting back to the reason for Reilly's original North Pole call. He'd wanted Santa to bring him a dad for Christmas.

I tried, buddy. Joel had been a great father—for his own kids.

"That's true. Luckily, the Murphys have a large support system—the entire town." Celeste patted Jenna's leg. "One thing you'll like about Eternity Springs is that we are family fluid."

"Family fluid?"

"What defines a family but the family itself? Eternity Springs is welcoming and generous. You and Reilly are spending your holiday with us so this season, you are part of our family. Now, see this bridge up ahead? Once we cross it, we're less than five minutes to the part of the forest where you can choose your tree. Do you know what kind you want? A Douglas fir? A lodgepole pine? A Colorado blue spruce?"

Jenna was glad to change the subject to Christmas. "I don't know. What do you think, Reilly?"

"I want one that's really tall!"

"We can do tall," Cam said. Less than ten minutes later, he pulled back on the reins and the sleigh slid to a stop. The boys scrambled down to the ground.

"We have a tall tree," Michael told Reilly. "You wanna come over and see it? Maybe you can come spend the night with me. Dad, can my new friend Reilly spend the night with me?"

Reilly went still and his eyes went round. He looked from Jenna, to Cam, and back to Jenna. Cam shrugged. "It's okay by me. We'll have to check with Mom, but I image she'll green light the idea. She won't be home tonight."

"It's Bunco night," Celeste explained to Jenna.

"Will you call her, Dad? Please?"

Cam looked at Jenna, his brow arched in silent question. Jenna's heart melted at the hope in her little boy's eyes. She nodded. Moments later, Michael's mom had given her blessing and the tree hunt began in earnest.

Jenna thought cutting a Christmas tree might be anti-climactic.

Celeste chose a five-foot spruce shortly after they stopped. While Cam removed a chain saw from a compartment beneath the driver's seat, the boys ran like banshees through the forest. Jenna gave up her attempts to chase them down when Cam told her not to worry. "As long as we can hear them, they're fine. That said, I didn't mean for my boy to crash your family moment. I'll make him sit—"

"No," Jenna was quick to say. "No. This is wonderful. It's just what we needed. What Reilly needed."

"Good." Cam braced his hands on his hips and slowly shook his head. "It's what I needed too, to be honest. Did you ever watch Bugs Bunny?" After she nodded he continued. "Remember the Tasmanian Devil? That's our Mike. And this time of year with all the excitement of Christmas . . . it's even worse. If your Reilly can drain some of his battery, I'll be a grateful man."

Jenna followed the path of his gaze and saw the boys playing tag. Wistfulness overcame her. Once upon a time, her son had run at life in a similar manner. Once upon a time—before a New Year's Eve SWAT raid.

The boys ended their game, and Reilly ran back to her. "Let's pick a tree, Mom. We need to get it back and decorated before it's time to go to Michael's house."

"Hey, I've been the one waiting on *you*."

Cam saw to harvesting the tree for Celeste while Jenna, Reilly, and Michael searched for the Stockton family's perfect tree. They narrowed it down to two trees, both fir, and Michael was running back and forth between them trying to make a final decision when he said, "What is Miss Celeste doing? Maybe she found a better tree for us."

He took off running toward the spot where Jenna could just see a speck of color that was Celeste's gold coat. With a sigh, Jenna trekked after them. What she discovered when she drew closer put a smile of wonder on her face.

It was a perfectly shaped noble fir that stood probably ten feet tall. In the middle of a forest in the middle of nowhere, it was trimmed like a Christmas tree, but with items made from natural elements. A garland of bright red berries encircled the tree. Carved wooden ornaments hung from the branches. Jenna spied twigs formed into stars and snowflakes, and acorn tops shaped into hearts. And at its top stood a most magnificent angel with a face carved from stone, a halo of silver, a gown of golden fur, and graceful wings of snow white feathers.

"What is this?" Michael asked, awe in his voice.

"It's my Christmas wishing tree," Celeste replied.

Reilly said, "I've never heard of that."

The smile that Celeste showed him was warm enough to melt the snow. "The Christmas wishing tree is a generations-old tradition in my family."

"How does it work?" Michael asked. "Do you ask for presents like with Santa Claus?"

"Well, not precisely. The Christmas wishing tree definitely has more of a spiritual aspect to it."

"Like ghosts?" Reilly asked.

"No, dear. While the term 'spiritual' means different things to different people depending on their worldview, in this case it refers to the sacred, that which is beyond ourselves, that existence that speaks to the soul."

Michel frowned. "I don't understand."

Reilly raised his hand like a schoolboy. "Sacred is Baby Jesus in the manger. That's what's Christmas is supposed to be about, we just forget about it because of all the commercials."

"Not commercials," Jenna corrected. "Commercialism."

Celeste laughed. "Commercials have something to do with it too. Let me try to explain it this way. Earlier when we entered the forest and you boys went still and quiet, do you know why you reacted that way?"

The boys looked at each other and shook their heads.

"Jenna, do you recall what you said to me?"

"I said it was like entering a cathedral."

"What's a cathedral?" Michael asked.

"A great big church," Cam told him.

"Why did the forest make you think of entering a cathedral, Jenna?"

The boys turned to Jenna expectantly. She took a moment to frame her response in a simple way the boys would understand. "Because when I go into a cathedral, it's so huge and beautiful and peaceful that it touches my heart deep down inside. Sometimes makes me cry good tears."

"My mom does that a lot," Michael offered.

Jenna smiled at him and completed her explanation. "Walking into a cathedral reminds me that I'm a tiny human being and the universe is huge and created by a power that is bigger than my mind can comprehend."

"That's an excellent description, Jenna. The Christmas wishing tree tradition came about because while we might not always have a cathedral handy, we can usually find a tree growing in the woods somewhere."

Reilly asked, "What about somebody's front yard? Would that count?"

"Why, yes. Yes it would. Although I will admit that a forest is beneficial to get the full effect."

He pressed. "What about fake Christmas trees, the kind you buy in a store?"

"Actually, I've never considered that question before, Reilly, but I believe that probably crosses the line. It needs to be a living, growing tree."

"So do you decorate the exact same wishing tree every year?"

"No. Each year it's a different tree. That's one of the things that are so wonderful about a Christmas wishing tree. It doesn't matter where I'm living or visiting, I can designate any tree to be my Christmas wishing tree.

"How does it work?"

"Reilly, that's what she's trying to tell us." Jenna made a zipping motion over her mouth. "Let her talk."

Celeste winked at Reilly, then continued. "Each year when I decorate my wishing tree, I make one special ornament that represents a particular challenge or circumstance I overcame during the past year and my biggest wish for the one upcoming. When I hang it on a tree, in the cathedral of a forest, I reflect on those two events. That's when the magic happens."

"Magic?" Cam asked, his green eyes watching Celeste closely.

"My wishes have a way of coming true."

"Because of magic?" Michael asked.

"Because I choose to live my vision, not my circumstance."

She focused her gaze on Jenna and continued, "All of us have circumstances. For some it's health related. For others, it's financial struggles. The choice each of us has is whether we allow circumstances to rule our lives, or whether we live according to our vision, how we want our lives to be. If I were the one who'd named my family tradition, I'd have called it the Christmas vision tree. Circumstances are temporary; vision lasts forever."

The words resonated inside of Jenna like a song. She had the sense that something important had just taken place, and she was still trying to think it through when Reilly asked, "Has your wish come true? The one you made when you hung your special ornament this year?"

BC Ferries
Coastal Inspiration

101955

Chk 5353 Oct21'18 10:56A Gst 0
---
1 CHRISTMAS WISHI   10.50
7812501317720
XXXXXXXXXXXXXXX0595
MASTERCARD   11.03

Subtotal   10.50
GST   0.53
Paid   11.03

Thanks for sailing with us!
GST# 89462 3206 RT0001

"Actually, yes. Yes it has. My wish came true yesterday, in fact." Then the older woman clapped her hands and added, "Now, we'd better see to finding your Christmas tree, young man, before the afternoon gets away from us. I remember seeing a tall, full, beautiful spruce over this way." She gestured toward the northeast. "Would you like me to show you?"

"Yes!" Reilly bounded after her with Michael close on their heels.

Jenna stood staring at the decorated tree, her gaze focused on a carved wooden angel ornament. Sensing Cam's gaze upon her, she said, "I get the feeling that something important just happened, though I can't really say what it was."

"That's our Celeste," he told her. "All I can say is ignore her at your own peril. She has an uncanny ability to offer up advice that a person needs to hear at exactly the time they need to hear it. I've seen it happen time and time again."

I choose to live my vision, not my circumstance.

My wishes tend to come true.

"Mom? Hey, Mom! We found it! C'mere, Mom! It's the perfect Christmas tree!"

Cam pulled the work gloves out of the back pocket of his jeans and said, "Sounds like it's time for me to get to work."

"Mom! Hurry!"

Jenna laughed and said, "Me too."

She followed her son's footsteps through the snow to where Reilly, his new friend, and a woman who seemed to have an inner glow about her admired a perfectly shaped Colorado blue spruce.

Two hours later it stood in front of Blitzen's main window sporting blinking lights, glass balls, dog bones, ribbon garland, Eternity Springs' Twelve Dogs of Christmas, and an angel tree topper that had the face of an Irish setter. The tree was so big it needed some fill-in decor, but all in all, Jenna decided it was the most beautiful Christmas tree ever due to the joy she saw in her son's face when he looked at it.

"'Where broken hearts come to heal'," she quoted softly. Eternity Springs was doing its thing.

The sleepover at the Murphys' house was a huge success. On Christmas Eve they attended church services and watched Michael shine in his role as a Christmas pageant shepherd. On Christmas Day Reilly did *not* find a puppy beneath the tree because Jenna judged he didn't need one. Neither did she. The reasons against having one had not changed. Instead, Santa brought him a remote control car as a surprise, and he was thrilled with the gift.

Between Christmas and New Year's Eve, they filled their days with activities. They went snowmobiling and sledding and horseback riding. During a day trip to Wolf Creek, Reilly learned to snowboard and made a good effort at learning to ski. They attended story time at the library and participated in the official Eternity Springs Boxing Day Snowball Fight. Michael spent the night with Reilly once at Blitzen, and Reilly returned to the Murphys' home for another sleepover the night before New Year's Eve.

Jenna changed her mind half a dozen times about how they should spend New Year's Eve. They'd been included in invitations for an adult party at Angel's Rest and a corresponding children's slumber party at a daycare center called Gingerbread House. Reilly desperately wanted to attend, but the thought of being separated on the swatting anniversary gave her cold sweats.

It was foolish, she knew. She had no reason to think that the stalker had traced them again. Nothing since their move to Tallahassee in September had given her cause for concern. She should allow Reilly to attend the party, go to one herself, and end their holiday trip on a positive note.

What finally made up her mind was finding Reilly sitting at the table in the cottage's kitchen with a pile of pinecones, stones, sunflower seeds, and a bottle of glue. "Whatcha doin' there, hot rod?"

"I'm making an ornament."

"To take home as a souvenir?"

"No. It's for my Christmas wishing tree. You can choose a wishing tree and decorate it anytime you want. I asked Ms. Celeste."

Jenna's heart did a little flip. "You did?"

"Yep. When we come back to Eternity Springs next year for Christmas I can add more decorations."

Choose to live your vision, not your circumstance.

Peace rolled through Jenna like an ocean wave. "That sounds like a plan. Looks like you have plenty of supplies there. Mind if I join you and make an ornament too?"

"Sure, Mom. You can come with me when I hang it. Just don't ask me what my wish is. Ms. Celeste said it works better if you keep it in your heart."

"Ah. Okay, then."

When Jenna hung her ornament on a tree in the cathedral of the Angel's Rest forest an hour later, she didn't try to keep the tears from her eyes. "Good tears," she assured Reilly.

They walked hand in hand back to Blitzen and got ready for their respective parties. Reilly left her at Gingerbread House without a backward glance, and Jenna enjoyed herself so much at Celeste's party that she stayed past midnight and even shared a friendly midnight kiss with a handsome lawyer named Boone McBride.

On New Year's Day with real regret for the end of their vacation and after Michael and Reilly secured promises from their mothers that phone calls between them would be allowed and encouraged, Reilly and Jenna headed home to Tallahassee.

As they passed the Eternity Springs city limits marker, Jenna promised them both. "We'll be back."

CAIRNS, AUSTRALIA

At five a.m. on the second of January, Devin filled his travel mug with piping hot coffee and prepared to head down to the marina. He had a busy day ahead. The dive boat tour was three-quarters full this morning and both fishing boats were fully booked. The three pharmaceutical executives from Boston going out with him on the *Out-n-Back* were repeat customers, and since fishing had been excellent the past three days, he had high hopes that he'd put them on to something big.

He'd just picked up his keys when his phone rang. He checked the number. "Hey, Dad. I'm just heading to work. Running a little late, in fact."

"I won't keep you. I just wanted to tell you about a phone call I had during the New Year's Eve party last night."

Cairns was seventeen hours ahead of Eternity Springs, so his dad was calling from New Year's Day afternoon. Devin wanted to ask about the college football games, but he didn't have time.

"Guess who phoned me a little before midnight? Your Reilly from Nashville."

In the process of reaching for his coffee, Devin froze. His lips stretched in a smile. "Oh yeah?"

"It was a short call and I'm afraid I couldn't hear him very well. Lots of noise on my end and on his. But what I did hear was him thanking Santa for his presents—I couldn't tell what—and he said something about believing."

Believing. Well, how about that? "Awesome. That's great. I'm glad you heard from him. Thanks for filling in for me."

"Glad to do it. I just hope that next year, you're here to serve this duty yourself. Your mother missed you terribly."

Just Mom? Devin rolled his eyes. "I missed being there too. But don't worry, I won't miss it. Christmas in Eternity Springs—I can't think of anything that sounds nicer."

TALLAHASSEE, FLORIDA

Reilly stood in the card shop with his hands clasped beneath his chin as he stared at the packaged valentines on the shelf. "I can't decide, Mom. I just can't decide! Do I get Minions or Paw Patrol?"

Jenna shook her head at her son's genuine distress over the momentous decision he faced. She was tempted to buy both, but she knew that would only complicate the issue when he went to choose which card to give to which friend at tomorrow's Valentine's Day party at his Sunday school. "I'm sure either one would be just fine, Reilly. Better make up your mind. We still have a lot to do this afternoon."

"Like cookies to decorate! Do you think they've cooled off enough, yet?"

"I expect so, yes." She and Reilly had spent the morning making two-dozen heart-shaped sugar cookies for tomorrow's party.

"Then we'd better hurry, Mom! We still have to go to the grocery store for sprinkles."

"I know," Jenna replied. "We need red food coloring too."

Thus motivated, Reilly made his choice, and as they walked toward the checkout counter, he said, "You know what I think, Mom?"

"What do you think, Reilly?"

"I think we should send a valentine to Santa at the North Pole. He was really nice to me and people shouldn't forget about Santa just because it isn't Christmas."

Jenna smiled down at her son. "I think that's an excellent idea, son."

Pride at Reilly's thoughtfulness warmed her heart, and during their stop at the grocery store, her thoughts drifted to a certain Santa. Too bad that a valentine sent to the North Pole wouldn't find its way to Australia.

They returned home with sprinkles and food coloring and a box of Paw Patrol valentines. Reilly donned his child-sized apron and chef's hat to help his mother whip up a batch of royal icing. After tinting one bowl of icing red and another pink, they sat at the kitchen table with cookies, icing, spatulas, and pastry bags before them. Reilly chatted like a magpie as he spread icing over golden brown hearts. Contentment rolled through Jenna like a tropical sea wave.

She was piping a red outline around a sugar cookie heart when the peace exploded. Light flashed, sound boomed, and men shouted, "We're in, we're in. Clear!"

Reilly screamed, "Mommy!"

Not again! Jenna lunged for her son and wrapped protective arms around him, bumping the table hard in the process. Cookies hit the floor.

Hearts broke.

Part Two

Chapter Six

JUNE

Traveling from Cairns, Australia, to Eternity Springs, Colorado, was no easy jaunt under the best of circumstances. This journey back to the States had been a nightmare of missed connections, crying babies, and mechanical problems that included a malfunctioning toilet on the Brisbane-to-Honolulu leg of the trip. By the time his plane from Denver landed in Gunnison and he exited security to see his mom, dad, and little brother waiting for him, Devin felt like wallaby roadkill.

"Devin!" Michael ran toward him, arms outstretched.

Devin dropped his backpack and stooped to scoop up his brother. "Hey, squirt. You've grown a foot since last October."

"Nope. I still only have two of them."

Sarah followed a few steps behind Michael. She wore her dark hair short in a style that framed her unusual violet eyes, eyes that gleamed with happiness and love as she wrapped Devin in her arms. "Finally. You're finally here. Oh, Devin."

He buried his face in her hair and inhaled the fragrance of . . . home. "Mom."

She looked up at him with tear-flooded eyes. "We've missed you so much."

Michael began to wiggle and Devin set the boy down as his gaze fell upon Cam. Tall and lean and broad of shoulders, his father had gone a little grayer at the temples, the laugh lines along his eyes carved a little deeper and stretched a little longer. His eyes hadn't changed. Mountain eyes, Sarah called them, because of their myriad shades of green. Neither had his grin, the devil-may-care pirate's smile that Devin had so admired and mimicked as a boy until he'd perfected it.

Devin extended his hand. "Hello, old man."

"Boy." Cam took Devin's hand in a punishing grip. "You look like you went ten rounds with a 'roo on a walkabout."

"Feels like fifteen."

"C'mere, son." Cam wrapped him into a bear hug and when they finally broke apart, Devin couldn't miss the sheen of tears in his father's eyes. "This has been too long a stretch. We have to do better."

"I won't argue with you."

After a late-season blizzard grounded his family in Eternity Springs at Easter, they'd attempted to reschedule their trip. Trying to coordinate schedules proved too difficult, however, and eventually they'd decided the best solution was for Devin to make a summertime trip home. Now, though, Devin was home for a three-week visit planned around the Callahan family's big Fourth of July celebration and an engagement party for Lori's sister-in-law, Caitlin Timberlake.

Sarah shoved her husband out of the way and swooped in for another hug. "Lori said to tell you she's sorry she isn't here. She wasn't feeling well this morning—she's had the stomach bug that's been going around town and she wasn't up to a car ride—but she and Chase are planning to come to dinner tonight as long as she's feeling better and Chase remains healthy."

"Are you killing the fatted calf?" Devin asked.

Cam shook his head. "She's killed the Crisco. You're mother's been baking for days."

Devin gave him a droll look. "She bakes every day. It's her job."

Sarah sniffed. "I'll have you know I made two extra batches of strawberry pinwheels and they're in the kitchen cookie jar. Of course, I could always take them back to Fresh."

"I love you, Mom."

"We're having Tex-Mex. Enchiladas, refried beans, Mexican rice, and chips with homemade salsa. Torie Callahan's recipe. It's your brother's new favorite food."

"Guacamole, too?" At his mother's nod, Devin stopped and put his hand over his heart. "That's almost enough to make me forget the horrors of the flights."

He shared the joys of the trip while they waited for his bag. Once they'd loaded into his dad's SUV for the two-hour drive to Eternity Springs, he asked for the local gossip update. That kept the conversation going for an hour. Then, as usual, his mother began grilling him on the status of his love life.

"I'm not dating anyone in particular, Mom."

"What about that schoolteacher you said you were seeing this spring?"

"That didn't work out." Lisa had been a nice woman, but the spark just hadn't been there in the bedroom.

"Oh. I'm sorry."

Devin shrugged. He'd been sorry too. Although he wasn't ready for a steady relationship yet, the dating scene was starting to grow tiresome. What had been fun when he was younger had become . . . well . . . work. Not that he wanted to settle down. He didn't. His flirtation with that idea two years ago had cured him of ever reaching for anything permanent. But he wouldn't mind having someone in his life who mattered for longer than a weekend or two—if he could find someone looking for a similar level of commitment.

Better not tell his mother that, though. She hounded him enough as it was. If she thought he might actually be ready for something serious, she'd dial it up to "incessantly."

He went for distraction. "So, Dad, let me tell you about the engine trouble I had last week on the *Out-n-Back*."

That got them all the way to Eternity Springs. At home, he took a long hot shower then surrendered to jet lag and fell into bed. He slept until his mother sent Michael to drag him down for dinner. The lively conversation with his family revived him, but he over-indulged on the delicious Mexican food and returned to bed when supper ended.

When he finally rolled out of bed mid-morning the following day, he took another long hot shower, and almost felt human again. Except the enchiladas lay in his gut like adobe bricks, and he knew he'd better get some exercise. He tugged on running shorts, an ancient Rockies baseball T-shirt, and his sneakers. Downstairs, he filled a water bottle and waved off breakfast.

He took off running down Aspen Street and decided he'd make the loop around Hummingbird Lake. The brisk morning temperatures moderated as the summer sun climbed over the mountains on the eastern side of the valley. Soon, Devin was sweating. By the time he'd completed the first half of the four-mile path around the lake, he'd taken off his shirt and draped it around his shoulders to use as a rag to wipe the sweat off his face. Too much beer last night. Too many carbs. Too much altitude. He felt like an out-of-shape runner twice his age.

So he had slowed to a walk as he approached the pier where the movements of a pair of fishermen caught his notice. They were a woman and a boy who appeared to be a year or two older than Michael. They kid wore his hair in a bleach-blond mohawk with blue tips. She wore jeans, a blue plaid flannel shirt with the cuffs rolled up over a V-neck white shirt, and hiking boots. A thick black ponytail was pulled through the back of her baseball cap and danced back and forth as she moved. A legal-size trout dangled from the end of the boy's line, which unfortunately appeared to be tangled with that of his mother's.

As a professional fishing guide, Devin had seen entangled equipment more often than he could count. While he watched, she grasped the fish—left hand, ringless—and the boy dropped his pole. She grabbed for the boy's pole—right hand, pretty sterling silver ring—and in doing so, dropped the fish.

This did not look promising.

Devin turned onto the fishing pier and sauntered toward them. "Looks like you have a rat's nest on your hands. Want some help?"

The woman stiffened and turned suspicious brown eyes in his direction. "No, thank you. We're okay."

Maybe so, but the fish wasn't. They were going to kill that rainbow trout if they weren't careful. "Are you guys planning to eat that 'bow?"

"No." Now, those big brown eyes flashed with annoyance. She lifted her chin. "We catch and release when we fish."

"In that case, you'd better let me help."

"Mister, we don't need—"

Devin cut her off. "The quicker we act to free him and get him back in the water, the more likely he is to survive." He reached for the tangled fishing lines. "Do you have a knife in your tackle box?"

At the question, the boy finally spoke in a voice barely above a whisper. "Are you going to kill him?"

"I'm going to save him," Devin replied as he wrapped

his fist around the fish. A glance at its mouth revealed it had two hooks in it. The one attached to the boy's line and another rusting barbed hook. "Or try to, anyway. This isn't this guy's first rodeo."

Moving quickly, he opened the tackle box and bypassed the knife for the needle-nose pliers he spied. At least Ms. Snippy had a well-stocked tackle box.

"Don't get me wrong," Devin said as he labored to free the trout. "I don't have anything against fishing. The opposite, in fact. Among other things, I make my living as a professional fishing guide. But fish are a precious resource and we need to be responsible fishermen."

"We weren't trying to be otherwise," the woman replied defensively.

"It's my fault," the boy mumbled, his voice barely above a whisper. He'd moved so close to the mother that he stood almost on top of her. "I got excited and didn't pay attention."

The woman frowned at the boy. "You did nothing wrong, RJ."

Having freed both hooks, Devin leaned off the pier and lowered the trout into the icy mountain lake. He gently opened his hand and was glad when the fish darted off.

Her tone as cool as the lake, the woman said, "Thank you for your assistance. We will handle it from here."

It was just the sort of challenge that appealed to Devin. He rolled back on his heels and shot his very best sexy-but-boyish grin up at her. "I don't mind helping. I love to help folks catch fish. I'm truly an excellent guide."

"I'm sure you are."

"I'm happy to give you a few pointers. No charge."

"How kind of you," she drawled, her smile one hundred percent fake. "However, my son hooked a fish within five minutes of getting his line wet. I don't believe we need any guidance."

"Five minutes, huh? Excellent work . . . RJ, was it?" Devin kept his gaze on the boy while continuing to take note of the mother's stick-up-her-ass expression. "So, I see you're fishing with salmon eggs. Ever try a fly?"

The boy stubbed the toe of his hiking boot and shrugged.

"It's tricky to learn, I'll give you that. I'm not nearly a pro, myself."

"What kind of a guide are you?" Mom murmured sotto voce.

Devin wanted to laugh, but he continued to talk to the boy. "I've been fishing all my life, but I was seventeen before I tried fly-fishing. See, I'm not from Colorado. I'm not even American. I'm an Aussie—Australian. Saltwater is my specialty, and it's a whole different kettle of fish."

The hint of interest in the boy's darting glance encouraged Devin to continue. "It wasn't until I visited Eternity Springs for the first time that my dad brought me to this very lake to teach me to cast a fly. You should have seen me. We were right over there." Devin pointed toward the shoreline about two hundred yards from where they stood. "I drew back my rod and let loose. Hooked a bird's nest in an aspen tree behind me. Yanked it right out of the tree and it flew through the air and whacked my dad's head."

The boy laughed softly and Devin thought he'd won a prize. He glanced at the mother and found her staring at him in shock. He arched a challenging brow. "What? You think I'm kidding? My dad was not a happy man with a head full of straw, I'm telling you."

"No. I . . ." Her voice trailed off and she stared at him, the look in her eyes unreadable. "You live in Australia?"

"Yes."

Following a long moment, her lips twitched. Her eyes softened like a mountain vista at sunset. "I . . . believe. You. I believe you."

Then her smile warmed and widened, and the act took her from attractive to downright stunning. Whoa. Talk about a difference. Icy Mom to Hot Mom in seconds.

Devin reacted like he always did in similar situations. He turned on the flirt, adding a twinkle to his eyes and flashing his famous grin. "I've learned a lot since the fly-ing bird's nest. To be a good fly-fisherman, one needs a soft touch and a great clinch."

She scolded him with a look.

"A clinch knot." He held up his hands palms out. "It's a knot. You need a clinch knot and a surgeon's knot."

The boy piped up. "Mom knows those. Mom can tie *any* knot."

"Oh really?" Devin gave her a measuring look. "Girl Scout?"

She nodded. "Among other things."

"Interesting." She *was* interesting. Wonder why she'd gone from frosty to friendly in a heartbeat? The bird's nest story wasn't *that* great.

Devin knew he probably should wish this mother and son well and go on about his business. He did have items on his docket. His mom would expect him to drop by the bakery. Odds were she had something special in the oven meant for him. He'd promised Michael that he'd play catch with him this morning, and Lori had guilted him into working a volunteer shift at the local pet shelter.

But he didn't want to continue his walk. He wanted to stand here and flirt with Hot Mom. So he extended his hand and said, "My name is Devin, by the way. Devin Murphy."

The boy made a strangled noise. His mother put her hand on his shoulder and gave it a squeeze. "Call me Jenna," she replied, accepting his handshake.

Devin waited a beat, but when she didn't offer a surname

or introduce her son, he inquired, "Are you visiting Eternity Springs, Jenna, or are you residents?"

"We're visitors."

"Well, welcome to Eternity Springs. I'd love to show you my skills. Fly-fishing skills, of course."

"Of course," she repeated, her tone dry, but her smile still in place. "I'm sure that my son would love to learn to fly-fish, wouldn't you?"

At his mother's question, the boy's mouth gaped. He stared up at her in shock.

Gently, she said, "It's true, isn't it?"

Hesitantly, he said, "Yes."

Jenna smiled regretfully at Devin and gestured toward the gear lying on the pier. "Unfortunately we don't have the right equipment."

Devin bit back a suggestive remark about carrying a rod around with him and rose to his feet. "See, we're in luck there. My dad owns the local outfitters shop and he'll let me borrow what we need. What does your day look like? I have time this afternoon for a lesson. Say, around two?"

"Two would be just fine. Do we meet back here?"

"Here will be good. Once your boy gets the hang of things, we can give creek casting a try. Now, I'd better finish my run and get home before my little brother calls the sheriff on me. I promised him a game of catch." Devin gave the boy a wink, tipped an imaginary hat to the pretty lady, and then took off running up the fishing pier. As he turned onto the lakeside trail, he turned back toward Jenna and called, "See you at two!"

She smiled and waved.

The boy looked up at his mother as though she'd lost her mind. *Huh. Wonder what that's about?*

It's him! I can't believe it's him!

And Santa Claus had an excellent ass.

Jenna stifled a semi-hysterica giggle as she watched Devin Murphy jog away in gym shorts, which were appropriately red. What were the odds? The first extended conversation she had in two months with a man who was younger than forty, and he turned out to be Reilly's Santa.

When she'd decided to bring her traumatized son back to Eternity Springs this summer, she'd known that they took a chance of crossing paths with someone they'd met during their Christmas visit. But she'd thought the potential benefit of basking in what Celeste called Eternity Springs healing magic would outweigh that risk. It had worked last Christmas, hadn't it?

She had hoped that by arriving at the height of tourist season when visitors crowded the streets and at a time when she knew that the Murphys were scheduled to be in Australia, she and Reilly could avoid being recognized. With their hairstyles significantly different and Jenna's colored contacts hiding the unique blue of her eyes, the plan had worked too. They'd made two trips into town in complete anonymity since their arrival yesterday.

She never expected to run into Santa Claus himself. And to meet him on their very first full day in town, no less. To have him approach them in a place where retreat literally was impossible and for him to be so darned friendly that her well-practiced cold shoulder didn't frighten him away before he provided enough clues to identify him . . . it was all simply incredible. Unbelievable.

Believe. Devin Murphy aka Santa Claus is the King of Believing. Wonder if—

"Mom!" Reilly interrupted her thoughts.

"Hmm?" Her gaze remained locked on Murphy's retreating form. His shoulders were broad and thickly muscled, fitting for a man who often battled big fish. He ran with a long-legged fluid stride. Bet he—

"Mom! You're not listening to me!"

"I'm sorry." She gave her son a distracted smile. "What is it?"

"What are you doing? That is Michael's brother! We can't go fishing with him. What if he recognizes us? That would be terrible."

Bless your heart, Reilly. You see danger everywhere you go now. "How would he recognize us?" Jenna asked in an effort to reassure her son. "We never met him."

"Maybe Michael told him about us."

"He probably did." When Reilly's eyes went round with worry, she put her hand on her son's shoulder and added, "And why would he connect a woman with black hair and brown eyes and a boy with a blue-tipped mohawk to the Stockton family who spent a few days here last Christmas?"

"You told him your name was Jenna. Not Jane or even J.C.!"

"I did?"

"Yes!"

"Oh dear." Jenna tried not to wince. For the past two months she'd gone by the name Jane Tarver, having used her most excellent Photoshop skills and a 3D printer to create a fake ID good enough to fool anyone but law enforcement. Since she studiously observed every rule of the road, she planned to never need to use her real ID.

But she'd forgotten all about Jane once she'd realized just who was tickling the trout. Her gaze shifted back to the running figure now on the verge of disappearing from view. "I guess I had a brain freeze."

Or a hormone flare.

"That's not good, Mom. And something else. If Michael's brother isn't in Australia today, then I bet Michael isn't there, either. He's probably in Eternity Springs too. Oh, Mom. What if Michael sees us? What if Devin brings Michael fishing with us? That would be a disaster. We have to go back to the camper right now and pack things up and leave right away! Something bad could happen to Michael!"

Oh, Reilly, you break my heart.

Plus, he did have a point. As much as she hated the thought of moving on from Eternity Springs, knowing that Cam and Sarah and Michael were around town changed things. She and Reilly had spent too much time with the Murphy family at Christmas.

"Why did you talk to him, anyway?" Reilly continued. "Devin Murphy was a stranger. Mom, that's so dangerous! You're not serious about meeting him later, right? You were just trying to get rid of him?"

Jenna used the act of picking up their fishing poles to buy time as she formulated a response. She walked a narrow line between seeing to her son's safety and feeding his fears. If not for Reilly, she'd go home to Nashville and challenge the stalker to come after her, goading him in every manner she could imagine. She'd buy ads on radio. Talk her way onto TV. She'd post on every Internet message board and social media site in existence, and she'd have an entire army of investigators ready to track his digital footprints back to his physical feet.

Then she'd show him what it was like to be baking cookies one minute and battling a SWAT team the next.

Except she *did* have her son to consider, and the boy's fears *were* justified. While she didn't worry that being recognized by the Murphy family or Celeste Blessing or even her New Year's Eve midnight smoocher, Boone McBride, would lead the stalker to their fifth wheel door, Reilly did. And who knew? He might be right.

Jenna had believed they were safe in Tallahassee and look how that turned out.

At the memory of that horrible afternoon, a shiver skittered up her spine. Better safe than sorry. As much as she would have liked spending time with Santa, it wasn't meant to be.

"Okay. Okay, honey. We will leave Eternity Springs."

Visible relief rolled over the boy, and Jenna knew she'd made the right decision. Thinking aloud, she added, "I'm a little concerned about where we'll go, though. It's tough to find a campsite vacancy this time of year."

That was a legitimate concern too. They'd lucked into the slot at Stardance Ranch. Jenna had called seeking a reservation minutes after the RV resort received a cancellation. "Let's head back to camp. I'll get online and see what I can find."

"You'll find something, Mom. I know you will."

They carried their equipment back toward the truck, which Jenna had left parked in a lot conveniently positioned between the fishing pier and the Hummingbird Lake Hike and Bike Trail. As they approached the trailhead, a group of five young Scouts scrambled out of a Jeep and into backpacks, laughing and poking fun at one another. Jenna didn't miss the yearning that flashed across her son's face. For what must be the three hundred millionth time since she'd put the clues together and realized she had a stalker, she silently cursed the bastard.

Reilly should be a member of a Scout troop, she thought as she stowed the fishing gear in the bed of the truck and climbed behind the wheel. He should have friends his own age with whom he roughhoused and made fart jokes and played Little League baseball.

All he has is me.

Jenna sighed as she waited for her son to buckle up, then turned the key, put the truck in gear, and pulled out onto the two-lane road that circled Hummingbird Lake. The situation wasn't ideal, but she was doing her best. Frankly, her best was pretty darn excellent. If life on the road was a little light on friends . . . well . . . that wasn't the end of the world. First things first. Safety and security first. Eventually, the rest would come. One day they'd no longer jump at loud noises. Strangers wouldn't make them nervous. Someday this permanent crick she had in her neck from constantly looking over her shoulder would completely disappear.

In the meantime, she'd make her living without using her medical license, and she'd pay for everything with cash. They would continue to conceal their real names and place of origin. Every day put more time and distance between them and the stalker.

Whenever she got down, Jenna reminded herself that the nomadic lifestyle suited them. She and Reilly had spent the last four months touring parks. National parks. State parks. Even local parks. What began as flight had evolved to an enjoyable way of life. The solitude soothed them. The anonymity reassured them. For the first time in a very long time, Jenna didn't schedule her life down to five-minute blocks. She provided for Reilly's basic needs—shelter, sustenance, and safety. Living out of a trailer tended to whittle away the fluff.

She'd homeschooled her son and educationally he was thriving. He'd mastered the third-grade curriculum and would begin fourth-grade work in September following their summer break. While she was pleased with his academic progress, she recognized that this lifestyle put obstructions in the path of his social development. Reilly could use a Scout troop. He needed friends. His social life was as barren as the moon.

So is yours.

True. Maybe that's why a shirtless Devin Murphy sent her heart thumping in a completely different way from what had become her new normal.

Maybe? Hah! Don't lie to yourself, Jenna. He's been your fantasy man for the past year and a half.

Reilly interrupted her brooding by asking, "Can I unbuckle for just a minute?"

"No," she responded automatically. A moment later, she asked, "Why do you want to unbuckle?"

"I have fish gunk on my hands and the wet wipes rolled under the seat. Can we have spaghetti for lunch, Mom?"

"Next time put the wipes back in the glove box where they belong. We'll be at the campsite in a few minutes. You can put up with fish gunk a little longer. Besides, why are you thinking about lunch? It's not even ten o'clock yet."

"I got scared. Being scared always makes me hungry."

Oh, Reilly. "I'd be happy to fix spaghetti for lunch, but I need to check the pantry. I'm not one hundred percent certain we have pasta. I'd intended to shop for groceries this afternoon at the Trading Post."

"Oh," her son replied, disappointment heavy in his tone. "You should keep more spaghetti in the trailer, Mom. Sauce, too."

Jenna's reply was a noncommittal "Hmm." Reilly would eat spaghetti every day if she'd allow it. However, she had learned early on during this odyssey of theirs to shop carefully with space limitations in mind.

During their first week on the run, she'd bought a pickup with a pop-up trailer off Craigslist in South Carolina. During their second month on the road, once they'd decided the lifestyle suited them, she'd upsized to a twenty-one-foot travel trailer—another Craigslist score, in Indiana. The truck had been dependable, and both campers had been clean and serviceable, but small. Then two weeks ago the wealthy retired couple parked next to them at a campsite in Wyoming had decided on a whim that they'd tired of the vagabond life. They'd made her a deal on the King

Ranch pickup and a thirty-two-foot fifth wheel that she couldn't pass up. This rig was a mansion compared to the others, but Jenna still tried to shop smartly.

She flicked her turn signal as she approached the entrance to Stardance Ranch RV Resort and bit back a sigh. She'd been looking forward to their stay in Eternity Springs. As much as she enjoyed life on the road and the fancy new rig, she could use her own summer break from towing a trailer.

Jenna drove slowly through the campground toward their slot, braking when a pretty golden retriever wandered into the road and stopped. Jenna rolled down her window and leaned her head out. "Move along, girl."

The dog didn't budge.

Jenna heard a loud whistle, and then the resort owner's annoyed voice call, "Sugar! Move your tail!"

Jenna gave Brick Callahan a friendly wave as his dog leisurely vacated the road.

"Sorry about that," Brick called. Sauntering toward the truck with a gas-powered weed-eater in hand, he added, "Sugar minds about as well as my wife does."

Having exited the laundry room moments ago with a stack of folded towels in her arms, Lili Callahan gave an exaggerated roll of her eyes. Brick's green eyes twinkled and his grin was unrepentant as he asked Jenna, "So, are you all settling in all right, Ms. Tarver? Everything to your liking here at Stardance Ranch?"

"It's very nice. We're settling in just fine, thank you." Jenna felt the weight of Reilly's questioning gaze, but these were not the circumstances to share their change in plans. Besides, she wanted to be sure she had a place to go before she gave up this campsite.

"Good. That's good. If you need anything be sure to let us know."

"I'll do that."

"And don't forget to check the bulletin board for changes to the weekly schedule. We posted an important one a little while ago. I'm afraid we've had to cancel pizza night this week."

"Pizza night?" Jenna asked.

He nodded. "It's our most popular event. You'll want to get in line plenty early, believe me." Ducking his head, he looked past Jenna to Reilly. "Saw you loading up your fishing gear earlier. Any luck?"

Reilly met his gaze quickly, and then nodded. "I caught one."

"Excellent. You did better than I did, in that case. I fished this morning and got skunked."

Reilly's eyes widened with alarm and he reared back away from the open window. Jenna deduced the direction of his thoughts. "He wasn't sprayed, RJ. That's slang that means he didn't catch anything."

"Oh."

She explained to their host. "When we were camping in Texas last month, the two dogs at the site next to ours had an unfortunate incident with a skunk. It made quite the impression."

"Ah. Sorry for the confusion." He winked at Reilly and added, "I had a similar situation with a dog of mine in the past. It's not fun, is it?"

"No. Not at all," Reilly agreed.

Since Brick had brought up fishing, Jenna took advantage of the opening. "RJ caught his fish on salmon eggs, but one of your neighbors has offered to give him a fly-fishing lesson this afternoon. Devin Murphy. Do you know him?"

"Devin? I do. He's a good guy. Lives in Australia now. I knew he was coming home this summer for a visit, but I didn't know he'd already arrived. He'll do a good job with the lesson. He's a professional fishing guide. Earlier this year he helped a guy catch a five-hundred pound marlin."

Reilly's gaze flicked toward his mother, then back to Brick. "There aren't fish that big in Hummingbird Lake, are there?"

"Oh no. Freshwater fish don't grow that big. But trout are good fighters and a lot of fun to catch. The welcome packet you received when you checked into Stardance Ranch has a copy of my favorite fishing holes map. Once you get the hang of using a fly rod, you should give some of them a try."

"We'll do that," Jenna replied. "Thanks for the tip."

She pulled into the parking spot beside their trailer. They exited the truck, and when Reilly started to run toward the camper, she said, "Slow down, hot rod. I need you to help me . . ."

Her voice trailed off as a motorcycle pulled to a stop at the foot of their lane. The driver wore silver and gold leathers and a sparkling gold helmet. Jenna thought, *Uh-oh.*

Reilly said, "Uh-oh."

The motorcycle rider removed the helmet to reveal a bob of gray hair. She waved at Brick Callahan and he waved back. Then the Angel's Rest innkeeper turned her attention toward Jenna and Reilly.

"What do we do, Mom?" Reilly asked, panic in his voice.

Jenna eyed the motorcycle and muttered, "Wing it."

"What?"

Jenna rested a reassuring hand on her son's shoulder as the newcomer approached carrying a package she'd removed from her saddlebags. "Hello," she called, a wide smile wreathing her face. "Ms. Tarver? My name is Celeste Blessing and I'm the Welcome Gold Wing."

"The what?" Reilly asked softly.

"That's the name of her motorcycle," Jenna murmured. "It's a Honda Gold Wing."

Her blue eyes gleaming with friendly earnestness, Celeste continued, "Lili Callahan shared the news that you are new seasonal residents of Eternity Springs."

Jenna hesitated, waiting for the expected moment of recognition. It didn't immediately come. *Okay, then.* "Well, we rented the space for a month. I don't know that it makes us residents."

"Absolutely! Anyone who remains with us longer than two weeks counts. The city council made a proclamation. Anyway, I am here to officially welcome you and your boy and give you a little goody box from some of our local merchants. You'll find discount coupons from shops in town including Whimsies and Heavenscents and Forever Christmas. The Yellow Kitchen restaurant has an offer for a free dessert with the purchase of an entree. Tarkington Automotive will balance and rotate your truck tires for free. Trust me, you won't go wrong taking advantage of the specials at Angels' Rest Spa. There's a coupon for a free fishing lure from our outdoors shop, Refresh, and one for two free cinnamon rolls from Fresh bakery."

Jenna watched Celeste closely, but saw only friendliness in her blue-eyed gaze. "We've heard the bakery is fabulous."

"You've heard correctly. You must try the cinnamon rolls. They are divine. Now, do you have any questions about Eternity Springs or the area? I am a veritable font of information. For example, do you enjoy hiking?"

"We do."

"Has anyone mentioned the Double-Dog Dare Trail up on Murphy Mountain?"

"No. I'm sure I'd have remembered that name."

"It's a public trail that recently opened."

Their visitor went on to talk at length about the trail that came about as a result from a football bet between Michael's dad, Cam, and another local landowner, Jack

Davenport. It was an amusing story and Celeste told it
with flair. Soon even Reilly was laughing.

The sound was more rare than Jenna liked and always
music to her ears. She wanted to reach over and hug the
twinkling-eyed innkeeper for the gift. That, and the fact
that she showed no sign of recognition. None whatso-
ever. Jenna and Reilly had spent almost as much time
with Celeste at Christmas as they had with the Murphys.
Maybe . . .

Her welcome complete, Celeste told them goodbye and
returned to her motorcycle. As she donned her helmet and
fastened her chinstrap, Reilly spoke with wonder. "She
didn't realize it's us."

"It appears not."

"Huh."

They both stood watching as she started the motor.
Once she pulled away, Reilly said, "Ms. Celeste is really
smart. I guess that means we have really good disguises."

"I guess so." As the sound of the motorcycle faded,
Jenna looked at her son. "Reilly, we spent of lot of time
with Ms. Celeste last Christmas, didn't we?"

"Yes. A bunch."

"If we fooled her, I'll bet we can fool most anyone."

Her son, however, wasn't easily fooled. He narrowed his
eyes suspiciously. "Not Michael."

Jenna shrugged nonchalantly. "No, probably not Michael. But what if we did a little investigating? What if we
met Devin Murphy for his fishing lesson and subtly
pumped him for information about his brother's schedule?
If we can find out where Michael is spending his time this
summer, we can avoid those places. If we're careful to stay
away from Michael, we should be able to remain at Stardance Ranch. This resort is a perfect home base for us as
we explore Mesa Verde, Black Canyon of the Gunnison,

and the Florissant Fossil Beds. When you think about it, we won't be in Eternity Springs itself all that often. Since Celeste didn't recognize us, I think it's safe to assume that nobody else will either. Except for maybe Michael."

Reilly shoved his fish-gunk smelling hands into the back pocket of his jeans. "What if Devin brings Michael with him to the lesson?"

"Well, we could stay in our truck until he arrives. If Devin is alone we go meet him and if he's not, we don't. Maybe we could use that opportunity to go into town and see about getting that certain late birthday present I promised you."

Michel's entire face lit up. "A dog? Mom, you're finally going to let me get my dog?"

"I told you we'd get one when we settled. If we stay here for a month, that's as settled as we'll be for the foreseeable future."

"That sounds like a bribe, Mom. You're making me choose between a dog and Michael being safe?"

"Nope." Jenna shook her head. "Not at all. I wouldn't put Michael Murphy at risk any more than you would. This is the same deal we've had since your birthday in March. I want you to have your puppy, but training is vital in order to have a well-behaved dog that will protect us both. Constantly changing campsites is not conducive to establishing an effective training schedule. However, if we decide to leave Eternity Springs, I intend to find somewhere else where we are able to camp for a month. I want to get you that dog, plus I need a break from windshield time with a trailer in tow. It's stressful now that the roads are crowded with tourists."

Reilly rolled back and forth on his heels. "I don't know, Mom."

"Well, we still have time to decide. Let's go inside and

you can wash up and I'll inventory the pantry. If the cupboard is bare, I believe I saw a grocery section in the office. They might have spaghetti supplies."

"I hope so."

She unlocked the camper's door and as was her habit, verified that their home had remained undisturbed in their absence. "All clear," she called.

Reilly dashed inside and disappeared into the bathroom.

Jenna checked her pantry cabinet, confirmed the paucity of foodstuffs, and then broke the news to a disappointed Reilly. "Here." She pulled a ten-dollar bill from her purse. "Run over to the office and buy something I can fix for lunch."

"Can I buy anything they have?"

Jenna was smarter than that. "You can buy anything that is something that is ordinarily on our lunch menu. So no sugary cereal."

"Okay." Reilly darted off to the Stardance Ranch RV Resort office, and Jenna grabbed her laptop and a notepad and pen. She took a seat at the table, booted up her computer, and logged into a VPN service, which allowed her to surf the Internet anonymously.

In the days following the Tallahassee SWAT raid, Jenna had spent her time studying up on how to go off the grid. Within a week she'd had bitcoins in the bank, a serious stash of cash, and a part-time job doing technical writing for a former colleague who'd left medicine for the nonprofit world and agreed to pay her in Visa gift cards. They'd hit the road and done their best to disappear.

She didn't fool herself that she was all the way off the grid, but she had moved significantly off center. Opening her browser, she searched for campgrounds within a hundred-mile radius of Eternity Springs, made a list in order of preference, and then began placing calls. Soon she'd expanded her search to two hundred miles and then to five hundred.

By the time Reilly returned with hotdogs, buns, and a can of beans, she had two less-than-ideal options to present to him. She did so when they sat down to their early lunch. "I don't guess the desert would be too terrible," he said as he squirted ketchup on his third hotdog. "It was hot in Florida."

"It was warm and humid in Florida. This will be hot and dry." Jenna shook her head in wonder as her son polished off the hotdog and spooned another serving of beans onto his plate. The kid's growth spurt was beginning to look like a growth geyser.

"Do dogs like the desert?" he asked.

"Dogs are adaptable. Giving them a loving home is the most important thing. That said, some breeds do better in extreme heat than others and vice versa."

"So we probably wouldn't want a great big hairy dog if we're going to camp in the desert?"

I don't want a great big hairy dog at all. "We'll have to see what dogs are available at the shelter and make the best choice possible for our particular circumstances."

Reilly licked ketchup from his fingers. "The mountains sound a lot better."

Jenna sipped her water and gave him a little more time to think before asking, "So, do you want to meet Devin Murphy for the fishing lesson and see what we can find out about Michael's summer plans? It's up to you."

"Can I have a cookie?"

"May I."

"May I have a cookie?"

"Yes."

In seconds, Reilly had his hand in the cookie jar. "I think we can meet Michael's brother, Mom. As long as we can hide first and make certain he comes by himself."

"We absolutely can do that."

With his mouth full of chocolate chip cookie, the boy added, "I hope we're able to stay in Eternity Springs."

"From your mouth to God's ears."

Reilly's expression brimmed with eight-year-old disgust. "I don't know that He would like having ears full of cookie crumbs."

Chapter Seven

Devin eyed the strawberry pinwheels in the bakery case and debated whether or not he should swipe one more. He *had* gone on a run this morning—but he'd reloaded what he had exercised off in the first half hour behind the counter at Fresh. If he had known then that he'd be filling in for his mom in Temptation Central, he would have run a second lap around the lake.

The jangle of the doorbell provided a distraction, and he gave a wink and a wolf whistle when two of Eternity Springs's downtown merchants walked into the bakery. Shannon Garrett owned and operated Murphy's Pub. Glass artist Gabi Brogan's Whimsies gift shop sold her art along with other handmade items. Both women smiled with delight upon seeing him.

"Well . . . well . . . well," Gabi said. "And here I thought Sarah's cinnamon rolls were the prettiest thing in Fresh. Boy was I wrong."

"Pretty!" Devin protested. "I don't think that's the proper term, do you?"

"He's right." Shannon flipped her sunglasses onto the top of her head. "Sarah's cinnamon rolls are downright beautiful."

The two women shared a look, and then laughed. Gabi

said, "Come around from behind that counter, handsome, and give us a hug."

He did exactly that, picking up each woman in turn and giving them a twirl. Shannon said, "Welcome home, Devin. I'll bet your folks are over the moon to have you back. I know your mom has been counting the minutes ever since their Easter trip got cancelled."

"Counting the minutes and baking all your favorites," Gabi added. She leaned left and peered through the doorway leading into the kitchen. "Is she in there whipping up some more strawberry pinwheels?"

"Actually, Mom is upstairs in bed. When I got home from my morning run she'd gone as green as guacamole. That's why I'm filling in here. Apparently Michael had a stomach bug last week, and she thinks he passed it on to her."

Shannon winced. "Poor Sarah."

"That virus has been making the rounds," Gabi said. "The Cicero kids have all had it. So have the Lancasters. I think your sister had it, too."

Devin nodded toward a plastic bottle beside the cash register. "I bought the last four bottles of hand sanitizer at the Trading Post before I rang up my first sale here today. Speaking of sales . . . what can I get you lovely ladies? I assume you came in for something more than a hug?"

"Absolutely. We're both here for our Saturday morning cinnamon rolls and milk. I don't know if you've heard the news yet, but Shannon and I are both eating for two." Gabi patted her stomach proudly.

"Babies?" A smile stretched across Devin's face as he gazed from one woman to the other. "That's awesome. No wonder the two of you are glowing. Congratulations. I take it everyone is thrilled?"

Gabi nodded. "Flynn is already knee-deep in baby-related inventions. We're not due until December."

"Daniel is thrilled," Shannon confirmed. "Brianna . . . well . . . let's just say she's reserving judgment."

"She's . . . what . . . two and a half?"

"She just turned three and we're having to work on the concept of sharing. It doesn't come naturally to her, I'm afraid."

"I could make an observation about women and sharing in general, but I think that instead, I should probably get you ladies your rolls."

"Good thinking," Gabi said, her tone dry. "We'll sit over by . . . oh look, Shannon. Sarah has done some redecorating since last week."

"She has! Isn't it cute?"

Devin served the rolls, then glanced around the shop, trying to decide what was different. Were the yellow gingham curtains new? He couldn't remember. The soda-shop tables were the same, and Mom had always decorated them with fresh flowers in clear glass vases. "The dry-erase board is new, isn't it?"

"Yes," Gabi said.

"'When life gives you lemons, decide yellow is your favorite color,'" Devin read aloud. "That sounds like something Celeste would say."

"It's a quote from her book *Advice for Aspiring Angels*. I think—" Shannon broke off when the doorbell jangled again and three more customers entered the bakery. Zach Turner, town sheriff and Gabi's older brother, led the way followed by Gabe Callahan, who was one of Devin's father's closest friends. A third man, someone closer to his own age that Devin vaguely recognized, brought up the rear.

"Well, look what the great white dragged in," Gabe said as Devin approached with his hand outstretched. "When did you get home, Dev?"

"Last night."

"Your mom already put you to work?"

"Yeah. It's like I never left. Never grew up."

"You grew up?" jibed Zach as he shook Devin's hand in turn. "Seems like just yesterday I arrested you."

Devin scratched his cheek with the middle finger of his hand extended. "Hardy har har, Sheriff Turner. So, how's that beautiful daughter of yours doing? Old enough to date yet?"

"Only if you want to die," Sheriff Turner fired back. He walked over to the women and kissed first his sister's cheek and then Shannon's. Then he grinned. "Welcome home, Devin. How long are you staying this visit?"

"Three weeks."

Gabe gave a satisfied nod. "So you'll be here for both of the big parties—the Callahan Fourth of July festivities and Caitlin Timberlake's engagement party."

"Yep." Devin nodded. "Wouldn't miss either one of them. Caitlin was like a sister to me even before her brother married my sister. Josh Tarkington is getting a princess."

"That's what her daddy believes," Sheriff Turner observed, his lips twisted in an amused smirk. "He's been grumpy about his little girl tying the knot."

The third man nodded. "That's because Caitlin and Ali are hip deep in wedding planning and the bills are beginning to hit."

Devin suddenly placed the newcomer—the lawyer who joined Mac Timberlake's legal practice. Devin extended his hand. "I know we've met before. You're another Callahan, aren't you?"

"A cousin. My name's McBride. Boone McBride."

"How are you liking life in Eternity Springs, Boone? You're from Texas, right?"

"Dallas–Fort Worth. It's been an adjustment, I'll admit, but for the most part, I'm loving small-town life."

The men placed their to-go orders, and visited with

Shannon and Gabi while Devin filled up white bakery bags. Talk returned to babies, and Devin learned that the sheriff and his wife, Savannah, could be counted among the expectant Eternity Springs families too. "Wow," Devin said with a knowing smirk. "That must have been some winter. Two grandbabies for your mother. Maggie must be in heaven."

Zach gave a rueful nod. "She's knitting like a madwoman."

Another group of customers entered Fresh—tourists this time—and Devin returned to work. Business remained steady all morning until he flipped the OPEN sign to CLOSED and started on clean up. His mother came into the bakery as he loaded the last utensil into the commercial dishwasher and turned it on. "Look at you, Devin. What a lifesaver you are. This is not the welcome home for you that I had imagined."

"Hey, no big deal. I'm glad I was here to help. Especially since Dad is tied up with tours this morning. Are you feeling better?"

"I am. The nap helped."

"Is there anything I need to do to get things ready for tomorrow?"

"Yes. I called the Trading Post, and they'll sell our day-olds if you'll bag them up and run them over there. I'm going to stay closed tomorrow. Eileen gets back from vacation tomorrow night and can handle things here on Monday if I'm not over this bug."

"Sounds like a plan. Anything else I can do? Do you need help with Michael? I have plans to go fishing, but I'm happy to take him along."

"Thanks, but he's staying up at the Rocking L with Chase all day. I didn't want to saddle you with too much on your first full day back when jet lag can be such a killer. I felt terrible asking for your help here as it was."

"I feel fine, Mom. Don't worry. You, however, still don't look too good."

"Gee thanks," Sarah grumbled.

"You know what I mean. Why don't you go on back upstairs? I've got this."

To Devin's distress, tears welled in his mother's eyes. "I just hate that I'm sick when you're home."

"Hey, as long as you don't give the crud to me, we're cool." He shooed her away. "Don't worry about me, Mom. I'm here for three weeks."

"That's hardly any time at all! What if I'm sick for more than a day or two?"

"Then I can tack a few days onto the end of the trip. I have some flexibility. That's one of the good things about being the boss."

Sarah sniffed. "That's not a good solution. It wouldn't make sense for you to return to Eternity Springs after we all go to the Caribbean for Mitch's wedding. Besides, being the boss means you work all the time. You know that."

His mother must really be feeling bad. Sarah Murphy didn't often play hostess of her own pity parties.

He shooed her away again and this time she left. By the time he finished at the bakery, he had a little over an hour to kill before meeting the ravishing redhead and her son.

He spent half of it at his father's outdoors store gathering up gear appropriate for the fishing lesson. He arrived at Hummingbird Lake ten minutes early, and it took him five to unload the truck. Really, he'd gone way overboard with the snacks. When Jenna and RJ had yet to arrive by ten after, he began to think his efforts might be for naught. The extent of his disappointment surprised him. It wasn't like he'd been stood up for a date. This had been a casual invitation to strangers. That's all. Nevertheless, when the pair emerged from the trailhead adjacent to the parking area, he found himself grinning.

"So sorry we are late!" Jenna called as they walked out onto the fishing pier. "We got here early and decided to take a hike and got distracted when we spied an elk."

"No problem. Being waylaid by wildlife is always a valid delay."

Devin got down to business and spent the next half hour on technique. RJ proved to be an attentive student who willingly followed directions and picked up things quickly. As Devin had expected, the boy did enjoy the act of throwing a fly much more than drowning salmon eggs. He wasn't all that interested in catching fish, either, which made it easy for Devin to flirt with lovely Jenna, who flirted right back. Subtly. After all, there was a kid within hearing distance.

He learned that she and RJ were from the South—she didn't say exactly where—and they were touring the western states in a fifth wheel currently parked at Stardance Ranch. She worked remotely for a health care–related nonprofit and she planned to homeschool RJ in the fall. However, the conversation revolved more around his life in Australia, the Caribbean, and Eternity Springs than it did on her world. Apparently Jenna was one of those women who preferred asking questions to talking about herself, and she appeared genuinely interested in his answers. Devin talked more about himself, his work, and especially his family than he had on a first date in . . . well . . . forever.

Not that this was a first date. He was working his way around to that. It's really too bad Mom sent his little brother up the mountain with Chase today. He had a feeling Michael and RJ would hit it off, which would free up the lovely Jenna for more adult activities.

And yet, why he was even considering spending his time pursuing the delectable Ms. Tarver was a puzzle. He had three whole weeks at home. Why was he spending his time with strangers instead of friends and family? His father often said that Devin had never met a pretty woman he didn't hit on, but that wasn't true. Devin's social life had been awfully dry of late. He couldn't recall the last time he'd been this interested in someone so quickly.

For all the good it would do him. Again, three whole weeks.

Maybe that was the appeal. For the past year and a half, he'd been working his butt off building the business. For the next three weeks, he had nothing to do but rest and relax. What was more restful and relaxing than sweaty, vigorous sex?

She sure had a kissable mouth.

He watched it closely as she shared a story about Celeste's Welcome Wing. He wondered what she'd do if he leaned over and covered those lips with his. Suddenly, he rather desperately wanted to find out.

He tore his gaze away from Jenna and tried to focus on what she'd said, not the way she'd said it. "Celeste is the most pure-hearted person I've ever met, and she is a fabulous ambassador for Eternity Springs. My mother says the town wouldn't have survived without her contributions."

"RJ says her smile warms him from the inside out."

Devin smiled at the picture and watched the boy work the rod and line. "He's gotten the hang of that quickly. How about we load up our gear and go up to the Devin Murphy super-secret fishing hole? It's about a ten-minute drive and then a five-minute hike. It's a beautiful spot and I took the precaution of packing a basket of snacks in case."

RJ's head whipped around. "Snacks?"

Jenna threw back her head and laughed. "He's a bottomless pit these days."

Captivated by the beauty of her joy, Devin drew in a sharp breath and hesitated a moment too long to say, "Growing boys."

"What sort of snacks?" RJ asked.

"For your mom I have cheese, crackers, fruit, and fresh-baked bread. For you I brought potato chips, corn chips, bean dip, beef jerky, and because I am a generous soul, one dozen of the best cookies ever to come out of an oven—my mother's strawberry pinwheel cookies. Oh, and soda pop."

Reilly turned a beseeching gaze toward his mother, and Devin knew he had won before she said, "We'll follow you."

"Awesome." Devin began gathering up the gear and RJ and his mother pitched in to help. A few minutes later, he led them away from Hummingbird Lake and back toward town, then took the turn onto Cemetery Road. The climb from that point was steep and the turn-off he desired easily missed, marked only by a sign that read PRIVATE ROAD.

She fell behind him a bit at that point, and Devin thought maybe he ought to have warned her about his fishing hole's remote location. He hoped she wasn't afraid he was a serial killer leading her toward her doom. He should have told her that the fishing hole was on private land—his father's land, to be precise—and part of a parcel of property the ownership of which went back to the founders of Eternity Springs. Upon occasion, his dad brought a tour up here to fish, but for the most part, the trout in this section of the stream didn't have to deal with anglers. In addition to being some of the best fishing in Colorado, the scenery was exceptional.

He parked his truck on the shoulder of the road at the usual parking spot, and when Jenna pulled in behind him few moments later, he figured she must have ruled out the serial killer possibility. RJ scrambled out of the truck and ran toward Devin. Jenna stepped down from the truck and then made a slow three-sixty turn, a look of awe on her face.

"Gorgeous," she said.

Devin knew she referred to the craggy, snowcapped peaks set against a brilliant blue sky, the hillsides painted with summertime in a dozen different shades of green, and the alpine meadow blanketed in a rainbow wildflowers that stretched out before them. However, he never took his gaze off her as he replied, "Absolutely."

The glance she darted his way acknowledged the awareness humming between them and revealed that the attraction wasn't one-sided.

"This looks like a place where we could see a bear," RJ observed. "What if we see a bear? He'll be a black bear, not a grizzly. They don't have grizzlies in Colorado. When we go to Yellowstone we might see a grizzly. We're going to Yellowstone in September after the crowds have died down. I can't wait. When Mom and I visited Rocky Mountain National Park we took a class about bear safety. The ranger told us to carry pepper spray. Do you have pepper spray?"

"I do."

"Mom does too. Are there berry bushes around here? Bears eat berries. We might see a bear if he's looking for food. If a black bear attacks you, you're not supposed to play dead. Have you ever been attacked by a bear?"

"No, I haven't, I'm happy to say. I've only seen a bear three times and two of those were in town when folks didn't practice proper food disposal."

"What about the third time? Was it at your fishing hole?"

"Nope, I've never seen a bear up here. I don't think there are berry bushes on this part of the mountain."

"Oh." RJ appeared disappointed. "I guess that's good."

Devin hated letting the boy down, so he offered, "I did see a mountain lion one time."

"A mountain lion!" RJ's eyes went round. "We haven't

taken a safety class for mountain lions. What are you supposed to do when you see a mountain lion? Is there mountain lion spray?"

Devin glanced at Jenna, wondering if he'd made a mis-
step here. He hadn't wanted to frighten the boy. "Um . . .
I don't think there is mountain lion spray. They don't tan-
gle with humans nearly as often as bears do. I only saw
one because I happened to spy him with my field glasses
as I was looking up at the rocks. He wasn't here in the
meadow."

"Oh."

Jenna asked, "You said we have a bit of a hike? What
can we carry for you?"

"A short hike. You can't see it from here, but we'll go
up over that ridge"—he pointed toward the north—"and
down the other side. The creek pools at the base." Devin
divided up the supplies and they started off. Within five
minutes of making their first cast, both Jenna and RJ
landed trout.

They fished for half an hour before Devin broke out the
snacks for RJ, and another half hour before he spread
the quilt he'd brought atop the boulder that had served as
the Murphy family picnic table in this spot for years and
set out the grown-up snacks. He pulled the cork on a nice
Sauvignon blanc and offered a glass to Jenna along with a
toast. "Here's to new friends."

"To new friends," she repeated.

They clinked glasses and he casually asked, "So, Jenna.
It hasn't escaped my notice that beyond telling me that
you're single, you've managed to dodge my questions about
RJ's dad. Are you divorced? Widowed? A single mom
from the git-go?"

She delayed her answer by taking a sip of her wine,
watching him over the top of her glass. The light in her
brown eyes reflected an inner debate he found intriguing.

What was so hard about the question? Did she expect him to be judgmental?

She licked her lips, then said, "RJ's biological mother was a single mom. I adopted him after she died. I've never been married."

Chapter Eight

As the words left her mouth, inwardly Jenna winced. *Why don't you just hand him a pencil to connect the dots?*

Just why she'd felt compelled to repeat a fact she had already shared with him during the Santa calls and thus play unusual-personal-facts roulette, she couldn't say. Except, Devin Murphy had proved himself to be a really great guy. She didn't like lying to him. She didn't like lying to anybody in Eternity Springs. She didn't like lying, period.

"Wow," Devin said. "That's a coincidence. My own situation is similar." He told her about his biological mother's death and Cam stepping up afterward. "He was a single parent for over ten years. It's not an easy job."

Jenna breathed a little easier. Devin's mind hadn't gone to Reilly from Nashville. She hadn't given them away. "No, it's definitely not easy, but it is rewarding."

Their conversation was interrupted when Reilly's cast went awry and his line got tangled in a bush. Devin hopped up to help and Jenna watched the summertime Santa assist her son. A pang of yearning twisted her heart. Would she and Reilly ever be able to have a normal life? Would she ever be free to have another romance or give Reilly that father he craved?

Her thoughts returned to that first Santa phone call. *Do you know how lonely your little boy is? Care to guess what his Christmas wish was? A daddy. The boy wished for a dad.*

Here it was a year and a half later, and she was no closer to making his wish come true than she had been that Christmas Eve.

Devin "Santa Claus" Murphy wouldn't approve. He'd been impatient with her reaction to being doxxed. What would he say if she told him that they'd been swatted two separate times? He'd probably be on the phone to his private investigator friend before she got the whole story out.

For all the good *that* would do. *Been there, done that, have the invoices and no fresh leads to prove it.*

After freeing the tangled line, Devin returned to the picnic quilt. "You know, despite my gypsy ways, I've always had a permanent address. Have you always been a camping aficionado?"

"My parents were campers," she replied, happy to be able to tell the truth about that. "We tent camped mostly, but when I was ten they bought their first pop-up. We spent at least one weekend a month and every vacation camping. It was heaven. I fell in love with the outdoors during those years and it's an interest I wanted to pass along to my son. Since I can work from anywhere that has an Internet connection and RJ was game for the adventure, we thought we'd give the camping lifestyle a try. Fifth-wheel living in RV parks isn't tent camping in a place like this, but it's a nice compromise."

Devin grabbed a grape and popped it into his mouth. "I like the way you think, Ms. Tarver."

The sound of her fake name on his lips dimmed her smile, but since his gaze had shifted to Reilly, he didn't notice.

"Although, I do have a question. If you grew up camping

in the great outdoors, how come you made such an amateur mistake taking the trout off RJ's hook this morning?"

Jenna's mouth twisted in rueful smile. "That's what men are for."

Devin gaped at her. "Seriously? Did you seriously just say that? What sort of modern-day self-sufficient outdoors woman are you if you can't take your own fish off the hook?"

"I can. I just don't like to. I don't like scales. That goes for snakes and lizards too."

"Snakes have skin, Mom," Reilly called, proving the truth about little pitchers having big ears.

Devin then proceeded to prove his maleness by launching into an in-depth explanation of snake "skin" and the protective properties of scales on reptiles. He had Reilly hanging on his every word. When he mentioned the six-foot long rattlesnake skin from the family ranch in Texas that Brick Callahan kept in his office at Stardance Ranch, it quickly became obvious that her son's interest in fishing was done for the day. Next stop for this outing of theirs was the RV resort office.

She started packing up the picnic supplies while Devin enlisted Reilly's help with the fishing gear, taking care to teach the boy best practices in the process. Soon they began the climb back up the trail with Jenna leading the way, her son in the middle, and Devin bringing up the rear, cooler in hand. She was a dozen steps from the top when she heard the sound that struck terror in her heart. Jenna halted abruptly. Behind her, Reilly gasped aloud.

Not a bear. Not a mountain lion.

"Hurry up, Dad," came a little boy's familiar voice. "Dev is gonna catch all the fish."

Jenna saw a flash of red as the figure topped the hill and raced downward. She had no chance to move out of the way before Michael Murphy barreled into her. He knocked

her backward, and her foot came down wrong on something—a root, a rock, she didn't know what. Pain exploded
in her ankle. She fell and began to tumble down the hill.

"Mom!" Reilly cried.

"Jenna!" Devin tossed aside the cooler and lunged for
her, but right before he reached her, she slammed into the
trunk of a tree and lost her breath.

"I'm sorry!" Michael exclaimed. "I didn't see . . .
Reilly? What are you doing here? What did you do to your
hair?"

Reilly emitted a low moan.

Cam Murphy topped the hill and took in the scene.
"Geeze, Mike. Jenna, are you all right?"

She closed her eyes against the pain in her ankle and
struggled for breath. Devin knelt beside her saying, "Obviously, there's a story here, but first things first. Got the
breath knocked out of you, did you? Take your time. Let
us know what hurts when you're able."

She used the seconds while she fought for breath to process what had just happened. Not a total disaster. The
cat was only halfway out of the bag. What happened to
Michael spending the day at summer camp with his sister's husband?

Oh, well. What's done is done. Deal with it.

"Mom!" Reilly was down on his knees beside her,
worry wreathing his face. "Are you okay, Mom?"

"I'm fine. I'm fine. Everything is okay, buddy. Go pick
up the things you dropped." She started to stand, but when
she went to put weight on her right foot, pain arrowed
through her. She sank back down. "Yikes."

"Your ankle?" Devin asked.

"Yeah."

"Broken?"

"I don't think so."

"You have ice in that cooler, Devin?" Cam asked.

"Yeah." Devin shrugged off the flannel shirt he wore over a plain white tee and tossed it to his dad. Cam used it to create a makeshift ice pack that he tied around Jenna's swelling ankle.

Michael watched the proceedings with narrowed blue eyes. "How come you and Reilly are at our fishing hole, Ms. Stockton? And why did you stop letting him do FaceTime with me?"

"Stockton?" Devin repeated.

Reilly groaned. Jenna grimaced. Cam said, "Michael Cameron Murphy, zip your lips. You've done enough for now."

"But Dad!"

Cam gave his younger son the father's hairy eyeball stare and, when the boy shut his mouth, continued. "Jenna, I think this will work best if Devin and I get on either side of you. At least until we get you up over the hill. Okay?"

"Yes. Thank you."

"Boys, pick up your gear. You go up first. Wait for us at the edge of the meadow." To Jenna and Devin, he muttered, "I want Michael out of the way. The last thing we need to happen is for him to get in a hurry and knock you down again."

Devin helped her to stand, and then the two Murphy men all but carried her up the hill. Nobody talked, a detail for which Jenna was grateful, and when they topped the hill and reached level ground, Devin said, "I'll carry her from here. Will you get the cooler, Dad? No sense baiting the bears."

He swept her off her feet and strode toward the spot where she saw Michael and Reilly sniping at each other. "Enough," Devin snapped as he walked past them.

As the boys fell in behind them, Jenna closed her eyes and tried to think. Under other circumstances she would have enjoyed being swept off her feet by Devin Murphy.

Actually, she had entertained a similar fantasy or two involving Sexy Santa in the past. But since she figured she had only a handful of minutes before the questions would begin, she needed to drag her mind away from the hard body cradling hers and come up with some answers.

When Cam caught up with them, Devin asked, "Did I miss the memo about you and the squirt coming fishing this afternoon?"

"My afternoon tour got cancelled. It's your first day home. We thought we'd surprise you."

"Mission accomplished."

"Yep." Cam gave Jenna a sidelong look and added, "Lots of surprises going around."

Okay, so she didn't even have a handful of minutes. *Too bad I didn't bang my head.*

Jenna knew what she had to do. She'd known almost since the moment she identified Michael's voice. Shoot, if she was being honest with herself, maybe she'd intended for the truth to come out all along. Why else come to Eternity Springs?

She needed help.

She lifted her mouth toward Devin's ear and spoke in a tone only he could hear. "Please don't react. Please don't ask questions. It's a long story and I need to explain . . . I will explain . . . when Reilly isn't around. Devin, do you remember the North Pole wrong number? He's Reilly from Nashville. I'm Reilly's Mom."

Santa Claus almost dropped her.

Devin's mind spun like the winds of Hurricane Danielle, which had taken out his boats in the Bella Vita Isle harbor. RJ was Reilly. Jenna was Reilly's Mom. Somehow, they knew his family. For some reason, they'd lied about their names. Changed their appearance—blue tips and black hair when she'd told him she was a redhead. Why?

What sort of trouble was she in? Something bigger than tangling with an asshat who'd doxxed her with pizzas eighteen months ago, obviously.

"You can't drive with that ankle. I'll take you into town and to the clinic to have it looked at. I'll drive your truck if you'd like." He halfway expected her to protest, but she simply nodded. "Dad can take Reilly home with him. We can come back for the extra truck tomorrow."

"No!" her son said, an edge of terror in his tone. "No, Mom. I'm going with you. You can't leave me!"

"I'm not going to leave you."

"I'm taking her to the clinic on Cottonwood Street to get that ankle treated. The clinic is only a block away from my dad's house. I'll bring her there as soon as she's finished. I promise."

"Mom!"

The plea in the boy's gaze convinced Devin that the boy would be coming with them. No way anyone could say no to those puppy dog eyes.

"Go with Mr. Murphy, sweetheart. It'll be okay."

"But, Mom. It's not safe."

Michael scowled with insult. "We won't hurt you, Reilly!"

Reilly rounded on Michael. "I'm not worried that you'll hurt me! I'm worried they'll hurt you. I got my arm broked the first time, and the second time Mom got a black eye. They have guns! Next time they could shoot somebody!"

As he burst into tears, Jenna said, "Put me down, please, Devin. Let me hold him. I need to hold him."

Guns? What the hell happened to them? Devin's jaw hardened. "We're almost to the truck. Dad, would you get the tailgate?"

"Sure." As Cam deposited the cooler into the bed of the truck Devin was using and lowered the tailgate, he looked as grim as Devin felt.

In a dozen long strides, Devin delivered Jenna to the truck. He set her down gently and then lifted Reilly up beside her. The boy buried his head against her breast and began to sob.

"Shush, honey," she said. "It's okay. It's gonna be okay."

"No, it's not. That's what you always say and it never is okay."

She stroked his bleached hair. "Well, this time might be different. I have a good feeling about it. I have a good feeling about this place and these people. I'm not giving up and I don't want you to give up either."

"But if he finds us—"

"He won't," Jenna was quick to deny. "Nothing has really changed, Reilly."

"They know!"

"The Murphys know. Nobody else. And Michael's dad and brother won't talk about us on the Internet, not after I tell them what happened. They're good people. They'll keep our secret."

"But I'm scared!"

"I know. I'm sorry about that, Reilly. I'm going to do everything in my power to make sure you're never scared again." She tilted his chin and directly met his gaze. "I promise."

She used the pad of her thumb to wipe away his tears and said, "Will you go with Michael? Please? You can tell him about our visit to the Great Smoky Mountains National Park, and Hot Springs National Park."

The boy hesitated.

Devin offered, "I'll bet my dad would take you to Stardance Ranch to see Brick's snakeskin."

That caught Reilly's interest. He darted a glance over toward Cam, who said, "We can do that. It is an awesome snakeskin. Six feet long."

"I would like to see it."

"Now is the perfect opportunity. After you see the snakeskin, if you want, I'll bet I could get us access to the special mountain animal exhibit room at our community school."

"Oh yeah!" Michael nodded enthusiastically. "It's super cool. There's a real bear and a mountain lion and mountain goat. Beavers and a hawk and a ton of cool things. They're stuffed and have glass eyes like the ones hanging on the wall at the Mocha Moose. Remember those?"

Reilly nodded.

Cam explained. "Our local taxidermist donated his collection to the school when he moved away."

Michael tugged Reilly's hand until he climbed down from the tailgate. "You'll like it, Reilly. C'mon. Let's get in Dad's truck. Bet we can talk him into getting us a snow cone too. Have you been to the snow cone stand? I like the blue ones best. They're coconut. Have you ever eaten a coconut? Devin says he had a coconut tree in his yard on Bella Vita Isle, but I don't remember it. That's where my brother used to live before he moved to Australia."

Reilly gave Jenna one more conflicted look. Gently, she urged him, "Go on, buddy. Have fun. I'm fine. Devin and I will find you once the doctor has examined my ankle."

The boy had one last concern. "Make him promise about the Internet."

Jenna gave Cam an apologetic smile. "Reilly and I appreciate all of your help, Cam. Do you mind reassuring him that you won't put our names on the Internet in any way this afternoon?"

"Of course I won't." Cam hunkered down in front of Reilly. "You have my word. Believe me?"

Reilly reluctantly nodded.

"Let's go!" Michael shouted, running toward his father's truck. "Wait until you see Mr. Brick's snake. It's awesome."

Cam rose and offered Reilly his hand. Devin spied Jenna's sigh of relief as he took it and they followed Michael to his father's truck. Devin waited until Cam had started the engine, made a U-turn on the road, and headed back toward town. Then he met Jenna's gaze. "Well, this trip certainly took an unexpected turn. How bad is your pain? I can't tell you how anxious I am to hear your story, but I'm willing to wait until after you've seen a doctor."

"I don't mind answering your questions." She tugged her keys from the pocket of her jeans and handed them to him. Devin opened the passenger door, gently lifted her off the tailgate, and settled her into the truck's front seat. By the time he climbed behind the wheel, she'd found her purse and dug a small bottle of ibuprofen from its depths. Devin spied the six-pack of bottled water in the back seat, reached for one, and handed it to her. "Thank you," she said and took two of the painkillers.

Devin adjusted the seat and mirrors and started the engine. But before he shifted into gear, he turned his head to look at her. "You're Reilly's Mom."

Her mouth twisted wryly. "Yep."

"Okay, then. Before we get everything else, there's one thing I need to get out of the way." He leaned toward her, cupped his hand on the back of her head, and without jostling her leg, gently pulled her face toward his.

Then he captured her lips with his for the kiss he'd been fantasizing about for the past eighteen months.

Chapter Nine

Jenna's head spun. Her body flushed with heat. Either someone had slipped something illegal into her bottle of ibuprofen or Devin Murphy's kiss packed a serious punch. *Sexy, sexy Santa.*

He took his time with it, his mouth gentle and firm, curious and exploring, stirring up a cloud of lust like an easy summer breeze through a mountain meadow. When he finally released her, he backed away slowly, his eyes closed, his lips pursed as if to savor the final trace of taste for the longest possible amount of time.

"Mmm . . . ," he murmured. "Thank you, Reilly's Mom. You don't know how many times I've thought about doing that."

"I . . . um . . ." No way would she clue him in that she'd entertained similar thoughts herself. "That was nice."

"Very nice." Shifting the truck into gear, he turned around and headed back the way they'd came. "So nice that I hate to put a damper on things, but I don't know how long this story you need to share takes to tell. We're twenty minutes from the clinic. Maybe you should get started."

And poof. There goes the mood.

Jenna leaned back against the headrest, shut her eyes, and attempted to gather her thoughts while ignoring the pain in her ankle. She'd rolled it and hit hard when she'd landed. She suspected an exam would rule out a fracture, and predicted a Grade 2 sprain. Possibly Grade 3. The bottom line was that the sprain was bad enough that it impaired her ability to drive safely, especially while pulling a trailer and with Reilly in the car. For the next week or so, anyway, their wings were well and truly clipped.

"Do you remember the last phone call we made to Santa? The one on New Year's Eve when I spoke to you and told you that Reilly had a broken arm?"

"I do."

She then told him about the New Year's Eve SWAT raid, their move to Memphis, the private investigator's lack of success, and the seven months of relative peace followed by a flurry of assaults that precipitated their flight to Tallahassee. She glossed over the reasons why they decided to spend last Christmas in Eternity Springs, but she went into some detail about SWAT raid number two.

With every fact she shared, Devin grew progressively more quiet and intense. His grip on the steering wheel tightened until the veins in his hands protruded and his knuckles went white.

"Reilly was traumatized and I was at the end of my rope. We had detectives assigned to our case who legitimately tried to help, but they couldn't promise me it wouldn't happen again. I knew what we had to do."

"Run," Devin said, firing the word like a bullet.

"Depend on ourselves. Only on ourselves. That's what we've done since February. We've done okay. Honestly, it's been a grand adventure, and in many ways, Reilly and I are better off because of it."

Devin cut to the heart of the matter. "Then why show up in Eternity Springs, where people know you?"

Jenna massaged her temples with her fingertips. A

dozen different reasons and excuses and justifications rolled through her mind, but in the end, she too cut to the heart of it. As the truck descended Cemetery Road and turned onto Aspen Street, she said, "Because Celeste Blessing assured me that Eternity Springs is where broken hearts come to heal."

They didn't speak any more after that. He carried her into the clinic and then into the examination room. He told her he'd wait for her outside and to ask someone to get him when she was ready to leave.

Jenna sat on the exam table with her leg outstretched and elevated as a nurse took her vitals and asked a series of general questions. Upon learning that her examining physician would be Dr. Rose Cicero, Jenna tried to recall if she'd met the woman during last winter's visit. She didn't recall the name.

Neither did she remember the face when Dr. Cicero introduced herself. Jenna chose not to mention her own medical degree during the initial workup or while the physician performed her subsequent exam. She didn't want to field the questions that bit of news would certainly elicit.

However, she liked Rose Cicero's competent, friendly manner, and had their positions been reversed, she'd have ordered the same diagnostic radiography and soft tissue ultrasound. Jenna agreed with Rose's diagnosis of a Grade 2 ankle sprain and the recommended treatment protocol that included crutches and a brace.

"We see a lot of ankle injuries around here," the nurse told Jenna as she fitted her with the brace and crutches. "Primarily hikers who get distracted by beautiful views and don't watch where they put their feet on our rocky mountain trails. Do you have experience using crutches, Ms. Stockton?"

"No, actually, I don't. This is my first ankle sprain."

"In that case we'll want you to take a couple of practice spins around the room to get comfortable before we turn you loose."

Jenna was halfway through her second circuit when Dr. Cicero exited the exam room across the hall and smiled at her. "Looking good. Walk on it as soon as you're able to tolerate it. You'll want to start physical therapy by the weekend. Lisa, did you give her the list of exercises?"

"Yes, Dr. Cicero."

"Good. I'd wait until Sunday to take advantage of the hot springs we have here in town, but then you'll find them a lovely treat. Now, do you have any questions for me?"

"No. I think I'm clear on everything."

"Great. Feel free to call if you need us."

"Thank you."

The doctor disappeared into another examination room and Jenna made her way toward the clinic's registration desk and fished for the debit card she habitually carried in her back pocket. The clerk said, "Mr. Murphy took care of your charges, ma'am. He's out back. I told him I'd give him a ring when you were ready."

"Don't bother," Jenna said. She slid the card back into her jeans. "I'll find him."

The rubber tips on the aluminum crutches squeaked against the tile floor as she hobbled toward the building's automatic doors. They *whooshed* outward at her approach, and she stepped into the warm afternoon sunshine. With her attention focused on the ground and the placement of her crutches, she didn't immediately notice the group waiting for her.

"Here she comes," she heard Cam say.

"Jenna!" Devin scolded. "They were supposed to call me when you were finished so I could help you."

She turned toward the voices—and darned near dropped a crutch. Men. A whole gang of them. A mountain range of tall, dark, and handsomes. Devin and his father and three or four more who seemed vaguely familiar. And another three or four who were total strangers. To a man, they turned to look at her. She saw irritation and indignation and concern. Devin looked angry enough to spit nails.

"I . . . uh . . ." Were she not on crutches, she'd have turned around and fled.

Devin met her gaze, smiled, and made a valiant attempt to gentle his expression. "So, no cast?"

"No break."

"Good. That's good."

Jenna's gaze slid past him, to Cam, and then back to Devin again. "Reilly?"

"He's with Michael at my sister's. She's a vet. Doing rounds at the local shelter and taking the boys with her."

Lori. Yes. Jenna had met her last year over their Christmas visit. "Reilly will like that."

"Jenna, I want to introduce you to some friends of mine. I'll start with the Callahans. You're staying at Stardance Ranch. Before the . . . um . . . accident, remember how we were headed there to see Brick Callahan's snakeskin? Well, this is Brick's family. His father Mark"—Devin gestured toward one of the men—"and Brick's uncles Matt, Luke, and Gabe. One of the Callahan family's primary businesses is security. And this is Eternity Springs' sheriff, Zach Turner. Daniel Garrett here is the private investigator who put us in touch with the investigator you hired in Nashville."

"Sorry that didn't turn out so well for you, ma'am," Daniel Garrett said, his expression serious, but his tone kind.

"And finally," Devin continued, gesturing toward the man who had yet to be introduced, "this is Jack Davenport. Jack is . . . well . . . Jack is a spook."

Davenport showed her a predator's smile. "Former spook. I'm retired."

Spook? As in . . . spy? Jenna pasted on a smile and tried to pretend that she was at a garden party instead of a . . . wait . . . what exactly was this? The back parking lot of a small-town health clinic? "Okay. Well. Nice to meet you all."

Devin said, "There's a park bench over hear where you can sit down. Will you please join us, Jenna?"

"You told them," she accused.

"I gave them a broad overview, enough to convey the severity of your situation. No one has taken his phone from his pocket, much less typed your name into a search engine. It's a happy circumstance that among the citizens of Eternity Springs we have a small army of brilliant, experienced professionals willing to offer their expertise and advice. We'd be fools not to listen to what they have to say."

We? So he considered himself to be part of this now?

Good. That's what you wanted, isn't it? You were hoping he'd magically make your troubles disappear.

Well, he is Santa Claus, after all.

"Where's this park bench?"

The mountain of masculinity parted to reveal a park and playground area with benches, picnic tables, a swing set, a jungle gym, and a wooden climbing fort. On another day, she'd have headed for the swings. Today, she went for the bench. The men gathered in a semicircle around her, leaning against trees, seated at or atop the picnic table bench. Cam took a seat in one of the swings. Devin helped Jenna get seated, her leg propped up, and her crutches stored out of the way but within reach.

He hunkered down in front of her and met her gaze. "If anyone can help, it's this group of guys. Share your story, Jenna, and let's get this monster off your back and behind bars once and for all."

Now that the moment was upon her, she hesitated. Maybe they should just keep running. They'd been doing all right. Why take the risk?

Because you can't run forever and you can't fix this alone. You know that. Trust your instincts, Jenna. They brought you here to Eternity Springs, didn't they?

She closed her eyes, said a brief prayer that she was making the right choice, and started at the beginning. They let her get all the way through the telling of it before the questions started. Different men seemed to naturally home in on different aspects of the story. Daniel Garrett's questions focused on the actions of the investigator in Nashville. Zach Turner asked pointed queries about the actions of the police. The Callahan brothers zeroed in on her digital footprints. Jack Davenport never said a word, but Jenna didn't doubt that he absorbed every detail.

The questioning went on for more than half an hour, until it finally appeared as though they'd run out of things to ask. The men discussed different aspects of the situation amongst themselves, but nobody offered a solution or even a path forward. Jenna was beginning to wonder if this had all been a waste of time when by some unspoken signal, everyone looked toward Jack Davenport.

"Should be easy enough to set a trap."

Devin straightened and his brow furrowed with a scowl. "What's the bait?"

"Who, not what," Jenna said, not taking her gaze off of Jack. "Me. I'm the bait, right?"

Davenport nodded.

"I won't have Reilly involved in any way," she warned.

"The boy can attend the next camp session at the Rocking L. Timing is perfect. It begins right after the Fourth of July."

Jenna knew that the Rocking L Summer Camp had been established to serve children who had suffered a significant loss. In addition to traditional camp activities, the Rocking L had special programs designed to help children learn to cope with and conquer their individual difficulties. She'd heard about the camp during their Christmas visit to Eternity Springs, and she'd gone through the application process upon their return to Florida. "That would be awesome. I know Reilly would love it. Unfortunately, I tried to get him a slot earlier this year and we were turned down."

Davenport flashed a grin, and his entire expression changed. Gone was the cool, intimidating predator and in his place stood a rogue with a gleam in his eyes. "Reilly will be welcome. I have particular influence with the head of the selection committee. I sleep with her."

Devin rolled his eyes and explained to Jenna. "He's married to her."

Ahh.

Cam asked. "What sort of trap are you talking about, Jack? I assume she'll stay here in Eternity Springs where we can keep her safe?"

Jack nodded, and the sheriff added, "Where swatting is limited to flies at the Fourth of July picnic."

Davenport spoke to the Callahans. "You'll submit a technology plan by the end of the day?"

The brothers shared a look, and then Matt nodded. "Can do, boss."

Davenport addressed Daniel Garrett. "I'd like you to touch base with the investigator she hired. We'll herd the stalker from that end too."

Garrett met Jenna's gaze. "I'll need you to sign some paperwork that I can fax him and get access to your information. If you'll come to my office when we're through here?"

"All right."

"What's our job in this, Jack?" Cam asked.

"You're the designated bodyguards. How long do you plan to be in town, Devin?"

"I planned to head home after Mitch's wedding. I can rearrange things if necessary. I *will* rearrange them." He met Jenna's gaze, daring her to protest as he added, "I won't leave until we've caught this asshat."

Jenna wasn't stupid. She wouldn't argue with Devin. Whether she'd recognized it or not at the time, this was why she'd come to Eternity Springs. She'd decided to put her trust in the Murphys and there was no going back now. The man would know how much time he could afford to be away from his life in Australia.

Davenport shook his head. "I can't imagine this taking longer than three weeks. I expect you'll make your flight without any trouble."

"Good deal." Devin nodded and folded his arms in satisfaction.

Jack Davenport said, "May I suggest we get about our business and reconvene Sunday afternoon at Eagle's Way? We'll cook out. Bring the wives and kids. We'll swim. Make it holiday pre-party. Does that suit everyone's schedules?"

"Maybe you should check with Cat first?" Cam suggested.

"His wife," Devin explained as Jack winced and nodded. He excused himself and stepped away, reaching into his pocket for his phone. Devin used the opportunity to move around from behind the bench and hunker down in front of Jenna. "You good with all of this?"

"Honestly, I don't know. My head is spinning."

"I could talk for hours about some of the challenges these men have overcome. To a man, they've walked some rocky paths. But the main thing you need to know . . . the bottom line for everything . . . is that you can trust them, Jenna. You can trust all of us. We won't let you down."

He gently stroked her cheek with the pad of his thumb and promised, "*I* won't let you down. You have my word on it."

Tears flooded Jenna's eyes and she blinked them back. The earnestness in his gaze, the offer of a burden shared after so many months of going it alone, spoke to the very center of her soul. Her emotions were too big, so she deflected with humor. "Your word or Santa's?"

"Both. All you have to do is believe."

Chapter Ten

Devin fitted his hands at Jenna's waist and lifted her into the truck. He stored her crutches in the cab's back seat and shut the passenger door. He didn't speak to her until he exited the medical clinic parking lot and turned the opposite direction from Stardance Ranch. "How's the ankle?"

"Grade 2 sprain. Partial ligament tear. Four- to eight-week recovery."

"Michael is such a hoon—a hooligan. He never looks where he's going. I can't tell you how many times I've seen him run into a wall because he's looking over his shoulder flapping his jaw about something instead of paying attention to what's in front of him."

"He was excited about spending time with you. When we were here last winter, he never stopped talking about his big brother."

Devin's mouth twisted with a rueful smile. "He's growing up so fast. That's the hardest part about living so far away. When we're apart, I can convince myself that I'm watching it happen through video calls, but when I'm with him"—he shrugged—"sometimes I want to kill him. I'm sorry he hurt you, Jenna."

"I'll heal. Where are we going, Devin?"

He drew in a bracing breath. "We are covering all the

bases. We don't want you living alone until we've taken care of this pizza jackass once and for all. The crutches are a limiting factor, but we found a good solution. It's actually the house where my dad grew up, where he and I stayed when he came home to Eternity Springs to win back my mother's heart. Celeste Blessing owns it now. It's a rental property, furnished and currently unoccupied."

"Wait a minute. What's wrong with my camper?"

"Quarters are a little close considering that we've yet to have our first official date, don't you think?"

He watched her work her way through it.

"You're planning to stay with me?"

"I wouldn't be much of a bodyguard if I didn't, would I? You're not going to argue with me about it, are you?"

Jenna opened her mouth, and then shut it. She closed her eyes. "This day has taken more turns than the switchbacks up Sinner's Prayer Pass. Was it only this morning when I seriously considered picking up Reilly and running when you approached us on the fishing pier? Now we're shipping my kid off to summer camp and moving in together?"

"Separate bedrooms," he was quick to say. "Reilly will love the Rocking L. Michael's gonna be pea green with envy. He loves his visits and gets to go as a camper for a week at the end of August with the other local kids, but he'd live up there all summer if he could."

"I do believe that it's a fabulous opportunity for Reilly, but I'm not one hundred percent certain I'll be able to convince him to go. His little world has been rocked time and again. It's left him insecure and angry and, in many instances, afraid of his own shadow. I don't think you realize what a big deal it was for him to leave the fishing hole with your father. This is the longest Reilly and I have been apart since before the last raid."

Devin darted a look at her. "Seriously?"

Jenna nodded. "I'm feeling a little like a new mother leaving her baby with a sitter for the first time."

"He got to see Brick's snakeskin. And now he's playing with puppies!"

"He's wanted a dog for a very long time. I'd decided to let him get one. If he's going to camp, we'll have to put that off."

"Not necessarily." Devin stopped the truck in front of the house where he'd lived when he and Cam first arrived in Eternity Springs. "Animals have held a prominent role in Rocking L therapies for some time now. My brother-in-law will be the first to tell you that working with his pup at the Rocking L helped save his sanity. Reilly wouldn't be the first camper who brought his dog with him."

"Really?" When Devin nodded, she added, "That might be the perfect solution."

"Let me show you the house. If it suits, we'll make a plan for going forward."

He opened the electronic lock using the code Celeste had texted. A second bathroom added during a recent remodel of the cozy, two-bedroom cottage along with new appliances and restoration of the three original fireplaces had turned the cottage into a showplace.

Jenna didn't try to hide her delight. "It's darling, and I won't pretend that I won't look forward to having a little elbow room, but I hate the idea that I'll be taking you away from your family. Your time with them is limited enough as it is."

"We'll see plenty of my family. I just won't be sleeping there. It's not a hardship, believe me." Devin gave her a droll look. "Michael likes to jump on me to wake me up."

"I won't do that," she said with a laugh.

It was a hanging curve ball Devin could have hit out of the park, but he refrained from taking a swing. Instead, he pulled a chair away from the kitchen table and gestured for her to sit. "Want to help me make a list of things we'll need?"

"Sure."

He grabbed a note pad and pen from the table beside the front door and placed it before her, then opened the fridge. "Milk. Whole milk. None of that sissy skim stuff. Butter. Real butter. Cheese. Eggs. Red meat."

"Not one to worry about cholesterol, hmm?"

Devin shrugged. "If you're one of those granola and tofu girls, more power to you. Just don't expect me to exist eating twigs."

Her lips twitched. "What about fruit?"

"I'm a fan of fruit. Berries and bananas are my favorites. But I'll warn you, we probably won't do much cooking here. My mother will insist on us joining them for supper, and on nights that she's not cooking, we'll be invited elsewhere. We should stock up on breakfast food and stuff for sandwiches, but beyond that, we'll be good."

Jenna glanced around the kitchen, her expression a little wistful. "When we lived in Nashville, I had an awesome kitchen. I make an excellent roast and a fabulous chicken parm, but I never had the time to invest in learning to cook the way I wanted. Maybe once I'm off the crutches, I can invite—"

Devin's phone rang, interrupting her thought. He pulled it from his pocket and checked the number. "Hey, Lori."

"Devin, Chase phoned and he needs me to run a couple of puppies up to the Rocking L. Reilly and Michael would like to ride up with me and hold the dogs. Is that all right with Reilly's mother?"

He relayed the question to Jenna, who signaled her permission and asked to speak to her son. Devin grinned to hear her speak the usual mother-cautions like "Behave" and "Mind your manners." When she handed the phone back to Devin, he arranged for Lori to drop Reilly off at the Stocktons' camper at Stardance Ranch upon their return to town.

Devin studied Jenna as he wrapped up the call, noting the weary lines around her eyes and between her brows. "How about we wrap up here and I take you back to Stardance? You should have time to get in a nap before Lori brings Reilly back."

"That sounds fabulous."

Devin made one final inventory circuit around the cottage and added "paper goods" and "coffee" to the shopping list. Then they exited the house and together picked a key code they would both remember. He helped her negotiate the three steps that led down from the porch. "If you're by yourself, there's a ramp to access the back porch so you won't have to worry about steps with the crutches."

"I suspect I'll be able to discard the crutches within a few days."

Jenna grew quiet during the drive through town that took longer than usual due to streets crowded with tourists. Devin noticed her pensive look and said, "Dollar for your thoughts."

"What happened to a penny?"

"Inflation."

Her lips twisted in a crooked grin. "I think I'm a little shell-shocked. This all happened so fast and I'm having a hard time processing it."

"You're accustomed to playing your cards close to the vest. I can understand why laying them down could be disconcerting."

"'Disconcerting' is a mild word for it. It's terrifying. I made a little small snowball of a decision to bring Reilly back to Eternity Springs for a summer visit, only the snowball started rolling downhill getting bigger and bigger, and now it's big enough to be the base of a snowman built by a giant. After months of going to great lengths to hide and remain hidden, I not only shared our entire story with a group of virtual strangers, I handed over control of our lives to them. This morning I wouldn't take Reilly into town to buy a cinnamon roll at the bakery. By suppertime, I'm sending him off to summer camp and moving in with Santa Claus? This isn't me, Devin. At least, not the 'me' who I've become since the first batch of pizzas arrived at my door."

Because he wasn't stupid, Devin bit back a suggestive comment about Santa's lap. Instead, he gently chided. "No one is trying to control you, Jenna. We're trying to help you."

"I know. And I appreciate it. I do. Don't get me wrong. But my actions today are completely out of character, and I'm wondering why I—oh."

She broke off abruptly and shifted her gaze away from him. She sat still and silent, and Devin could all but see the wheels turning in her mind. They'd traveled half a city block and were approaching the intersection of Spruce and First streets when she repeated a pained, "Oh."

"Jenna? Everything okay? Is the ankle bothering you?"

She glanced around as though trying to get her bearings. "Where are we? Are we near Angel's Rest?"

He hooked his thumb over his shoulder. "That way."

"I think . . . can I go back? Please? Would you take me to Angel's Rest?"

Along with not being stupid, Devin had enough experience with women to know the best course of action to take at times such as this. Without protest, he made a left at the corner onto Spruce, headed north, and waited for further explanation.

And waited.

And waited.

"Oh," she said a third time as they approached the entrance to the resort.

Devin spared her a quick glance and saw that her focus was directed inward. *Patience, Murphy.* He gave a friendly wave to guests fishing from the bridge over Angel Creek and slowed the truck to a crawl as they approached a fork in the road. "We're here, Jenna. Is there a particular part of the resort you want to visit?"

"Yes, please. Take me to Blitzen."

At his clueless stare, she grimaced. "Sorry. The cottages at the back. Celeste said she renamed them for the holidays. We stayed in Blitzen. If you'll drive around to the cottages, that would be perfect."

He did as she asked and stopped in front of the cottage she indicated. "Looks like someone is staying there, Jenna. Angel's Rest cottages stay booked all summer long as a rule."

"I don't need to go in." She opened her door and started to reach for a crutch.

"Hold your horses!" Devin said. "I'll help. Let me help." He scrambled from the truck and hurried around to assist her. Moments later, she was hobbling across the resort grounds, going exactly where he hadn't a clue.

She was acting peculiar. Had they given her something stronger than Tylenol at the doctor's office?

When she entered the forest, he fell in behind her. Twice he started to ask her what she was up to and twice he thought better of it, silently repeating his new mantra. *Patience.*

Then she veered off the trail and his concern grew. "Jenna . . ."

"Almost there."

"Okay," he murmured, half beneath his breath.

She finally stopped . . . somewhere. In the middle of the forest. She was staring at a tree. One of millions of trees.

Devin shoved his hands into his pockets, rocked back on his heels, and glanced around. *Okay, she officially has me baffled.* Then she started mumbling and his bewilderment only grew.

". . . can't believe . . . *mumble mumble* . . . clueless . . . *mumble mumble* . . . ostrich . . . *mumble mumble mumble.* Seriously, I actually believe this . . . this . . . what, am I a seven-year-old?"

Devin cleared his throat. "Um, Jenna, this is getting a little strange. Want to tell me what we're doing here?"

The look she gave him was faintly accusing. "I'm a scientist."

"You are?"

"A physician. I'm a doctor."

"Cool." Devin nodded thoughtfully. "Although, I've always considered doctors to be part artist."

"I believe in what I see before my face. Not . . ." She waved her hand around in little circles.

Devin had no clue what the hand circles meant.

"The stress must have taken its toll."

"That's understandable."

"I've been delusional."

"Did Dr. Cicero give you something for pain? You're seeing things? Maybe you're having a reaction."

"Oh, I'm having a reaction, all right," she said, a note of hysteria hovering at the edge of her voice. "My brain freeze finally thawed."

"I don't mean to be dense, but I'm lost. I don't have a clue about what you're trying to tell me."

"I'm telling you that I am a fool. I got the wool pulled over my eyes. Conned by a flimflam artist."

Devin frowned. Did she think someone from Eternity had screwed her around?

"I suppose you think that today's events occurred by chance, that our meeting you at Hummingbird Lake was spur-of-the-moment happenstance? Nothing more than coincidence?"

He rolled his tongue around his mouth. Did she really want him to answer or was this simply a rant?

Well, it was one thing to go along to get along, but that scornful note in her tone rubbed him wrong. "I don't see how it could have been anything but chance. When I went out for my run, I almost took the route that goes up Cemetery Road, not around the lake. I wouldn't have seen you two fishing. I wouldn't have taken you up to our fishing hole. Michael wouldn't have run like a heathen and knocked you down. What is that if not happenstance?"

"See, that's what's sneaky about it. I tried to tell myself too. It's safe to go to Eternity Springs. The Murphys will be visiting Michael's brother in Australia. We won't run into them. They won't be around to recognize us. No one else knows us well enough to see past colored contacts and purple tips."

Distracted, he asked, "Reilly wears colored contacts?"

"No. I do. And I don't like them. I don't need them to see and my eyes are dry all the time. I won't be sad to ditch them, I'll tell you that. They were a lie. Another lie. Here's the deal, Devin. What happened today wasn't coincidence. It wasn't happenstance."

"It wasn't?"

"No! What we have here is the power of suggestion at work. That sweet, but ditzy woman's power of suggestion and I—a scientist—fell for it."

That woman? When anybody in town said "that woman" in that tone of voice, they invariably referred to one person—Celeste Blessing. Suddenly, Jenna's nonsensical ramblings began to make a little sense. Celeste had her fingers in this. Exactly how, he didn't know, but something told him he was about to find out.

"I can't believe I was so dishonest with myself," Jenna continued. "I'm deliberate in my decisions and calculated in my actions. I don't lie to Reilly and I never *ever* lie to myself. But I've been lying to myself for the past four months. This morning if you had asked me when I made the decision to come to Eternity Springs this summer, I'd have said a week ago last Thursday. That's when I called Stardance Ranch searching for a campsite. But that's not the truth. I see that now. Do you know when I really decided to come here, Devin? When I heard Reilly's screams and saw broken hearts lying on my kitchen floor, that's when."

"Oh, Jenna."

"You see, above all else, I must protect my child. I had done my best. I had used logic and reason and followed the rules, and I failed him. I failed him miserably. He was terrorized while decorating cookies in his own kitchen."

"It wasn't your fault, Jenna."

"Wasn't it? I did something, sometime, to cause a crazy person to fixate on me. Who knows what? Maybe it's something as random as I cut him off in traffic. So, in a very real way, what happened to us was my fault. My fault, and my sweet boy went from decorating cookies to non-medical shock. I knew how to diagnose and treat that, but I didn't know how to neutralize the threat."

"I'll bet you were so frightened."

"Yes. But on top of being scared, I was angry. Furious. In the aftermath, Reilly was exhausted and fell asleep. I put him to bed, but he was restless and I didn't want to leave him. I paced his bedroom like a caged tiger, and I didn't know what to do or where to turn. When I get nervous or angry or scared, I clean. I needed to clean the kitchen and deal with the cookie mess, but I needed to be with Reilly more so I started cleaning his room.

Tears pooled in her eyes she turned toward Devin. "I straightened his bookshelf. You want to know what book I found? *The Christmas Angel Waiting Room.*"

He recognized the title, of course. *The Christmas An-*

gel Waiting Room was a children's book written by Eternity Spring's own Claire Lancaster. Hollywood had made a movie out of the story that had become an instant Christmas classic. "I'm not surprised. Claire has sold a bazillion books."

Jenna nodded. "I didn't put it together. Not until ten minutes ago. I stood in Reilly's bedroom that evening and swore I was done asking anyone else for help. From then on, we would take care of ourselves, by ourselves. We couldn't . . . we wouldn't . . . depend on anyone else. It was Reilly and me against the world. Self-sufficient. Self-dependent."

"That's completely understandable."

"I planned how we would disappear, and we hit the road. We made no reservations. Followed no set itinerary. Going where the wind blew us. I was so . . . smug. So stupid. What I did was drive halfway across the country with my head buried in the sand. I was lying to myself and to Reilly, and that's inexcusable."

"Lying about what, Jenna?"

"I bought it. Hook, line, and sinker. I picked up *The Christmas Angel Waiting Room* and I bought"—she waved her hand toward him in a flourish—"Santa! And I bought Celeste and her"—she hooked her thumb over her shoulder pointing toward a fir tree she stood before—"Christmas wishing tree!"

"What's the Christmas wishing tree?"

"A myth. A fairy tale. It's a fairy tale just like Santa and safety and a CIA agent who runs a children's camp! Oh, no." She closed her eyes. "What have I done?"

Had a meltdown, that's what. The woman still wasn't making sense, but Devin recognized when someone needed a hug. Careful of her crutches, he put his arms around her and guided her head onto his shoulder. "You've done an amazing job, that's what you've done."

"Because I bought into the myth? Because this small town is somehow going to make everything right again?"

"Because your son is safe, Jenna. He has food on his table and shoes on his feet and a roof over his head—even if it does roll. Now, I'm not sure what this wishing tree business is, but I take my Santa duties seriously. You need to believe it when I tell you that you made the right choice today. You've put your faith in a group of men who are worthy of your trust. We will keep you and Reilly safe while we locate your tormentor and eliminate the threat he poses."

Jenna remained silent for a long moment. Finally, in a small voice she asked, "Why? Why would you do that for us? We're nobody to you."

"Ah, now that's where you are wrong." Devin tilted up her chin and stared down into her eyes. "You are Reilly's Mom. You've been important to me for a year and a half. Now that I know your story, I can understand why trust might be a scarce commodity. But how or why it happened aside, you are in Eternity Springs now. You're not alone anymore."

He sealed the promise with a kiss.

Chapter Eleven

After Devin helped her climb the steps of her camper and said goodbye, Jenna removed the blasted contact lenses, dug the hair color remover shampoo from the back of her cabinet, and took a long hot shower. She pulled on her favorite yoga pants and a Hot Springs National Park T-shirt, dried her hair, and crawled into bed for a nap. Exhausted, she fell right to sleep and didn't wake up until . . .

Something licked her cheek.

She let out a screech and her heart pounded and her eyes flew open. She stared into the blue eyes of a little black and white bundle of fur and heard her son's delighted giggles. The sound was so welcome, such music to her ears, that she smiled instead of scolded.

"What do we have here?" she asked, sitting up.

"Isn't he cute? I wanted to show you because he has eyes like yours. I've never seen a dog with blue eyes before. He's one of the puppies Dr. Lori took up to the summer camp. She did show-and-tell on how to give dogs a bath. It was fun."

"Oh yeah?" She scratched the pup behind his ears. "Is this a puppy from the animal shelter?"

"No. They don't have any puppies in the shelter right

now. He belongs to one of Dr. Lori's customers. She borrowed him for today. He's a borador, which is a mix of a border collie and a Labrador. We're taking him home now, but I wanted to show you first. Isn't he cute?"

"He's a doll. What's his name?"

"Sinatra. It's a weird name, but so is Mortimer. That's Michael's dog. Do you remember him, Mom?"

"I do." Mortimer, bless his heart, had to be the ugliest Boston terrier ever born. "Frank Sinatra was a singer whose nickname was 'Old Blue Eyes.' Maybe that's why his owner picked it."

"Maybe. Whatever. But he's cute, isn't he? Mom, when I get back from taking Sinatra home, can we talk about my birthday present?"

"Sure, buddy. We'll do that."

"And can I make my hair normal again too?"

"Absolutely."

"Great." His eyes bright with happiness, Reilly scooped the puppy into his arms and headed for the door. "I'll be back soon."

"Hold on a minute, buddy. I'd like to talk to Dr. Lori before she leaves."

Jenna managed to make it out of the camper with her crutches without hurting herself, and followed her son toward the van sporting an Eternity Springs Animal Clinic logo on the side. With her attention on Reilly, she was slow to notice that the van didn't appear to be occupied. Michael lay on his belly in a swing on the swing set, twisting the chains so he'd spin like a top when he lifted his legs. Lori Timberlake was on the Stardance Ranch office porch, bent over and vigorously rubbing the Callahans' dog's golden coat as she spoke with Devin, Brick and Lili Callahan, and Boone McBride—Jenna's New Year's Eve midnight kiss.

"Well," Jenna murmured. "This could be awkward.

Would Boone remember her? Recognize her? Lori had

been informed about the day's developments, but what about the Callahans? Had Brick's father or uncles given them the lowdown?

Devin noticed her first and his eyes went wide. He made a thumping motion over his heart and said, "Wow, Reilly's Mom. You were gorgeous as a brunette with brown eyes, but now . . . whoa. I'm speechless. Did you get to rest? Feel better?"

"Thank you, I did," she said with a hesitant smile. "I do."

Lori straightened and gave her a curious once-over, wincing as her gaze lingered on her ankle. "Ouch. Bet you thought the only wild animals you needed to worry about were bears and bobcats. Someone should have warned you about baby brothers."

"I'm not a baby!" Michael called from the playground, where he'd slid off the swing and knelt beside Reilly, who was playing tug-of-war with the puppy and a stick.

"Your hair is gorgeous, Jenna," Liliana said. Her eyes twinkled as she added, "Pretty name, too."

Okay, that answers one question. "I'm sorry for the deceptions."

Brick waved the apology away. "Hey, forget about it. I'm impressed as hell that you managed so well in the face of all of your challenges."

Boone glanced from Jenna, to Devin, to Brick, then back to Jenna again. "It's obvious I'm out of the loop about something here. I'll be curious to learn what I've missed. In the meantime, though . . ." He stepped forward, leaned down, and gave Jenna's cheek a friendly kiss. "Jenna, welcome back. I've thought of you often since New Year's Eve."

"Hello, Boone," she replied, ignoring Devin's sharp look. "I hope the new year has treated you well."

"It's been downhill since midnight, New Year's Eve, I'm afraid."

"I take it y'all met last Christmas," Devin said.

"No," Boone replied, not taking his gaze off Jenna. "On a memorable New Year's Eve."

Devin's eyes narrowed.

Jenna decided a change of subject was advisable so she focused on Lori. "I'm sorry to interrupt your conversation, but I wanted to say hello and thank you for your help with Reilly today."

"I was glad to have him along. Having Reilly around makes dealing with Michael half as much work."

Devin sidled up beside Jenna and placed a proprietary hand at her back. "Why don't you come sit down? You probably need to keep your ankle elevated, don't you?"

Boone smirked, but took a step back as if surrendering the field. Yet Jenna didn't miss the quick little wink he gave her.

"Actually, I'd like to speak with your sister alone for a moment. Could you guys distract the boys for a few minutes? Is there another super-cool snakeskin you could show Reilly?"

"No. I wish there was."

"I made chocolate chip cookies earlier," Lili said. "I have some in the office that are still warm from the oven. Think that would work?"

"Works for me," Boone said. Then he glanced at Brick. "You have a super-cool snakeskin?"

"I do. Something I found on the ranch. Want to see it?"

"Cookies first."

Brick called. "Boys, y'all come with us. Lili is going to give us some homemade cookies and then I'm gonna get my snakeskin out to show my cousin."

"Cookies!" Michael exclaimed, hopping to his feet. "I love cookies and Mom hardly ever lets me have any."

"It's true," Devin said to Jenna. "We're limited to two a day."

Lori snorted. "Two plus all the ones you sneak. And don't think Michael isn't following in his big brother's footsteps."

"I'm afraid Sarah's cookies put mine to shame," Lili said with a note of regret. "But sometimes a girl just needs a bite of chocolate chip cookie dough. You know?"

"Amen, sister," Lori replied before turning to Jenna. "You might not need to sit down, but I do. How about we adjourn to that picnic bench by the playground?"

Jenna nodded, and as Lili and the men headed for the office, the boys rose to join them. Lori called, "Reilly, why don't you let us hold Sinatra."

"Okay, Dr. Lori."

Jenna added, "And wash your hands before you eat."

"But Mom, a dog's mouth has fewer germs than a human's."

"You've been playing in the dirt."

He rolled his eyes and handed the puppy to Lori, then scampered after the others.

Lori watched them go and smiled. "I like the hair."

"I think he and I are both ready to be done with dyes." She blew out a breath, then asked, "How much of Reilly's and my story has your father or brother shared with you?"

"Dad hit the highlights. Or lowlights, to be more exact. I'm so sorry this has happened to you, Jenna. And poor Reilly."

"It's been terribly hard for him. Children should grow up feeling safe and secure, and that's been stolen from him. My goal is to give that back. We had a shaky start today, and I didn't know if sending him off with your father was the right thing to do. He and I have been together twenty-four seven since Valentine's Day. But in these last few minutes, I see my old Reilly. He's forgetting to be afraid. What was he like when he was with you this afternoon?"

Lori tilted her head and considered the question. "I see what you're saying. I did notice a moment or two when he seemed to withdraw. That was when we were at the shelter and someone came in with a stray they'd found on the Gunnison highway. He opened up again once we were alone."

"How did he act up at the camp?"

"Reilly was too busy playing with the puppies to be nervous. Plus, Chase met us when we arrived, and Reilly remembered him from your visit last Christmas. He did act a little shy at first around the other children, but it was nothing out of the ordinary. I will say that he impressed me with his kindness toward our two wheelchair-bound campers."

Jenna's heart warmed. "Thank you for sharing that. He's always been a tenderhearted boy, and I'm glad for the reminder that there is value to that trait. I'm afraid I lost sight of that during the past four months as I've concentrated on trying to toughen him up."

"He's a good kid, Jenna. He's a good influence on my little brother, which is something I know my parents appreciate. Michael can be a little monster—but then, that's no news to you since he put you on crutches. As a veterinarian I probably shouldn't admit to this, but I believe it's Mortimer's fault."

"Michael's dog?"

"He's actually my father's dog, and a troublemaker like none other. When Michael was born, Mortimer became his shadow. I think he knew he was getting old and slowing down, so he transferred his devilry to the baby."

Jenna looked for a teasing light in the other woman's eyes, but Lori appeared to be serious. *Okay. Well. Hmm.* "Speaking of dogs, that's something else I wanted to discuss with you."

She told Lori about her plans to finally get Reilly the

dog he'd wanted. "Devin mentioned it might be possible for Reilly to take a dog with him to camp?"

Lori nodded. "We've done it at other sessions. Pets are excellent therapy. I will confirm with Chase, but I'm ninety-nine percent certain that Reilly could attend camp with a dog."

"In that case, I'd like to move forward with this. Considering our situation and with the possibility that we may be living in our camper for some time to come, do you ~~~ ly available dogs that might be a good fit for us?"

~~~ pends. How much exercise could you commit to for ~~r dog?"

"Honestly, more now than when we lived in an apartment. Neither Reilly nor I tolerate being cooped up very well. My son might not be quite as active as Michael, but he's not far behind."

"In that case, then why not this little guy?" Lori gave Sinatra a good scratch.

Jenna's brows arched in surprise. "Reilly said he's not a shelter pup."

"No, but he is up for adoption. The dam's owner wanted her to have one litter of puppies so that the owner's children could have the experience. I know both the dam and the sire. They're good dogs. I expect that Sinatra will be smart and friendly and an excellent companion for Reilly—as long as he gets plenty of exercise. He'll be ready to leave his mama next week."

"The same time Reilly will leave me to go to camp. The timing couldn't be any more perfect. Oh, I hope this works out."

Lori held up a finger, pulled her cell phone from her pocket, and called her husband, then Sinatra's owner. By the time the boys spilled out of the office with milk mustaches and giggling like fools, arrangements had all been made.

Later that evening after Jenna trimmed the blue from Reilly's hair, he brought up the subject of his birthday present.

"Yes, we need to talk about that," Jenna replied.

He slumped onto his seat at the table and buried his head in his arms. "You're gonna tell me no. It's because of what happened today, right? Did Michael's dad and brother break their promise and put us on the Internet? The bad man is on our trail and you're going to hook up the trailer and sneak out of town after dark. It's not safe, all, is it? I'll never see Michael again."

"Oh, Reilly, no. Slow down." Jenna sat opposite him, reached out and placed her hand on his shoulder. "That's not it at all. No one broke his or her promises. I actually have a pretty spectacularly wonderful surprise for you."

Now the boy lifted his head. Hope filled his expression. "The police found the bad guy?"

"No. No. I'm afraid not. If that was my news I wouldn't wait until after your shower to tell you. Honey, I told Devin and Mr. Murphy about what happened to us and then we talked to some of their friends who are investigators. They have promised to help us."

"But we've had an investigator."

"True. But instead of one investigator looking or a handful of policemen working our case and dozens of other cases, we have ten people ready to help us."

"Ten?"

Jenna nodded. "Yes. From what the Murphys tell me, these men are really sharp and they're experienced and they have the tools it will take to track the bad guy down. I don't know about you, but I'm tired of always looking over my shoulder. Wouldn't it be nice to put this behind us and have a normal life?"

"But I like living in the camper. We still have lots of national parks to visit."

"Hey, you and I have a deal. We are going to visit every single national park whether we're living in this camper or a penthouse condo in New York City."

"I don't want to live in a condo."

Jenna licked her lips and asked, "What about a log cabin?"

Reilly's brow knitted as he narrowed his eyes in suspicion. "What log cabin?"

"One at the Rocking L camp. You liked what you saw up there today, didn't you?"

"Well . . . yeah. It was cool, I guess. Mr. Chase is nice and he has a really awesome dog. His name is Captain."

"Reilly, you've been offered a slot there in the session that begins next week. I'd like you to go."

Reilly's eyes got round and worried, so Jenna was quick to press on. "It will be so much fun. They have horseback riding and rock climbing and swimming and hiking."

"Where are you going?"

"Nowhere. I'll be right here in Eternity Springs. I promise."

"All by yourself?"

"Actually, I won't be by myself. I'm going to have my own personal bodyguards—Devin and Mr. Murphy. And the sheriff is on our team too. He's not going to fall for any bad tricks."

"It scares me, Mom. I don't think I like this. I think we should stay together. I think we probably *should* leave Eternity Springs."

Jenna smoothed Reilly's still-damp bangs away from his brow. "Honey, I don't expect there to be any trouble. Things are different now. This is a small town where people know us. It's like living in our own little castle and we have knights standing at the ready to protect us. You'll be up in the parapets at camp and if you get too lonely for me, I can climb up to see you or you can come down to see me."

He gave her a droll, *Really, Mom?* look and she decided it was time to roll out the big guns. "However, you'll be so busy taking care of the puppy that I don't think you'll have time to be lonely."

He sat up. "What puppy?"

"There's a puppy who will be sleeping apart from his mother for the first time. He'll need a lot of love and care and company. I thought that would be a good job for you—if you're interested."

"Like, to babysit?"

"Like, for that birthday present I promised."

"Mine! A puppy? Not an older dog?"

"A puppy. And yes, he can be yours if you want him. This little guy will be ready to leave his mama next week, and Mr. Chase said you can bring him with you to camp—if you're prepared for the responsibility."

"I am! Oh, I am!" He clasped his hands prayerfully, but the frown lines between his brows showed he wasn't ready to believe. "But Mom, Dr. Lori said they don't have any puppies at the shelter. We didn't see any when we visited."

"Sinatra needs a home."

Reilly's mouth dropped open. His eyes went round as saucers. "Sinatra? Really, Mom? For me?"

"It's a little bit of a bribe. I need you to go to camp, Reilly. Will you do that?"

"And take Sinatra with me?"

"And take Sinatra with you."

"Yes!" He launched himself out of his seat and into her arms. "I'll do it. I can do it. I'll be super responsible. I promise. I'll be the best ever."

Jenna's heart swelled with happiness as she hugged her

son and absorbed his joy. Through the camper's window, she saw the evening shadows fade to full night. What a wild ride this day had been.

Riley pulled away from her. "We have to get him a bed and food bowls and a collar and a leash. And treats. Lots of treats. What day do I get him, Mom? Can I go visit before then? And we need to get him a tag for his collar that has his name. Can we go get one tomorrow?"

"Maybe. It'll depend on if we can catch a ride to town. I won't be able to drive for a few days yet because of my ankle."

"I'll bet Devin will drive us. He's your bodyguard, right? In the movies, bodyguards drive people around."

"Well, we'll see. We took up a lot of his time today, and he's here to visit family. We don't want to intrude more than we already have." Looking for a distraction, she added, "About Sinatra. You do know that it's okay if you want to change his name? He'll be your dog and you get to name him."

"Oh. I'll have to think about that."

"You do that. Now . . ." Jenna rose and ruffled his hair. "Get your book and get into bed. Quiet time officially begins in"—she checked her watch—"seven minutes. Lights out in thirty-seven."

For once, he gave her no argument. Jenna got ready for bed and settled down with her own current read, a cozy mystery by one of her favorite British authors. They read for their usual half hour, though she noticed that Reilly did more staring out the window than page turning. At nine thirty, she said, "Lights out. Good night, buddy. I love you."

"G'night, Mom. Love you too."

From outside, she heard the faint sounds of laughter and farewells as the campsite settled down for the night. Worn out from the day, she drifted easily toward sleep.

From out of the darkness, she heard her son murmur, "This was the best day in forever."

"Amen." For the first time in longer than she could recall, Jenna fell off to sleep with a smile on her lips.

Devin fixed bacon and eggs for the Murphy men for breakfast. Sarah didn't come downstairs due to the slow bounce back from her bug. Afterward, he spent some quality time with Michael shooting baskets in the driveway, then met his dad for lunch at the Mocha Moose coffee and sandwich shop. Finally, a little after two o'clock he ran out of reasons not to wander out to Stardance Ranch. He turned into the RV resort entrance just in time to see the local florist van stop in front of Jenna's trailer.

Like many camping enthusiasts do, Jenna had set up a patio that looked homey and inviting beside her fifth wheel. With an outdoor rug and chair cushions in earth-tone stripes, she'd accented the space with splashes of yellow. Wearing khaki shorts, a pepper orange V-neck T-shirt and a floppy brimmed hat, she sat in a rocker with her foot propped up on a matching ottoman. A tall glass of what looked like iced tea sat on a table beside her. She was reading a paperback book.

When the driver removed a huge bouquet of sunflowers from the back of the delivery van and carried them toward her, she set the book aside. The smile that bloomed across her face was almost as bright as the sunflowers.

"Boone McBride," Devin muttered beneath his breath, knowing in his gut who'd sent them. "That sonofanoilman."

I should have thought to send flowers.

Devin parked his truck and sat stewing for a moment, drumming his fingers on the steering wheel. He should probably think this through. He'd just met the woman yesterday. Flirtatious phone calls a year and a half ago did not a relationship make. Not that he was in the market for a relationship, because he wasn't. Especially not with a woman who lived . . . well . . . not in Australia.

So what was he doing getting so . . . territorial?

It was the Santa thing. They'd formed a bond during those phone calls, he and Reilly's Mom. He'd bonded with Reilly too. Shoot, he'd remember that first phone call until the day he died.

"So, Reilly. What is your Christmas wish?"

"A daddy. I want a daddy of my own."

Devin's eyes closed and he heard the echo of his own words. *"It's a good wish. You hold onto it. Keep wishing it. Believe it will come true."*

Believe. Devin wondered if Reilly remembered that conversation. He wondered if the "believing" had been crushed out of Reilly's little soul by the events that followed their week of Santa calls. He'd wished for a daddy of his own. Had it ever come close to happening? Jenna hadn't mentioned leaving anyone behind when she gave her summary of events. Had she found anyone special, someone she regretted leaving behind when she had to leave Nashville or Memphis or Tallahassee?

Or Eternity Springs.

Devin's gaze drifted toward the Stocktons' fifth wheel. *"A daddy. I want a daddy of my own."*

In the echo of his memory, he heard Celeste's voice as clear as a Christmas bell. *"Open your eyes and heart and imaginings to the possibilities that await. You must believe. Wishes can and do come true. And when the Christmas bells ring, Devin Murphy, don't you fail to answer."*

What the heck was the thought nibbling at the edges of his brain?

Santa Claus.

"I want a daddy of my own."

Whoa. Whoa. Whoa. Whoa. Back this truck up. That way there be dragons.

Devin let out a nervous little laugh. Must be delayed jet lag. He'd met Reilly and his mother yesterday. Yesterday! What the heck was wrong with him? He should probably turn his truck around and head back into town. Go home and take a nap. Shoot, maybe he was coming down with whatever was plaguing his mother.

The unexpected peal of a bell startled him. He turned toward the sound and saw a little girl decked out from helmet to sneakers in red and green teetering on a bike with training wheels while she flicked the bell mounted on the handlebars. *Brring brring. Brring brring.*

"When the Christmas bells ring, Devin Murphy, don't you fail to answer."

"Oh, man. No. Celeste! Don't tell me I'm having a Celeste Blessing moment."

"Is this Santa Claus? I want a daddy of my own."

Devin's gaze returned to Jenna's camper, the same camper where moments ago, the local florist had delivered a big honking bouquet of flowers.

Boone McBride.

Wait a minute. This was June, not December. It was a bicycle bell, not a Christmas bell. He didn't have snowy white hair and a belly that shook like a bowl full of jelly. *You soon will if you don't stop eating so many strawberry pinwheels.*

Maybe so, but he wasn't there yet. He didn't leave presents under a tree, and he didn't grant little boys their Christmas wishes. He wasn't effing Santa Claus.

He'd come home to Eternity Springs for three short weeks to visit his family. Period.

"I want a daddy of my own. Are you Santa Claus?"

Slowly, Devin reached up to the dashboard and twisted his key, cutting the engine. He blew out a heavy breath.

What the heck was he thinking? He'd let Celeste Blessing get in his head, that's what. Did he truly believe some cosmic force was at work here? Did he believe?

Well, he'd definitely had a front-row seat to many of the Eternity Springs' more woo-woo moments. And what he didn't witness himself, he'd heard about firsthand. Everything from Gabe Callahan's now-ancient boxer, Clarence, just happening to show up in time to save Gabe's life to Hope Romano finding her lost child to the reunion of long lost lovers—his own parents—after Sarah won a vacation to Australia that brought her face-to-face with Cam. They all had one thing—one person—in common. Celeste Blessing.

And how had Jenna and Reilly found their way to Eternity Springs?

Through a cell phone of Celeste's.

"There's your sign, dumbass." The clues were right there in front of him, clear as a Christmas bell. Only an idiot—or someone who didn't believe in Eternity Springs woo-woo—would fail to connect the dots. Reilly called Santa and asked for a dad. Devin said enough to attract them to Eternity Springs for Christmas vacation and then, unless he was totally off on the clues he picked up yesterday, Jenna ended up at a local's party on New Year's Eve and locked lips with the lawyer at midnight.

Then she comes back to town with trouble on her tail at the exact same time that Devin happened to be here—after a freak snowstorm changes the family's plans. "Can Celeste control the freaking weather?"

Devin wouldn't put anything past her.

So now here he was about to move into close quarters with Hot Mom for whom he definitely had a thing and the sorry Christmas bells ring. Goodbye hot tub daydreams. So long vacation-fling fantasies. Arrivederci any idea of taking advantage of Jenna while Riley was away at camp.

Because Devin wasn't The Guy. Devin didn't dream about finding The One. His MO was The Many. He liked having a harem, to use his father's term. He was a love 'em and leave 'em kind of guy, and the ladies knew that from the beginning. He was always up front when he started dating. He didn't lie about his intentions—or lack thereof. He didn't lead anyone on. Because . . . he would leave. He always left. That's what he did.

The one time he'd considered doing it differently had bitten him in the ass. He'd learned a hard, bitter lesson, one that he'd never forget.

And now that he'd heard the Christmas bells, he knew what was what. He wasn't meant for Jenna. He certainly wasn't meant to be Reilly's dad. He was home for three weeks and then he'd be history. He would be her bodyguard. He would be part of the team to solve the stalker problem. But he wasn't the answer to Reilly's Christmas wish. Reilly and Jenna needed something different. Some*one* different.

The clues were too many, the Christmas bells too loud to ignore. The Eternity Springs woo-woo was at work with Jenna and Reilly Stockton, and Devin couldn't help but believe. He had to do his part.

He was Santa Claus.

Santa's job was to play Cupid. For Jenna and Boone McBride.

Well, if that's not a kick in the balls, I don't know what is. Maybe he'd better stop by his dad's shop and get a bow and some arrows.

He'd take aim at Boone McBride first.

Chapter Twelve

The handwritten card read, *Keep your face to the sunshine and feel better soon! Boone*

Jenna had always been a sucker for flowers, and bright cheerful sunflowers invariably brought a smile to her face. They couldn't have come at a better time either, since she'd been sitting on her patio and pretending to read, while in reality she'd been staring at the pages, brooding and second-guessing her decision to send Reilly to camp.

While part of her was positively giddy at the thought of having a month to herself, another part feared she'd spend the entire time missing Reilly and fretting about how he was managing without her. Intellectually, Jenna recognized that living in each other's pockets these past four months had changed the dynamics of their relationship in a way that wasn't good for either of them. But since the February SWAT team invasion, in matters that involved her son, emotions ruled the day more often than not.

Now she had a big, bright, beautiful bunch of flowers to distract her from her doldrums. "Keep my face to the sunshine," she murmured, smiling. "Don't you know that gives a girl wrinkles?"

Nevertheless, she took off her hat and tilted her face toward the sun. As sunshine warmed her skin, she tried to recall the last time a man had sent her flowers. It had been a long time, that's for certain. Joel Mercer brought her a red rose when he picked her up for a date one night, but he never had a florist deliver to her. If she tried to name a flower-sending man who she hadn't been sleeping with at the time . . . whoa. That took her all the way back to high school.

And honestly, she wasn't certain she would call her sweet, shy nerdy boyfriend a man. He'd been a boy learning to be a man.

There was nothing left of the boy in Boone McBride.

What did she think about this overture? Was it an advance or just a gesture of friendship? Or, maybe these flowers had more to do with Devin than with her. She hadn't missed the posturing between the two men yesterday. The feminist in Jenna had been annoyed. The woman in her had been secretly thrilled.

"Hey, pretty lady."

Startled, Jenna opened her eyes to see the figure dressed in Hawaiian board shorts and a Refresh Outfitters T-shirt standing just beyond her patio. "Devin."

"You look relaxed. Enjoying the weather?"

"I am. It's a gorgeous afternoon."

He gestured toward an empty chair. "Mind if I join you?"

"Please, be my guest. Would you like something to drink?"

"If that's iced tea in your glass, I wouldn't turn it down—as long as you'll let me fix it myself."

Jenna gestured toward the camper. "Make yourself at home."

Moments later, she heard the sound of ice hitting a glass from inside the camper. When he rejoined her, she saw that he'd chosen Reilly's Scooby-Doo glass. "Okay, now *that* amuses me. Care to guess where we got that particular glass?"

Devin gave the tumbler a closer look, then grinned. "Mikey. He is a Scooby fiend."

"He gave it to Reilly when they got to be friends over Christmas."

Devin lifted the glass in toast. "To friendship."

After they clinked glasses, Devin sat and stretched his long legs out in front of him, crossing them at the ankles. Ray-Ban sunglasses hung from a cord around his neck. On his feet, he wore flip-flops. She couldn't quite read the look that came into his hazel eyes as he studied her.

He took a long sip of tea, then asked, "How is your ankle today?"

"A little better. I expect that by tomorrow I'll be down to using one crutch. I'll be much more mobile at that point."

"Good. I'm glad to hear that." Devin made a broad gesture toward the surrounding campground. "So where's the squirt?"

"In town visiting the puppy. Liliana had a few errands to run in town, so she offered to take him along."

"I heard through the pinecone telegraph that he's whittled his list of possible names down to seventeen."

Jenna laughed. "The pinecone telegraph?"

"Your son my our brother to our sister to her husband to his sister to her fiancé to my father to me."

"Well, you can add another link in your chain. I happen to know that as of twenty minutes ago, the list was down to eleven."

"You have a prediction on the winner?"

"I do. I think he'll decide against changing the puppy's name. Reilly was never comfortable with changing his name by using his initials. I think he'll take Sinatra up to camp with him."

"It's a good name." Devin lifted his sunglasses and slipped them on. "Pretty flowers you have there. Got a secret admirer?"

"A get-well message from a friend."

The nosy man reached over and plucked the card off the bouquet and read it. "I figured as much. So I gather you and McBride have a past?"

Jenna rolled her eyes. "Yes, it was quite scandalous. We met at Celeste's New Year's Eve party and made small talk. He handed me a glass of champagne and kissed me at midnight."

The words Devin spoke next were at odds with the slight thinning of his lips. "McBride is a relative newcomer to town and I don't know him well personally, but he has an excellent reputation. Have you met Mac Timberlake, my sister's father-in-law?"

Jenna nodded.

"Mac is a former federal judge and he's an excellent judge of character. He convinced McBride to move here from Fort Worth and take over his law practice. Scuttlebutt is that he tried to set McBride up with his daughter Caitlin. That's about as good a recommendation as you can get around here."

And you are telling me this why? "It was nice of him to send flowers."

"He's related to the Callahan clan, too. A distant cousin or something. I'm not exactly sure how. I met him at Brick and Lili's wedding."

Jenna had other things on her mind than Boone McBride, so she changed the subject. "How is your mother feeling today? Better, I hope?"

"I think so. She has more color in her cheeks than she did yesterday."

"Good." Jenna made a mental note to call in her own order of get-well-soon flowers. Sarah Murphy had been nothing but kind to her and Reilly, and Jenna would like to brighten her day with some sunflowers. "I hope she's not upset about the change in your sleeping arrangements during your visit home."

"No, not at all. She did bring up family dinners, though, so I was right to warn you about that. She said Lori will join us more often than not too, since Chase stays up at the Rocking L when camp is in session."

"Please let her know that I'm happy to help with the cooking. Reilly doesn't exactly have a sophisticated palate. It'll be a joy for me to make something other than spaghetti."

"I'll do that. So, any idea when Lili and Reilly will be back?"

Jenna glanced at her watch. 2:38. "Any time now, I imagine. Lili said she needed to be back by three. She and Brick have an appointment."

Devin gave a satisfied nod. "I'll wait then, if you don't mind. I have a little something to give him. A birthday gift."

"That's sweet of you, but his birthday is in March."

"I remember. But I also understand that Sinatra is a birthday gift."

"How do you know . . . oh. The pinecone telegraph?"

"Nothing in Eternity Springs stays secret for long."

They both turned to look when three quick beeps of a horn announced Liliana Callahan's return. Devin set down his drink and then rose and said, "I'll be right back."

Jenna watched as her son exited the Jeep sporting the Stardance Ranch logo and started running toward their campsite. Upon spying Devin, her son veered in his direction. "Hi, Devin. Guess what?"

"You've whittled your list of puppy names down to ten?"

"You know about my dog?"

"Everyone in Colorado knows about your dog. Come with me. I need help carrying some things."

"Yessir."

Devin reached into the bed of his pickup and lifted out a shopping bag and then another and another and another. He handed two of the bags to Reilly, and then reached back for two more and a box.

Jenna murmured, "What have you done, Devin Murphy?"

Reilly bobbed from side to side as he carried the obviously heavy bags. Although she couldn't hear what he was saying, his mouth never stopped moving. Devin grinned down at him and said something that caused Reilly to giggle in such a carefree manner that it took her breath away and brought tears to her eyes. What a difference a couple of days—and a dog—could make.

"Set the bags down by your mother," Devin said as the pair drew near.

Reilly did as instructed then pulled a phone out of his pocket. "Look what I have, Mom. Don't worry. Ms. Lili gave it to me. It's an old phone she had in her car but it's not connected to the Internet or anything and the camera works. I took a whole bunch of pictures of Sinatra."

"Oh yeah?"

"Let me see 'em," Devin said as he deposited his packages on the patio beside the two that Reilly had dumped. He sat in the chair he'd vacated earlier and motioned Reilly to hand over the phone. He flipped through the photos. "Those are some blue eyes on that pup. Maybe you should call him Sky. Sky is a good name for dog."

Reilly's lips pursed. "Sky. I hadn't thought of that."

Devin then rattled off another dozen names that had Reilly finally clapping his hands on his head and wailing. "I can't decide!"

Devin's chortle had a smidgen of evil in it. "Or you could just call him Sinatra and be done with it. While you're thinking about it, why don't you open your birth-day presents?"

Reilly blinked. "My what?"

"I know. I know. Your birthday is in March and this is June, but I didn't know you this past March and next March is too far away and besides, you need this stuff now."

"You're giving me a birthday present?" Reilly repeated, awe in his tone. "Why?"

A private smile played on Devin's lips as he replied, "I like to give presents to good boys and girls."

"I try to be good."

"So your mom tells me. I heard she was giving you a belated birthday gift so I thought I'd get something to go along with it."

"Thank you so much! I'm so excited! Which bag is the present?"

"All of them."

Reilly's jaw dropped.

Devin folded his arms. "Now, I don't want any whin-ing because they're not wrapped. They're in bags and boxes, and you can't tell what they are until you open them. I seriously don't understand why a person needs to take something out of one bag and plunk it into another. Oh . . . wait. Before you dig in I have one thing . . ."

He reached into one of the shopping bags that sported the Forever Christmas logo and removed a small white bakery bag. "I thought about getting you a cake or a cup-cake, but believe me, this is better. You turned eight on your birthday, right?"

"Yessir."

"Inside this bag are eight pieces of heaven—my mother's strawberry pinwheel cookies. I'll have you know I took them from my private stash. Want us to sing to you?" Without waiting for a response, Devin launched into song in a pleasing tenor. "Happy birthday to you, you belong in a zoo. You look like a monkey, and you smell like one too."

Reilly giggled happily as Devin finished by saying, "Happy birthday, Reilly. Now, share your cookies."

"Okay. Thank you. Thank you so much." He took three cookies from the bakery bag and passed them out.

Devin popped one into his mouth. "Mmm. I could eat my weight in these. Have at it, kid. Tear into those bags."

In that Devin was doomed to disappointment, Jenna knew. Reilly had never been one to "tear in." He opened gifts reverently. He wanted to make the moment last as long as possible. He picked at tape and tugged gently at ribbons. Even with these bags, he'd find a way to go slowly. The boy reached tentatively for the nearest bag. "All of them? They're all for me?"

"Yes."

Reilly filled his cheeks with air then blew out a slow breath. Jenna recognized that he was overwhelmed by the moment. When was the last time that anyone had treated him with such kindness and generosity? Not since their original trip to Eternity Springs. *He's never going to want to leave here.*

That's something she probably should spend a little time thinking about.

Devin snagged a second cookie from the bag. "Hurry up, boy. You're slower than Christmas."

Reilly looked up at Devin and grinned. "If these were Christmas presents instead of birthday presents, that would make you Santa Claus, wouldn't it?"

In the process of reaching for his iced tea, Devin jerked and came close to knocking Scooby-Doo over. He met Jenna's gaze and his lips twisted in a rueful smirk. Reilly didn't notice because he'd finally pulled something from the bag. A Scooby-Doo dog leash. It took him ten more minutes to unwrap the rest of the gifts—a Scooby snack treat jar and Scooby-themed dog bowls, collar, tag, toys, and, finally, a deluxe dog bed. When the boy threw himself into Devin's arms and declared his undying thanks, Jenna blinked back tears. Needing to lighten the moment, she cleared her throat and said, "Now I understand. Michael isn't the only Murphy who likes Scooby-Doo."

Now Devin's grin turned sheepish. "What can I say? I'm a fan."

Jenna watched her son hug his Santa Claus and murmured, "Me too."

Everyone in Eternity Springs knew that Jack Davenport was a descendant of one of three partners who had discovered the Silver Miracle mother lode in the 1880s. Townspeople knew that he and his wife Cat ran a charitable foundation named after their deceased daughter Lauren, and one of its numerous projects was the Rocking L summer camp, which had been built on Davenport family land. The grand estate Jack had built in a picturesque valley on Murphy Mountain was more of a mystery. Rumor had it that Eagle's Way had a level of security that rivaled Camp David's, and the handful of people in town in position to know the veracity of that rumor didn't talk about it.

They did, however, gather at Eagle's Way on Sunday afternoon with potluck offerings, swimsuits, and pieces of a plan to rid the Stocktons of the threat under which they'd been living. Because they came with a whole gaggle of children in tow, the decision had been made to party first, thus giving the little ones a chance to wear themselves out.

Eagle's Way boasted an outdoor living space and swimming pool worthy of a five-star resort with floating step pads, chaise lounges on a tanning ledge, a spillway spa and rain curtain, and a bar table inside the pool. Every time he visited, Devin wondered why the Davenports only spent about half their time in Colorado. If he owned Eagle's Way, it would take a bulldozer to get him out of this valley. That was saying a lot, considering how far away this place was from an ocean.

In keeping with his bodyguard role, Devin had volunteered for lifeguard duty. The boy in him chortled with glee when Jack produced a whistle and a red throw float to assist in the effort. "Cool. Thanks, Jack. Though I'd have brought zinc oxide for my nose if I knew I'd be in uniform."

With more than a dozen young people in the pool, Devin did pay close attention. He blew his whistle judiciously and used his stern voice to demand obedience, but the only time he got seriously sidetracked was when Jenna emerged from the pool house in a one-piece swimsuit. His mouth went dry and he'd have licked his lips except that he felt the weight of his mother's interested gaze. Due to his beachfront lifestyle, Devin was accustomed to seeing women in scraps that barely covered anything. How was it that a conservative one-piece in a gray-blue that matched Jenna's eyes and complimented her creamy skin distracted him so thoroughly?

"You feeling a little hot?" his father asked, his tone brimming with innocence. "Want me to take over as lifeguard so you can cool off?"

"Gee thanks, Dad." Devin shoved the float at his father and started to walk away.

"Hey! What about the whistle?"

Devin rolled his eyes, tugged the whistle chain over his head, and tossed it to his dad. Then he strolled toward the end of the pool where the women had congregated, tugged off his T-shirt, and kicked his flip-flops beneath a chair.

Then a splash from one of the Callahan girls caught him by surprise, and he had no choice but to cannonball in beside them. He played with the kids until his father blew the whistle loud and called everyone out of the water to eat. After dinner, Cat Davenport took the children inside to the theater room, and Jack asked the adults to gather around. He called the meeting to order by asking Jenna if she had anything she wished to say before individual team members began their presentations.

Jenna glanced at Devin, who gave her a reassuring nod. She blew out a breath, then said, "I'm even more over-whelmed by your kindness and generosity today than I was last week."

Jack's answering smile to her was gentle. "We're happy to help you, Jenna. Those of us here have benefit-ted from the efforts of friends in the past. It's good to be able to give back in some small way. Now, why don't we start with your report, Daniel? I trust you were able to speak with your colleague about Jenna's case?"

"I was." Proving that old police detective habits die hard, Daniel removed a small notebook from his pocket. "He faxed me your file, Jenna. After studying it and mak-ing a few follow-up inquiries, I don't see any glaring mistakes. He identified three suspects."

Daniel looked toward his wife and nodded. Shannon Garrett drew a handful of manila folders from a briefcase and passed them out to team members. Daniel continued. "First, we have Nashville attorney Jeremy Tomlinson, whose wife was an obstetrical patient of Dr. Stockton's."

"Wait. Excuse me." The sheriff's wife, Savannah Turner, stepped forward. "You're a doctor? An obstetri-cian? I missed this piece of news." She turned a scolding gaze toward her husband. "Zach, you didn't tell me that."

The sheriff gave his wife an apologetic smile. Savan-nah waved dismissively, then said, "I'm sorry, Daniel. I'll be quiet."

He gave her a blue-eyed wink. "Jeremy Tomlinson

accosted Jenna in her office building parking lot and
struck her with a slap to the face following his wife's first-
trimester miscarriage. Another physician witnessed the
altercation and called the police. Dr. Stockton refused to
press charges."

Everyone looked at Jenna, who shrugged. "He was
grieving. I didn't take it seriously. Besides, he apologized."

"Tomlinson's firm learned about the incident and he lost
his job."

"Serves him right," Luke Callahan muttered.

"I've never believed he was my stalker."

Devin imagined his own expression mirrored the skep-
tical looks he spied on the faces of the people around
him.

Daniel continued. "Our second person of interest is
Dr. Alan Snelling. Jenna reported the surgeon for sexual
harassment to hospital administration. He denied it and
started a campaign of innuendo against her. But after seven
more women came forward with similar charges, he lost
his hospital privileges. At that point, word of the scandal
made it onto social media, and that apparently was the last
straw for his wife of"—Daniel checked his notes—"thirty-
four years. She filed for divorce. Jenna, anything to add?"

"I know that surgeons often have the reputation for being egotistical jerks, but in my experience, that's seldom
true. Dr. Snelling, however, is a different animal. He's an
egotistical pig. While I could easily picture him hiring
someone to torment us, I still don't see him doing it himself."

"Which brings us to the third suspect identified by Jenna's investigator, Adam Zapel," Daniel said. "Mr. Zapel is
a singer-songwriter whom Jenna dated briefly three months
before the first harassment incident. He was unhappy when
she told him she didn't want to see him anymore. He con-
tacted her three subsequent times in an effort to change

her mind. And"—Daniel glanced her way.—"he wrote a song about her."

"Jenna!" Sarah said. "A song? This was in Nashville. So, a country music song? Did he record it? I want to hear it."

"No. Please, no." Color stained Jenna's cheeks. "It's so embarrassing."

"He's cute," Savannah said, peering over her husband's shoulder at the file.

Devin flipped through his own file folder to a picture of Zapel. Huh. He didn't look like a country and western singer. More of a used-car salesman, to Devin's way of thinking. Of course, he could be prejudiced.

"He's also married now with a baby on the way," Daniel continued.

"So does that take him off the list?" Maddie Callahan asked.

Daniel shook his head. "Actually, it makes me want to dig even deeper. Here's what I propose to do."

He outlined a plan of investigation that revisited these three characters, doing a deeper dive with the technological assets the Callahan family was able to bring to the table. During a pause in the discussion, Jenna asked the question that had occurred to Devin. "Is what you're suggesting legal? That seems awfully intrusive."

"We're fighting fire with fire, Jenna," Mark Callahan explained. "The law hasn't caught up with technology, I'm afraid. However, you can be assured that law enforcement will be able to use any information we give them to aid in the prosecution of the man—or woman—who has caused you such grief."

"Woman?" Savannah repeated. "You think this person could be a woman?"

"We'd be foolish to ignore the possibility," Daniel observed.

Mark nodded. "We won't do anything that jeopardizes the end goal, which is putting this jackwagon in jail for a very long time."

"I appreciate that, but—"

Seated beside her, Devin placed a hand on Jenna's knee and spoke one word. "Reilly."

She closed her mouth.

After Daniel wrapped up his presentation, Zach outlined his security plans. "The music festival presents a unique challenge. On one hand, we'll have all the extra security the Callahan family has arranged, and they'll obviously be brought up to date on this situation. On the other hand, our town will be busting at the seams, and my guys will have their hands full. You and Mac will need to be on your toes, Devin."

"With any luck, this will all be over by then," Jack said. "It's quite possible that our prey will reveal himself shortly after we start the clock ticking."

"All we need is a nibble," Mark Callahan said. "We'll be on him like ducks on a June bug."

Jack asked, "Do you foresee any problems having your monitoring in place by the fifth?"

Luke Callahan stretched out his legs and laced his fingers over a belly still admirably flat for a man in his fifties. "None at all. We have a few last things to tie up tonight, but we'll be ready when the clock starts ticking on Thursday."

"That's one thing I'm not clear about," Jenna said. "How exactly do we kick things off?"

Daniel responded. "We have an eight-point list to return you to the grid, Dr. Stockton. First on the list, and most important, is for you to apply to practice medicine in Colorado."

"Awesome," Shannon Garrett said. "Do you know how badly Eternity Springs needs our own obstetrician?"

Chapter Thirteen

Retail businesses in Eternity Springs counted the Fourth of July as one of their busiest and most profitable days of the year because they benefited from the crowds who collected to watch the parade travel the length of town on Spruce Street. Members of the public were invited to join the parade, the sole requirement being that the entry be decked out in red, white, and blue. As a result, led by the Eternity Springs Community School band, it was patriotic conglomeration of motorized vehicles, pedestrians, and pets.

"If we're here next Fourth of July, I'm going to put Sinatra in the parade," Reilly declared.

"It's fun," Michael said. "Last year we dressed up dogs from the shelter and took them."

With her ankle much improved and numerous offers for a ride to and from the day's events, Jenna had invited Michael to attend the parade with her and Reilly, thus freeing Devin to help his father at Refresh and Lori to spend time alone with her husband before the second summer session at the Rocking L began the following day.

Jenna was glad to have the distraction. She was nervous about sending Reilly off to camp and borderline paranoid about launching the effort to find the stalker.

Not that she doubted the talents of the people on their team, because she didn't. Especially not after witnessing them in action. However, reliving the stalker-related events during a three-hour interview with Daniel yesterday had stirred up the memories of all those fear-filled moments and left her with a lingering sense of discontent. Dare she hope that Jack Davenport was correct in his assessment that this nightmare might possibly end within a week?

On the way back to town last night, Devin had told her to believe. *Well, he is Santa Claus, after all.*

Reilly tugged on her arm. "The parade is over. Is it time to go to the party yet?"

She checked her watch. "Not yet. Another hour and forty-five minutes."

"Oh."

Jenna smirked at his obvious disappointment. Reilly would just as soon skip the picnic and fireworks. He was counting the minutes until morning when he picked up Sinatra on their way to the Rocking L. He'd lobbied hard to get the puppy today, and Jenna finally put the matter to bed by asking Lori to explain to Reilly about the trouble dogs have with fireworks. Of course, after that he'd tried to convince Jenna to pick up Sinatra and head up into the mountains away from the noise. She'd finally used her Mean Mom stare, and the boy got the message.

"What are we going to do for an hour and forty-five whole minutes?" Reilly asked.

"We're not far from the park. We could go to the playground."

"That's a great idea," Michael said.

Ten minutes later Jenna sat on a park bench watching the boys as they climbed on a wooden jungle gym. The park was crowded, the children loud. She didn't notice the man approach until an ice cream cone appeared in front of her face. "Ice cream solves everything."

She smiled up at Devin. "Hello."

"For you. It's strawberry and vanilla with blueberries."

"Thank you." She took a lick and said, "Mmm. Delicious *and* patriotic."

"It's the theme of the day. I like the sock."

Jenna lifted her leg, showing off the toeless, flag-themed sock she'd slipped over her brace. "Thank you. It was Reilly's idea."

"You're still on one crutch, I see. So all the activity yesterday didn't adversely affect you?"

"No. I'm fine as long as I'm careful. Steps give me a challenge, and I certainly won't be dancing anytime soon, which is a shame because I hear the band tonight is supposed to be fabulous and I love to dance." She paused to savor another lick from her ice cream cone, then asked, "I thought you were helping your dad?"

He was staring at her mouth. "Huh? Oh. Yeah. I am. I had time to tie a few flies that a customer ordered before we opened this morning. I was going to deliver them to him before the picnic, but when I saw you and the boys, I called and asked him to meet me here."

From the playground Michael yelled, "Devin, what are you doing here?"

"I'm looking for a brother to spank."

Michael stuck out his butt, daring Devin, then when another child called his name, promptly ignored the adults. Devin gave his ice cream cone a lick and wryly observed, "He might as well just say 'Go on back to Oz.' So, did you enjoy the parade?"

"I did. I especially liked the Krazy Kazoo Bicycle Band."

"Aren't they awesome? Mom usually rides with them, but she decided to skip the parade this year." A frown knit his brow as he added, "I'm getting a little worried about her. She's just not acting like herself."

"She said she was feeling great yesterday. She certainly held her own in pool volleyball."

"Yeah." He considered a moment and shrugged. "You're right. I think that flu bug really knocked her back. Maybe once she . . . oh . . . here comes my customer."

Hearing the odd note in his tone, Jenna followed the path of his gaze to see Boone McBride strolling toward them.

She hadn't seen Boone since he sent her the flowers, so she needed to thank him. But wow, this again would be a little awkward. Why did she only see the man when she was with Devin?

"Red, white, and blue ice cream. I like it," Boone said when he drew near.

"It's delicious." She lifted her cone up to him. "Want some?"

"Thank you." He took a testing bite. "Okay, that tastes a lot better than it looks. Where did you get it?"

She dipped her head toward Devin. Boone drawled, "What . . . none for me?"

"The lady gets ice cream. You get flies."

"Story of my life," the lawyer said with an exaggerated sigh.

He really was a fine-looking man, Jenna observed. "I want to thank you for the flowers, Boone. It was a lovely surprise, and the sunflowers make me smile every time I look at them. That was so sweet of you."

"You are welcome." He gave her a flirtatious wink and added, "I'm sweet as ice cream."

The sexual innuendo was obvious, and judging by the gleam in Boone's eye, another place, another time, he might have offered to let her lick him. Devin must have noticed too, because he warned, "Gotta be careful with ice cream. Listeria can be a problem. Wasn't there a Texas ice cream maker than shut down due to listeria?"

Boone ignored that and extended his hand. "Let's see my flies. I'm hoping to do a little fishing during the picnic. There's a great little spot on a creek that runs through the North Forty."

Devin handed him the bag containing the flies. Boone opened it, and while he studied the contents with interest, Devin nonchalantly asked. "So you are going to the Callahan picnic?"

"Wouldn't miss it."

"I hear Branch Callahan made it up to Colorado again this year."

"He did. I'm pretty sure Branch will outlive us all."

Devin spoke to Jenna. "You should have seen how Branch threw every single woman in attendance at this cowboy last year. Between Branch and Mac Timberlake's shenanigans, it's a wonder he didn't end up married to Caitlin Timberlake before the fireworks ended."

Boone smirked. "It was an interesting event, to say the least."

"So, are you bringing a date today in self-protection?"

"No, I'm going stag. Probably a mistake on my part, though."

Devin took a deliberate bite of his ice cream, and then pursed his lips as though it tasted sour. He cleared his throat and suggested, "In that case, you should take Jenna as your date."

Jenna almost dropped her ice cream cone. Did he just say what she thought he'd said? This from the man who'd kissed her socks off more than once? The man with whom she was moving in with tomorrow?

Yep.

Hurt rolled through her and it took every bit of acting talent to keep it out of her expression. Now she saw why Cam joked about Devin's harem. He bargained away women like rugs at a bazaar.

Boone was obviously caught off guard by the suggestion too, but the interest on his face proved a soothing balm to Jenna's raw feelings. "Now there's a fabulous idea. My bad for not thinking of it myself. Jenna, would you and Reilly do me the honor . . . and solid . . . of attending the Callahans' Fourthfest with me?"

Jenna didn't bother to spare Devin a glance. "I'd love to, Boone. Thank you. Although I've promised to take Michael also. His parents aren't planning to arrive until later in the day."

Boone's smile beamed like a camera flash. "That's one Murphy I don't mind tagging along on our date." Giving Devin a pointed look, he added, "I trust you have other plans?"

He shoved his hands into the pockets of his jeans. "Yeah. I'm going with my parents. My time here in Eternity Springs is limited, and I want to spend as much time with them as possible."

Well. That only made it worse. Jenna gave Boone her brightest smile. "What time are you planning to go to the Callahans'?"

"Actually, I was on my way now. Branch requested I come early to visit. Personally, I think he wants to grill me. Do you mind going this soon?"

"Not at all. The boys are anxious to head that way."

"Cool. Do they like to fish?"

Jenna recalled Michael's excitement the day of the accident. "Definitely."

"Excellent." Boone clapped Devin on the back. "You just made my holiday, Murphy."

"Oh joy," Devin muttered

"Shall we go?"

As Jenna started to stand, both Boone and Devin reached to help her. When she had her crutch securely beneath one arm—and her churning emotions locked away—she gave Devin a cool smile. "Thank you for the ice cream."

"Sure. You're welcome." He hesitated a moment, then said, "Jenna, I . . ."

She waited, but it quickly became obvious that the thought was to remain unfinished. Abruptly, he turned away. "I need to say goodbye to my brother."

Watching his long-legged strides eat up the distance between the bench and the playground, Jenna stewed. Devin Murphy ran more hot and cold than the shower room at Stardance Ranch at the end of square-dance night. He called Michael's name, and while he spoke to the boy, Jenna mentally focused on dismissing him. *Forget Devin Murphy. I'll go have a wonderful time with Boone and . . . and . . . and set off some fireworks.*

She looked away from Devin to find Boone watching her with a knowing look in his eyes. "It's the Aussie accent, isn't it?"

Jenna winced. "I'm that obvious?"

"I'm an extremely observant guy."

She tossed what was left of her ice cream cone into a nearby trash can. "It's not the Aussie accent. It's a long story and I'll have to tell you when the boys aren't around. Let's just say I'm having Santa Claus issues."

"On the Fourth of July?"

"Pitiful, isn't it?"

Leaning against the white bark of an aspen tree at the edge of a grove off away from the picnic goers, Devin watched his father approach with two bottles of a local microbrew in his hands. "So what put the bee in your Uncle Sam hat?" Cam asked as he handed Devin a beer.

"I'm fine." Devin took a pull on the bottle. Though he didn't know why the heck his mother had chosen to lay out their picnic within spitting distance of the Callahan clan.

Their spot was crowded to begin with because the Timberlake and Murphy families blended at all events ever
since Chase married Lori. Today, in addition to his parents, his brother, and his sister and brother-in-law, their
picnic spot included Mac and Ali Timberlake, their old-
est son Stephen and his wife and three kids, and Caitlin Timberlake and her fiancé Josh Tarkington. And of
course the Callahans had about a million people as part
of their group.

A million and one, because they had Jenna. She sparkled like a firecracker in a sleeveless, flag blue summer
sundress, and she really lit Devin's wick. He cleared his
throat and added, "I'm accustomed to an ocean of water
rather than an ocean of people. I just needed a little space."

"Uh-huh." Cam gave Devin a look that said he didn't
believe a word of it.

"Everything is great. The weather is beautiful, the food
excellent, the beer cold. I'm enjoying the holiday with
family and friends. What do I have to be pissed about?"

"That's my question."

"I'm *fine*."

Cam sipped his beer and chose not to argue.

A full minute passed before Devin said, "Maybe it
sticks in my craw a little bit to see everybody worshiping
at the feet of that lawyer. He's a nice enough guy, but he's
not the star of the Second Coming."

"Everybody? Or one body?"

Devin took another long sip of his beer. "I'm going
home in two weeks."

Now it was Cam's turn to scowl. "I wish this place was
home to you."

"It is. When I'm there. When I'm here, home is there."

"That's not the way it should be, Devin. That tells me
that your life is missing something vital."

Devin shrugged. He couldn't argue with his father about

that. He agreed with it. He simply hadn't figured out the way to fix it . . . yet. "That's a problem for another time."

"Bull. Are you forgetting every lesson I ever taught you? Life is short, Dev. Only a fool ignores that."

"I have a good life," Devin defended. "My business is growing. I love what I do. I'm a damn good captain."

"I know. Been there, done that. I had a good life in Australia. I had a thriving business that I loved. I had a family—you. It was a good life and I thought I was happy. But it was half a life."

"Gee, thanks."

"Stuff it. You know I'm not talking about you. If Sarah and Lori hadn't won that vacation to Australia and booked a snorkeling trip on my boat, you and I would probably have had a decent life. We might have even thought we were happy. But I will tell you this, son. My life would have been missing the biggest and best part of it."

Devin shrugged. "Not everybody has a high school sweetheart who they were in love with for most of their lives."

"If you like Jenna Stockton, you should explore the possibilities, not shuffle her off to—" Cam broke off as his daughter caught his attention with a wave.

"Dad? Devin?" Lori called to the Murphy men. "Would you please join us?"

"A Texan lawyer," Cam finished. "I'll share one last thought, son. The biggest mistakes I made in my life were the decisions I rushed. Take your time and be sure to keep your eyes open. Life presents more possibilities than are readily apparent. Now, it looks like we're being summoned."

Devin trailed his father back toward his family. Cam took a seat in the empty lawn chair next to Sarah, who sat beside Ali. Mac Timberlake sat next to his wife. Lori and Chase stood and faced their parents.

Chase said, "Lori and I had a conversation the other day about how lucky we are with regard to our families. We realized that whenever we refer to you all, we use the singular, not the plural. We really have become one big happy family, and that makes life even sweeter for Lori and me. Since the entire family is with us here today, we decided to take this opportunity to acknowledge and recognize what a great job our parents have done."

He gestured for Lori to continue. She smiled at the Timberlakes and then at Cam and Sarah. "You guys are the greatest. You've done an awesome job as parents. In fact, you've done such great jobs, that we think you should be promoted."

She reached into the picnic hamper at her feet and pulled out two small boxes wrapped in Old Glory paper and tied with red, white, and blue ribbon. She handed boxes to the mothers.

Sarah and Ali shared a curious look, and then began tugging the bows. Ali got hers open first. She removed a smaller box wrapped in Christmas paper and ribbon. "What's this?" Sarah asked when she revealed a similar box.

"Open them," Chase suggested.

Ribbon slid. Paper tore. Sarah and Ali each opened her box.

Sarah gasped aloud. Ali laughed.

"What is it?" Michael demanded. "Let me see."

Chase and Lori clasped hands as their mothers pulled Christmas tree ornaments out of their boxes. Written across Sarah's ornament was the word NANA. Ali's read MIMI.

Tears spilled down Sarah's face and she launched herself at Lori. Grinning like an idiot, Chase said, "There are ones for you, too, Dad and Cam. Or should I say, Grampy and Poppy."

"Well, Merry Christmas to us," Mac said, his smile wide.

"I don't understand," Michael wailed.

Devin slung an arm around his little brother. "You're gonna be an uncle, Mikey. Lori's going to have a baby."

Lines of worry carved across Michael's brow. He stared hard at Lori. "But I'm not old. How can I be an uncle?"

"I'm not old either, buddy," Cam said. Having had his turn hugging his daughter and shaking Chase's hand, he stepped back and rested his hand on his youngest child's shoulder. "How can I be a grandfather?"

"You are too old, Dad. You have some gray hairs."

"And you gave me every last one of them," Cam fired back.

Once the 'rents backed off, Devin added his congratulations to his sister and her husband. The festive atmosphere kicked up a notch and banished Devin's foul mood. When talk turned to the due date—December, thus the Christmas wrapping—and morning sickness and swollen ankles and heartburn, he bailed and joined a game of Frisbee being played by a group of teens and other young adults. After that, he joined a horseshoes tournament and got his butt whipped by an eighty-seven-year-old.

An hour before sunset, Branch Callahan and his sons congregated on the outdoor stage and officially welcomed everyone to the celebration. Mark Callahan said, "We're about to fire up the band, but before the dancing kicks off, my son has requested a moment of our time. Brick, the floor is yours."

Brick sauntered onto the stage and took the microphone from his father. "Thanks, Dad. Howdy, everyone. Hope you're all enjoying yourselves."

The crowd responded with cheers and whistles.

"I'm going to try to keep this short, so I hope you'll bear with me. Most of you probably know that I am the chairman of the Chamber of Commerce fundraising committee to benefit the Eternity Springs Community School. The Fall Festival remains our primary fundraiser, and I know y'all are looking forward to the third weekend in October. In the past few years the town's and, subsequently, the school's growth rate has skyrocketed. The Chamber has accepted the challenge to fund the addition of a new wing onto our school without raising taxes."

"Good luck with that," someone called.

Brick gave a dismissive wave. "Today, I'm announcing a new fundraiser to help us achieve that goal. I want to ask a few fellow citizens to join me here on the stage. Daniel Garrett, Sheriff Zach Turner, Flynn Brogan, and Chase Timberlake—y'all come on up here."

The men must have been tipped off to the request, because they all joined Brick onstage. Brick waved his hand in a gesture that encompassed all of them. "So . . . the five of us here . . . anybody know what we have in common?" Without giving the crowd time to respond, he answered his own question. "We're all fans of blizzards."

Zach got it first. He folded his arms and grinned at Brick. "You and Lili are expecting, too?"

"We are."

The crowd erupted in cheers and catcalls with a few risqué comments thrown in. Off to the side of the stage, Brick's father and uncles grinned, "So, there are five families with babies due in December. Unless . . . is there anyone else who's part of this club whose news I've missed?"

No one joined them, so Brick continued. "So, back to the fundraiser. Because I always think events are more fun when wagers are involved, we are going to hold a contest. I have two words for you: permutations and combinations. Entrants have dozens of opportunities to win. We're picking genders and weights and lengths. Birth dates and times. Chamber members are donating lots of prizes, including a brand new ATV—let's all hear it for Poppy Murphy!"

Cam waved. Devin saw his mother twist around to look at her husband. "Did you already know about Lori's baby?"

Cam turned his wave into a gesture of innocence, holding up his palms out toward Sarah. "No . . . no . . . that was a complete surprise. I knew about Brick and Lili's baby and the others were already public news."

"Of course, the biggest prize we will award is bragging rights. Those are important here in Eternity Springs. Don't you agree?"

The crowd cheered.

Brick continued, "We have five babies on the way, all due about the same time. Pick up your baby parlay entry form and make a predication and a donation before you leave here today. They'll also be available from any Chamber member beginning tomorrow. Again, all proceeds benefit the Eternity Springs Community School expansion project. Now, I'm gonna get off the stage so the band can get going. Y'all come on and dance. Fireworks will begin in about an hour. Happy birthday, America!"

As soon as Callahan vacated the stage, the band kicked off with an up-tempo medley of patriotic songs. Following that, they segued into dance tunes and the dance floor began to fill up.

Devin's gaze drifted back toward the Callahan group, where Boone McBride knelt on one knee talking to Gabe and Nic Callahan's twin daughters. He appeared to be folding paper into origami figurines and delighting the girls. Was there anything Mr. Perfect couldn't do?

For once, Jenna wasn't glued to his side. She sat in a lawn chair with her ankle propped on top of a cooler, talking with Cat Davenport and three of the Callahan wives. Devin didn't consciously make a decision to approach her, but all of a sudden, there he was, standing in front of her.

When she noticed him, the light in those gorgeous blue eyes went a bit frosty. She lowered her foot to the ground and stood. "Devin, I've been hoping I'd have a chance to speak with you. Please excuse me for a few minutes, ladies."

With her crutch beneath her arm, Jenna walked toward the aspen grove where Devin had sought refuge a little earlier. She held her back ramrod straight. Devin had enough experience with women to recognize when one was about to chew his ass. He shoved his hands into his pockets and braced himself for the onslaught.

When they walked far enough away that their conversation wouldn't be overheard, she faced him and surprised him. She didn't snap at him for embarrassing her or being a clod or serving her up to McBride like a steak. No, she tried to weasel out on him.

"I feel terrible, Devin. I appreciate the sacrifice you were willing to make on my behalf, but I can't in good conscience take you away from your family. We need to call off this move tomorrow. I'll stay where I am. I've managed just fine so far without a live-in bodyguard. That's really overkill."

"And that's a really poor choice of words," he fired back. "For one thing, living with you will be no sacrifice. An exercise in willpower, maybe . . . definitely . . . but in no way a sacrifice."

She pursed her pretty little lips. "Willpower?"

Devin's gut churned. He glanced toward the crowd and saw that they were the object of his mother's and sister's attention. He muttered a curse and said, "Let's dance."

"I can't dance."

"Sure you can."

He took her crutch and leaned it against a tree, and then he swept her up into his arms and headed for the dance floor.

"Devin!" Jenna protested. She tugged at her skirt and tucked it close.

Having Jenna Stockton in his arms and away from Boone McBride lightened Devin's heart in a dangerous way. As they reached the dance floor, the band began a country waltz. He stepped into the song, turning and twirling in time with the beat.

She followed his lead gracefully and he pulled her close. They didn't speak. Devin was vaguely aware that the other dancers moved aside to accommodate them, but his attention remained on the woman in his arms.

He recognized the fragrance she wore—a lightly floral, old-fashioned scent with a French name. L'Air-something, it had been called. He'd always liked it and had gifted it to women he'd dated in the past. On Jenna, it smelled heavenly.

At some point during the afternoon she'd taken her hair out of its customary ponytail, and now it brushed against the skin of his arm like a silken waterfall. She was soft in all the right places, but hardly any heavier than Michael. Devin couldn't remember the last time he'd enjoyed a dance so much. The song ended way too soon.

When the opening bars of the next number sounded, he swallowed a sigh and moved toward the edge of the dance floor. Navigating the choreographed moves of a line dance with Jenna in his arms was more than he figured he could manage. But he didn't want to put her down. So, he didn't.

He was on shaky ground here. He should cart her pretty little ass back to McBride and deposit her in the pretty-lawyer-boy's waiting arms. Devin needed for those two to become a couple. Devin had many faults, but he wasn't a poacher. Once Jenna Stockton was officially some other guy's lady, the buzz zipping through his veins would surely fade. He just needed to let things play out.

But dammit, he'd delivered the gift this morning. He shouldn't have to hang around and watch it being opened this evening. How much responsibility did Santa have? McBride could take it from here.

And Santa should get his cookies and milk.

The shadows deepened as twilight descended on the forest. The music and sound of partygoers faded. When it became obvious that this wasn't simply a shortcut back to her date, Jenna slightly stiffened. "Now where are we going?"

"Too many people. I need some space."

"Space for what?"

"Being."

He took half a dozen more steps before she said, "What does that mean?"

"Have you ever been out on the ocean and surrounded entirely by the water?"

"No."

"There's nothing like it, especially if you are the only person on the boat and drifting on the current. It'll make you feel like the smallest, most insignificant creature in the universe. At the same time, it's empowering because it makes you one with the universe. I never feel alone when I'm on the ocean. Sometimes when I'm in a crowd, I need the ocean."

She thought about that a moment, and then asked with a knife edge of insult, "You felt alone when you were dancing with me?"

"No, not at all. I wanted to *be* alone when I was dancing with you. Alone with you."

"Oh."

He carried her into the woods away from the music and the people. They'd hiked three or four minutes before she spoke again, this time with wariness instead of slight. "I don't know about this, Devin. It's getting dark. I shouldn't leave Reilly, and Boone will be looking for me."

"We're almost there. Technically, Reilly left you because he went out on the houseboat to watch the fireworks from the water with Michael and the Callahan kids. As far as your date goes, McBride can take a flying leap off the fishing pier for all I care."

"You were the one who suggested the idea. You—"

"Yeah. Yeah. Yeah," Devin interrupted. "Can we not talk about him please? At least for the time being?"

"Fine." She gave a snooty little sniff.

"Don't worry. We won't miss the fireworks." The postage-stamp-sized meadow he headed toward had an excellent angle on the pertinent part of the sky.

"I'm more worried about missing the bears."

"Honey, a bear isn't the animal you need to worry about tonight," he muttered beneath his breath.

Since his mouth was inches from her, she most likely heard him—and that shut her up. Moments later, he reached his destination and was pleased to discover that none of the other Fourthfest guests had beaten him to it.

"We're here."

"Where's here? Other than the middle of nowhere?"

"It's a hot springs pool like the ones at Angel's Rest. You can soak your ankle."

"Oh."

The purr of delight that replaced the wariness in her voice sent a shudder of lust racing through him. Devin knew he was in trouble. *Don't do this. Don't be stupid.*

I won't be too stupid. This can't go too far. We might be isolated, but it's still a public place. Just a little nibble, a little sip. I'm just so damn hungry.

Gently, he lowered her to a grassy spot on the ground beside the pool. He knelt beside her and slipped off the red flat she wore on her uninjured ankle, then carefully untied the ribbon from her brace and pulled the Velcro tabs.

"You make me feel like Cinderella," Jenna said, her voice soft and husky.

"I'm no Prince Charming." He set the brace aside. "There . . . I have you naked. Dip your toes and see how you like it."

Jenna sank her ankle into the hot springs pool and released a sensual groan. "That's fabulous. It makes me want to go all the way."

"Jenna, please! You're killing me here."

She laughed like a wicked, teasing siren as he sat beside her and took off his boots and rolled up the legs of his jeans. In a soft, Eve-in-the-Garden voice, she said, "Devin?"

"Hmm?"

"Come here." She cupped her hand at the back of his neck and pulled his mouth down to hers.

Chapter Fourteen

What better time to play with fire than the Fourth of July?

Jenna knew she shouldn't bait the bear—or whatever animal Devin purported to be—but the man sent more mixed messages than a drunk-texting coed. She was tired of it. Her nerves were shot. She was on edge. Tomorrow was a big day, what with sending Reilly off to camp and launching their offensive operation against her stalker, and she needed a distraction.

She was lonely and he'd held her close and with tenderness. And she did love the way he kissed. Hungry and hot and wild as a mountain thunderstorm. His hand plunged into her hair and anchored her. His lips crushed hers, devouring her, as if the taste of her drove him into a frenzy.

The taste of him certainly fired her hormones. Lust snapped through her like a whip. She wanted to crawl on top of him, she wanted contact and friction and the glorious heat of combustion. She moaned with desperate pleasure when his teeth nipped and scrapped at the sensitive skin at the base of her neck.

She melted back onto her elbows when he murmured her name and his kisses trailed lower toward the scooped neckline of her dress. Thrill zinged along her nerves as his hand swept up the length of her thigh. Need became an aching, clawing animal inside her, and she arched her back and . . . gasped in pain when she banged her ankle on a rock.

Devin muttered a curse and pulled away from her. "Jenna. I'm sorry. Are you okay? I'm so sorry."

"No. Not your fault." She closed her eyes and grimaced as she absorbed the waves of pain. "Mine. I started it and then I forgot about . . . everything."

"I know. Me too. Is there anything I can do to help? I don't guess I can kiss it make it better?"

She groaned a laugh. "I think you'd best keep your kisses to yourself."

"Yeah. This spot feels isolated, but we're just a stone's throw away from a hundred people. We were playing with fire."

The first skyrocket of the night shot into the air and burst in a shower of red, white, and blue sparks in the sky above them. She let out a shaky sigh. "I know. But it *is* the Fourth of July. It's a night for it, don't you think?"

"Fourth. Fifth. Fifteenth." Devin released a long sigh. "I don't think the date is going to matter. I tried. I am trying. But we have lots of hours of darkness ahead of us to make it through. Alone together. You and me. I don't know about you, Jenna, but after tonight, I don't think I have that much willpower."

Jenna's heart began to thunder anew as a scandalous notion took hold. She liked this man so much. It had been so long.

He lives in Australia.

So what?

Without giving herself any more time to consider, she asked, "I don't know that you need it."

He went still. With a whiz, whistle, and bang another skyrocket exploded overhead. Sparks of purple and green lit the night, and Devin cleared his throat. "Are you suggesting we . . .

Jenna wasn't quite brazen enough to proposition him outright, so she looked up into the sky and gave a whistle of admiration. "Wow, look at that one. Those gold chrysanthemums are my favorite."

He waited for a full minute before picking up a stone and chucked it into the hot springs. "Jenna, you know that I'm leaving the country in two weeks, right? My work . . . my life . . . is in Australia. I have to go back. I *want* to go back. Don't lose track of that detail, because I'm giving you fair warning. I'm not a forever guy."

"If I may point out that except for that kiss a moment ago, I haven't asked you for *anything*, much less forever?"

"I'm not saying you did. Although I think we should observe a moment of silence in honor of that kiss because it truly was in my top five all-time favorite kisses. Okay, top two. And you can't hold it against me that it's competing for number one with the kiss I got from Angelina Jolie when I was sixteen, and she chartered Dad's boat for a day. That was a kiss on the cheek, so it's an entirely different category, but I'm trying to be honest here."

"You're crazy."

"You don't know the half of it. I did something today that went against every instinct I possess. I failed pretty spectacularly at it, but I did try."

"What did you do?"

"Put my foot in it," he grumbled.

She folded her arms and glared at him. Dark though it was, she felt certain he sensed it. "Well?"

"Let's enjoy the fireworks."

"Oh, I'm about to show you fireworks. This has something to do with Boone, doesn't it? Is that why you manipulated him into bringing me to this party?"

"You know, if you ever get the chance to watch New

Year's fireworks over Sydney Harbor, you should do it. It's just spectacular."

"That's a pitiful attempt to change the subject and an insulting action you are attempting to cover up. Just because I asked for assistance finding a stalker doesn't mean I need help finding someone to date!"

"Look. That makes it sound worse than it was. Besides, it's not you. It's me."

"Oh, brother."

"Okay, fine. You know what I did? I'll tell you what I did. I set you down in front of McBride like a fly in front of a trout."

"Excuse me?"

"No, excuse *me*." Above them a rapid series of explosions lit the sky. Devin raked his fingers through his hair. "Dammit, it's true. I won't deny it. But I have my reasons and they're good reasons, but I don't want to tell you because you'll think I've lost my ever-loving mind."

"Try me."

Two more rockets burst up in the sky before he acquiesced and launched into a convoluted tale about cell phones and Eternity Springs and Christmas bells and wishes. When he finally wound down, Jenna attempted to summarize. "Let me bottom line this. You think some sort of Eternity Springs mojo means you're supposed to find a father for Reilly? And you decided that father needs to be Boone McBride?"

"The McBride part isn't set in stone."

"Okay, I agree. You have lost your mind."

"Call me Santa Cupid," he grumbled unhappily.

Jenna laughed and they both looked skyward as a starburst set off an extended number of crackles and pops. When the sounds finally faded, Devin continued. "I know it sounds unbelievable, but that's part of it too. In my very first conversation with your son, I talked about believing."

"I remember him telling me that."

"I don't know where the words came from, Jenna. They just appeared on my tongue out of the blue. Kind of like his call appeared on my phone——the brand-new phone given to me by none other than Celeste Blessing. Maybe you're too new to Eternity Springs to recognize when woo-woo knocks on your door, but believe me, it happens. This town has a long history of strange experiences and coincidences, especially when Celeste is involved. I don't bet against them."

Loud booms accompanied a rapid series of fireworks. Devin raised his voice to be heard above the noise.

"And think about it. You didn't, either. You chose to come to Eternity Springs as a result of one of those coincidences, didn't you?"

She couldn't argue with that. However . . . "I'm not interested in Boone and he's not interested in me."

"Bull."

"It's true. We discussed it. You weren't exactly subtle with the set-up this morning."

"He sent you flowers."

"As a friendly gesture."

"Yeah. Right. Are you always this naive?"

She wasn't going to argue the point with him, but Jenna knew she was right. Boone didn't hesitate to flirt, but he didn't mean it. A woman could tell these things. After spending a bit of time with him, she sensed that there was much more to Boone McBride than he let on. He carried some serious baggage.

Devin continued, "Even if neither of you are interested right now, that could change. Or maybe somebody new will come to town tomorrow. Who knows? One thing I do want to stress, though. I don't want you to worry that I'm so far off my rocker that I won't protect you like I promised. I vow that I will guard you with my life until the stalker is caught."

Jenna couldn't resist commenting, "Or for the next two weeks, anyway."

"If this takes longer than Jack expects—something I can't imagine because Jack and the Callahans managed to track down Chase outside of a remote mountain village in Chizickstan—I'll stay longer. I'm not going to abandon you. Although, do you have a passport?"

"A passport!"

"Yeah, a passport. Do you have one?"

"Yes, why?"

"My friend Mitch is getting married on Bella Vita Isle. I planned my trip home around the wedding. You can be my plus one if worst comes to worst. A bunch of us are going." He paused as if a new thought had just occurred to him. "Lori and Chase are going. Wonder if the baby news changes their plans. Is there a reason she couldn't travel?"

"I'm a doctor, but I'm not your sister's doctor. However, unless she's had a problem with her pregnancy that she hasn't shared, I know of nothing that would prevent her traveling."

"Cool. I'm excited about the baby. Lori is gonna be a great mom. You've seen how fabulous she is with animals. Imagine how she'll be with her own little one. And Mom and Dad as grandparents? That'll be a hoot to watch." He hesitated a moment then added, "From afar. Good thing the world has Skype. I can have a front-row seat even from the other side of the world. Although, this news will change the family travel plans again. Guess I'll be hauling myself back to Eternity Springs again for the holidays, after all."

"Can we go back to this passport and wedding issue, please? I could not go out of the country and leave Reilly behind at camp."

"Why not? He'll be doing whatever he's doing whether you are in the mountains or at the beach."

"But . . ."

"It's the Caribbean, Jenna. Not the South Pacific. The flight isn't bad at all. I've made it plenty of times. But we are getting ahead of ourselves worrying about that. Although, consider yourself officially invited to join me. Bella Vita is an awesome place. I'll take you out in a boat and show you what I meant about being one with the universe."

"I'm not going to crash a wedding."

"You wouldn't be crashing. My invitation includes a guest, and I accepted for two figuring I'd invite somebody when I'm there. I hate going to weddings alone, don't you?"

"Yes, but . . ."

"Mitch is good friend of mine and the woman he's marrying is super nice. You'll like them both. Mitch lived in Eternity Springs for a while when he apprenticed with our resident glass artist. Have you met Cicero?"

"I met him tonight. His son Galen is a couple years older than Reilly."

"His wife is one of Eternity Spring's doctors."

"Rose Cicero. She treated my ankle. I liked her."

"They're great people. Have four children. They're adopted, too. Reilly has that in common with the Cicero kids. Anyway, my friend Mitch was Cicero's apprentice. When I ran boats out of Bella Vita, he and I spent a lot of time together." Devin threaded his fingers through hers and brought her hand to his mouth for a kiss. "Say yes. Say you will come whether we've found the stalker or not. It's a beautiful place. Tropical breezes, sugar sand beaches, umbrella drinks. We'll take moonlit walks on the beach."

"I do not understand you, Devin Murphy. One minute you're telling me you're playing Yente trying to marry me off and the next you're inviting me on a Caribbean get-away?"

"Yente?"

"Fiddler on the Roof. The matchmaker."

"Oh. Okay. I like 'Santa Cupid' better, but whatever works. What can I say? I can multi-task. Come with me to Bella Vita Isle, Sugar Cookie."

"Sugar Cookie? Really?"

"Yep. C'mon. Let Santa have a nibble." He laid her back against the grass, and when the grand finale burst across the sky a few minutes later neither of them noticed.

Sitting in his truck in the parking lot at Eternity Springs Community School, Devin reached across the console and awkwardly patted Jenna's knee. Tears had been rolling down her cheeks ever since Reilly had climbed into the Rocking L bus for the trip up to the summer camp ten minutes earlier. Devin hadn't felt this helpless since a tour last year when a little girl's teddy bear blew out of her arms and into the Coral Sea during a trip out to the Great Barrier Reef. "Reilly will be fine, Sugar.

"I know."

"He wasn't upset."

"I know! That's what was so bad. He's not going to miss me at all."

"That's a bad thing?"

"No. Not at all. I'm happy!" She covered her face with her hands and released a little sob.

Devin sighed and twisted the key, starting the ignition. "I can tell."

"I'm being silly. I know. And I never cry. It's just that Reilly and I haven't been apart in months and months. It's a good thing that he's gone to camp. I just wish he could have acted the tiniest bit sad to leave me."

"I'm sure that inside he's sobbing his little heart out. But he's a guy. He has to show a stiff upper lip."

"That's true, isn't it? I tend to forget just how silly males are no matter what their age. Thank you."

"You're welcome."

"He was awfully cute with Sinatra, wasn't he?"

Devin nodded. "He and that dog are going to be great friends. Now, Daniel will be expecting us, so we need to get going. Are you ready?"

"Yes. Let's go."

He put his truck into gear and exited the parking lot. The plan was to meet at Daniel Garrett's office, where Jenna would file the paperwork that would launch the team's effort to track down the stalker. By the time they made the short trip to the office building, Jenna had herself under control.

The Garrett Investigations office was located in the three-story building on Pinion and Fourth that also housed Timberlake and McBride law offices, Rafferty Engineering, and a few other professional concerns. As they climbed the narrow wooden staircase to the second floor, Jenna observed, "What a neat old building."

"It started out as a saloon and whorehouse. Every mining town needed one or two. Various remodels over the years have made it a hodgepodge, but it's hodgepodge with character." Devin rapped on the frosted glass panel of Daniel's door before opening it. Daniel was on a phone call, but he waved them inside and gestured for Jenna to take the chair behind his desk.

"Thanks, Bob," Daniel said into the phone. "I appreciate that. You've been a tremendous help." He listened a moment, then replied. "She's doing well. We're very excited. Yes. Eternity Springs has been very good to me."

Daniel pointed toward a single-serve coffee maker on

a credenza, and Devin made two cups while Daniel completed his call. Once he'd disconnected, he offered them a welcoming smile. "Good morning. So how did the bus drop-off go?"

"As well as could be expected," Jenna told him. "Reilly barely spared me a look back. I managed to hold off the tears until I made it to Devin's truck."

"Never mind that he told her she was the best mother in the whole universe ten minutes before that when we picked up his new puppy. I've never seen a kid so happy."

Reilly had thrown himself and his arms full of puppy into Jenna's. He'd said the whole universe line and added, "This is my number-two biggest wish in the whole world."

Jenna and Devin had shared a silent look that acknowledged they both knew which wish was the boy's number one.

To Daniel, he added, "I don't know whose tail wagged more, Reilly's or Sinatra's."

Daniel grinned. "I hope he's ready for all the mewling that pup will do for the next few nights as he adjusts to being away from his mom. You're lucky to be missing that, Jenna."

"True," she replied. "I'm definitely counting my blessings today, and you are on my list. I can't thank you enough for helping us, Daniel."

"I'm happy to be of service. Are you ready to get down to it?"

"I am."

She spent the next hour and a half filling out online forms and hard copy paperwork for Daniel to file. She made a series of phone calls from a list he had created. If her hand trembled a time or two while affixing her signature to documents, well, Devin didn't point it out. Before the job was done, she'd applied for a Colorado driver's license, subscribed to three professional journals and four general magazines, signed up for a credit card, and submitted her credentials in order to become licensed to practice medicine in Colorado.

The last one shifted the steadiness needle from "tremble" toward "shaking." She murmured, "I guess it's too late for second thoughts now. Anything else?"

"I think that takes care of it," Daniel replied. He checked his watch and added, "Right on time, too. I need to beg your indulgence, Dr. Stockton. My wife arranged a little reception in the wake of this morning's events. I hope you won't mind joining her and her friends."

"Of course I won't mind," Jenna replied.

"Devin, if you'll wait here, there's a few things I'd like to go over with you. We can join the ladies in a bit. Jenna, if you'll follow me?"

While he waited for Daniel's return, Devin checked his cell and was pleased to see the text from his brother-in-law. Camp Director Chase had sent a trio of photos of Reilly's arrival at the Rocking L. So far, so good. The kid was all grins and giggles. He'd show Jenna the photos when they finished up here.

When Daniel reentered the office, he asked, "Do we have a problem? Are these things you need to go over bodyguard-duty related?"

"No. No problem. Actually, what I have to go over isn't all that important. This was mainly an excuse to send Jenna into the lion's den alone."

"Uh . . . lion's den?"

Daniel took his seat behind his desk. "Remember how your mom and her friends held what they called interventions when they thought one of their lives needed interference from people who cared?"

"Oh, yeah. They were big on that."

"Shannon decided your Jenna needs one. At the picnic yesterday, she told the Callahan wives that she has no intention of staying in Eternity Springs and practicing medicine. Well, the wives want an OB/GYN in town and they have no intention of letting her get away. Shannon has gathered the prego parade to work on changing Dr. Stockton's mind."

Devin let out a long, slow whistle. "Jenna doesn't stand a chance."

And maybe Boone McBride will get a second one.

Chapter Fifteen

Jenna loved her profession. She loved working with women and being their sounding board and their source of information during one of the most important events of their lives—pregnancy and childbirth. Few experiences in life equaled that moment when a child slid from his mother's body into her waiting hands.

But as she left Daniel Garrett's office building, she seriously needed a break from pregnant women. "Can we go do something physical?"

Devin stumbled and she realized that she had too. "Not *that* kind of physical. I want to go running or hiking. I need to move!"

"You have a sprained ankle. You're in a brace."

Yeah, yeah, yeah. She could pretend otherwise, couldn't she? "There has to be something I can do."

He opened his mouth.

"Other than that. What about rowing? I could do that, couldn't I? Does somebody rent rowboats on Hummingbird Lake?"

Devin suddenly understood her agitation. He rolled his tongue around his mouth and asked, "So which was more difficult? Spitting in your stalker's face or telling my sister and her cohorts that you don't want to be their doctor?"

Jenna shook her head. "They're an amazing group of women. Intimidating when they're all together."

"Did they change your mind?"

She sighed. "I promised to think about it. So, about that rowboat?"

"I got a better idea. How about we go four-wheeling? Daniel told me about a new trail that's opened up since the last time I've been back. Dad has raved about it too. Riding an ATV isn't as physical as rowing, but it's not like sitting on a sofa knitting an afghan, either. You should be able to manage it just fine with your ankle braced. I can promise it will clear the cobwebs from your head."

"I've never ridden an ATV."

"Well then, Sugar, you are in for a treat."

"We have time? Remember, we promised to have dinner with your parents."

"I haven't forgotten that. Mom is making lasagna using Ali Timberlake's recipe. Her lasagna is the best you can eat this side of Rome. No way I'll be late for dinner tonight."

"In that case, let's go."

The outing sounded like just what she needed. Her head was full of, if not cobwebs, then of arguments and ideas and decisions waiting to be made. On top of that, her heart had problems of its own. She didn't know why sending Reilly off to camp had reawakened all the fears and insecurities she'd experienced when he was wounded, but it had. Add in the incessant pull of her attraction to Devin and the possibility—no, probability—that she was about to embark upon a short-term affair with him, and she was definitely a basket case.

Devin drove to his father's shop and pulled around to the back lot where the Murphys stored their personal outdoor toys, which included ATVs, a fishing boat, and a pop-up camper. He sent Jenna to the sandwich shop across the street with instructions to "buy lunch and lots of it" while he hooked up the trailer and got directions from his dad.

She placed an order, and then took a seat at a table to wait for it. She was scanning a copy of the *Eternity Times* when she heard her name and looked up with a smile. "Hello, Celeste."

"Hello, dear. I was so pleased when I spied you crossing the street a few minutes ago. I was looking for you at the school this morning, but I apparently just missed you. I have a little something for you—a gift I stumbled upon in Claire's shop that made me think of you. Since you were sending Reilly off to camp this morning, I thought you might need a little pick-me-up." She sat at the table and pulled a box sporting the Forever Christmas logo from a sparkling gold tote bag and handed it to Jenna.

"Aww," Jenna said. "How sweet. That's so thoughtful of you, Celeste." With the box in her hand, Jenna hesitated. "Before I open this, I want to say something. About your Welcome Wing visit to us at Stardance Ranch . . . I feel terrible about misleading you . . ."

Celeste interrupted her with a touch on her arm. "Now, honey. Don't give that a second thought. I knew you had your reasons, and it wasn't my place to interfere."

"So you recognized us?"

Celeste chided her with a look. "Open your gift, dear."

Jenna opened the box and pulled back red tissue paper to reveal the thick round glass of a snow globe. She lifted it from the box and saw that the scene inside showed a Christmas tree in a forest. "It's beautiful."

"It's a Christmas wishing tree. One that's portable."

"I love it." She gave it a shake and watched the snowflakes float. "Thank you, Celeste."

"You are very welcome. I was so pleased to learn that Reilly wanted to adopt the tradition after I shared it with you. I hope you will continue it in years to come."

"We definitely will. It's a lovely idea and it really struck a chord for us." As she reached across the table to give Celeste a hug, the young woman behind the sandwich shop's counter called her name.

"That's a large sack of sandwiches," Celeste observed.

"Devin told me to buy a lot. He's taking me four-wheeling. I've never ridden an ATV before."

"Oh, you'll love it." Celeste rose and kissed Jenna's cheek. "Go have fun. I hope you'll stop by Angel's Rest one day soon for a cup of tea."

"I'll do that."

Jenna tucked the snow globe into her purse, paid for her sandwiches, exited the shop, and crossed the street to find Devin tucking water bottles into the storage compartment of an ATV. "Hey, beautiful. Are you ready?"

"Let's do it."

During the drive up to the trailhead, they talked about music and movies and monotonous highway drives. Upon reaching their destination, Devin pulled his truck and trailer onto the shoulder of the road. A few moments later, he fired up the ATV and backed it off the trailer. Then he handed Jenna a helmet and told her to climb aboard and wrap her arms around his waist. "Or, you can use the handholds, but I'd really enjoy it a lot more if you held onto me."

For the next forty minutes she bounced, swayed, squealed, and giggled her way up a mountain trail with her arms wrapped tight around Devin's waist.

He stopped at what felt like the top of the world, the vista beyond a patchwork of color from craggy snow-capped peaks to forests in varying shades of green to wildflower-dotted meadows. "Now, isn't this pretty," Devin said as he took off his helmet. "I think we've found our picnic spot, don't you?"

"It's fabulous." Jenna set her helmet beside his atop a boulder.

"Did you enjoy the ride?"

"I did. Much more than I expected to, to be honest. Riding a four-wheeler is a lot more fun than it looks."

"I know *I* enjoyed it. Feel free to hang onto me anytime, Sugar Cookie." He opened the ATV's storage compartment and removed their sack lunch and a thin tarp.

She snorted a laugh "That's the silliest nickname."

"Hey, I like it. And it's totally appropriate." He spread out the tarp and gestured for her to sit down.

She passed out sandwiches and chips while he pulled bottled water from the storage space. They ate in silence, enjoying the peace of the place. When she finished her sandwich, she pulled the dessert she'd purchased from the bag—iced sugar cookies in the shape of a hammock. Devin laughed and polished off a third of the cookie in a single bite.

She stretched out her legs and leaned back with her weight resting on her elbows. "This has to be one of the most beautiful places I've ever been."

"Have you not done much traveling?"

"Until this road trip, no. I attended a symposium in London when I was in medical school, but since I adopted Reilly, trips have been limited."

"Wait until you see Bella Vita."

Jenna took a bite of her own cookie. She had not told him she'd make the trip. "Is it something in the water?"

"Excuse me?"

"You're not a lot different from those ladies who spent an hour pressuring me to become their doctor."

"Hey. Wait a minute. I'm not pregnant and I'm not asking you to be my doctor. I'm not opposed to playing doctor, mind you, but . . ."

A grin on her face, Jenna dropped her head back and lifted her face toward the sun. "I'm not going to be pressured. I have enjoyed life on the road. It's really nice to work the hours I want to work. I don't make much money, but we don't need much money. I don't know that I'm ready to give this up."

"That's understandable." He took another bite of his cookie. "It's nice to check out from the hassles from time to time. I've done it myself."

"We have reservations at a campground in Wyoming beginning the week after Labor Day. I've never planned to stay here permanently."

"You went to school a long time to become not just a doctor, but a specialist."

In a warning tone, she said, "Don't try to education-shame me."

He made a zipping motion over his lips.

"How can I say no when this town is doing so much for me? How selfish is that? What kind of person does that make me? Those women have every right to lobby for their interests. And, the salary they threw out—whoa. I'm shocked they don't have obstetricians streaming over Sinner's Prayer Pass in hope of securing the job."

"May I ask a question that has nothing to do with shaming of any sort?"

"Okay."

"Why not stay? It's a great little town. You've already made friends here. Reilly has already made friends here. You can't remain on the road forever."

"I know." Jenna shoved to her feet. "But I don't make snap decisions. Even deciding to go on the road four months ago took me three days to decide. I think things through. I'm deliberate." She paced back and forth. "Everything has happened so fast. I've been dealing with this stalker for a year and a half. A year and a half! I can't make a life-altering decision over tea and crumpets with a room full of hormonal women."

"Okay. Okay, that's fair enough," Devin said.

"I have time to think about it. Even if I loved the idea of establishing a practice in Eternity Springs, I couldn't do anything about it yet. There's the little detail about my license. Until I'm licensed to practice medicine in Colorado, I won't so much as tell anyone to take a Tylenol."

"You're right. You do have time to think about it. I just wonder . . ."

When his voice trailed off, Jenna waited for him to finish his thought. He didn't, so she prodded, "You wonder what?"

"It's nothing. How did you like your sandwich? Ham and cheese, wasn't it? Are you a mustard and mayo girl, or mustard only?"

She narrowed her eyes and repeated, "You wonder what?"

He scooped up a rock from beyond the tarp, and threw it out into the nothingness. "I wonder why your reaction to the notion of staying in Eternity Springs is so intense. Could it be that it has more to do with what you don't want to do than what you do want?"

"I don't follow you."

"All indications suggest that the obsessive loon we're chasing intersected your life in some way through your work. I'm no psychologist, but it's understandable that you'd be gun shy about hanging out your shingle once again."

"You think I'm afraid to return to medicine?"

He shrugged. "In your shoes, that's probably how I'd feel."

Jenna frowned. "That would be letting my enemy win."

"I don't think it's that black and white, but perhaps something to consider as you think about what you want

to do when this is over. Now, how about we change the
subject to something more pleasant? Do you know how
beautiful you look with that gorgeous hair of yours on fire
with sunshine and roses in your cheeks from the ride?
One thing's missing, though. Your lips need a little puff
and shine to them."

He leaned over and took her mouth in a slow, sweet kiss
that scrambled her pulse and heated her blood. Her arms
lifted and wrapped around his neck, and he pulled her onto
his lap. She was lost, drowning in him, when suddenly, he
set her aside with a curse. "This is insane. We have to stop
doing this in public.

Even as the protest formed on her lips, she heard the
chug of approaching engines. A moment later, five ATVs,
each carrying two people, rounded a curve in the trail. The
lead vehicle pulled to a stop behind Devin's four-wheeler
and as the riders disembarked, Devin asked Jenna, "Ready
to go?"

"Yes."

Devin helped her to her feet and they exchanged greet-
ings with the newcomers—tourists from Texas riding
ATVs rented from Refresh—while packing up their picnic supplies. Jenna pulled on her helmet, fixed the chinstrap, and then wrapped her arms around Devin's waist for
the trip down the mountain. The ride down was as exhila-
rating as the trip up. Nevertheless, Jenna was unable to lose
herself in the activity like she had on the ascent.

Had Devin hit the proverbial nail on the head? Was she
afraid? Was that why she was so conflicted by the notion
of making Eternity Springs her home?

Perhaps. Something certainly had her hesitant to buy
into the idea, despite the fact that the town had so much to
offer. Really, in many ways it was a perfect solution. She
and Reilly couldn't be road rats forever. They liked it here.
The outdoors lifestyle it offered suited them. They both

already had friends here. Once the stalker threat was eliminated, why wouldn't they settle down?

Reilly could go to school. He could join a Scout troop. He could play baseball and basketball and soccer.

And you? What will you do if you put down roots in Eternity Springs? Sit around and wait for Devin Murphy to pay a visit home from Australia?

Ding Ding Ding Ding. The ATV hit a dip hard and her stomach followed suit.

Jenna closed her eyes. That's what this was all about. She was already halfway in love with him.

Which was crazy. She didn't believe in love at first sight. True love didn't happen in a week. She couldn't be in love with him. In lust, sure. Definitely in lust. She had a serious case of the hots for him. She would have had sex with him last night had they been somewhere private.

They had tonight. They had the next two weeks.

She'd been planning to have an affair with him. A nice short two-week fantasy, then he'd be off to Oz and she'd roll on down the road. But if she had an affair with Devin, she couldn't stay in Eternity Springs. It was one thing to love 'em and leave 'em and something else entirely to love 'em and run into his mother in the grocery store.

This was his world, even if he only occupied it for a short time on rare occasions. Eternity Springs was his mother. His father. His sister and brother. She knew her own heart well enough. If she had an affair with Devin, feeling like she did about him already, she'd be setting herself up for real heartbreak.

She couldn't sleep with Devin Murphy and make a home in Eternity Springs. So until she made her deliberate, well-considered decision, she couldn't sleep with Devin Murphy at all.

Her heart twisted. Her eyes filled with moisture. While she couldn't remember the exact moment, she had a sneaking suspicion that this was how she'd felt when she learned that Santa Claus wasn't real.

Devin stepped into his parents' house that evening a happy man. He had an excellent bottle of Chianti in one arm, a beautiful, smart, sexy woman on the other, and the promise of homemade lasagna on the menu. Sarah would serve tiramisu for dessert and Devin planned to eat his share, but he intended to have his real dessert upon returning to the rental house. Hopefully it would be an early evening.

He had clean sheets on his bed and a bottle of champagne chilling in the fridge.

"Hello, 'rents," he called as he walked through the living room. "We're here."

He strode into the kitchen expecting to see his mother at the stove or the island or even in the depths of the large walk-in pantry. She wasn't there. "Mom?"

Jenna touched his arm and nodded toward the floor, where the sight of a broken wine glass and a puddle of red wine spilled across on the floor brought him up short. He took a step toward the glass. "Mom? Dad?"

Michael burst through the door, his expression wreathed in fear, and started babbling. "Devin. Mom fell down. For no reason. She just dropped. Boom! Now Mom and Dad are fighting because Dad wants to call the ambulance, and Mom says no, that she's fine. But Dad doesn't believe her."

"Where are they?"

"He carried her to their bedroom. She said if he called an ambulance she'd never forgive him."

Devin was walking toward the stairs before his brother finished talking. He was halfway up the stairs when Cam exited the master suite. He stopped Devin by holding his palm out. His gaze went directly to Jenna. "Will you come talk to her, please?"

"Of course." Jenna started for the stairs.

Cam continued. "Just convince her to let me take her to the clinic. This has gone on way too long. I think she's scared because our friend Mac Timberlake had a serious health scare last year, and it's made us aware of our mortality."

"Let me see what's going on."

"Can I get you something?" Devin asked as she climbed past him up the stairs. "Your black bag?"

"I'm not her doctor, Devin."

"It won't hurt you to have it, though, right?" Cam asked.

Devin nodded. "It's an emergency. Is your bag at the trailer or did you bring it to the house?"

"Fine. It's in my bedroom closet at the house. A blue nylon messenger bag."

"I'll be back in five."

Devin flew from the house. His hand trembled as he twisted the key in his truck's ignition, and his tires spun as he gunned the gas pulling away from the house. *Mom. Mom. Mom.* He said her name like a litany. She couldn't be sick. She couldn't! This couldn't happen again. Michael was just a kid. He still needed her. *I'm* still a kid. *Her* kid. God wouldn't be that cruel as to take a second mother from him, would He?

"Don't go there," he muttered. "Do not go there. That's bad juju."

Fear rolled through his belly like an ocean wave. A stomach bug. What sort of stomach bug lasts this long? And comes and goes? She'd been sick ever since he came home, and what had he worried about the most? Not catching it. *Selfish bastard.*

Mom. Mom. Mom. Mom. She can't leave us. She can't. She can't. Please, God. Don't take her. Not again.

At the house, he ran to Jenna's bedroom and threw open the closet door. The bag was on a shelf at eye level. He grabbed it and ran, and was back at his parents' house within minutes.

"I'll take it up," Cam said, meeting him at the door. He took the stairs two at a time climbing to the master suite.

With his task accomplished, Devin suddenly felt adrift and alone and . . . hell . . . abandoned. Then Michael slipped his hand into Devin's. Devin forced a smile as he gazed down at his little brother, and in the boy's terrified blue eyes, he saw himself. *You've got me, Mikey. You'll always have me.*

"I'm scared, Dev."

"It'll be okay, Michael. I believe that. I really do."

The master bedroom door opened and closed. A grim-faced Cam came down the stairs. "How is she?" Devin asked.

"I don't know. She was in the bathroom. Your doc lady wouldn't tell me a damn thing and I can't read her face, but I don't think she's calling an ambulance. She said they'd be down in a few minutes, and your mother asked us to set the table and toss the salad."

"Toss the salad!" Devin exclaimed.

Michael scampered toward the kitchen. "I'll set the table."

Cam dragged a hand down his jawline. He looked like he'd aged five years in the past five minutes. "Thanks, buddy. Devin, would you clean up that mess on the kitchen floor, please?"

"Sure, Dad. I'll do anything you need."

"In that case, maybe pour me a bourbon too."

Upstairs, Sarah Murphy stepped out of her bathroom in a zombie-like daze, her complexion as pale as the Murphy Mountain snowcap. "You were right," she croaked.

"Yes," Jenna replied. "I know."

"This can't be!" Sarah whined. "I'm old! I'm going to

be a grandmother! I had hot flashes. Mood swings. Weight gain. I thought it was menopause. It's supposed to be menopause!"

"Perimenopause, and you'd be surprised at how many surprise pregnancies we see in women over forty. People get lax with birth control."

"Not me! Not since I was a teenager. Been there, done that, and had a bouncing baby girl as a result of it. I learned my lesson. Cam and I always . . . well . . . except . . ."

"It only takes once." Jenna's mouth twisted wryly. "That was some snowstorm. At Easter, wasn't it?"

"Yes. An Easter blizzard. An Easter miracle. Oh my. I have to sit down." Sarah sank onto the edge of her bed. "Oh my. A baby. Another baby. *And* a grandchild." She looked up at Jenna with a wild look in her eyes. "If Cam dyes his hair and starts wearing turtlenecks, I'll lose my mind. I need to throw away the sleeping pills right now!"

"Sarah, what are you talking about?"

"It's *Father of the Bride Part II*. The movie. I'm married to Steve Martin."

"Ah. Yes."

"You know, sometimes he even sort of looks like Steve Martin. Well, Steve Martin when the movie was made. Young Steve Martin. Except, Cam is old. Like me. We're in our forties! That's too old to be having another baby."

"Mother Nature didn't think so, obviously."

"Oh my." Sarah waved her hand in front of her face. "Oh my. What am I going to tell Cam?"

"Not to shop for turtlenecks?" Jenna suggested, trying to stifle a grin.

Sarah's eyes widened, then she burst out in a laugh. The tinge of hysteria didn't worry Jenna. Neither did the tears pooling in Sarah's eyes. Many women cried upon learning of impending motherhood—sometimes in joy, sometimes in despair. Hormones running amok combined with the realization of a major life event tended to bring emotions close to the surface.

But regarding emotions . . . "Your family is worried. Shall I ask Cam to come up so you can share your news?"

"Yes, thanks. No, wait. Maybe I'll go down. Tell them all at once. Which should I do?"

"It's totally up to you."

"He'll have questions. I'll be a high-risk pregnancy because of my age, won't I? When Nic Callahan was pregnant with the twins, she was high risk and she had to go to Denver to be near doctors and a state-of-the-art medical facility. But that was before the new clinic was built. And you're here now. You'll have your license back. You'll stay, Jenna, won't you? You'll stay in Eternity Springs?"

Jenna's heart gave a little wrench. She thought about Devin and the cozy rental house and clean sheets on her bed. She thought about two weeks without Reilly underfoot.

She thought about Gabi Brogan and Savannah Turner and Lili Callahan and Shannon Garrett. She thought of Devin's sister Lori.

"You will be my obstetrician, won't you, Jenna?" Sarah asked.

Sarah, Devin's mother. His beloved mother, who had been so kind to Jenna and Reilly. This whole town had been a gift to her. A gift. In her mind's eye, she saw herself pulling back red tissue paper to reveal Celeste's Christmas wishing tree snow globe.

She made her deliberate, well-considered decision with only a twinge of regret. "Of course I will, Sarah. I'll be honored to be your doctor."

Sarah filled her cheeks with air then blew it out in a puff. "Okay, then. Let's do this. Let's go downstairs and give my husband something different to worry about. You know, he thinks I have a tumor. That's his default whenever something is wrong." With a snicker, she added, "I guess, in a way, he's right this time."

"I probably wouldn't use that terminology tonight," Jenna suggested.

"Probably not."

Sarah paused in front of the bedroom mirror to fuss with her hair. In the past few minutes, color had returned to her cheeks, and Jenna thought she was as pretty an expectant mother as she'd ever seen.

Cam paced at the foot of the stairs, and his head jerked up when he heard them coming. His forest green eyes lasered onto Sarah as he murmured, "Honey?"

"I'm fine," she said as descended the staircase. "I'm not sick, Cam."

"There's no tumor?"

"No." Sarah snorted and glanced over her shoulder toward Jenna. "See, I told you so."

"Then what's wrong? I still think you need to go to the clinic. They have night hours, you know. Why have you been so sick? This isn't normal."

Devin exited the kitchen and looked at his mother with an assessing gaze, then focused on Jenna. Sarah reached the bottom of the stairs. "Actually, it is. It's totally normal and I should have realized it. After all, I've done this twice before."

The furrows in Cam's brow deepened. "Done what?"

Sarah rested her hand on his chest and smiled up at him, an impish light in her violet eyes. Their gazes locked. She waited.

The color drained from Cam's face. The crystal highball glass he held slipped from his hand and shattered on the wood floor. He croaked, "You're kidding."

"What?" Devin asked.

"Tell me you're kidding," Cam added.

Sarah shook her head. "Nope. I'm not kidding."

"Are you okay, Mommy?" Michael asked.

"I'm fine, Michael. Watch your feet. Don't step on the glass."

"What are you talking about?!" Devin demanded.

Cam reached out and swiped the glass out of Devin's hand. He chugged back the contents and said, "She's not kidding."

"About what? She hasn't said a damn thing!"

"Don't curse, Devin. I'm pregnant! We're having another baby."

"A baby!" Michael exclaimed. "Cool."

Devin's jaw dropped. "But . . . but . . . you're too old."

It was just the observation Cam needed to hear to bring his world back into focus. He pulled his gaze away from his wife long enough to shoot his son a smirk.

"Apparently not." Then he pulled Sarah into his arms and kissed her thoroughly before adding, "This grandpa still has game."

Chapter Sixteen

Five days after his mother's big surprise, Devin still had trouble accepting that his parents' sex life was playing so much havoc with his own. The mood hadn't been right for him to make a move on Jenna that night, so they'd said their good nights and retired to their respective rooms. The following morning, she'd cooked him breakfast and proceeded to ruin his appetite by explaining that barring any unforeseen problems, she intended to keep the promise she'd made to his mother and remain in Eternity Springs, at least through Christmas and possibly for good.

Because of that, she didn't think it was advisable to start an affair.

"It would be awkward, Devin. If I'm trying to make a life here for Reilly and me, if these people are going to be my friends and neighbors, I don't want to open myself up to slut-shaming. If we don't sleep together, I can hold my head up and speak with truthfulness and authority when I deny that you and I have something more than friendship here."

He'd wanted to protest, but he understood her argument. One of the drawbacks to small-town living was that everybody knew everybody's business. That said, just because he sympathized with her point didn't mean he had to like

it. Just because he tried to ignore the whole Santa bell-ring-
ing revelation about finding a father for Reilly didn't
mean it didn't slither and shake its rattles in his mind. He'd
whined a little and made an attempt to change her mind,
but his heart wasn't in it. He knew she was right. So every
night they retired to their respective rooms and he
yearned—and cussed the very thought of blizzards.

On this Tuesday morning at his mother's and sister's
urging, they were on their way to participate in a mid-
morning yoga class. Devin might have preferred a hard run
or, let's face it, a bout of athletic sex—but he had nothing
against yoga. He needed physical activity and it was better than nothing. Though he'd made a mistake lining up
behind Jenna. There wasn't anything downward about his
dog when she stuck that sweet little butt in the air right
in front of him. He was damn glad that he'd worn a long
T-shirt over loose-fitting gym shorts or he'd have embar-
rassed himself in front of his mom and sister.

When class ended, the prego parade congregated around
Jenna. She prefaced her answers to their questions with her
standard line, "I am a doctor, but I'm not *your* doctor and
I'm not licensed to practice in Colorado." That didn't stop
anyone from trying to pin her down. When the hen party
finally broke up and they left the studio, Jenna bubbled
with happiness. Devin gave a crooked smile and said, "You
are such a fake."

"What?"

"You tried to say you were happy doing your online job.
I eavesdropped on you this morning as you were taking
your calls and I listened to you just now. Sugar, you are
meant to work with patients. You're a natural."

They walked half a block before she responded. "I've
missed it. I didn't realize how much until today."

They had exited the studio with Lori and his mother and
walked north on Aspen. Their plan was to spend an hour

or two doing yard work at his mom's. Or, as Jenna happily called it, playing in the flowerbeds. He had discovered the previous day that she had a thing for digging in the dirt, and he knew his parents would be happy to indulge her. Mom could never have enough posies.

They stopped at the local lumberyard, which kept a nursery and a landscaping section stocked during the spring and summer. Jenna picked out garden gloves and shoes and tools, and then debated over flowerpots and annuals as a gift for his parents' patio. "Do you think Sarah would like this rustic-wood look, or is the clay pot better?"

"Which do you like best?"

"I like the clay, but—"

"Get it. From what I've seen, you and my mom have similar tastes."

It was true. Jenna shared a lot of common interests with his mother. She didn't bake, the only mark against her that Devin could see, but the two of them could go on for hours about the pros and cons of youth sports and decorating trends and movie soundtracks and technology rules for their boys.

Sarah and Lori were as close as a mother and daughter could be, but there were some parts of their relationship he'd never understood. They could make each other bristle with nothing more than a look. War had started over a single word.

For them both to be pregnant at the same time . . . whoa. *Dad might want to move back to Australia with me.*

And yet, a part of Devin regretted that he wouldn't be around to watch. How would his parents be with their first grandchild? What sort of relationship would Lori develop with her youngest sibling?

What will mine be like with the new kid? Will I know him at all?

The ringing of his cell phone jerked Devin from thoughts

that had turned brooding. He checked the number. The Yellow Kitchen? Who was calling him from the restaurant?

"We didn't have a lunch date I forgot about, did we?" he asked Jenna as he thumbed the green dot and brought the phone up to his ear. "Hello?"

"Devin, it's Ali. It looks like we just had a bite on your plan. I assume Jenna didn't actually place an order for thirty-four pizzas to be delivered to the medical clinic?"

Devin halted mid-stride. "Hot damn. Phone order or online?"

"Online."

"Even better. Thanks for the heads-up, Ali. I'll call the team."

Ending the call, he met Jenna's gaze. "It's on."

"What happened?" She covered her mouth with a hand as he explained. "Thirty-four? Why thirty-four? Why any of this? Oh." She waved her hand in front of her face. "I need to sit down. This is actually happening. Oh, wow. I think I'm going to faint."

"Don't do that!" Devin turned a large flowerpot upside down just in time to provide the seat she needed. "Around here, people will think you're pregnant. Put your head between your knees, Jenna." He patted her back. "It's okay."

"Make sure that Chase gets the news. I know Reilly is safe and happy and having fun at camp, but please, make sure everyone at the Rocking L knows what's happened."

"I will. I'll start making calls right now if you promise you won't topple off your flower pot and crack your head on the floor."

"I promise." She breathed deeply and exhaled loudly once, twice, three times. "Why thirty-four?"

"It's a curious number. Think about it, Sugar. Maybe there's a clue there."

Jack Davenport made the same suggestion later that day

when the team gathered at Daniel's office to discuss the development. "If you think of anything at all, even the slightest possibility of a connection, reach out to me or Daniel. You never know what seemingly obscure bit of information will be key."

"I will," Jenna vowed.

Jack turned to the Callahans and said, "I trust that with today's contact, your worker bees are already hard at work?"

"Absolutely," Mark said. "Our best hackers . . . I mean . . . professionals are on the case."

"Good. Daniel, you want to summarize where we stand with our guys on the ground?"

"Sure. We've had our three persons of interest under surveillance since the fifth. I've let our guys know that we've had movement on our end, though I expect since we're dealing with online contact, your hackers will be the ones who hit pay dirt."

"Professionals," Mark repeated, giving Jenna a wink.

Daniel continued, "I'll admit that a part of me figured you'd never hear another word out of this guy. The fact that he's continued his pursuit this long suggests that this guy's mind is seriously disturbed. I still feel confident in your safety, Jenna, and I have absolutely no doubts about Reilly's, but it's not the time to get lax. Don't go anywhere in public without Devin or Cam or one of the rest of us."

"She won't," Devin declared. "I'll make sure of it."

The rest of that day and all the next they waited for something to happen. The phone didn't ring. Pizzas didn't arrive. The deliveryman didn't show up with dozens of packages. By the third day, Jenna's nerves stretched tight as a guitar string. Devin's nerves weren't exactly loosey-goosey either. His time in Eternity Springs was quickly drawing to a close. He wanted this stalker situation settled so he could leave in good conscience, but at the same time, he didn't want his time with Jenna to end.

He *really* didn't want his time with Jenna to end.

Five days after the pizza order, Jack called another team meeting and this time they met up at Eagle's Way, where Jack had electronics that allowed the Callahans to illustrate the points they were trying to make.

Mark Callahan led off the meeting with disturbing news. "We got bubkes. I do not believe it because our guys are seriously good at what they do, but this guy is obviously no amateur. We will track him down eventually. Of that I have no doubt. But it's going to take some time or another event for us to find him. Unless you have something new for us, Daniel?"

"What I have is bubkes part two." He met Jenna's gaze with an apologetic smile. "We've basically confirmed your original investigator's conclusions. Based on a thorough examination of their records combined with both electronic and physical surveillance, we eliminated the lawyer and the songwriter as suspects almost immediately. I wanted to finger the surgeon, believe me. The guy is a total prick. Two more women have accused him of sexual harassment since you left Nashville, Jenna. However, we can't find anything that suggests he's our guy. So we're back to square one."

Jenna closed her eyes. Devin muttered a curse beneath his breath before saying, "This totally sucks."

"I won't argue the point," Jack observed. "That said, we knew that might be the case. Daniel and I talked it over before you all arrived, and we want to come at this from another direction. Perhaps this isn't about Jenna, after all, but about Reilly."

"Reilly!" Cam exclaimed. "I get that kids grow up fast these days and cyberbullying is a thing, but at this age? Seriously?"

"My questions are about his biological father. We only brushed on him during our initial conversation, Jenna. What can you tell us about . . . ?" He checked his notes. "Steven Caldwell?"

"Oh. Well . . ." Jenna took a moment to gather her thoughts. "I guess it's possible. At this point, anything is possible, isn't it? I only met him once. Actually, we didn't officially meet. I saw him once when I testified against him in court. Reilly's mother was a patient of mine. Early on in her pregnancy she confessed to me that the father didn't want the baby. He wanted her to end the pregnancy, but she refused to do it. She was eight months pregnant when he started beating her. She went into labor and delivered three weeks early."

"Did he kill her?" Mark Callahan asked, his expression carved in granite.

"No. She called a lawyer and filed for divorce before leaving the hospital. Reilly's father was charged and convicted of assault and a few other crimes . . . I don't recall exactly what. He went to jail. I honestly don't recall what his actual sentence was, but I remember the lawyer warned her that he'd probably be out before Reilly's first birthday. He signed away parental rights and as far as I know, he never once came to see Reilly."

"What about child support?" Daniel asked.

"She came from money and didn't need it. We stayed friends. She was happy. Loved motherhood. She was diagnosed with pancreatic cancer when Reilly was eighteen months old. Shortly thereafter, she asked me to be his guardian."

"Grandparents?" Daniel asked.

"None on either side. No extended family on her side. I honestly don't know about his."

Daniel looked pointedly at Mark Callahan, who opened his computer and started typing.

They quizzed Jenna at length, and by the time the meeting broke up, Jenna was obviously exhausted. Devin wasn't feeling all that chipper himself. When they climbed into his truck for the trip back to town and Jenna reminded him of the stop he'd intended to make, he considered calling it off.

"Maybe we should skip it."

Jenna gave him a hard look. "You're not going to tell Reilly goodbye before you leave?"

He tightened his grip on the steering wheel. "Maybe I won't leave."

"What are you talking about? Of course you'll leave."

"Well, I'll go to Mitch's wedding, but maybe instead of going on to Cairns, I'll come back here."

"For heaven's sake, why?"

"I'm not comfortable leaving before your stalker is caught."

"Devin, you have a business to run. You can't put your life on hold like that."

"The business can manage without me a little longer, and I don't look at it as putting my life on hold. Just because I like to wander the world doesn't mean I don't keep my word. I promised to protect you and that's what I'll do. I don't bail. That's not who I am."

Jenna folded her arms. "Welcome to the nineteen-fifties where the little lady really needs a big strong man to protect her."

"Now, Jenna."

"No! Stop it. You know, I wish this bastard would come after me. I'm not afraid of that. I took self-defense classes after Alan Snelling started harassing me. I'll put him down and make it hurt."

"Good. I hope you do. But what will you do if an FBI agent shows up to arrest you for money-laundering or child porn?"

"What?" she screeched.

"Can you definitely claim that someone who thinks doxxing and swatting are good ideas wouldn't take it a step further? What if he created a digital trail that ties you into a real crime? Or some dark web scenario that gets some real bad actors after you? I can imagine you being hand-cuffed and swept off to a secret room full of rubber hoses and an interrogator named Hans Gruber."

She blinked once. "A *Die Hard* reference? You're bring-ing up *Die Hard*?"

He shrugged. "It's my favorite Christmas show."

She burst out with a laugh, though it was filled with ten-sion rather than joy. "What kind of man are you that you'll change your life plans so drastically for a woman you barely know, a woman who isn't even sleeping with you?"

"Yeah, that last part is dodgy, I'll admit. But the rest of it . . ." He shrugged. "I can't do anything different. I don't want to do anything different. I'm trusting my instincts on this one."

"But what if they still don't find him?"

"I'm trusting Daniel and Jack and the Callahans on that."

"Okay, so what if they find the stalker while you're at your friend's wedding?"

"While *we* are at the wedding. You're coming with me."

"I can't. I won't. Look, all along I've assumed that the stalker focused on me, but the idea that Reilly's biological father might be involved changes everything. I still believe Reilly is safe at camp, but I can't travel thousands of miles away if there's any possibility that he's the stalker's target."

"Fair enough. However, you shouldn't underestimate the team. If Steven Caldwell isn't involved, they'll elimi-nate him fast. That question could well be solved before it's time to leave for the island."

Jenna shrugged. "Nevertheless, that's not the issue at

hand. If the team solves my problem while you're in the Caribbean, you won't come back here, which brings me back to my original question. Are you going to leave town without telling my son goodbye?"

He drummed his fingers on the console between them. No, he couldn't do that. But dang it, he didn't want to see the boy right now. "Here's the truth, Jenna. The story you told about his prick of a father has my stomach churning. How could anyone with a heart act that way?"

"I don't consider Steven Caldwell to be Reilly's father. He's a sperm donor. That's all. Reilly doesn't have a father."

"Which is why he asked me to bring him one for Christmas," Devin said glumly. "Look, I'm afraid if I go see him right now, I'll take one look at him and start bawling like a baby. That's not how I want Reilly to remember me. I'm a tough guy."

She gave him a tender smile. "You're Santa Claus."

"Hey, he doesn't know that. I have to keep up my rep."

Jenna reached across the console and gave his forearm a squeeze. "You'll manage, Murphy. I know you will. I believe."

He gave her a sidelong glance and a doubtful smirk.

"We told Chase to expect the visit and he might well have told Reilly."

"Okay. Okay. We'll go up to the Rocking L. But if I start to blubber, I expect you to cover for me. I think—"

He broke off when his cell phone rang, and a glance at the screen revealed Jack Davenport's number. Devin accepted the call. "Hey, Jack."

"Devin, is Jenna with you?"

"Sitting right beside me. You're on speaker."

"Good. I thought she'd want to know what we've learned ASAP. Steven Caldwell isn't our guy."

Devin shot Jenna a quick *I told you so* look. "Oh, yeah?"

"He's dead."

Jenna's eyes rounded and she covered her mouth with her hands. Devin pulled off the road and parked. "What happened?"

He expected to hear that the bastard had been knifed in prison or OD'd on crack. Jack surprised him. "He settled in a small town in California following his release from jail. Worked in a hardware store and joined the volunteer fire department. He was killed fighting a wildfire the summer before last. He's credited with saving three lives."

"You're certain you have the right Steven Caldwell?" Jenna asked.

"We're positive," Jack replied, his tone gentle. He provided further details about what the team had learned about Reilly's biological father and, when Jenna had no further questions, ended the call after giving his reassurance that the search would continue.

Devin did not immediately resume their drive. Instead, he studied Jenna closely. Tears had pooled in her eyes. "Sugar, you okay?"

"Yes. I just . . . whew." She exhaled a heavy breath then wiped the corners of her eyes with the pads of her fingers. "It's so sad. He's lost both parents."

"*Biological* parents. He has you, the lucky little boy."

A smile flickered across her lips. "It's just a lot to absorb. I've worried about this in the past. I know he'll ask about his parents someday, and I worried about what I would say about Steven Caldwell. Now I'll have something good to say, won't I? He saved three lives. That's a good thing."

"Yes, that's a very good thing." Devin leaned over and kissed her lightly on the cheek. "And you are a very good person, Jenna Stockton."

"Thank you."

Devin checked the traffic, then pulled out onto the road.

They made the rest of the drive in comfortable silence, and it was only when the log structures of the summer camp came into view that Devin posed the question burning in his brain. "So, are you going to tell Reilly that you'll be away for a few days? You'll come to Bella Vita with me?"

She waited until he'd parked in a visitor space and switched off the engine to respond. "Yes. Yes, I'll go to Bella Vita with you. As long as we can find room in your sleigh, that is. How booked are flights to Bella Vita Isle as a rule? You said quite a few people from Eternity Springs are attending this wedding?"

Devin pursed his lips and considered the question. Because it was still tourist season in Eternity Springs, which made it hard for his parents to get away for long, they'd decided to go down just for the weekend. He'd planned to fly commercial with them, and he didn't worry about there being an open seat for Jenna. But Flynn Brogan was flying down tomorrow in his Gulfstream.

"I have an idea." He reached for his phone, scrolled through the contacts, and made a call. "Hey, Flynn, Devin here. Are you guys still heading to BV tomorrow?"

"We are."

"You're flying your Gulfstream, I assume?

"Yep. Sure am. Do you need a ride?"

"We do. Plans have changed, and Jenna Stockton and I would like to get to the island a couple days ahead. Do you have room for a couple of tagalongs?"

"Sure, we'd be happy to have you join us. Gabi's clan is flying down with us, so fair warning, my wife and Savannah may well talk the doctor's ear off with pregnancy questions."

"I'm sure she won't mind."

"Will Jenna want a ride back on Sunday?"

"Actually, we both need a ride back on Sunday. I'm extending my stay in Eternity Springs for a bit."

Devin glanced at Jenna, who was gaping at him in surprise. "When and where do we meet you?"

They made plans, and then Devin ended the call. He grinned at her. "We're all set."

"Flying in a private jet. Tomorrow. Not Friday. That's a long weekend, Devin."

"Yeah, doesn't it sound great? I am ready to be back on the water. Which reminds me. I don't have a boat there anymore. Cursed hurricane." He called a friend on Bella Vita who owed him a big favor and made arrangements for a boat, which banished the last vestiges of the black mood that had started sucking on him as he listened to Jenna speak of Reilly's father.

Devin whistled cheerily as they exited the truck and went in search of Chase. They found him on the phone speaking to the parent of a camper who'd changed his mind about wanting to participate in a hike into the national forest for overnight tent camping. The camp needed a signed permission slip before the boy would be allowed to go.

When the call ended, Chase greeted Devin with a handshake and Jenna with a hug. "Any word on your license? When you'll be official? Lori likes her doctor in Gunnison well enough, but we're all anxious to have a local specialist."

"Jack told me he's been pulling some strings and maybe by next week I'll be good to go."

"If anyone can pull strings, it's Jack Davenport."

"So, is Reilly behaving himself? How is he doing with Sinatra?"

"He's doing great. The puppy has been so helpful. He uses Sinatra's needs to verbalize his own insecurities, so his counselor is making real progress with him. The fear we saw in him those first couple of days hardly makes an appearance now."

"That's so good. I'm so relieved." Jenna exhaled a heavy sigh. "I believed camp would be good for him, but you always have a niggling worry."

"I'll give you one warning. If you've come up here expecting him to want to spend much time with you, you are headed for disappointment. Reilly is a busy boy."

"Nothing could make me happier than to have him snub me," Jenna responded.

Chase checked his watch and then his clipboard. "He's due at the stables in fifteen minutes. Why don't you meet him at the bonfire site? You know where it is, Devin. I'll message his counselor to send him on. Does he know you were planning to visit?"

"No. Not unless you said something about it."

"I did not. I'll send for him now and I'll make sure he knows there's no emergency."

Five minutes later, Jenna sat on one of the logs set in an octagon around the fire pit. Devin had picked up a stick and was drawing in the dirt when Reilly came running up. He wore jeans and the red Rocking L uniform T-shirt and ball cap. He gave her a hug and then asked, "Mom, why are you here? Is something wrong?"

"No, everything's fine."

"Did they find the bad man?"

"Not yet, but they're looking hard for him."

"Okay. That's good. Look, I don't have much time. I have to go to the stables so we can go horseback riding."

"Okay, we won't keep you. I just wanted see how you were doing and tell you that I'm going to go with the Murphys and some of our other Eternity Springs friends to an out-of-town wedding this weekend. We'll leave tomorrow, and I'll be back on Sunday."

"Okay. That's cool. On Friday we're going to go hike up in the mountains and go camp in a tent for two nights. Sinatra is going to stay here. Not all the kids want to go, so

Miss Cheryl will be here and Sinatra is going to stay with her while I'm gone. I think he'll be fine, don't you, Mom?"

"I think he'll be absolutely fine."

"All right. Well, I better go." He started edging away. "Today I get to ride Bubba. That's the horse's name. Bubba."

"Whoa there, cowboy," Devin said past the lump of emotion that had formed in his throat. "Don't go yet. I gotta say . . . I need to . . ."

Reilly peered up at him, expectant and impatient. "What?"

Damn. Devin dragged his hand across his mouth. "Say goodbye. See, once we find the bad guy, I'm going to have to go back to work. So it's possible, by the time you come home from camp I'll be gone.

"Oh." The boy's expression fell. "That makes me sad, Devin."

"Yeah, I know. It makes me sad too. But you know, we can always talk on the phone. You can call me whenever you want."

"We can FaceTime."

"Yep. We sure can. I can tell you this right now. I'm going to want to hear all about this tent-camping trip you're about to take. I'll bet that's a real adventure."

"Yep. We have bear spray to carry."

"Always be prepared." Devin went down on one knee and held out his arms. "C'mere and give me a hug, Reilly."

The boy ran into the man's embrace. "I'll give you a bear hug!"

Devin closed his eyes and gritted his teeth against the emotion rolling through him. Then he growled like a bear and squeezed Reilly tight. When the boy giggled and wiggled, Devin released him and stood. "Take care of yourself, Reilly James Stockton."

"I will. I gotta go now. Bye, Devin. Bye, Mom."

"Wait!" Jenna called. "I need a hug."

Like any healthy, happy eight-year-old boy, Reilly rolled his eyes in disgust. "Mo-om."

Reilly gave her a fast hug, then pulled away and headed toward the stables in a run. Just before the path took him out of sight, he stopped, turned around and waved. "I love you!"

"Love you too, buddy!" Jenna called.

Devin swallowed hard. His eyes stung. His heart twisted. Softly, he said, "I love you, Reilly."

Damned if he didn't mean it.

Chapter Seventeen

Bella Vita Isle was a feast for the eyes, an emerald island awash in tropical flowers and surrounded by a turquoise sea. Colorful birds flittered from tree to tree, bloom to bloom, and as Jenna sat on a porch swing watching one bird the size of a robin sporting a bright blue breast, shocking yellow neckband, and fire-engine red crest perched on the weathervane atop the house next door, she felt a little like Cinderella at the ball. Flying on a private jet, vacationing at a beachfront cottage, and now motoring about the Caribbean on a private boat? "Dr. Stockton, you're not in a trailer park anymore."

They were staying in the house that had been Devin's home. The darling three-bedroom, two-bath structure had sustained only minor damage during Danielle, and rather than sell it when he moved to Australia, he'd chosen to repair it and market it as a vacation rental.

Jenna found it easy to picture Devin living here. Although he'd removed all personal items from the property, the house was decorated in a nautical theme that included photos of the vessels he'd lost to Hurricane Danielle— *The Office*, the *Outcast*, and the *Castaway*. Moored at the marina on the opposite end of the island, the boats had taken a direct hit from the dirty side of the storm.

The wistful look on his face when he talked about them made her want to give him a comforting hug. She didn't do it. Jenna was being extra careful not to touch him too familiarly.

They hadn't kissed since she'd made the decision to stay in Eternity Springs. They rarely touched. However, sexual awareness remained a constant hum in the background whenever they were together, and as a result, her nerves remained strung tight. More than once she'd caught him watching her with that heavy-lidded gaze that spoke more loudly than words ever could. More than once, he'd caught her at it too.

They didn't acknowledge the tension by either word or deed, but it was always there. She had thought that getting away from town and the stress of the stalker hunt along with being in a new setting might ease the edginess. Yeah, right. And tomorrow she'd be able to play a Beethoven concerto on the piano when she could barely manage "Chopsticks" today. *Stupid. Stupid. Stupid.*

It didn't help the situation that during the two days they'd spent here on Bella Vita, she'd seen Devin in a new and even more intriguing light. He was in his element in the tropics. He was at home on a boat. Yesterday, they'd joined one of his friend's fishing tour operations for a half-day trip. Despite being a paying customer, he'd taken on the role of a crewmember, assisting and advising the person in the fighting chair, rigging the outriggers, and baiting the hooks. Jenna had caught two fish—a wahoo and a yellowfin—and while she'd enjoyed the experience, she thought he'd had more fun than she.

Last night, they'd met a large group of his friends at a local restaurant for dinner. She'd met the bride-to-be and the groom, Mitch, who'd told her stories about Devin that had her helpless with laughter. Toward the end of the evening, when she'd stepped outside to get a breath of air, Mitch had followed her out. "Ya like our mon Oz, don'tcha now?" he'd observed, his voice heavy with the lilt of the Caribbean. "Ya really like him."

"Devin has been very kind to me and my son."

"Kind, eh? He's a good man. He told me about being your boy's Santa Claus. Him, he loves the little ones. 'Tis not right what that evil witch Anya"—he paused and spat on the ground—"did to him."

"Anya?"

Mitch tilted his head in a considering manner. "Not my story to tell. Ask him, pretty lady. You should understand why he will not toss an anchor."

Jenna had been digesting that remark moments later when Devin came outside looking for her, and the conversation turned to the couple's upcoming honeymoon in Paris.

"Evil witch Anya," Jenna murmured, wondering for the dozenth time since last night just who Anya was and what she'd done to Devin.

The thought evaporated when the bird spread his wings and flew away at the same time the sound of an approaching car engine reached her ears. Devin was back.

Jenna had returned from a shopping trip to the local market with Gabi Brogan, Savannah Turner, Hope Romano, and Maggie Romano to find a note from Devin saying he'd gone down to the marina to ready things for their excursion and would return shortly. She'd relished the time alone, but seeing him climb out of the Jeep he'd rented for the duration of their stay nevertheless sent her heart going pit-a-pat.

"Hey there, Sugar. Did you and the girls have fun shopping?"

"We did. I bought way too much, but I blame it all on

Gabi because she assured me that I don't have a luggage limit since I'm flying back to Eternity Springs with the Brogans."

"Bet I can guess one of your purchases. A mandolin."

"How did you know?"

"Last week at dinner I heard you tell Mom that you wanted Reilly to learn to play a musical instrument. I knew that if you saw them at the market they would catch your eye. They're fabulous, aren't they? The man who makes them is a real artist."

Jenna nodded. "I'm going to save it and give it to Reilly for Christmas."

"He'll love it."

"I hope I can find someone who can teach him to play."

"Get him a good beginner book and once he learns the G, C, and D chords, he'll be playing simple songs on Christmas Day. I picked it up quickly."

"You can play the mandolin?"

Devin nodded. "My dad has one. I gave it to him a couple years ago. If I'm still in town when Reilly comes home from camp, I'll give him a lesson or two if you don't think it would spoil the surprise."

Reilly doesn't come home until Labor Day. I can't live with Devin for another six weeks. She'd be so far gone by then there'd be no coming back.

Jenna hesitated so long with her response that he said, "But if you'd rather I didn't . . ."

"No. No. That'd be great." Jenna smiled brightly and changed the subject. "So, before I forget. Do I need to bring anything special for the boat ride this afternoon? Towels? Sunscreen? Snacks and drinks?"

"The *Windsong* is fully outfitted. All you need to bring is your swimsuit." His eyes took on a devilish glint as he teased, "Though if you want to leave it off, you'll get no complaints from me."

Jenna rolled her eyes.

Devin continued, "Are you ready to go?"

"I am. I just need to grab my tote. I bought a new one at the market today."

"Let's do it."

During the twenty-minute drive to the marina, Devin quizzed her about her opinions of the various vendors in the market, their wares, and if she thought a demand for any of it might exist in Eternity Springs. They were enthusiastically discussing the possibilities of importing the mandolins when she caught sight of dozens and dozens of boats moored at the marina. "Wow. For a small island, that's a lot of boats."

"Danielle thinned 'em out, but the marina is coming back. I'm glad to see it. Of course, this time of day, this time of year, fishing boats and tour boats are all out. They'll be back tonight and even some pleasure craft will have wandered in when we return this evening."

He pulled the Jeep into a parking spot and switched off the motor.

"Which boat are we using?" Jenna asked.

"The *Windsong* is there. The blue and white one. She's pretty, isn't she?"

"Wow. You said we were taking out a boat. You didn't say a yacht."

"In my world, yachts are sailboats. She is a big boat, I'll give you that, at sixty-five feet. Let's go aboard, Sugar, and we'll have us a cruise."

They cast off the lines with the assistance of dockhands and Jenna took a seat beside him in the lower helm. "We'll move up to the flybridge once we're out on open sea." He explained the workings of the instrumentation as he guided the *Windsong* out of the harbor. "I thought we'd take a leisurely three-sixty around Bella Vita first and then head out to sea. Does that work for you?"

"Sure." Jenna was back to her Cinderella-at-the-ball moment. This boat was utter luxury with teak decking, a wet bar and barbecue, a dining area, and a convertible sundeck on the flybridge. The main deck had three cabins with a chef's dream of a galley, a living/dining area, a full-standing head, and a full-beam stateroom.

Devin captained the boat with familiar ease. Jenna asked, "Tell me about your boats."

"My boats aren't anything this fancy-schmancy, that's for sure," he told her. "This is a pleasure boat. Mine are workboats. I make my living with them. That's the most basic difference."

"But what type of boats are yours? Sailboats? Catamarans? Fishing boats like what we were on yesterday?"

"We've had each of those at different times. When I was growing up, Dad ran snorkel and dive tours out to the Reef off of catamarans and sailboats, but I learned early on that I preferred fishing charters."

"The three that you have hanging on the wall were like the one we took out yesterday."

"Basic sport fishing boats. Workhorses. Two of the three I have now are the same thing." A satisfied smile stretched across his face. "The *Out-n-Back* is different."

"Tell me about it."

"Her. She's a fine, fine boat that began as another man's pleasure boat. For me, she's a workboat—a dream of a boat—but she's still a fishing boat, a Boston Whaler. Her original owner had her less than a year when he ran into some financial problems and needed out fast. I'd just received my insurance check from Danielle so I was able to manage the down. I have earned a reputation as a guide, and between that and the accommodations, I can charge a pretty penny for charters. But the nut is steep. As long as I can keep the little boats going out, I'm okay but—" He broke off abruptly.

Jenna realized he'd said more than he'd intended to say and she gave him a knowing look. "It *will* hurt you financially to stay longer in Eternity Springs than you'd originally planned."

"I'll be fine. The little boats are doing great. Now look, we're on the windward side of the island. Look up at about ten o'clock and you'll see the restaurant where we had dinner last night."

Jenna decided to allow the change of subject—for now. She couldn't in good conscience allow him to be hurt financially by assuming responsibility for her problems out of some sense of Santa psychology. If the problem wasn't solved by Sunday, he needed to go home to Australia just like he'd originally planned. She'd have to do whatever was necessary to make it happen.

But Sunday was still three days away. She wasn't going to worry about it. She was going to enjoy her Cinderella Thursday aboard the *Windsong*.

They moved up to the helm on the flybridge, where Devin could captain the boat with the wind in his face. Jenna sat beside him, her gaze shifting between the beauty of the island and that of the man who was so in his element here on the water. And she was so out of her own.

When they rounded the southern tip of the island and started up the leeward side, he said, "The Brogans' place is on this side of the island. See that stretch of beach there? The red clay roof behind the hedge?"

"I see it."

"They got hit pretty hard from the hurricane, but Flynn wanted to redesign the place anyway, so he was glad to have the excuse."

"Gabi said he's always designing something."

"True, that." When they'd puttered halfway up the island, he asked, "So, you want to take a turn at the wheel?"

Jenna instinctively drew back. "Oh, I couldn't. I've never driven a boat."

"No worries. We're in eighty feet of water here."

"How do you know that?"

"Here." He released the wheel and stepped back.

Panicked, Jenna grabbed the wheel. He chuckled and began teaching her to read the electronics and gauges. Accustomed to reading machines in the operating room, she caught on quickly. As they neared the southern tip of the island, she asked, "How many miles per hour is five knots?"

"About five and three quarters."

"It feels like we're going faster than that."

"Because your face is in the wind. Go below and it won't seem so fast."

"We went a little slower when we were trolling yesterday."

"Yes. About three knots."

"And when we were going faster? Out toward the spot where we started trolling?"

Devin pursed his lips and considered it. "Eight to ten."

"It was fun." Jenna waited a few moments, then confessed, "Yesterday was the first time I'd been on a boat."

He glanced over at her and his chin dropped. "Seriously?"

"Not even a rowboat on the lake."

"Now, that's just wrong. Why didn't you say anything?"

"I don't know. I just didn't want to admit it. I was too busy worrying that I'd get seasick."

"Seas were a little rougher yesterday than they are today. Boat a lot smaller. You didn't mention feeling queasy. Did you?"

"No, not at all."

"Then hold on, Sugar." He stood behind her, covered

her left hand with his, and rested his right hand on the throttle. "I'm going to open her up."

He applied pressure, the engines accelerated, and the *Windsong* shot forward like a thoroughbred at the starting gate. Soon they were flying across the sea, the wind whistling a song as it rushed past her ears. Devin's eyes gleamed and he gave her a pirate's smile.

What a rush this was! She could get used to this—with Devin and being free upon the sea. Jenna had the wayward thought that this might be what having sex with Devin Murphy was like. Maybe she should throw caution to this whistling wind and really enjoy herself.

After a while, he slowed the boat to cruising speed, set a waypoint on the autopilot and declared it was time for lunch. They went down to the galley on the lower deck, where Devin set out fruit, cheeses, and sandwich fixings from a well-stocked fridge and pantry. Jenna took her ham sandwich and grapes to the dining table, where she tried to listen to Devin's conversation about the engines powering the boat. However, she truly didn't care about motors of any sort as long as they started and ran when she wanted them to run. Also, she kept popping up from the table to look out of the window.

Devin asked, "What in the world is wrong with you?"

"It's the autopilot. It sort of freaks me out. What if there's another boat coming?"

"This is the most sophisticated system on the market." He began ticking items off on his fingers. "We have radar, sonar, radio, stereo, DVDs, MP3s, telegraph, duotronic transporter . . ."

"A *Star Trek* reference? You are so funny. Laugh at me all you want, but wasn't the U.S. Navy involved in a collision or two in recent years?"

"Fine. I'm not laughing. Your concerns are valid and

understandable. I should have demonstrated the system when we were around traffic and you'd have been more comfortable with it. Tell you what." He nodded toward her sandwich. "How about after lunch, we turn off the autopilot, stop the boat, and go for a swim."

"Is it safe? I won't be fish bait?"

"We're in good swimming waters. That's why I took us this direction.

A swim sounded fantastic. Between the heat of the afternoon and the never-ending strum of sexual tension, she could use a cool dip and some exercise. She polished off her lunch and went into the stateroom where she'd left her bag upon their arrival to change into her swimsuit. There, she hesitated over her choice. She'd brought the modest one-piece she usually wore, but she also had the bikini she'd purchased yesterday at the market under peer pressure from Gabi and Maggie because they said it was made for her.

"It matches your eyes," Maggie had said.

"You have the body for it too," Gabi added. "I'm so jealous of your curves. Your hips are made for the matching sarong."

In the end, Jenna had bought the bikini and the sarong and a wide-brimmed hat with a matching scarf. Now as she pulled the items from her tote, she wondered if she'd be playing with fire to wear them.

Maybe. Probably. She'd wear the one-piece. She kicked off her deck shoes, pulled off her T-shirt and bra, and slipped out of her shorts and panties. But somehow when she left the stateroom, she wore her new bikini.

The sound of steel guitars and reggae music drifted from hidden speakers. Devin stood on the swim deck deploying the second of two coral-colored foam floats behind the boat. Attached to the *Windsong* by ten feet or so of line, they bobbed up and down on the turquoise waves. Shirtless and shoeless and wearing board shorts that hung low on his hips, he looked tanned and toned and so sexy that she felt itchy and needy inside. She almost moaned aloud. Instead, because she was both physician and mother, she asked, "Did you put on sunscreen?"

He turned around and, upon seeing her, froze. Then he lowered his sunglasses and gave her a long, smoldering look. "Sugar Cookie," he said, drawing it out to about twelve syllables. "Don't you look fine?"

"Thank you. So . . . my question. . . . Sunscreen?"

He tilted his head, still considering, and took a long time to answer. "Will you get my back?"

That's when she realized she'd made a mistake. Talk about playing with fire. As she stepped down onto the swim deck, he opened a compartment at the back of the boat and removed a bottle of sunscreen. Solemnly and without saying another word, he handed it to her and presented his back.

Devin was tall, his shoulders broad and roped with muscle. Yesterday she'd witnessed firsthand just how those cords had come to be. Devin was no gym rat who jerked a barbell. He jerked around thirty-pound groupers and mahi-mahi.

Jenna's mouth went dry and, as she squirted white, coconut-scented lotion into the palm of her hand, she suddenly thought of high school English and Coleridge's "Rime of the Ancient Mariner." "Water, water everywhere, nor any drop to drink."

"Hmm? You're thirsty? There's a cooler right behind you. The center cushion. There's water, juice, soft drinks. Beer if you want it. I'm serving mojitos at cocktail hour."

"Thanks." Jenna wouldn't mind a bottle of water, but the Coleridge quote had referred to a totally different type of thirst. Bracing herself, she slid her hand across his back. His skin was warm and taut, neither smooth nor rough, just normal. Lovely. Scarred here below his left shoulder. *Wonder what happened here?* An old scar, long healed. She lingeringly traced it with her index finger. Six inches long. It had been stitched.

"About done?" Devin asked, his voice sounding strained.

"Oh, sorry. Let me just . . ." With quick, clinical motions, she smoothed lotion over the places she'd missed, and then stepped back.

"Thanks." Devin cleared his throat and held out his hand and wiggled his fingers. "My turn."

Oh. Well. Oh. She gave him the sunscreen and whirled around, happy not to have to face him as heat flushed her cheeks. "Just . . . um . . . right above my . . . um . . . strap. I could . . . um . . . reach everywhere else."

Her bikini top didn't have a strap. It had a string. A thin, tiny string she'd secured with a bow. A bow he could easily untie if he pulled on one of the knotted ends. She closed her eyes. She heard the squish sound of lotion leaving the bottle. For a long moment, nothing happened.

She shivered in anticipation. Goose bumps rose upon her flesh. She felt his index finger grasp one of the knots on her bow. His voice low and gravelly, he asked, "You don't want to get burned, do you, Jenna?"

Her voice escaped in a squeak. "No, but—"

He tugged once, quick and hard. The bow slipped. Instinctively, her arms lifted to clasp the triangles of her top against her breasts.

The lotion was cool. His fingers were hot. They stroked across her skin slowly, back and forth. Back and forth. Jenna held back a moan.

When finally he spoke, it was in a low, throaty tone from right beside her ear. "Seems to me we have a choice here, Jenna. Do we go swimming?" His lips brushed across the sensitive skin of her neck. "Or . . . not?"

She wanted him. Oh, how she wanted him.

His finger trailed down the base of her spine and the edge of the sarong. Moisture pooled between Jenna's legs. He tugged at the knot at her hip and the sarong drifted to the *Windsong*'s deck.

Jenna turned around. Devin's gaze made a slow, hot crawl up and down her body, desire turning his eyes dark and dangerous.

Swim? Or sink? That was the question here, wasn't it? She tried to recall all the reasons why this would be a mistake. Only one hovered like a half-formed protest in her mind—Eternity Springs.

Well, Dorothy, you're not in Kansas right now, are you? Much less Colorado. And he's not in Oz. Not yet.

And, oh, she had the feeling that he likely was a wizard.

She was Cinderella on a genuine-freaking-yacht and if she wanted to mix her metaphors and movies and fairy tales, well then she had until midnight before Jaws ate her glass slipper and she had to put on her red glitter shoes.

She wanted Devin's mouth on her. Every inch of her.

"You told me being on the ocean is empowering because it makes you part of the universe. You said you never feel alone. When you asked me to come with you to Bella Vita Isle, you said you'd show me. I'm tired of being powerless, Devin. I'm tired of being alone. I want to swim . . . later. Now, just for today, while we're here on the ocean aboard the *Windsong,* make me part of your universe."

He put his hands on her waist. "Just so I'm positively certain, you're saying yes?"

"Yes, I'm saying yes."

His lips twisted in that slow pirate's smile. His fingers

tightened and he lifted her off her feet. He crushed his mouth to hers and turned in a slow circle once, twice, three times.

Jenna felt him lift her and she expected to find herself seated on the sundeck, where he'd lay her back and have his wicked way with her. She nearly laughed aloud.

So to find herself sailing through the air caught her completely by surprise. Screeching, she caught her breath just before her head sank beneath the surface of the cool Caribbean.

She surfaced sputtering to find Devin treading water beside her, laughing maniacally. "What in the world did you do that for?"

"Look around us. See all the steam rising from the water? Sugar, you and I have been on slow burn for weeks. Without a bit of a cool down I'd have gone off like a rocket."

"So you throw me in the ocean?"

"Yeah." He continued to laugh. "You should have seen your face."

"Why . . . you . . . you"—she drew back her hands and splashed him—"pirate!"

"Well, this *is* the Caribbean." He grabbed her hand and pulled her close. "C'mere, me pretty. Give us a kiss. Later I'll let you walk my plank."

"Oh, for heaven's sake." Her mouth curved against his as he kissed her and they sank beneath the waves.

When they came up for air, he stared deeply into her eyes and said, "Welcome to my world, Jenna Stockton. Let's play, shall we?"

Chapter Eighteen

Devin opened his eyes. The moon was a tiny sliver of a fingernail in a midnight blue sky awash with stars. Underway at four knots with a following sea, the *Windsong* rocked gently on the waves, making her way slowly along the course he had plotted after dinner—a large circle around Bella Vita Isle. He lay stretched out on the lounge on the flybridge with Jenna tucked up against him.

What a great day.

Great weather. Great boat. Great sex. Really great sex. Really great woman.

He had just enough energy left to turn his head and nuzzle her behind the ear. "Not again . . . ," she groaned. "I have to sleep."

Bravely, Devin worked up enough strength to smile. "I just don't want you to miss the Milky Way, Sugar. It's at its best this time of year."

She angled up on her elbows and dropped her head back to gaze upon the filmy cloud of stars arching across the sky. "Oh, wow. How fabulous is that? Do you know the constellations, Devin?"

"I'm a mariner. Of course I know the stars. If all the electronics on the *Windsong* were to fail, I could get us home with a compass and a sextant."

"Point some of them out to me?"

They spent the next twenty minutes stargazing, and she shared with him a childhood memory of her father. "We lived in a small town in Mississippi. I was about Reilly's age. It was summer and our air conditioner was broken. It was so hot that we gave up attempting to sleep in our beds and moved to the lawn furniture in the backyard. My dad tried to help me see the constellations, but I just couldn't mentally draw the pictures. I did see the Milky Way, though." After a moment's pause, she added, "Thank you for the nice memory of my father, Devin."

"My experience wasn't all that different from yours, except Cam and I were on a boat. I was around the same age, maybe a little younger. I could see the Southern Cross, but beyond that, forget it."

"Seeing the Southern Cross is on my bucket list. Crosby, Stills, and Nash, you know."

"Great song." Devin pressed a gentle kiss against her hair. "Maybe you should plan a visit to Cairns. I'll show you the Southern Cross."

She stiffened ever so slightly, and even before she spoke, Devin knew that the magic of the night had been broken. She rolled away from him and reached for one of the white terrycloth bathrobes they'd donned at the end of their late-night swim and then discarded during lovemaking.

She slipped it on, belted it, and faced him. It was too dark to see her expression, but he thought he could hear tears in her voice. "I can't, Devin. This has been a fairy tale of a day, but Cinderella has to leave the ball. I need you to keep to your original plans and return to Australia on Sunday."

"But the stalker—"

"Isn't as big a danger to me right now as you are."

"Excuse me?"

"I am on the verge of losing my heart to you, Devin. I

have to put a stop to it. There's no future in it and I need a future. I need to give Reilly a future. I need to give Reilly a father."

Well, if she'd wanted to shut him up, she'd chosen the best possible way to do it. He didn't have a comeback for that.

"I am going to return to Eternity Springs with the Brogans, and I'll take Jack Davenport up on his offer to stay at Eagle's Way until my stalker is identified. From the beginning, everyone said that was the safest thing for me to do. You won't need to worry about me and you can return to Australia and get back to business making payments on the *Out-n-Back*. I'll get my Colorado medical license and set about giving your mother and sister and friends the best possible prenatal care."

"And get married," he grumbled, unable to help himself. He grabbed up the second robe, shoved his arms into the sleeves, yanked the belt around his waist, and tied it.

After a significant pause, she asked, "Who is Anya?"

The name came right out of left field to sucker punch his gut. While he was still recovering from the blow, she continued, "Last night at dinner, Mitch said I should ask you about the 'evil witch Anya' so that I would understand why your boat has no anchor."

"Now? You have to ask now?" He exhaled sharply, angry at his friend and at himself. "Anya is nobody. Someone I used to know is all."

"Someone from Bella Vita?"

"Dammit, Jenna." He yanked open the wet bar's fridge and pulled out a beer. "She doesn't matter. She never mattered. The baby was all that mattered."

At her audible gasp, he literally bit his tongue. *I'm gonna kick Mitch's ass next time I see him.*

"You have a child?"

He had enough experience with women to recognize the

futility of attempting to avoid spilling the beans at this point. He might as well open the can and start pouring.

"I started seeing a woman here on the island. She got pregnant and I'm old-fashioned about such things, so I offered to marry her. She moved in, but she wanted to wait until after the baby was born to get married. Said she wanted the wedding gown and photos, and I bought her story. Turns out I was her backup plan. I wasn't the baby's father. He'd left her, left the island. After the hurricane hit he had a change of heart, returned, and they rode off together into the sunset. End of story."

"Oh, Devin. That's despicable. I'd use a much stronger word than 'witch' to describe her."

He shrugged. "I dealt. It was okay. I didn't love her. It's not like losing her broke my heart."

Losing the baby, now . . . He'd been a boy. Devin had believed he'd had a son on the way. He gave his head a shake, took another pull on his beer, and then said, "It was for the best. I'm a rolling stone, or, to keep it nautical, a spinning prop. So, that's the story—but why did you pick now to ask about it?"

She'd sure as hell managed to spoil the mood.

"It was the tone of your voice when you said the word 'marriage.' It reminded me of Mitch's cryptic comment."

Jenna reached up and framed his face in her hands. "Devin, thank you for this fairy-tale day. Thank you for caring for me and for my son and for being our champion. Being our hero. Being our Santa Claus. You've taught me to believe again."

She pulled his mouth down to hers and gave him a kiss so sweet, so honest, so full of an emotion that he dared not name that it staggered him. When it ended, he drew her unsteadily away. "Jenna . . ."

"Take me back to port, sailor. I'm afraid Cinderella's clock is starting to chime.

* * *

By mid-morning the following day, what seemed like half of Eternity Springs arrived for the wedding. It didn't happen a moment too soon as far as Jenna was concerned. She had thought that being around Devin was difficult before she had traveled to Bella Vita Isle with him. Following their day aboard the *Windsong,* she found it to be sheer torture.

By the time the boat docked at the marina in the early hours of the morning, she'd realized she had lied. She wasn't on the verge of losing her heart to him. It had happened. It was a done deal. She was toast. She'd fallen head over heels in love with Devin Santa Claus Murphy.

She believed, all right. She believed she was an idiot.

His family's arrival on the island had been a welcome distraction, and she'd happily joined Lori and Sarah on a visit to the market despite having so recently shopped until she dropped there.

It helped that Devin didn't appear to want to be alone with her anymore than she did him, and he spent the majority of his time doing activities with his brother, including building a large and intricate sand castle. In fact, once his family arrived, the two of them didn't exchange a word in private until just prior to their departure for the wedding. "Pretty dress," he said. "You look beautiful in yellow. You look beautiful in everything. In nothing . . ."

"Devin," she'd protested. "Off-limits. That's the other universe."

"Yeah. Yeah. I know. Sorry." His grimace held a bit of yearning that served to soothe her lovesick heart. He might not be one to permanently trailer his boat, but that didn't mean he didn't want her. Crumbs, true, but at this point her feminine ego would take them.

The wedding was a sunset beach ceremony on the Brogan property, a beautiful meld of traditions from the heritages of both the bride—a Minnesota native educated at Michigan—and the groom—Caribbean born, raised, and educated in the island studio of a master glass artist. Mitch made a stir when he appeared without his customary Rastafarian braids—a promise to his bride, he'd declared to the shocked assembly. She floated up the beach in diaphanous white on her father's arm, and bride and groom said their vows against a pallet of orange, rose, and gold as the sun slipped into the turquoise sea.

Jenna seldom cried at weddings, and she barely knew this couple, but while watching Mitch pledge his undying love to his bride, she teared up nevertheless. Her emotions were a jumble of grief and yearning and acceptance and anticipation.

This was the worst, standing beside Devin in these circumstances. Once she got through tonight it would get better. Maybe not out of sight, out of mind, but out of sight and in Eternity Springs, where broken hearts go to heal.

She couldn't think of a better place for her to be. From now until Christmas at least, she would nurse her broken heart while she doctored the women, her new friends who were in need of her professional services.

Following the ceremony, the guests moved off the beach to the poolside garden and lawn where a buffet dinner was to be served. In the midst of all the people, Jenna was able to relax and enjoy herself. Obviously, friends and family hadn't picked up on the fact that she'd been intimate with Devin, so she need not fear facing those uncomfortable questions. She caught Lori looking at her curiously once or twice. The gaze Sarah leveled upon her son when he was looking at Jenna was downright suspicious. Such things Jenna could withstand. What happened on the *Windsong* had stayed on the *Windsong*—and for that, she was grateful.

It wasn't until Devin smoothly led her off into the garden

at the end of a dance that her tension returned. "How's your ankle doing?"

"It's okay. Devin, we shouldn't leave. They'll be doing the sendoff any time now."

"We won't be long. I just need to speak with you alone, and with the family at the house, I might not have another chance. Jenna, I've been thinking about your idea to stay at Eagle's Way. The more I turn it over, the less I like it. I think we should keep to the original plan. I'll go back to Eternity Springs tomorrow and—"

"No."

"Hear me out. I think that—"

"No! We settled this, Devin."

"But I want you to be safe. I need you to be safe."

"I *will* be safe. You know it's true."

"But I won't be there to see it!" He shoved his fingers through his hair. "Look, I'll be the first to admit that I don't understand what's happening here, Jenna. I have all these questions spinning around in my heart."

His heart? Not his mind?

"Jenna . . ." He took both her hands in his. "Jenna, I need answers, and I'm afraid I'm not going to get them in Queensland."

She closed her eyes against the turmoil his words created inside her. What if she took the risk? What if she believed—

Cam's excited voice interrupted them. "There you are. We've been looking all over for you. Neither one of you is answering your phones."

"What's the emergency?" Devin asked, frustration in his voice.

"No emergency. News. Great news. Jenna, Daniel has been trying to reach you. The FBI in Nashville has your stalker in custody."

"What? Oh, my . . ." She covered her mouth with her hands and swayed as her knees went a little weak. As Devin caught her elbow and steadied her, she asked, "Who is he?"

"He's someone connected to the surgeon," Cam replied. "Daniel has all the details. Devin, why don't you show her to Flynn's office and she can return his call. I'll tell Zach where to find us. I know he's as curious as I am."

"But the sendoff . . . ," Jenna said. "Devin, you need to . . ."

He placed his finger atop her lips. "Mitch won't miss me. And I'm not missing this. C'mon. This way. We can reach it by going around through the garden."

Flynn Brogan's office was more workshop than traditional office space, with gleaming stainless-steel work tables and an array of tools to leave most men of Jenna's acquaintance drooling. Devin escorted her to a chair and as she pulled her phone from her evening bag—silenced for the wedding—he moved a chair close to hers and straddled it.

She drew a deep breath, and then placed the call. Daniel answered on the third ring. "Congratulations, Jenna. You can once again order a pizza without any hesitation."

"Who did this? Why?"

"Is Devin with you?"

"Yes." She glanced toward the door as it opened. "Cam and Zach too. Shall I put you on speaker?"

"Good idea. The Callahans and I are up at Jack's. You're on speaker here. Sounds like we have the whole team together, which is fitting. Jenna, I think the most efficient way to do this is to allow me to summarize first, highlighting the pertinent details. Then I'll take questions. Okay?"

"Of course."

"Your stalker is Jonathan Reid."

Jenna blinked. Her gaze flew to Devin's. The name meant absolutely nothing to her.

"He is sixteen years old. The connection to you comes through Dr. Snelling and the boy's father. Allan Reid had secured financial backing for his medical-device start-up from Snelling, and the deal fell through when Mrs. Snelling filed for divorce. Reid lost his shirt, and the family lost their home. A mention of you during his ranting in the aftermath led to his son's obsession."

"Sixteen," Jenna said. "That means he was fourteen when this started."

"Yes. Thirteen when they lost their house."

Jenna took a moment to digest that information. Stalkers were invariably disturbed individuals, and she'd expected her stalker to be young due to his use of doxxing and swatting. But . . . fourteen?

Daniel turned over the conversation to Mark Callahan, who explained how they'd tracked the boy down. Honestly, her thoughts wandered as he spoke of digital footprints and technologies about which she had no knowledge or interest.

It was over. Reilly was safe.

Reilly was safe.

She came back to the conversation and realized that Mark had concluded his explanation. Zach and Cam were asking questions. Devin was looking at her. She smiled shakily at him. She was having a hard time taking this all in.

"Do you have any questions for us, Jenna?" Jack Davenport asked.

"What's going to happen to him? To Jonathan?"

"That remains to be seen. Unfortunately, Jenna, you are not the only person he has tormented. We turned over evidence of three more victims. He's a troubled young man."

Daniel added, "Something you need not worry about . . . he won't be allowed near a computer for a very long time. And now that his issues are known, he'll get help."

"Good. That's good." Her thoughts drifted off again as she tried to imagine the Reids' reaction to their son's arrest. Then something Daniel said jerked her back to attention. ". . . to apologize for missing Jonathan Reid the first time."

"Whoa. Whoa. Whoa," Jenna interrupted. "Excuse me, Daniel. Please. I've been fighting this for two years. You guys have found him in less than a month. And you did all this . . . went to all this effort . . . just because . . . because . . ."

"You're our friend, Jenna," Jack Davenport said. "We value friends in Eternity Springs. You are part of our family."

The Eternity Springs family.

A knock on the door sounded and Gabi Brogan stuck her head into the room. "Mitch and Elizabeth are about to leave if you all can join us."

Zach nodded. "Thanks, Gabi. I think we're about done here. Last word, anyone?"

"Yes!" Jenna said. "The last word . . . words . . . are mine. Thank you. On behalf of Reilly and myself, from the bottom my heart, thank you. You all have changed our lives, and that is a gift beyond words. So . . . thank you."

Her mind fired in spurts and sizzles just like the sparklers she held a few minutes later, ushering the bride and groom into the car that would carry them to their honeymoon bower. It was over. Over. Over.

The following day at the tiny Bella Vita Isle airport where she watched Devin hug and kiss first his sister and then his mother, the words played a litany through her mind. *It's over. It's over. It's over.*

He shook his father's hand, they pounded each other's shoulders, and then Cam pulled him into his arms for a hug. "Fair winds and following seas, son."

"Thanks, Dad. Love you, too."

Both Lori and Sarah had tears in their eyes when Devin went down on his knee to speak softly to a sobbing Michael for a few moments before hugging him long and hard.

Michael turned to his mother for comfort when Devin rose and finally looked at Jenna.

It's over. It's over. It's over.

"Well, Jenna," he said in a voice that was gruff with emotion. "Tell Reilly I know he's going to love Ms. Jenkins—she's the second-grade teacher."

"I'll do that." She worked to keep her tone light.

It's over. It's over. It's over.

"I . . . um . . ." He tossed his parents a pleading expression.

Sarah took the hint. "Michael, let's pop into the store and buy some snacks for our flight. Cam, here come the Romanos. You should go help them with their luggage."

"Why would I want to do that? Lucca is younger than me."

She hooked an arm through his elbow and dragged him off. Lori shook her head sadly at her older brother, and then turned to follow her parents, saying, "I need to buy a paperback for the flight. A romance. With a happy ending."

Devin muttered a curse. "She's such a smart-ass."

"She loves you. They all love you. You are blessed in your family."

"I know," Devin said, watching them go. "I know. My growing family." Then he turned back to her and said, "I can't tell you how much comfort it gives me to know that you'll be there to watch over them. I trust you'll take good care of my ladies."

"You have my word on it."

"I think this is why it happened . . . the wrong number. I think we were meant to help each other."

Not meant to love each other?

It's over, it's over, it's over.

"I believe you're right."

His lips twisted. "Believe. That reminds me. With all the excitement last night, I didn't get a chance to say good-bye to Celeste. Though knowing her, she's liable to be on my flight in the seat next to me."

"She's flying back with the Brogans. She told me last night. She said she has pictures of a house that is coming onto the market that she wants to show me. One she thinks I should buy.

"Oh, yeah? Are you ready to buy a house in Eternity Springs? Put down permanent roots there?"

"Maybe. We'll see. I told her I might be interested in a rent-to-own scenario. See how Reilly does in school before I commit to a house. If it's the perfect house for us, I'd hate to miss out on it."

"Where is it? In town?"

"On the lake. Next to Boone McBride's house, I believe."

Devin scowled. "Why are we talking about houses? Why are we talking at all?"

He closed his lips over hers, and just for a moment she allowed her senses to steep in the taste of him, in the firm warmth of his masculine form, in the scent of salt and sand and sea that clung to him. For just a moment, Jenna allowed herself to kiss him goodbye.

Then she pulled from his arms and put the first few feet of distance between them. "Thank you for a lovely cruise, Devin Murphy. Safe travels as you continue your journey."

Jenna turned and left him. It was time to take her broken heart home to Eternity Springs.

Chapter Nineteen

LABOR DAY WEEKEND

Boone McBride eyed the half-dozen boxes, each big enough to hold a full-grown St. Bernard, that were lined up in his next-door neighbor's living room. He softly whistled. "Wow. Exactly how do you code the billing for this, Dr. Stockton?"

"Oh, hush. This was a labor of love."

"Appropriate on this Labor Day.

"Hey, we are all about labors today." Jenna fussed with one of the bows, then took a step back and surveyed them with a critical eye. "I think we're good, don't you?"

"Well, little lady," he said in an exaggerated Texas drawl, "I think we're safe from getting them mixed up."

"That was the idea." All the boxes were wrapped in glossy white paper and tied with big red bows. Rather than use tags to indicate which box was intended for which couple, Jenna and Reilly had played Picasso and decorated the paper on each box with permanent markers, drawing not only names but other details to personalize each one. "I loaded one box at a time and we wrapped and decorated it before starting another box. It wouldn't do to mix them up."

"That would not be good," Boone agreed. "So, are you ready for me to start loading them into the Jeep?"

Jenna glanced at the clock. "Yes please. Thanks again for the help, Boone."

"Glad to do it. That's what neighbors are for."

As Boone carried out the first box, Jenna began gathering up the rest of what she'd need for the afternoon. She had sold her extended cab pickup along with the fifth wheel last week, and she had a nifty Jeep in her driveway and a new trailer on order to replace the behemoth they no longer needed to live in.

Boone quickly returned for the second box and then the third. He saw the tote bags she'd filled. "Those going too?"

"Yes, they're the entries we received at the clinic this week and more entry blanks."

His brows arched and then he laughed. "Brick's idea to turn this whole thing into a contest was brilliant."

"Wait until after today. He has his entire family ready to whip out their checkbooks to find out the baby news. Before he's done, Brick will have raised enough money to build an entire new school, much less fund the expansion."

All of Eternity Springs had been invited to the Back-to-School event to celebrate the beginning of the school year. The highlight of the party was to be the update on the school expansion fundraising contest that Brick Callahan had announced at the Fourth of July party and subsequently dubbed the "Maternity Springs" contest. The update consisted of a gender reveal moment for each expectant family.

Two of the couples had elected to receive their happy news in private. Three wanted to share their big moment with family and friends. Cam and Sarah were being old-fashioned about the news.

"A gender-reveal party?" Cam had repeated in a voice laced with disgust when Sarah had shared the idea with him during their last prenatal appointment. "No. That's not natural. That's a personal, private moment meant to happen when we take our first good gander at the squiggling little rat and see what sort of equipment he's got."

"I'm not giving birth to a squiggling little rat." Sarah's lips had twitched with amusement. "Gender-reveal parties have become quite popular the past few years."

"Yeah, well, so has kale. I rest my case."

Despite his traditional views, Cam had been amenable to the idea of participating in the Labor Day fundraising event. Today, they'd be opening a box filled with yellow and green balloons. Lori was going to be disappointed. She was almost as excited to find out whether her baby was expecting an aunt or an uncle as she was to learn the sex of her own child.

The past month had been a busy one for Jenna. She'd loved the house Celeste had shown her upon her return from Bella Vita, and she'd negotiated a six-month lease with an option to buy. Her license to practice medicine in Colorado was approved the first week of August and she'd begun seeing patients immediately. The joy she found in the process revealed the truth that she'd hidden from herself during their months on the road—she loved her work, loved her profession, and she'd missed it rather desperately.

She'd also missed Reilly rather desperately, but the healthy, joyful boy she'd visited at the Rocking L to share news of their stalker's apprehension had made every lonely moment worth it. Eternity Springs had certainly worked its magic on her son.

She was still waiting for that healing magic for herself.

She missed Devin. He'd cut a big jagged hole in her heart when he'd returned to Australia, and it wasn't going to heal overnight. Maybe now that Reilly was home from camp and her loneliness not so acute, the intensity of the ache would soon begin to dull.

Reilly burst into the room from the backyard, Sinatra close on his heels. Both dog and boy raced in mad circles

around the remaining boxes. The two were all but insepa-
rable. Jenna wondered how both of them would manage
the stretch of separation necessitated by the school day.

"Is it time to go yet, Mom?"

"Almost. We're loading up. Why don't you make sure
Sinatra has plenty of water and put up the doggie gate?"

"Can't I take him with me? I'll watch him really close
and keep him on his leash and he'll behave. I know he will.
Besides, we'll be in the park."

"No, my love. You're doing very well with his training,
but there will be too many people in the park today. He'll
be happier here."

"But Mo-om!" he whined.

She gave him her stern mother look. "Tend your dog."

Ten minutes later, she and Reilly pulled out of their
driveway and followed Boone's truck. The park was already crowded upon their arrival. The Chamber of Commerce had been set up accepting entries and donations for
the contest since mid-morning. Brick and the other fathers-
to-be were out working the crowd. "This is kinda fun, isn't
it, Mom?" Reilly observed.

"It is."

"Michael is really excited. He hopes he's going to get a
brother and a nephew." He looked at her closely then sighed
heavily. "You never give away anything, Mom."

She laughed, shifted the Jeep into park, and then
reached into her tote for her wallet. She pulled out a twenty.
"Here, go make a donation and a guess."

"Blue or pink?"

"Your guess."

He scrambled out of the Jeep and took off. Approaching the Jeep with Zach and Savannah Turner's box in his
arms, Boone asked, "Does he ever slow down?"

Jenna lifted Cam and Sarah's box from her back seat,

then smiled warmly up at Boone and laughed. "Only when he's sound asleep."

At that moment, Reilly let out a loud squeal. Alarmed, Jenna turned toward the sound—and went numb. The box slipped from her fingers and fell to the ground. Unprepared, Boone stepped right into the middle of it.

A yellow balloon bulged from the hole his foot made.

"Seriously?" Devin said, his arms full of Reilly. "I come all this way for the big surprise, and get yellow?"

All that yellow and Devin was seeing red.

He was jet-lagged, exhausted, feeling light in the pocketbook after purchasing the last-minute ticket, and hungry. For Jenna. And thirsty. For Jenna.

And she shows up all sunny and grinny with Mr. Next-Door-Neighbor. Devin grumbled, "I need a beer."

His big surprise was looking like a great big mistake.

All flustered, Jenna had barely glanced at him as she fussed over repairing his parents' box before the cat climbed any further out of the bag, so to speak. After that, the hoards spotted her and her boxes and descended, and Devin had no chance for any sort of private conversation with her at all.

His decision to travel to Eternity Springs for the big baby-reveal extravaganza had come after a phone call with his sister during which she'd expressed her deep regret that he wouldn't be there in person to share the big moment. Then he'd called home to talk to his folks and Michael at a time when his brother's BFF was over to play.

Talking with Reilly about his time at camp and hearing his enthusiasm for life in general had made Devin feel like a million dollars. Neutralizing the threat that had been Jonathan Reid had made a significant difference in Reilly's life. While Devin had been busy patting himself on the back, the boy began talking about his mom and their new house and new neighbor. Devin learned that McBride got out and threw a football with Reilly almost every afternoon. Before Devin quite knew how it had happened, he'd been on an airplane back to the States.

He watched the box-opening spectacle with sincere interest. Brick made the whole process entertaining. The Garretts had a boy on the way, as did the Turners. A bouquet of pink balloons sailed out of the Brogans' box. It was too fun to watch his parents' reaction to the news that they had a granddaughter on the way. And Lori . . . well . . . she beamed and got teary-eyed, and if Chase smiled any wider he'd have broken his jaw. *A niece. I'm going to have a niece.*

When the family swept him into the circle for a group hug, he was truly glad he had made the trip.

The final reveal of the afternoon was Brick and Lili's box. Showman and fundraiser that he was, he whipped his family into a frenzy of last-minute check writing before opening the box. Blue balloons sailed out . . . and so did pink.

"Very funny." Brick cast Jenna an annoyed glance. Despite all his campaigning, it was obvious he was ready to find out if his child was a boy or a girl. "Now where's our real box?"

But beside him, Lili started to giggle. "This *is* our real box. Use your brain, Callahan."

It took him about ten seconds, but then the color drained from his face. Frantically, he grasped his wife's hand.

Brick's father Mark fist-bumped his twin brother, Luke, and said, "I knew it. I just knew they were having twins."

For the next hour, Devin watched and waited for his chance to talk to Jenna. That chance never came.

The woman was avoiding him. Oh, she spoke to him.

Then he put his arm around her shoulder and escorted her toward the ring of spectators before joining the participants on the field of play: Brick Callahan, Josh Tarkington, Zach Turner, Lucca Romano, Gabe Callahan, Daniel Garrett, Chase Timberlake, Flynn Brogan, and . . .

Devin Murphy.

Chapter Twenty

"Who starts a fight at a cakewalk?" Jenna demanded before slamming her front door in his face.

Devin wasn't about to let that stop him. He opened the door and stepped inside, then followed her to the great room where she paced like a caged lioness. He glanced around. According to what he'd gleaned from the Internet, Jenna's house was a four-bedroom, three-bath, six-year-old log cabin built as a second home for an architect out of New Mexico. "Nice digs."

She whirled to face him. "You smashed Maggie's cake!"

"Yeah," Devin grimaced, then wished he hadn't. The movement hurt his swollen eye. "That was unfortunate. But since I was the winner, the only person I hurt was myself. Besides, I scored pinwheels."

"You broke Boone's nose!"

"Well, he deserved that. He put his mouth on my woman."

Jenna sucked in a breath, and then narrowed her eyes. "Your woman?" She took three steps toward him then punched him in the chest with her index finger. "Your woman! Did you just say 'your woman'?"

His mouth quirked. "Yeah."

"You arrogant, conceited, loathsome"—eyes flashing fire, she shouted—"cake killer!"

Cake killer? Good one.

"Why are you here? No, it doesn't matter. I don't care. I'm getting over you. I want you to leave."

"Not until we talk. I've allowed you to avoid talking to me for the past two months and that was a huge mistake."

"Allowed? You didn't *allow* me to do anything, Devin Murphy. What do they have in the water in Cairns that has turned you into a troglodyte? Haven't you heard? Alpha males are politically incorrect." She put her palms against his chest and shoved him hard.

"Let's keep politics out of it. This is romance."

"Romance! This is not romance. This is . . . this is . . ."

"Love. This is love, Jenna."

She went still. He took her by the shoulders and held her, his grip firm. He met her gaze with a steady one of his own. "You turned my life upside down and you have brought me to my knees. I love you, Jenna. I can't live without you. I want you to marry me. Please marry me."

Speechless, she stared up at him, her wide gray-blue eyes shimmering with tears.

"I can give you and Reilly a good life. The business is doing great. One of the reasons it took me two months to get here is that I have a deal cooking with a group of investors that will set us up to make great things happen."

"You want us to move to Australia with you?" she asked.

"I do. Not before the babies are born, of course, but after Christmas. I've looked into it. We'll have some hoops to jump through, but you'll be able to practice medicine. I want to give the ocean to Reilly like Cam did to me. I want to give him brothers and sisters."

"Plural?" she squeaked.

"I'd like at least three, but it's negotiable. Say yes, Jenna. I know you're crazy about me."

"Somebody's crazy," she muttered, not yet willing to relent.

Devin decided to tease her a little more. "This thing you have with Boone was just an effort to get over me. Maybe in time, it would have worked, but I wasn't stupid enough to give you time, and despite Big Tex's taunting kiss, I know I'm not too late. Reilly told me he doesn't sleep over."

"You did not ask him that!" She slapped his shoulder.

"No. I didn't." Devin grinned and took her back into his arms. "I didn't have to ask because I know you love me too."

"You are so conceited."

"I am so in love with you. Head over heels, until death do us part, in love. Marry me, Jenna. Say yes. Repeat after me, 'Yes, Santa.'"

"Santa?" Her lips curved.

"You didn't think this was plain old Devin Murphy who just proposed marriage, did you? I'm Santa Claus, and it's my business to make wishes come true." He slipped his arms around her and pulled her against him. Gazing intently into her yes, he kissed her once lightly. "Believe, Jenna." He kissed her again. "Believe in me." He kissed her a third time. "Believe in us."

She hitched in a breath and licked her lips. "Yes. Yes. I'll marry you."

He gave a murmur of triumph as he closed his mouth over hers. The homecoming of the taste of her soothed away all the aches in his body and soul. "I've missed you. Oh, woman, how I have missed you. Where's Reilly?"

"A sleepover."

He drew back, and a smile of pure delight spread across his face. "I love the boy like my own, but damn, do I have timing or what? Which way is your bedroom?"

He lifted her into his arms and carried her from the room whistling "I Saw Mommy Kissing Santa Claus."

Jenna had stars in her eyes the following morning when she woke snuggled in Devin's arms. A glance at the clock showed she'd slept half an hour later than her usual six a.m. wake-up time after sleeping very little during the long, delicious hours of the night. Now, she'd better get her sated little self in the shower and dressed because Reilly would be home before she knew it.

Ten minutes later she stood at the stove frying bacon and reliving moments of the previous night. In the middle of the night in the darkness of her bedroom, he had painted her a picture of Australia, of Queensland and Cairns and the Great Barrier Reef, so vivid that she'd all but seen the images on her ceiling. They spoke at length about his charter operation and the opportunities that had come his way in the past few weeks. His excitement was infective.

"The boats make the *Windsong* look like the S.S. *Minnow*—after it wrecked on Gilligan's Island," he'd told her around two in the morning. "We'll have personal use of one of them too. I'll take you to Tahiti and Bora Bora . . . all over the South Seas. And we have more than five hundred national parks in Australia. Reilly is going to love it."

Jenna hoped so. Reilly was the only real reservation she had. He had sunk his roots quickly in Colorado. How would he feel about picking up and moving? He wouldn't be happy about leaving Eternity Springs, but he would be getting his number-one wish in the deal—a dad. He would adjust, wouldn't he?

Hands came around her waist and lips nuzzled her neck. "Mmm. Bacon." Devin nipped her neck.

"Are you calling me a pig, Devin Murphy?" Jenna asked as a thrill ran down her spine.

"I was talking about breakfast, but now that you bring

it up your sexual demands last night might be considered excessive."

"They might be, hmm?"

"Have I mentioned how much I love bacon? Any chance I can get some scrambled eggs to go with it?"

"You'll find a carton of eggs in the fridge. Get to crackin'." When he leaned over to peer into the fridge, she swatted him on the butt with a wooden spoon, and then laughed when he shot her a narrowed-eye scowl. She'd have laughed at just about anything at that moment. She couldn't recall the last time she'd been so happy.

She started humming a certain Christmas song along to the sizzle and spit of the bacon. He cracked eggs and sweet-talked her into making biscuits.

"It's amazing how taking care of one hunger can work up another," he observed just as an unfamiliar ringtone sounded from her bedroom. "That's work. It's midnight at home. Wonder what this is about?"

"Take your time."

She had just put a sheet of biscuits in the oven when Reilly opened the front door. "Hey, Mom. How is Sinatra? Did he do okay without me?"

"He did great. I put him outside a few minutes ago and he's probably ready to come in. How was the sleepover?"

"It was sooooo much fun." He went to the back door and called his dog. A few moments later he was sitting on the floor playing with the puppy as he rattled on about the movies they'd watched and popcorn fights and on and on. When he finally ran down, Jenna decided the time had come to broach the subject uppermost in her mind.

She rinsed her hands and wiped them on a dishtowel, then said, "Hey, hot rod. I need to talk to you about something."

"Uh-oh." Warily, he looked up at her. "That's never good."

"No . . . this is good. *Really* good. Reilly, remember when you made the first phone call to Santa a couple years ago? Do you remember what you asked him for?"

"Well . . . yeah. I told you about that. I asked him for a dad."

"Well, this is my really great news. Reilly, Devin asked if he could be your dad. He asked me to marry him."

Reilly put his puppy aside and went up on his knees. Hope filled his voice. "Devin? Devin is going to be my dad? I love Devin! This is the best news ever!"

He pushed Sinatra off his lap and leapt to his feet and threw himself against his mother for a hug. "Michael's brother is going to be my dad! So does that make me and Michael brothers? Oh, no." Reilly pulled away and looked wide-eyed up toward his mother. "He won't be my uncle, will he, like with Dr. Lori's baby? He's real obnoxious about being an uncle."

Jenna laughed. "I'll have to look into it to see what the relationship will be. I wouldn't worry about it though, Reilly."

"Okay. Oh, I'm so excited. I wanted a dad more than anything, even more than I wanted Sinatra."

"I know."

"When is Devin coming home to live in Eternity Springs? Will you have a wedding? Do I have to wear a tie?"

"Yes, we will have a wedding and yes, you'll have to wear a tie. And no, Devin is not moving back to Eternity Springs." Jenna drew in a bracing breath, sent up a quick, silent prayer, and explained. "Devin has asked us to join him in Australia."

It took a moment, but the light in Reilly's eyes died. "You mean . . . like . . . move there?"

"Yes." Jenna told him about the five hundred national parks and the rain forest and the Great Barrier Reef. She told him that Devin loved him and loved her and wanted them to be a family. "He says his dad—Michael's dad—gave him the ocean, and he wants to give that to you too. It's his favorite place in the world and he wants to share it with you."

In a little voice, Reilly said, "But I like Eternity Springs. I don't want to leave."

"We've only been here a few months. Not nearly as long as we spent in Nashville or Tallahassee."

"I didn't make friends there. I have a lot of friends here."

"I thought you wanted a dad."

"I do. I really do. I love Devin. But why do we have to move to Australia? This is the best place in the whole world! I get to be a camel in the Christmas pageant and Ms. Gabi is going to teach me how to make a glass ornament for our Christmas tree."

Jenna's teeth tugged at her bottom lip. She'd figured he wouldn't be thrilled about moving, but obviously this wasn't going to be as easy as she'd hoped. "We won't move before Christmas, honey. It'll be sometime after the first of the year."

"I don't want to move to Australia ever! Why can't Devin move to Eternity Springs and stay here with us?"

"He can't do his job here."

"Why not? Other dads have jobs here. *His* dad has a job here. Devin could work with Cam."

"It doesn't work that way, Reilly. Look, I'm sure you'll love it there. Devin will make sure of it. You'll make new friends and the three of us will have new adventures. You just need to give him and Australia a chance."

"I don't want to! I want to stay here."

"We'll come back to visit."

"I don't want to visit. I want to live here! I hate jobs! A dad was supposed to make things easier because of you working all the time. Not make everything worse! I hate

Australia! I'll be scared there. I'm never scared here! Everybody knows me here and they're not going to break my arm or point a gun at me. You go without me, Mom. You're not my real mom, anyway. You can unadopt me. I'll find another mom."

Tears streaming down his face, Reilly whirled around and dashed for the back door, failing to wait even long enough for Sinatra to catch up with him.

Jenna groaned and muttered, "That went well."

Hearing a sound behind her, she turned to see Devin standing in the great room just beyond the kitchen door. By the stricken expression on his face, it was obvious that he'd heard everything.

Jenna went to him and wrapped her arms around him. "It's okay. He'll come around."

"Hearing that ripped out my heart."

"I know." She closed her eyes and heard the echo of his hurt little voice saying, "Unadopt me." Tears flooded her eyes. Here she'd thought he'd healed. Guess she'd gotten ahead of herself.

"I can't do that to him, Jenna. He's been through so much. I can't put him through more traumas. I won't be able to live with myself."

"We'll find a way to make it work."

"How? I can't make a living in Eternity Springs. If I tried to work for Dad again, we'd be at loggerheads and it would ruin our relationship. My higher education took place aboard a boat. It's all I ever wanted. All I know."

He closed his eyes and rested his forehead against hers. "I've considered it, you know. When I learned about these babies coming and knowing I wouldn't be part of their lives, I considered my options. Family does matter. It matters a lot. That's one reason why this new deal matters so much. The deal gives me the financial resources to come home when I want. Let me tell you, three flights since June has made my credit card bill a thing of horror."

The timer went off. They stepped apart, and Jenna moved to take the biscuits out of the oven. She tossed the hot pads down onto the counter, closed her eyes, and rubbed her temples. "I suspect what we saw a few minutes ago is simply a case of too much change in too short a time. Reilly probably needs to talk to a counselor too. I wanted to do that last summer, but moving around the way we did didn't make it feasible."

"Moving around the way you did," Devin repeated. "See, that's what makes this so bad. I knew he liked it here, but I didn't realize he'd fallen under the Eternity Springs spell. Dammit, Jenna, I wouldn't have . . ."

She folded her arms and faced him. "You wouldn't have what? Fallen in love with me? Risked your heart on me?"

"Taken so long to figure it out."

"Long? We've only known each other four months."

He shook his head. "I fell in love with you long before I spotted you on the Hummingbird Lake fishing pier. I knew from our very first phone call, Jenna."

"That's sweet, but silly. You don't fall in love with a stranger during a phone call."

"Don't be betting against the Eternity Springs mojo."

"I'm not going to. That's why I'm sure we will find a way to make this work. Listen, Devin, you and I can be sensitive to Reilly's needs—we should be—but we should be fair to ourselves too. Families make sacrifices for one another. That's what families do."

"But he's just a boy and he's already been through so much."

"I know. And if he was truly in danger like before, that would one thing, but this situation is different. Families all over the country—all over the world—face this same problem every day. Sometimes, kids have to move for their parents' job. That's life. Children have to learn that the world doesn't revolve around them. Otherwise they grow up to be selfish and self-centered and narcissistic, and I want better than that for my son."

Devin took Jenna into his arms. "Reilly isn't selfish, he's scared."

"Yes, but those fears are not based in reality. Not this time. Moving him to Australia will not put him into danger. I wouldn't do it if it would. But I also won't let my eight-year-old son dictate my life. I love you. I'm not going to walk away from that. We will give Reilly some time, but he will just have to learn to deal. You asked me to marry you. I'm not letting you take it back. You're stuck with me, Devin. We will find a way to make this work."

He pressed his lips to her forehead. "I'll make him happy. I'll make you happy. I swear."

"I believe you, Devin. I believe in us, in the family we will form."

"Okay. I trust you. I believe in us too. The bad news is . . . that phone call . . . there was a fire at the marina office. This wasn't a hurricane that sank my boats, but my paperwork is a mess. I have the meeting with the investors next week. I'm going to have to recreate a lot of records. I have to go back."

"Oh, Devin, no. When? When do you have to leave?"

"Right away. I've already called the airlines, and connections are gonna be a bear." He glanced toward the back door. "I want to talk to him, but what can I say in a couple of minutes? I'm afraid I'll only make things worse. Dammit, Jenna. I don't know how I went from such great timing yesterday to such sucky timing today. I don't want to leave here, not like this, but everything I own is tied up . . ."

She rested her index finger against his lips. "You'll be back for Christmas, right? After the babies are born?"

"Yes."

"Then go take care of business, Devin. Reilly and I will be waiting here for you when you return."

"I wish . . ."

"I know. Me too."

"I'll call you from the airport. From all of them. I'll call you every day." He kissed her once, hard and quick. "Why are we always saying goodbye?"

He'd just shifted into reverse to back out of Jenna's drive when she ran out of the house with a paper bag in her hand. He rolled down the window. She shoved the bag at him. "Breakfast. And not goodbye. Never goodbye. I'll see you at Christmas, Santa. Don't forget to believe."

Chapter Twenty-One

Elsewhere in the country the day after Thanksgiving was known as Black Friday. In Eternity Springs, things were different. Here the day was known as Deck the Halls Friday, and everyone turned out to dress up the town for the holiday season. As always, spirits were high, the cinnamon-spiced cider was hot, and by noon, wreathes decorated doorways, garland graced lampposts, and thousands of twinkling white lights set the scene. Citizens pitched in to decorate the town's official tree in Davenport Park, and once the mayor and honorary Deck the Halls chairwoman Celeste Blessing placed the angel atop the tree, they dispersed to trim their family trees and put up their personal holiday decorations.

At Angel's Rest Healing Center and Spa, Celeste and her helpers had been busy little elves. When Reilly and Jenna arrived for their three o'clock appointment, she had the old Victorian mansion that served as the headquarters of the resort glistening and twinkling and glittering in silver and gold. Angels sat on every nook and cranny and post and beam throughout the house.

"Everything looks beautiful," Jenna told her as Celeste descended the staircase carrying a large canvas tote.

"Thank you. I so enjoy decorating for the holidays."

Celeste lifted a down-filled white coat from a hall tree near the front door and asked, "Where is Reilly?"

"He's outside with Sinatra."

"The boy does love his dog, doesn't he?" she observed, slipping into her coat.

"Yes." It was the one thing Jenna could count on where Reilly was concerned these days.

This past month with Reilly had been a challenge, to say the least. The first week after Devin returned to Australia, Reilly would hardly talk to her. The second, he spoke with her, but pretended their conversation about Devin had never happened. She'd gotten him in to see a counselor in Gunnison that week, but she knew better than to expect too much too soon on that front. Trust in counseling relationships took time to build. During the last two weeks, she'd begun to hope that they'd made some progress. Her son hadn't bolted from the room every time she'd brought up the subject of their future.

Devin had called daily. They'd decided to keep news of their engagement to themselves until he returned at Christmas. His family had been curious about his unexpected brief trip home, but when he'd asked them for patience, they'd given it to him. With their due dates fast approaching, the Timberlakes and the Murphys both had babies uppermost on their minds.

"I'm so glad you invited me to join you this afternoon, Jenna," Celeste said. "It warms my heart to know that you and Reilly have chosen to adopt my family's Christmas wishing tree tradition."

"It's a lovely tradition. I'm grateful and honored that you shared it with us."

When they stepped out onto the front porch of Cavanaugh House, the sound of Reilly's unbridled laughter reached Jenna's ears. She watched her son and his dog play together in the snow and a sense of peace washed through her.

Everything would turn out okay. She knew that. After all, hadn't that been her wishing tree wish?

Jenna picked up the backpack she'd left on the porch swing upon arriving at Angel's Rest and slipped her arms through the straps.

"The sun has come out," Celeste observed as they started down the front steps. "Isn't this lovely? We had just enough snow to freshen everything up. I do love sparkle and glisten."

Celeste had a treat in her pocket for Sinatra, and the puppy wiggled and yipped with delight upon seeing the biscuit. As they hiked toward the forest, she chatted with Reilly about school as Sinatra raced in mad circles around them. Then as they entered the hushed cathedral of the forest, even the pup quieted and fell into step at Reilly's feet.

They'd hiked for about ten minutes when Celeste abruptly stopped. "I think we've found it. That looks like a perfect Christmas wishing tree."

In front of them stood a majestic blue spruce about twelve feet tall. Frosted with snow, heavy with pinecones, and with a beautiful shape.

"It's close to last year's tree," Reilly said. "It's right over there. See it? I can see it." He pointed toward a spot some twenty feet away where an angel remained standing at the top of the tree. "They can be wishing tree friends."

"I like the sound of that. So, let's get to work, shall we?" Celeste set down her tote and began pulling out an amazing number of trimmings for the size of her bag. For the next ten minutes she, Jenna, and Reilly draped garland and hung ornaments upon its branches. When the tote bag was finally empty, Celeste used a folding extension tool to place a simple straw angel atop the tree.

"There. We're all done but for the final touch." She reached into her coat pocket, and as she withdrew one last ornament a small gold velvet bag fell into the snow.

"You dropped something," Reilly said, diving for it.

Celeste hung an intricate woodcarving of a snowflake on her tree, then smiled down at Reilly as she accepted the bag. "Thank you, Reilly. I would have hated to lose this."

Then with quiet ceremony, Celeste hung the snowflake on a branch. The trio stepped back and observed the tree. Following a few moments of reflection, Jenna observed, "It's simple and lovely."

"Yes, isn't it?"

"I like your tree, Ms. Celeste," Reilly said. "Whose are we doing next, Mom? Yours or mine?"

"You pick."

"Let's do yours. We'll save the best for last."

"Okay. But I want you to help me pick out the perfect tree."

"I can do that."

"We'll follow you."

The path the boy led them along took them past Celeste's wishing tree from last year. Jenna was surprised to discover that the tree's decorations appeared unharmed by a year's worth of wind and rain and snow and squirrels. She spied only one bit of damage.

Reilly saw it too. "Oh no. The angel you hung last year has a broken wing."

"No problem," Celeste said in a chipper tone. "I have a few more wrinkles and creases this year, myself. But she's hanging in there, isn't she?"

"What if she'd disappeared? What if a bear knocked her out of the tree and stomped on her? Would your wish be ruined?"

"Oh, Reilly." Celeste gave him a quick hug. "Don't forget that she's only a symbol, just as the wishing tree itself is symbolic. Don't forget that what matters is what was in my heart when I hung her on that branch."

The boy continued to look at the broken angel for a long

moment. "What is in your heart matters most of all. I remember." Glancing up at his mother, he said, "I remember there's a pretty tree next to the wishing tree I chose last year. You might like it."

"Why don't you show me?"

"It's this way. I remember." Reilly headed off through the forest with Sinatra, as always, at his heels.

"How does he know where we are?" Jenna wondered aloud. "We've wandered a lot of different woods in the past year."

Celeste slipped her arm through Jenna's. "It's amazing what our young ones recall when it comes to everything Christmas."

That much was true. A few minutes later, he stopped in front of a Douglas fir just a little bit taller than Jenna. "What do you think, Mom? Do you like it?"

"It's perfect." Jenna slipped off her backpack and started unloading decorations. Yesterday after sharing a Thanksgiving meal up at Heartache Falls with the Timberlakes and Murphys, she and her son had passed a pleasant hour creating their wishing tree ornament. Reilly had made a snowman from pinecones and twigs.

Jenna would have loved to know what the snowman symbolized for her son, but she remembered the rules. Ms. Celeste said it works better if you keep you wishes in your heart.

Personally, Jenna was wearing her wishes on her sleeve these days. She'd carved a whole, healthy wooden heart from a piece of firewood she'd filched from the Murphys' woodpile, decorated it with sparkling gravel gathered from the banks of Angel Creek, and tied a leather band around it that roughly—very roughly—symbolized eyeglasses.

Reilly had looked at the ornament and then at her with an expression that said, *Really, Mom?* but he didn't comment. He knew the rules too.

With her tree trimmed, Jenna carefully unwrapped her heart from its protective tissue paper. She hung it on the tree, and then looked at Celeste. "Because I choose to live my vision, not my circumstance."

Celeste's answering smile warmed Jenna from the inside out. "And for that, I have a little something for you to carry with you wherever you go. It's a bit easier to carry around than a snow globe."

Jenna opened the bag and removed a delicate angel's wing pendant on a chain. She knew what this was. She'd seen her friends wearing it. Her eyes flooded with sudden tears. "It's the Angel's Rest blazon."

"That it is. Awarded to those who have accepted love's healing grace."

"It's beautiful, Celeste. Thank you. But . . ." Something else remained in the small gold bag. Jenna looked again. "Two more?"

"Live in your vision, not your circumstance." Celeste looped her arm through Jenna's and spoke to Reilly. "I think it's time to decorate your Christmas wishing tree now, don't you?"

"Sure! I have one all picked out. It's right this way."

Jenna scooped up the backpack and followed her son through the woods to a spot along the forest's edge. "What do you think, Mom?

He'd stopped in front of what could best be described as a Charlie Brown Christmas tree. Its trunk was bent but unbroken, and the branches sparse. It grew from the midst of a rocky section of land that offered little soil for roots. Despite the less than ideal circumstances, the tree survived.

Just like Reilly survived. Survived, ready to thrive.

Tears flooded Jenna's eyes. Her voice sounded a little shaky as she said, "I think it's the perfect tree."

"You couldn't have found a better choice!" Celeste agreed.

Reilly took off his own backpack, and as he began to pull out the decorations he'd assembled, Celeste snapped her fingers. "Oh, posh. Do you know what I did? I left my mittens back at my wishing tree. Reilly, do you mind getting started without me while I run back to get them?"

"That's okay."

Jenna looked down at the abundance of trimmings he'd set out. She couldn't for the life of her imagine how they'd all fit on that little tree. "Where do you want me to start, hot rod?"

"You can wrap the ribbon around it."

After much debate on what constituted "natural" as far as tree trimmings went, they'd decided that one hundred percent cotton ribbon counted. Jenna had made one loop around the tree with the red ribbon when Riley threw her a curve ball. "I don't believe in Santa anymore."

The ribbon spool slipped from her hand and landed in the snow. Her heart twisted. He was eight years old. She'd expected this subject might come up this Christmas, but she wasn't ready! "I don't know . . . um . . ."

"It's okay. You don't have to pretend. I know that you're the one who buys the Santa presents and puts them under the tree. I know you fill my stocking. Santa doesn't come down the chimney, and he doesn't answer the telephone when somebody calls North-Pole-One."

Jenna started to reach for him, but his body language shouted, *Stay away*.

"Oh, Reilly." Jenna scooped the ribbon spool up off the ground and tried to recall all the parenting advice she'd read on this subject as she made another loop. "It's true that I'm the person who puts Santa gifts under the tree, but that doesn't make me Santa. It also doesn't mean that Santa doesn't exist. Santa does a really important job because he teaches children a really important lesson. He teaches them how to have faith in something that they can't see or touch. He teaches them to believe, and that is something important to have as you grow up."

"I know."

"You do?"

"Uh-huh. It's like the Christmas wishing tree. Santa is a symbol. The real magic of Christmas isn't wishes or reindeer. The real magic of Christmas is . . . are you about done with the ribbon? I'm ready to hang my special ornament."

Jenna gave her head a little shake, glanced at the pile of decorations on the ground, and saw that while she'd been occupied with one of the traumas of parenthood, her son had decorated his tree. "Okay. Sorry."

She made one final circuit, then stepped back and surveyed the tree. Darned if he hadn't balanced his decorations in such a way that the crooked little Charlie Brown tree stood a little straighter.

Reilly reached into his backpack, but the ornament he hung on the tree was not the pinecone snowman he'd made the previous day, but a little wooden boat.

"Reilly?"

"Don't ask, Mom. You know the rules."

"Okay. I won't. Only . . . finish what you were going to say. What's the real magic of Christmas?"

"Geez, Mom. Don't you know anything? It's love. The real magic of Christmas is love."

After his father mentioned the upcoming sleigh ride during one of their calls, Devin planned his surprise with the precision of a battlefield general and kept knowledge of it strictly need-to-know.

It was the first Saturday in December and "any time

now" was the phrase of the week. In a half-dozen houses across the small mountain town, mothers-to-be couldn't sleep—their backs hurt, and they had heartburn, swollen feet, and moods that swung from rage to tears to joy to despair on the basis of . . . well, anything. These were a half-dozen women who wanted to not be pregnant NOW.

And a half-dozen fathers-to-be who dearly loved their wives but whose nerves were frayed to the point of breaking. Something had to give.

Enter, Santa Claus.

The first salvo was a mano-a-mano confab to be held over cookies and milk at Fresh. Cam delivered the goods shortly after the bakery closed at noon. "Where's Michael, Mr. Murphy?" Reilly said when he spied the table set for two. "I thought he was going to be here."

"Well, I tricked you, Reilly. I said *my son* is waiting for you."

"He meant me," Devin said, stepping into the room.

Reilly folded his arms and frowned at Devin.

"Good luck," Cam said as he tipped an imaginary hat and left the room.

Now that the moment was upon him, Devin was a little nervous. "Would you sit down and share some cookies and milk with me?"

It appeared to be touch and go for a moment, but eventually, Reilly shuffled over to the table and took a seat. He didn't touch his snack.

Devin forged ahead. "Before we dive into this, I need to say something flat out so that there is no ambiguity. I love you, Reilly. I love your mother. I want us to be a family. I want to be your dad and to be your mother's husband. That's the bottom line."

Reilly dipped his head, but not before Devin caught the sheen of sudden tears in his eyes. Was that a hopeful sign or a problem? He wasn't sure.

So he hurried on. "Everything else is open for negotiation. That's why I invited you here today. I have a proposal to make, man to man."

"Aren't you supposed to propose to my mom?"

"I did. Sort of. I have plans to make an official, more flashy one later today if you and I can come to an agreement here." Devin pushed the plate of strawberry pinwheels closer to Reilly.

Reilly picked up a cookie and took a bite.

That was something, anyway. At least he hadn't thrown it at him. Yet.

Devin breathed just a little easier and launched his argument. "I can't go back in time and change my decision to make my living from the sea. Now, because I'm shooting straight with you, I probably should mention that I'm not sure I would change it if I could time travel. You see, Reilly, I love what I do. The ocean is part of me. It's such a fascinating, amazing place, and every day offers something new. It's exciting. Going out on the ocean, diving and snorkeling and fishing, it's like visiting a new world every single day. I truly believe you will love it, Reilly. I think you'll love the ocean as much as you love national parks, and maybe even more. I want to share it with you and your mother."

"Australia is really far away from Eternity Springs," Reilly pointed out in a small voice.

"Yes, it is. It truly is." Devin paused and took a sip of milk. "I recognized that the distance between Australia and Eternity Springs was one of the main problems facing us, so I set my mind to finding a solution. That brings us to my proposal."

He picked a notebook off the seat of the chair beside them and set it in front of Reilly. It was a three-ring binder with a leather cover. Embossed across the front of the journal were the words REILLY JAMES MURPHY'S CARIBBEAN ADVENTURE.

"I can't move to Eternity Springs, Reilly, but I can move my business back to Bella Vita Isle. It's a whole lot closer than Australia. When I used to live in Bella Vita, I visited Eternity Springs all the time. Michael and my parents used to visit me a lot too. The Brogans have a home there and so do the Ciceros. People are always going back and forth between Bella Vita and Eternity Springs."

"This says Reilly James Murphy. Not Reilly James Stockton."

"Well, yes. When I marry your mom, I would like to adopt you. I want very much for you to be my son and carry my name."

"Michael and I would be like brothers."

"Almost."

Reilly ate the rest of his cookie and took a drink of milk. He opened the notebook and began flipping through the pages behind tabs that read ANIMALS OF BELLA VITA and CARIBBEAN SEA MARINE LIFE and PIRATES OF THE CARIBBEAN. Reilly paused at an illustration of Blackbeard's frigate, *Queen Anne's Revenge*, flying the skull and crossbones. "Pirates?"

Devin nodded sagely. "It's not just a ride at Disney."

"Cool!"

"I think we could make it work, Reilly. If you'll give me your permission to marry your mother and become your dad, I'll give you my solemn oath that you'll get to spend plenty of time in Eternity Springs each year."

"And Michael can come visit us?"

"Of course."

"He'll probably want to get away from the babies. Especially if they're both girls."

"Hey, we Murphy men will have to stick together."

Then, with his heart in his throat, laying it all on the line, Devin extended his hand. "So, Reilly James Stockton, do we have a deal?"

Reilly stared at Devin's hand. "Two years ago, I asked Santa to bring me a dad."

"I know. Merry Christmas, Reilly."

The boy took his hand. "Merry Christmas . . . Dad.

Devin's heart took flight.

The twenty-minute sleigh ride up to a high meadow on Murphy Mountain meadow proved to be just the medicine her patients had needed, Jenna decided as Cam reined in the horses and the sleigh glided to a stop. To a woman, each expectant mother was more relaxed upon arrival than they'd been at the beginning of the ride. Nothing like shared misery and commiseration to ease one's burden.

The fathers-to-be had traveled ahead by other means, primarily snowmobiles, and the women arrived at the meadow to find a bonfire burning brightly. Playing with both speed and fire had mellowed the men's moods too, so everyone was relaxed and happy as hot chocolate and warm apple cider was passed around.

"It's a pretty day, isn't it, Mom?" Reilly asked her.

"It is. Did you enjoy your snowmobile ride with Mr. Chase?"

"It was *so* much fun. Michael and I wanted to go faster but he said maybe next time, because Dr. Lori made him promise six ways to Sunday not to be one bit reckless."

"Six ways to Sunday, hmm?" Jenna grinned over the top of her steaming cup of chocolate at her rosy-cheeked, sparkling-eyed son. He was one happy boy today. He'd been happy ever since last week's wishing tree outing, but today his little light seemed to shine exceptionally bright. *Wonder if he snooped and found his stash of Christmas presents?*

"The sky is sure blue, Mom, isn't it?"

"It is."

"No, look at it! You gotta look at it."

The insistence in his voice caused her to follow the path of his pointing finger. Only then did she see the small single-engine plane flying high over the meadow.

And something fell out of it. *Holy cow, are we witnessing a drug drop?*

A minute after the object started falling, a parachute popped. Soon everyone in the meadow had his or her gaze glued to the sky. As each moment ticked by, Jenna was able to identify a bit more. First, she saw that it was a human, not a box. So, not a drug drop. Then she recognized what the figure was wearing. A red suit? With black boots? A snowy white beard?

"It's Santa Claus!" Michael Murphy exclaimed.

Jenna glanced around the group, wondering who had arranged for a visit from Santa. Must have been Cam since he'd put together this sleigh ride. Plus he had a knowing smirk on his face, although Sarah obviously wasn't in on the surprise. She looked as baffled as Jenna.

Santa managed a near-perfect landing some fifty yards from the bonfire. At exactly what moment she recognized him, Jenna couldn't say, but by the time he'd dealt with his chute and somehow turned a backpack into Santa's bag, her heart began to pound.

"Ho ho ho," Santa said, striding toward them, the unmistakable twang of Australia in his tone. "Merry Christmas."

"Devin!" Michael protested. "You're not Santa." He turned to Reilly and said, "That's my brother. He's just dressed up. He's not the real Santa."

Lori reached for her mother's hand. Emotion cracking in her voice, she said, "He's here. He came to be with us when they're born."

"I'm not surprised. I don't care what he said." Tears

rolled down Sarah's cheeks. "Devin is such a marshmallow when it comes to family."

"Ho ho ho. Merry Christmas." Devin's cheeks were rosy and his eyes surely twinkled, and while he didn't pull off the Santa belly, he did find a booming voice when he added, "I hope everyone's been behaving because I have presents for the good girls and boys. Where's my helper elf?"

To Jenna's surprise, Reilly said, "Here I am, Santa."

"Where'd he get that elf hat?" Jenna murmured as her son ran to meet Devin.

"And ears!" Lori said with a laugh. "Look at the pointed ears."

"He was in on this," Sarah observed. She glanced up at Cam. "You were, too. You dog, you. You didn't say a word!"

"You would have worried about the skydive part of his plan," Cam defended. "You always fret when you know that he's going to jump out of a plane."

"True." Sarah glanced toward Jenna. "I think it's a stupid hobby. Why, once—"

"Gifts!" Devin interrupted loudly. "We have gifts galore." He opened the bag and fished out two small packages. "Hmm . . . this one appears to be for Baby Turner and this one"—he read the tag—"Baby Brogan."

Reilly delivered the gifts to the parents, then ran back for more. "Baby Timberlake and Baby Garrett. Baby Murphy and the Babies Callahan."

As Reilly took the gift to the Turners, Lori asked, "Santa, can we open them now or do we have to wait for Christmas?"

"Whatever you'd like. Feel free to open them now if you wish."

He'd brought them each a little koala bear, and Jenna

grinned at the chorus of oohs and aahs. Santa started to pull the drawstring on his pack when his little elf said, "Wait, Santa. Isn't there one more thing in your bag?"

"Is there?" Santa asked.

"I hope so," Reilly said. "Because there's one very good girl who didn't get a present."

"Oh. Well. Hmm." Santa made a show of peering into his bag. Then he said, "Aha, elf. It appears that you are right.

He reached deep into the bag and pulled out a black velvet ring box. Jenna's heart pounded like reindeer paws on a rooftop as he made a show of reading a tag. "For the love of my life." He glanced down at Reilly. "I think I'd better deliver this one myself, don't you?"

"Yep, sure do, Santa."

Finally for the first time since his arrival, Devin met Jenna's gaze and held it. He walked slowly toward her and went down on one knee. "Jenna Stockton, my love, my heart. Will you marry me?

"Yes, Devin Murphy. Of course I'll marry you. You're my Christmas wish."

He slipped a beautiful solitaire diamond ring on her finger, and his mouth had just touched hers in a kiss when his mother interrupted the moment. "I hate to do this, but Devin, I need to borrow your fiancée. It appears that my water just broke."

With his black belt discarded and his red jacket unbuttoned to reveal a plain white T-shirt, an unkempt Santa Claus paced the hospital waiting room. What a crazy day and night this had been.

His mother might have kicked things off, but it hadn't stopped there. They'd no sooner got her down off the mountain and settled into a room at the clinic than the same thing happened to Shannon Garrett. After that, it was like dominoes. All six women . . . every last one of them . . . went into labor.

Devin wondered just what his father had put in that hot chocolate he served up on the mountain.

With so many patients involved, it was all hands on deck at the clinic. But all the rush and hurry quickly became hurry up and wait. Hours crawled by in a waiting room packed with friends and families. Devin was excited for his sister and parents and the other expectant couples, truly he was. However, would it have hurt any of them to hold things off for just a couple of hours? He'd barely had the chance to kiss his fiancée, much less share a proper hello.

He visited with the Timberlakes and Celeste and the Chamber of Commerce members who stopped by for updates on the big Maternity Springs contest. He pillowed Michael's head in his lap and Reilly's against his chest as both boys slept. At one point during the long night, his soon-to-be son looked up at him and said, "Don't worry, Dad. Sometimes Mom's work hours stink, but you'll get used to it. And from now on, we'll have each other."

Yes, from now on, they'd have each other.

Dawn the following morning broke on six inches of new snow. Devin stood at a waiting-room window watching a new day dawn over Eternity Springs, his heart full of quiet anticipation. So much to look forward to. So much to be grateful for.

His sister and his niece were born within half an hour of each other.

It was noon before he made it home and got the boys settled and fell into bed for a much-needed nap. When he heard the phone ring, he almost didn't answer it.

What phone was that, anyway? He lifted his head from his pillow. His Santa pants that he'd left pooled in the middle of Jenna's bedroom floor were ringing. Why were his pants ringing? He glanced at the bedside table where his phone silently lay.

But his Santa pants were ringing.

Devin stretched out an arm, snagged the red velvet, and tugged it toward him. Damned if there wasn't a phone in the pocket. A flip phone.

He flipped it and cautiously brought it to his ear. "Hello?"

"Santa, this is Reilly from Nashville again, only this Christmas I'm Reilly from Eternity Springs and next Christmas I'll be Reilly from Bella Vita Isle. I have another Christmas wish for you, Santa. You did so good bringing me a dad that I figured I'd better get this on record. My poor best friend Michael got stuck with two girls today. If you have any pull in the baby department, could you see about getting my family a boy?"